Magnetic Mansion

Acknowledgment

Many thanks go out to Mrs. Katie Barrett for her first edit and to Ms. Carol Woods for her brilliant final cut. I salute Rabbi Asher for his converting ancient Hebrew into English. I'm always grateful to my bed buddy and green-eyed beauty—my wife who without I am nothing!

Magnetic Mansion

by

FORREST HASKELL

Top Publications, Ltd.
Dallas, Texas

Magnetic Mansion

Top Publications, Ltd.
3100 Independence Parkway, Suite 311-349
Plano, Texas 75075

ISBN #1-929976-42-9
Library of Congress # 2007929143

PART I

Be careful what you wish and pray for;
you may get it…and sometimes it's not good!

The words written on the following pages are a
perfect example of this.

1

"Honey, wouldn't it be wonderful to have a nice little cottage at a lake? It would be a great place to escape next summer's heat and the kids certainly would enjoy the swimming and boating."

Just a simple, sincere statement such as this certainly doesn't sound like the beginning of an eight-year journey into bizarre and haunting experiences that would envelop me, my wife and my four children—but that's exactly what it would become.

"You know we have talked about this before, so why not?" was my quick reply to my wife's question. "We can certainly afford it, and one might be less expensive this time of year. Why don't you keep your eyes peeled in the newspapers for something that might go up for sale."

Little did I know at the time that I was letting myself and my family into a strange vortex surrounding an isolated old mansion that easily could cost us our sanity and possibly our lives.

My name is Zachary Heikel. I'm in my mid-30's and happily married to my teenage sweetheart, Peggy Sue. We have four wonderful children, and I consider myself a happy-go-lucky kind of guy. My life has been progressing merrily along, as if following a perfect script on how one should succeed in life. There was no way I would knowingly change it's course for the worse; but that's exactly what I was about to do on this fine February afternoon in 1971 when Peggy Sue dropped the Ann Arbor newspaper in front of me at the dinner table. There was a large circle drawn around an ad stating "Cottage for Sale."

The ad was worded persuasively and covered everything we had been considering when discussing the perfect summer cottage. We particularly liked the fact that the cottage was situated high on a hill with its own private lake and a panoramic view of the surrounding area. We decided that even if the cottage was just a tumbledown shack, we could complete the demolition and pitch a tent or buy a small pop-up tent for shelter. We could picture in our mind picnics on the site and going swimming and boating on the lake mentioned in the ad. Even though there was no sale price listed, we both got very excited at the prospect. We decided we had to see this place and perhaps purchase it at a "steal." We agreed to drive over the next morning to have a look-see.

When we awoke the next day, we found it had snowed heavily during the night. Our plan of going immediately to see our dream cottage had to wait until the roads were cleared and rock salt placed on the roadways had melted some of the ice and snow. Brilliant sunshine hid the fact that the temperature outside was still hovering near zero degrees. I was more concerned about whether my new Cadillac would start than if I was going to see the cottage right away. I threw on my heavy parka and boots and hiked out to the car.

We were living in the small village of Dexter in southern Michigan. Our house sat on flat open-range land where the wind and snow blew almost constantly. The car was covered with several inches of new-fallen snow. When I hopped in the car and shoved the key into the ignition, I crossed my fingers as I turned the key. To my surprise, the engine made just a couple of revolutions and started with a huge roar. After a few minutes, the car's heater had warm air flowing into the passenger compartment. Soon it was warm enough to get Peggy Sue out of our cozy, warm house for the 50-mile trip to look at the cottage. Roads were soon passable, and we were on our way.

It took us almost two long hours in the slow-going road conditions to get to the cottage location. Peggy Sue was navigating, using the directions she had written down during a conversation she had with the gentleman who answered the telephone number in the ad. There were no expressways or multi-lane highways in our area of the state, just small country back roads, some of them just dirt. We were lucky that the longest stretch of the trip was on US 12, a two-lane, blacktop road that had once been the main highway between Detroit and Chicago but was now seldom used. Now, the new East-West expressway about 50 miles north of US 12 carried most traffic between the two cities.

The further we drove into the backwoods country, it became increasingly evident that we were heading into a very remote area known as the Irish Hills. These hills are located in the extreme south-central area of Michigan, near the Indiana state line. These hills were very reminiscent of the Berkshires in Massachusetts and were created several thousand years ago by the glaciers that plowed the land and dumped massive piles of dirt. As we drove along, it was easy to see what the glacial plow did as it furrowed out the Irish Hills. There were huge thousand-foot-high hills and also yawning kettle holes that were miniature Rose Bowls. As the glaciers had melted, they left shiny silvery lakes of fresh water spread across the southern part of Michigan.

The area was densely overgrown by towering evergreen trees as well as oaks and hickories. Anyone fond of the outdoors would cherish the wilderness of these wooded hills and valleys. Vegetation struggled with its neighbors to reach upwards for the sunlight. A strange vegetation grew in the bogs, tamaracks and swampy areas that abounded in these ancient lowlands that appeared to be almost untouched by man.

Peggy Sue and I were impressed with these remote, but exceedingly beautiful surroundings. Even though a veil of white fluffy snow covered virtually everything, I could visualize how it would look in the springtime. I knew the area would be crawling with all sorts of wildlife because of the dense cover of the tall trees and vegetation and the abundance of fresh water.

As I took in this incredible scene, a thought passed through my mind and I asked Peggy Sue, “Are there bears in this part of Michigan?”

In her partially mesmerized state, she answered, “There could be. This area is so out of the way that probably every wild thing native to Michigan lives here. I only hope I never run into one. A little Bambi would be all right; but not a bear!”

As we approached the area with the steepest hills, I was thankful for the road crews that had cleared the snow. This area could be quite treacherous when slippery. As we drove I thought this had better be a good deal on that summer cottage because, if not, this trip was turning out to be more trouble than it was worth. I felt the Caddie drop down into second gear as the incline began to get steeper. Peggy Sue said that since we had passed through the small town of Clinton about 12 miles back we should be preparing to turn left very soon. When we reached the top of the hill, we could see for miles. Directly in front of us, however, was an even larger hill that we still had to climb. Peggy Sue’s scribbled notes showed this was where Collier Drive would be located, after making a sharp turn on the upper part of the hill.

There wasn’t much traffic on US 12 and soon we made the sharp curve and saw the road we were looking for. It quickly took a downhill turn that would bring into view an area that appeared to us as if it were another world!

Collier Drive was a dirt road that plunged down so

steeply that I had to apply the brakes to get ready for a curve that was fast approaching at the bottom of the hill. On both sides of the road was water, frozen right now, but still showing a swamp on the right, reminiscent of the bayous of Louisiana. Instead of cypress trees, however, there were evergreen, so tall they blocked the bright sunlight and plunged the area into semi-darkness.

Onward we drove and soon we could make out a lake through the trees and underbrush. I noticed a small shack on the edge of the lake and was so intent on looking at it that I didn't notice the base of a huge hill on our left until a startled Peggy Sue uttered, "Oh, my God!"

I quickly backed up to see what had caused her startled outburst. Two massive stone pillars marked the entrance to a large estate. Twisted iron gates between the pillars were closed, blocking an asphalt driveway that wound its way several hundred yards upward to the top of the hill. Standing above the wooded valley was a solitary manor house of unbelievable grandeur. It was built of brick with a number of severely sloping roof lines that appeared to be made of slate. There appeared to be hundreds of windows that lined the front of the mansion. There was a huge chimney that rose four stories high and was topped by a vent that from a distance appeared to have been the size of a Volkswagen car.

My wife and I realized this certainly could not be the house in the ad. Clearly it was not a cottage. However, we were on the right road and, right in front of us, was the address from the ad. Driven into the ground beside the mailbox was a sign that read, "Cottage for Sale." Peggy Sue and I both had an overwhelming urge to drive to the top of the hill and find out exactly what kind of joke was being played on us…if we could just get through those closed gates!

I hopped out of the warm Caddie and ran up to the gates. I pulled on them with a huge tug and, to my surprise, the gates swung open wide while the hinges creaked for oil all the way. Our next challenge in solving this "joke" was to make it to the top of the steep, winding, snow-covered driveway. We started up the long drive, slipping and sliding with our tires spinning; but with a final lunge, we reached the top.

I knew I probably could not afford to buy the place, but I wanted to get in the face of the guy who made me take this long journey as some kind of strange or twisted joke. He deserved a piece of my mind!

I brought the car to a stop in the middle of a large circular driveway centered by a huge fountain with its water frozen into a giant ice sculpture. This was obviously the front entrance to the house and I determined then that the back of the house, which we had seen from the bottom of the hill, actually faced the lake. To the left of the drive were what looked like an old carriage house, stables and a large stand of trees that appeared to be a fruit orchard. I didn't worry about blocking the driveway, because I didn't think anyone else would be stupid enough to inquire about the "cottage for sale" ad once he saw this house.

There did not appear to be anyone around, but smoke was coming out of the massive chimney and there was a four-car garage on one end of the mansion that probably contained the occupant's automobiles. Peggy Sue noticed a single light coming from a window beside a small courtyard. There must be people inside.

We got out of our comfortable and warm car and headed toward the massive, solid oak door. It was so cold and I could feel the icy wind. I saw that the wind was bending the thick column of black smoke horizontally as it exited the chimney, making an inky streak across the sky. We huddled together as we approached the entryway. Peggy Sue seemed to be intimidated not only by the size of the house, but by the huge door looming in front of us. The door resembled the entry to a medieval chateau and was a real work of art. I guessed the door was at least seven feet tall and probably four feet wide. It came to a peak at the top and three hinges supported its enormous weight. They were handmade of beaten iron. The large oak planks that made up the door were held together by strips of the same material, nailed together with square-headed nails, making the big door airtight. At eye-level in the middle of the door was a small window with its glass protected by steel and wire mesh. I lifted the wrought-iron door knocker and dropped it twice with a loud "thud, thud." Shortly, a face appeared in the small window as it opened. "Yes," said a deep voice from inside.

"I'm here about your ad in the *Ann Arbor News* and the 'Cottage for Sale' sign at the foot of the hill," I said loudly, trying to be as sarcastic as possible.

We heard several noises emanating from behind the door, like bolts being slid open and a key turning in a lock. The door swung open just wide enough for us to step through. At the voiced invitation of "Please, come in," we entered the mansion.

I was ready to pounce verbally on the person who opened the door, but the size of the man made me realize I'd better take a little softer tone of voice—and leave the sarcasm completely out of our conversation! The man was at least 6 feet, 6 inches tall, and he must have weighed well over 400 pounds. He was nearly as massive as the door he had just opened.

We gingerly stepped into a large entryway, adjacent to a dimly-lit, extremely large living room floored in polished ash and wainscoted to the ceiling in knotty pine. Beams supporting the ceiling were hand-hewn and larger than railroad ties. They must have weighed several hundred pounds each. A large fire was roaring in an enormous fireplace, flanked on either side by large steel-framed, multi-paneled windows. Over the fireplace was an antique-looking, four-foot by five-foot oil painting of an old man, whom the artist had succeeded in making appear almost non-human!

For some strange reason, the first words out of my mouth were, “My, what an unusual painting.”

The giant standing beside me replied, “Oh that, it’s been hanging there since the house was built, I guess. It’s somehow attached directly to the wall and you can’t move it even an inch. So, it stays with the house.”

Peggy Sue, standing somewhat behind me as if for protection, said in a low voice, “If that painting is so unusual then what’s that? Is it real?” She motioned with her head to a corner directly behind the massive front door, next to a cloakroom.

Standing there on a wooden pedestal covered in red leather was a seven-foot tall antique suit of armor, complete with a five-foot engraved sword in one hand, its end resting on a steel plate which protected the leather from punctures. This thing was almost as spooky as the painting. The helmet and the entire suit of armor was made of a highly-polished metal that reflected the lone bulb in the light fixture hanging over our heads in a manner that made it appear the eye sockets were lit from inside the suit. I felt the hair on the back of my neck stand straight up because it seemed the eyes were looking directly at me!

I walked closer to get a look at the inscription on the sword, which read, “Whoso Pulleth Out This Sword Of this Stone is Rightwise King Born of All England.”

“Hey,” I said, “that’s the same inscription that’s on the Excalibur or ‘Singing Sword’ of King Arthur, like in the Knights of the Round Table.”

The giant responded again, “That’s also been here a long time and it also goes with the house. Where else could one put something like that? It’s hideous.”

“Goes with the house?” was my startled reply. “You mean *this* is the ‘cottage” and it really is for sale?”

“Yes, it is and, by the way, my name is Jake,” he said

as he extended his hand toward me. We shook and I was happy to find him docile because his hand completely surrounded mine and part of my wrist.

"I'm Zachary Heikel and this is my wife Peggy Sue" who just nodded her head in an effort to save the bones in her right hand.

Jake said that evidently the ad he had placed in the newspaper was a bit misleading. It had run for two months and he had not received even one inquiry about the house. He had thought it would be a novel sales approach to call the mansion a "cottage," in the hopes of sparking interest in a prospective home buyer when he actually saw the house. It was certainly a unique approach, and it worked with me.

"This place is really unbelievable," I said. "How long have you lived here and why do you want to sell it?"

He replied that he had lived in the house for only a few months. "My health is getting so bad I can hardly move around the place. It has gotten to the point that I can barely make it upstairs," Jake complained while touching his knee.

Peggy Sue spoke up, "We sure would like to have this house, but I don't know if we can afford the price you must be asking for it." Jake responded by telling her he would make us a good deal.

Earlier, while driving up the steep driveway, I had taken a guess as to what a possible selling price must be for such a place. I had that figure in the back of my mind when I asked Jake to give me the selling price. "I'm only asking $125,000 so I can move quickly to a warmer climate and take care of my health. I know it's a very low price, but I'm hoping for a quick sale. The price includes the surrounding 224 acres."

"Jake," I responded after I picked my jaw off the floor, "Did you say $125,000?"

"Yes, that's right," he said rather sternly, "but it has to be cash and as quickly as possible and the house must be accepted in its present condition with no stipulations." I stopped for a moment, thinking his price was only a small fraction of what I had thought the property was worth.

In my best "lawyerly" voice, I asked Jake what was wrong with the house and whether or not he had a clear deed to the place. "Nothing's wrong with it that a little elbow grease won't cure and yes, I do have a clear title as well as the original abstract. We could make a deal as soon as you would like," he said very matter-of-factly.

Certainly, this was the "steal" Peggy Sue and I had been hoping for, but it was coming too fast and seemed to be way too easy. The home we now occupied was located on 16 acres and was worth about $175,000, but I felt we could move it quickly it we needed to. From her facial expression and the look in her eyes, I could tell Peggy Sue wanted this property. We have always been impulse buyers and usually buy anything we want as long as we have the cash to pay for it. We had never really been stung on any of our impulse purchases, but this was something out of the ordinary. This purchase would mean a real lifestyle change as well as a change in residence and new schools for the kids. But, it was just too good to pass up. I had enough money in the bank to buy the house and property outright and, at this price, we could use it for our summer cottage as we had planned. A voice in my head said, "I'm going to buy this place and just take it one step at a time." I decided we could get used to the area and maybe later we could move here permanently when we sold our old home.

"Jake," I said, looking him right in the eye and letting the small voice in my head do the talking, and "I'll take it if, and only if, you have a clear title and no back taxes owing."

During a moment of silence, we looked at each other; then Jake spoke: "Zachary, you've got yourself a real bargain," he said as he extended his hand to seal the deal. I shook it vigorously and hoped I had not jeopardized my family with my decision. From experience, I knew that good deals don't wait, so I felt I had to jump at this opportunity, and responded to Jake's reference to my getting a real bargain with a simple, "I hope so."

"Joyce," Jake shouted from his enormous lungs, "Someone here wants to buy our house." Apparently, Jake's wife had been in the anteroom all during the negotiations. As she approached us she said, "I didn't even realize anyone was here. What's this about the house, Jake?" Our feeble attempts at "how do you do" were drowned out by Jake's response. "Zachary and Peggy Sue are going to buy the place." Not giving me time to reply, Jake went forward with "Could we make the deal in the morning? I have a friend in the real estate business who could prepare the deed transfer and bill of sale."

"I don't see why not," I replied, still trying to make his wife's acquaintance. "I just need time to get to the bank for the money. I hope a cashier's check will be all right with you? It's the same as cash."

"Sure," Jake said enthusiastically. "Just have them make it out to Jake Kendall." I agreed, and turned to shake his hand again as further acknowledgment of the deal, when he asked me if we would not like to see the rest of the house.

"Nope," I said, "this room and the acreage alone is well worth the price and I don't care if the rest of the place is made of paper mache. I'll see you tomorrow at noon."

Peggy Sue appeared to be in a state of shock, but she knows I'm a wheeler-dealer and she didn't say anything. Finally, she was going to get the "cottage at the lake" she had always wanted. I'm sure, however, she would never in her wildest dreams have imagined the mysteries that moved about in the walls and halls of the house on the hill.

As we drove away from the house, we left two very shocked people standing in their living room. When we looked back at the house from the bottom of the hill, there was only darkness. Jake and Joyce must have turned out the lone light bulb.

Had this really just happened, or were we dreaming? We pinched ourselves to be sure we were awake. In little more than an hour after seeing the "cottage" on the hill for the first time, we had managed to buy a huge mansion for a steal of a price. Something was definitely too good to be true…but what was it?

2

In no time at all, it seemed, we were back at our home in Dexter. I was about to drive the baby-sitter home when the telephone rang. Jake Kendall was asking for me. I took the phone and asked Jake if we had forgotten something. "Yes, Zachary," he replied, "I forgot to ask you for a deposit."

"Jake, I'm about to give you a check for a ton of money so why don't you just call me Zack…and what's this about a deposit?"

"Sorry, but I have to have some good faith money in hand."

"My God Jake, I'm coming over there tomorrow with a cashier's check for the whole amount. Isn't that good enough? You know we shook hands three or four times and that should be a good enough deposit!"

"No, Zack, I want a cash deposit and I want it tonight," Jake replied. He sounded frightened, as if I might renege on the deal.

I told Jake that we had just arrived home after the long drive from his house and I didn't want to make that drive again to give him a deposit. I reminded him one more time that we would be meeting at noon the next day to finalize the purchase.

"No, that's not good enough," he said. "I'll meet you halfway in the town of Chelsea and you need to bring as much cash money as you have on hand." After some thought I finally agreed to meet him in Chelsea but advised him, I had only a few hundred dollars for a deposit. He said that was acceptable and we agreed to meet at the Chelsea Restaurant and Bar at 10 p.m.

Arriving at the restaurant, I found Jake's demeanor completely different and so was the look of his face. He had very dark circles around his eyes, his face was beet red, he was perspiring profusely and his breath was very foul. I handed him the small roll of bills and without looking me in the eye, Jake said, "Zack, you just don't know what this means to me. Thanks so much. Maybe I can finally get some sleep tonight. Here's a receipt and I'll see you tomorrow." With that, Jake hurriedly left the restaurant, leaving me alone to finish a cup of coffee and pondering why this meeting was necessary. It was beyond me why a small deposit of a few hundred dollars would hold something as valuable as that mansion. Something or someone had scared the hell out of Jake. He was terrified that this deal might fall through and seemed desperate to complete the sale. I was not yet aware of the bizarre things that can happen to people while in the house on Irish Hill.

It was nearing midnight when I got home and I was exhausted. After a quick shower, I jumped into bed knowing that tomorrow would be a rough day. I didn't sleep well, tossing and turning all night, thinking constantly about having decided so quickly to buy the house without taking time to think it through. Never one to second-guess myself, I finally slipped off to sleep, waking early the next morning grumpy and knowing I had not rested. I knew I had to be sharp if I was going to complete the deal of a lifetime.

All I could think about was the house as I made my way to the bank early that morning to pick up the cashier's check. I waited nervously for the bank to open and then headed straight for the bank president's office. Lance Van Sickel was a very good friend and we exchanged a few pleasantries before I told him I needed a cashier's check for $125,000 "Because I'm going to buy a cottage at a lake."

"A hundred and twenty-five thousand dollars for a cottage! Must be some kind of cottage," Lance said jokingly. "I've really gotta see this one. I didn't even realize you were in the market for a lake cottage, this one must have really caught your eye."

I agreed that it had and told him I wasn't going to apply for a home mortgage but planned to close out one of my savings accounts and buy the place outright. I also explained that I had decided to take some time off from my company and help Peggy Sue decorate. "This will be a good opportunity for me to see if my Vice President can run things for a while. Not only is this a fabulous deal, but something is just drawing me to possess this house."

Lance mumbled as he took out some papers. "Okay, it's your money. It appears you want to move very quickly on this one since they say that good deals don't wait. That does sound familiar." As Lance prepared to draw up the cashier's check, he asked me where the property was located.

"It's just outside the town of Clinton and it's actually not a cottage but a house on 224 acres, set high on a hill with a private lake in the Irish Hills," I said rather nonchalantly.

Lance replied enthusiastically, "You know, Zack, I'm very familiar with the town of Clinton. My parents live there and have for most of their lives and Ruth and I visit them almost every weekend."

"Well then, Lance, you must know the place. It's the one that's out near the lookout tower about 30 miles west of town."

"Man," Lance exclaimed, "you don't mean that big old mansion out near Lake Misty? If that's the one, my dad and most every older person in town can tell you some stories about that place that are plenty puzzling! You know he delivered most of the wood and materials they used to build that house by horse-drawn wagon. The hill is so steep they had to use double teams to pull loads up to the top. It must have cost a fortune to build back before the depression. Dad said only the very best materials were used in the construction."

"Well, that's the place," I replied, "and it's nice to know that your dad is familiar with it. I'd like to visit with him as soon as I close the deal."

Lance asked when I planned to do it. "Well, as soon as you cut me that check. I'm meeting with the owner and will make the transaction today. He's in a hurry for some reason. Said something about being in poor health and needing to move to a warmer climate."

As soon as I signed all the necessary papers, Lance prepared the $125,000 cashier's check payable to Jake Kendall. Handing it to me, he smiled and wished me luck. "I'll tell Dad you are going to be the proud owner of the haunted Mansion on the Hill!"

Startled out of my skin, I asked, "What do you mean, haunted?"

Jokingly Lance replied that he was just kidding, "But there are rumors," he said, "Rumor has it that the old man who built the house died a few months ago and some guy from out of town bought it but is very unhappy living there. He says he hears strange noises and sees things so he spends most nights at the local hotel. I'm sure this is just a bunch of bologna and you'd better hurry or you'll miss your appointment. Drive safely. Those roads can be pretty tricky with all those curves."

I said my goodbyes to Lance and headed out with the check in my pocket, all the while wondering whether Lance was kidding around and just trying to scare me, or trying to ruin my day. Even though he was doing a good job of it, nothing anyone could say or do was going to stop me from buying that house! However, I was certain that I would quiz Jake extensively about the rumors. He would have to convince me he really was selling the house for health reasons; but just maybe he would slip up and tell me the real reason why he was ridding himself of such a fabulous property so cheaply and in such a hurry.

As I pulled out of the bank parking lot, I flipped on the radio to listen to the news or hear some music. About halfway through the drive, I realized I had not heard a word of the news. My mind was completely occupied thinking of the right questions to ask Jake regarding those rumors Lance had mentioned. Once I arrived at the real estate office, I was ready with my question-and-answer session with Jake. As I entered the office, he greeted me warmly and, once again, we shook hands. He noticed the stern expression on my face and quietly asked, "Zack, is everything all right?"

In an abrupt voice I answered, "I think so, but we need to talk for a moment in private." As we headed for a conference room, I could see by his nervous actions that Jake was concerned about my negative attitude. As soon as we closed the door to the small room, I came right to the point, "Jake, I've got some questions for you about a rumor I heard about things that go on in the house."

Jake's worried expression grew worse and he asked, "What rumors? What do they say goes on in the house?"

I told Jake about the rumors of his hearing strange noises and seeing things during his short stay in the house. Jake answered as if trying to lighten the moment, "The only noise I hear is my wife bitching about not being able to make it up the driveway because of all the snow…and when am I going to plow the driveway."

"Jake, this is no time for your jokes," I said. "I'm dead serious. I'm not going to wake up some night in that upstairs bedroom and have the shit scared out of me!" Then continuing in almost the same breath, "Are you absolutely certain there are no strange goings on and that everything is perfectly normal at the house? Will you give me your word?"

With a completely serious look on his face, Jake

answered, “Absolutely Zack! The only reason I’m selling the house is to get to a climate that I can stand and to move into a home all on one level. I just can’t take stairs any longer because of my weight and that’s the truth.”

By this time, we were both serious and I came right back at him. “Jake, you know I want this house and I’m prepared to make the deal with you. If there is anything unusual that has happened at the house, just tell me now so I can be expecting things and not have my family scared out of their wits.”

With a half smirk on his face Jake said, “Well, there is Ice Pick Charlie, but he’s very old and harmless.”

“What the hell are you talking about?” I yelled. “Who in the hell is Ice Pick Charlie? Are you kidding around again or is there actually such a thing?” Even before I got the final words out of my mouth, Jake was already laughing heartily and trying to talk over my questions.

“Zack, Zack, there is no Ice Pick Charlie. There’s nothing wrong at the house, there are no ghosts, no goblins, and there is nothing supernatural. You have my word on it.” He said these last words with a straight face and looked me right in the eye. I wanted so much to believe him, but I had only known him for a couple of days and his face was not one that gave me confidence. For some reason, I thought he would make a fine carnival barker or excellent used-car salesman! He seemed sincere, but I still wasn’t sure I should believe him. My nerves had been completely rattled by Lance and talk of the rumors. Jake’s nonchalant attitude did nothing to boost my confidence or assure me strange things were not occurring in the house on the hill.

Jake left the room and soon returned with Rita Fitzvasser, an elderly real estate agent who was going to handle the sale and transfer of title. She was a pleasant woman and spoke to me in a motherly tone as she asked if I wanted coffee or a soft drink.

"No, nothing at all," I replied politely. "But I would like to get right on with the business at hand."

"So, you are going to be the new occupant of the house we call the Mansion on the Hill," she observed. I responded with a question, asking Rita Fitzvasser why she referred to the house as the Mansion on the Hill.

"Well, I guess we've always called it that because it's the largest and most prominent residence in the area. You can see if for miles away when you are driving on US 12 and at night from the highway, when they have the house lights on, it looks like an ocean liner just hanging in the sky. It's an awesome sight," she explained.

"Rita, is there anything strange you know about the house, that you might like to tell me? I realize you are doing this transfer as a favor for Jake and you don't have any part in selling the home, but are there any rumors circulating in town about this property?" I asked Mrs. Fitzvasser.

"Actually, Zack, it's the kind of place that would be easy to start rumors about because people in town know very little about the house. After all, it is thirty miles away, is in a very secluded area, and is quite old, over fifty years I'm sure. Most of the time the iron gates at the bottom of the hill are closed and locked so no one goes up there. The old man who lived there for so many years was almost like a hermit and very few people had actually ever seen him.

"As far as anyone knows, he had no domestic help. No one knew how he cared for himself and that enormous house. We all thought it must be terribly filthy inside. He did have a man that everyone believes is the groundskeeper that lives out there and comes to town occasionally to shop and do errands. They say he is very strong the way he throws a 100-pound bag of potatoes into the truck.

"This big guy's face is very disfigured," Rita continued. "He has a bad speech impediment that makes it difficult to understand him. Needless to say he is very quiet and keeps pretty much to himself. He lives in that small shack on the other side of the hill and drives an old black pickup. I believe his name is Bruno. He would be your best bet to ask about anything unusual going on at the house, if you are able to communicate with him. He's lived in that shack for years and probably still does."

Rita continued her tale of the disfigured man in the shack on the other side of the hill. "The old man from the mansion deeded the shack to him along with two acres of land a few years before he died. I think he sold it to Bruno for something ridiculous like $25.

"Another person you might want to talk to is Outhouse Van Sickel who helped with the construction of the place about 50 years ago. I hope he's not too old to remember it because he's probably in his 80's by now."

"Wow, Rita, that's a coincidence," I said. "I know a banker with that same last name."

"Of course," Rita interrupted, "that would be Lance. He's Outhouse's son. I know him."

"That's amazing," I replied. "Lance told me his dad lived here in Clinton but he never told me his first name. Did you say his name is Outhouse? That's a very unusual first name to say the least."

"Yes, his name is unusual and so is he. He's the oldest person in town and little senile, but he knows everything that's going on and a lot about the house you're buying," Rita said matter-of-factly.

At this point, Jake jumped into the conversation after having sat quietly through Rita's tale. "Zack, I live there and I'm telling you that nothing unusual or strange is going on. You can talk to these other people if you want to, but I don't know how that would help you. They can't possibly know what it's like to actually live there."

Jake's last comment convinced me and the check was burning a hole in my pocket by this time. I told Rita I was ready to get on with the signing of the paperwork. At the price I was paying for the property, I was certain I could unload it on another unsuspecting soul like myself! If I heard noises or wasn't happy, I felt I could get my money back with very little trouble.

Having convinced myself, I whipped the check for $125,000 out of my pocket and got on with the signing of the deed transfer and other documents. Every time I looked up at Jake, he was smiling. I felt like he might have "something up his sleeve," but I put my final signature on the closing statement, handed Jake the check, did still another handshake and the deal was done! The house on the hill was mine.

Still smiling, Jake looked at the check, folded it in half, and stuck it in his shirt pocket. With his other hand, he handed me a set of keys to the massive front door and said abruptly, "I'll be out of the house in a week."

I assured Jake there was no need to move so quickly because Peggy Sue and I were in no hurry to take possession. Still, I could tell he was in a hurry to get gone.

After saying my farewells to Rita Fitzvasser, Jake walked me out to my car and still smiling said, "Thanks for your quick action on the house and I hope you will happy with the purchase."

I couldn't ever remember seeing anyone so genuinely happy as he was to sell a house. As I drove home to Dexter, I kept trying to determine if I had done everything correctly in the transaction. I had the bill of sale, I had the deed, and I had the old, yellowing, dog-eared original abstract of the house and the surrounding 224 acres. All those things were safely beside me on the front seat of my Caddie.

Peggy Sue was anxiously waiting for me when I arrived home. She said she had been making so many plans for the redecorating of the "cottage" that her head was in complete turmoil. She mentioned that she needed room and window dimensions so she could get on with her planning. As

I handed her the keys to our new "lake cottage," she looked a bit confused.

"You know," she said, "I have no idea what the rest of the house looks like or even how many rooms there are or what the basement looks like. I didn't even look at the kitchen; and I'm sure we will need all new appliances. I have a million questions. I wonder if Jake and Joyce would mind if we went through the house in the next couple of days. I have so much planning to do, drapes, wallpaper, carpeting, painting, you name it…I really have plans for that place."

Peggy Sue barely took a breath before she continued her staccato pace. I could see by her enthusiasm that she was going to have a grand time decorating; my only concern was whether or not my checkbook could take the strain!

3

The following morning Peggy Sue mentioned that she had not slept well because of all the questions running through her mind. I figured right away that I'd better call Jake and ask if we might visit during the next few days. I needed to put my wife's mind to rest and answer some of her questions. I dialed the number Jake had scribbled across the top of the bill of sale, but there was no answer. I tried several more times during the day with the same result. By this time, I had also begun to dream about the possibilities for the 224 acres. I could finally get some horses for the family to enjoy. I could see myself as a John Wayne figure, riding across those Irish Hills.

I told Peggy Sue that in the morning after the kids were off to school that we would just take a drive out to the property. I was sure Jake and Joyce would not mind our coming just to take some measurements.

Our morning drive was wonderful, with temperatures well above freezing and the sun bright on the melting snow. The scenery seemed much friendlier, revealing the vibrant, dark green colors of the evergreen trees that were in such abundance in the Irish Hills. As a matter of fact, the drive relaxed me because I no longer had to worry about which hill to climb or which road to take. The tensions of our first trip in the snow and ice evaporated as we traveled the roads that were now clear and dry.

As we reached Collier Road and were turning into the driveway, we noticed the gates unlocked and standing wide open. We proceeded up the dirt driveway that had revealed itself after the snow melt. I could see that this driveway would need quite a bit of attention. The dirt and cinder drive was full of large potholes, but we reached the top of the hill without incident. I was surprised to see there were no vehicles at the top of the hill. I was concerned that no one would be at home and we would have to suffer through another few days with the questions we had about the layout of the house.

I was able to look at the immediate area around the house. I noticed there were two old barns and a garage to one side and I could see the fruit trees that surrounded the back of the house. The air was clear and I could see miles in all directions. I noticed an observation tower about two miles west. I knew it would be fun exploring all the hills and places of interest with my family. I was becoming really eager to take possession of our property so we could get on with our plans.

As Peggy Sue and I approached the front door, she was commenting on the beautiful shrubs and the flowers that would be blooming in the spring. We lifted the large doorknocker and let it fall several times. There was no answer so Peggy Sue peeped through one of the windows and said the place looked deserted. I walked around the side of the house, looked through one of the large windows and noted the same thing. The house was completely vacant. I had given Jake 30 days to move out, but he had moved out in less than three. Man, they must have been in a big hurry!

Well, we decided, it was our house—bought and paid for—so we wasted no time in putting the key in the lock of the front door and stepping into our new abode. With tape measure in hand and with Peggy Sue and her legal pad and pencil at my side, we started to examine and measure what we had purchased so impulsively.

The large entryway was the same as I remembered, with the suit of armor still standing in place where we had last seen it. Now, however, it was acting as a silent sentinel to the empty house. A small niche in the knotty-pine paneling surrounded by finely carved woodwork held an old style, pencil-thin black rotary telephone with its separate earpiece connected to a long cord in the telephone's base. This was a true antique and I wondered if it worked. When I picked it up, surely enough there was a dial tone.

I next glanced at the fireplace and the painting hanging directly above it. It did not seem as menacing in the bright daylight as it had when I first saw it. The old man in the portrait did not look nearly so sinister.

Peggy Sue wanted to see the kitchen immediately, so we started down a long hallway that seemed to double as a cloakroom. On one side of the hallway, there were two rows of double doors that opened in the center and extended from the floor to the ceiling. These closets were large enough to hold more than 100 coats. On the other side of the hallway were large windows in steel casings and a small bathroom was visible at the end. A left turn took us into the large kitchen with a very high ceiling. One entire wall was filled with shelves and china cabinets with glass doors.

Peggy Sue had certainly been right about one thing: we would definitely need new kitchen appliances because the ones in place were old enough to be original to the house. I figured the appliances did not work, but obviously Joyce had been cooking on something!

The view from the kitchen's large, steel-framed windows was as magnificent as it was from the living room. Beautiful green hills were everywhere and a brilliant sunlit blue sky, dotted with fluffy white clouds, came down to meet the horizon way off in the distance. At the foot of our hill was our small lake. Directly behind it, we could see a rather large lake with the sun glistening beautifully on its still, silvery waters. Further in the distance was the tower I had noticed earlier. Peggy Sue and I stood there for several minutes, taking in the landscape and its awesome scenery that surrounded our house. This place was already mesmerizing and we found it difficult to pull ourselves away from the windows to get on with the job ahead of exploring the house with its anticipated surprises and taking the necessary measurements.

There was an archway on the end of the kitchen that led into a small mudroom with shelves on either side, a small closet and a single door that led to the large four-car garage. When I entered the garage, I was impressed with the four oversized doors, each one of them a work of art. The doors were so heavy they required a large wheel on the end that supported the weight when the door was pushed open. I noticed small hot water radiators running along the base of the garage walls, so this must be a heated garage. The same steel-framed windows seen elsewhere in the house also adorned the front and side walls of the garage, showing the breathtaking view from that direction. On the wall next to the house, the same beautiful knotty-pine paneling had been installed. In the fourth bay of the garage, there was a large steel door jutting out of the floor. I could hardly wait to lift that door to see what it covered.

When I lifted the door and the sunlight poured in, I saw three steps that dropped down into a pool of dark, clear water. At first I thought this was just an old cistern, but it appeared to be much more elaborate. There was mosaic tile all around the top of the pool at the water line with a light bulb surrounded with wire mesh.

I asked Peggy Sue to turn on the light switches, which were near the kitchen door where she was standing. After tripping several of them and turning on various lights, suddenly the light above the water flashed on, revealing a beautiful pool, large enough for swimming. I reached down to touch the water and found that even in February the water was warm to the touch. This under-floor pool appeared to run the entire length of the four-car garage. I guessed the pool was about eight feet deep, with plenty of headroom for a swimmer. I considered several scenarios to explain the pool, thinking it might be just a large reservoir of fresh water that was replenished from gutters when it rained; or that it was a pool to be used in a drought or if the electricity to the pump malfunctioned.

I looked over at Peggy Sue who was sill standing by the light switches, clutching the wall as though she was afraid she might fall in the pool if the floor suddenly cracked beneath her feet! I called her over to look at the amazing sight.

Peggy Sue moved toward the open steel door, walking lightly on her tiptoes as she approached the pool. "It's kind of spooky down there. Do you suppose someone actually swam in that water? This place is unbelievable and I can't wait to see the rest of it. We've only looked at two rooms and have already found something that is hard to explain. But don't ever ask me to get in that water! We need to padlock the door because the kids might get curious and could fall in someday. Close it up and let's look at the rest of the house."

Making a mental note to get a padlock for the pool door, I began to lower the 25-pound door when the handle slipped out of my hand. The door dropped with one helluva bang, vibrating the windows and our eardrums as well.

We continued our exploration of the house, going back through the mud-room, the kitchen, and past the enormous fireplace in the living room until we came to a wall at the end of that cavernous room. On that wall was a large steel casement of double glass doors with fixed-pane-window sidelights on either side. Rows and rows of bookshelves continued down the wall, partially filled with dusty old books that appeared untouched for many, many years.

Peggy Sue grabbed the two door handles and pulled open the doors. When we stepped through, we found ourselves in a large sun parlor that ran the full width of the house. Even without a tape measure, I guesstimated the room to be at least 40 x 50 feet! The exterior walls were made of painted brick, once brightly painted, but now faded to a sickly yellow color. Crank windows ran halfway up three walls, offering a tremendous panoramic view of the hills and valleys to the east, and lots of fresh air when opened.

Peggy Sue commented that there appeared to be nothing highly unusual about the room and that it would make a great playroom for the kids. I could visualize making one end of the room into a music area that would easily hold our Wurlitzer Organ and our grand piano.

Deciding to check out the upstairs, we climbed the wide staircase just adjacent to the entryway by the cloakroom. More casement windows were located on the small landing at the top of the stairs, but these also had a cozy window seat. To the right of the landing was a door leading to a small empty room with only a solitary window.

Another six steps led us to the second floor that featured a long hallway with a hand-painted mural, faded and cracking. The scene appeared to depict the early days of the house—people arriving in old, open-topped autos and in horse-drawn carriages. The men were dressed in 1920's-style suits and the women were arrayed in flapper dresses and unusual hats. Many were smoking cigarettes in long, stylish holders; others were lying about on blankets, enjoying a picnic. The mural was unsigned.

There appeared to be six bedrooms opening off this hallway. All six doors were closed, leading Peggy Sue to say, "This is just like "Let's Make a Deal," so which door should we choose?" We agreed to start at the far end of the hall and work our way back to the other end of the house. The door at the end of the hall opened into a large room with windows on three sides. We decided the room would be a perfect bedroom-playroom for our two boys. "They could even store their bicycles up here, it's so large," Peggy Sue commented.

I noticed small hot water radiators on the floors just beneath the windows and a large walk-in closet. Wallpaper was separating from the walls in several places and was generally dirty. A large, corner bathroom with an old pedestal sink and iron and porcelain tub and fixtures was sure to appeal to the kids. The toilet was very old-style with a water chest above it and a pull-down flush chain.

The bathroom walls were wainscoted in black-and-white ceramic tile and held two medicine cabinets, one mirrored in a manner that distorted your image when looking into it. A large laundry chute was located on another wall behind a small door. Its size was very unusual, particularly when I looked into it and found that it not only led downward, but continued upward into the attic.

At the far end of this bathroom was a heavy locked door with a glass knob. Retracing my steps to the hallway, I found another locked door that also appeared to lead to the same room. The lock was old and looked like it could be opened with a skeleton key. Peggy Sue said she would be on the lookout for a key in one of the drawers or nooks and crannies in the house.

Even though I was still very curious about what was behind the locked door, we continued on to the other rooms. One room, with a huge double walk-in closet and large fireplace, was beautifully decorated in ornate fashion and held a spectacular view of Lake Misty through its large bay window. The room's only drawback was the exact replica of the hideous oil painting that was hanging in the downstairs living room. The thought crossed our minds that the old guy really enjoyed seeing his own image and he must have been vain as hell!

A corner door in the bedroom opened into a bathroom, identical to the one off the other bedroom with one exception. Just above the heatalator, and to the right of a mirror that distorted its images, was a small steel encased window with a hand crank, recessed into the wall as if it had been an afterthought. A door with a glass knob was located at the end of the room. When I turned the knob and opened the door, I was surprised to find Peggy Sue standing there. She had apparently gone back through the bedroom into the hall and entered one of the doors that led into this room. “Man,” I said, “you can get lost in a hurry in this place.”

Peggy Sue was excited about the room she had found. “Wait till you get a load of this room. It’s unbelievable,” she gushed. Apparently, Peggy Sue had found the Master Suite, complete with an attached, but much-neglected, small library. The shelves still contained old volumes of books and many old papers scattered about in helter-skelter fashion under a thick layer of accumulated dust. I stepped into the library and tried to shut the door in an effort to get the full effect of the small room. Apparently the door had been stuck in open position for many years because it squeaked and groaned as I forced it closed. Another door in the room was partially hidden by the bookshelves that were on dried out, rusty rollers. I managed to move the shelves enough to reach the doorknob, but found the door would not budge. The keyhole also looked like a skeleton key might fit it.

As I pondered all the locked doors, Peggy Sue called out to me and I hurried into the master bedroom to see what new discovery she had made. She was standing at the far end of the massive room in an area recessed into the floor by three steps. A beautiful ornate wrought iron fence surrounded this recessed eight-foot square space that contained a kneeling bench just below a small altar. An impression on the wall showed that something had hung there for years and left its image on the wallpaper when it was taken down it resembled two triangles set side by side. To the left of the altar was another door, its top half made of ventilated woodwork. It concealed a smaller room that had a built-in wooden bench and seat, reminiscent of a Catholic confessional.

Could the original owner have been a very religious man? I wondered about that, but felt uncomfortable thinking about having a confessional in what was to become my bedroom. However, the sensation left me almost immediately as I looked out the windows of the small room and saw the stunning view of the surrounding countryside. I decided the place was just too beautiful to be evil, but my mind continued to ponder the many oddities we were finding in what Peggy Sue had begun to call our "House of Doors and Mysteries."

We decided to look at the basement and save the unlocking of the doors and solving of the mysteries until another day. It was hard to remember just how to get into the basement. Which door was it? Peggy Sue and I decided to split up so we could explore the rest of the house more quickly, find the entry to the basement, and get home before the children returned from school. We went down to the first floor and separated. I remembered seeing a small window outside in the foundation of the house and decided that would enable me to look into the basement and find its entrance.

Once I found the window and cleaned off the glass with my hand, I tried to peer in, but found only total darkness. Because this was the only window, I went back inside to see if Peggy Sue had found the entry to the basement.

"Hey, Babe, I found the window, but I can't see anything down there. You find anything?" I asked as I came back in the front door. Nothing. Only silence. "Peggy Sue, yoo hoo, Peggy Sue." Still nothing. Like I said, you can get lost in this place real easy. "Peggy Sue, where are you? Peggy Sue, where in the hell are you?" My voice showed my concern and I took a fast run upstairs and again called out to my wife. Still no reply, and now I'm getting a little scared. Thinking she might have managed to get into one of the locked rooms, I tried those doors. I headed back downstairs to look out the front door, hoping she was waiting outside by the car. Man, she was nowhere!

I hurried back inside and called out to her again as loud as I could. “Peggy Sue, can you hear me?” Very faintly, I heard her answer, “I’m here.”

“Here, where is here?” I shouted. She replied that she was in the basement. “How do I get to you?” I hollered. “How do I get into the basement?” I was running down the hallway, putting my ears against the closet doors and, finally, I was able to hear her quite plainly.

“The entrance is outside by the door next to the small courtyard,” she said. “It blends in with the woodwork. Just push on the woodwork and the door swings open.”

I was relieved to know where Peggy Sue was located, but I was still not certain I could find the outside door. I moved up the hallway toward the small bathroom, made a left toward the kitchen and to the door that was on my right. I looked out into the small courtyard and saw the oak paneling that blended into the kitchen wall that held the glass china cabinets. I started pushing and kicking on the panels in a sort of panic when I heard Peggy Sue’s voice, “Over here, Stupid.”

She had opened the door from the inside and was standing only six feet away from me. She closed the concealed door and proceeded to show me how to get into the basement. She pressed on a long strip of wood on the side of the wall and the door swung open. “See, you just push here and presto! It’s really simple if you know where to look.”

“How did you know where to push?” I asked, expecting some explanation of her investigative expertise. “I didn’t,” she replied, “I just leaned against the wall and the door opened. It’s not very hard to find.”

We talked about how much trouble the builder had gone to in an effort to hide the door to the basement and were wondering what he might have had to hide. Because we needed to get home to the kids, we headed back to Dexter, leaving the solving of the mysteries for another day.

On the drive home our excitement was at a fever pitch. The "cottage" at the lake was proving to hold lots of adventure.

4

We were up early the next morning and were on our way back to the new house on the hill as soon as the school bus drove out of sight. Our conversation rambled on and on about what we might find in the basement and in the two locked rooms upstairs.

When we reached the foot of the long, winding driveway that wound up to our Mansion on the Hill, I looked up, hardly able to believe the place was really ours. The early-morning sun hitting the windows gave them a golden cast that made the place look more majestic than ever.

I dropped the Caddie into low gear and we cruised effortlessly up the driveway, occasionally glancing at the changing colors in the windows of the house. When we arrived at the rear of the house, everything looked so beautiful that we just sat there and took in the view. Soon, however, our excitement got the best of us and Peggy Sue said, “Let’s go exploring.” We hurried to the front door of the house, jammed the key into the lock and stepped inside. We could hardly wait to get to the hidden doorway to the basement. I got there first and asked Peggy Sue not to touch anything but to let me try to do it.

I had to know if I remembered where the trip board was located. I pressed on the wooden strip I thought would activate the door. I guessed right! Just like yesterday, the door swung open by itself. We both peered down into a long, dark stairwell. “You know we should have brought a flashlight,” I said.

Peggy Sue replied quickly, "It's okay; there's a light switch on your right that turns on the light at the foot of the stairs. I found it by accident yesterday."

I ran my hand along the wall in the darkness, found the switch, and turned on the light at the bottom of the stairs. As we descended into the basement, I counted the steps. After 22, we arrived at the bottom where the air was damp and stale. I calculated that the 22 steps had placed us about fifteen feet underground, deep even for a Michigan cellar. We were standing in a room about 20-feet square, and dust and cobwebs were everywhere. The lone light bulb cast an eerie shadow over everything.

"Man, it stinks down here like a toilet has backed up or something," was my first reaction. "And, we're gonna have to have more light. I have a small flashlight in the car and am going to get it…and you, Peggy Sue, do not move!"

I was glad to see that Peggy Sue had stayed put when I returned to the basement with the flashlight. "Let's get on with this. I can see a huge room through that archway," she said impatiently.

"Now let's not get in a hurry," I said gingerly. "What's this over on the wall to our left?"

The entire wall was a wooded structure completely outfitted with old wooden doors. A few of the doors had fallen off, revealing shelves with small pigeonholes that held wine bottles. Several bottles were still in place but were covered with so much dust and spider webs they hardly looked like glass.

"Man! There is some old wine here, and I'll bet it's worth a fortune," I laughed. We moved closer to get a better look when I noticed another archway that led into still another darkened room. I played the small beam of light about the walls, hoping to see a light switch. Unsuccessful in adding light to the scene, we moved into the room. "Stay close to me, Honey," I said to Peggy Sue, taking her by the hand.

We stepped into what once had been a large shower room. In the beam of the flashlight I could see drains in the floor, a few showerheads and pipes jutting from the walls. These walls were covered in the same blue and gold ceramic tile we had seen surround the pool beneath the garage floor. I counted nine shower-heads, enough to accommodate a large group at any one time. On the back wall there was an oak door with a large wooden handle. We moved to it, Peggy Sue clinging to my shirttail, and opened the door. Through all the spider webs, I was surprised to see the remains of an old sauna. Wooden benches surrounded the walls of the small room and the remains of the wooden box that held the warming rocks were now scattered about the floor. I could also see that the room was crawling with big spiders and knew we would have to set off insect bombs in the entire basement area. Peggy Sue was ready to leave immediately. “Let’s get out of here; my skin is crawling.”

Our small flashlight with its single battery was losing power and the lone light bulb didn’t help much. “Let’s take a drive into town. I can buy a new flashlight and a couple of insect bombs to fumigate this basement—unless, of course, you want to let the spiders live. This basement would make a great Halloween fright house,” I said in an attempt to break the tension of the moment.

“Very funny,” was my wife’s response as she hurried up the stairs and away from the black widows. "I can’t come back down here again knowing those things are still alive. Gas the hell out of them! Let’s go to town and get those bombs. Maybe we can explore the town and have a nice lunch at one of those quaint little restaurants downtown.”

Forty-five minutes later, we had completed the drive on the long, twisting road that led into Clinton. We stopped at the Clintonia Inn, an old hotel on the outskirts of town that featured a nice atmosphere and elegantly-set tables. We were approached by an attractive, silver-haired lady who asked us what we might like for lunch.

"Well, since we are new in town, we really don't know. What's the special?" I asked, while looking around the attractive dining room.

"I guess I could bring you a menu," the elderly lady replied, "but the special is liver and onions, corn and mashed potatoes for $4.95." Since that was Peggy Sue's very favorite meal, we agreed to the special while admiring the antique dinner plates on the tables.

The restaurant was filled with customers, indicating it was a favorite eating place in town. Guests included a few couples, some men in business suits, two giddy young school girls who had probably skipped out on algebra class, and a large number of farmers, dressed in bib overalls, flannel shirts and baseball caps set at ridiculous angles on their heads.

Our meal was served family style with a large bowl of mashed potatoes and another filled with corn. Our plates were delivered with a large helping of liver, smothered with an inch of onions. I turned to Peggy Sue and asked, "How's our supply of Tums?" She told me not to worry, we had plenty—and then she dived right into the hearty meal.

As soon as we tasted the food, we could understand why the place was full of customers. After our delicious meal, we finished up with coffee and homemade apple pie—way better than mom ever made!

When I signaled for the check, the lovely silver-haired lady came right over. The tab read $12.85, no charge for the coffee. I thought this place must be stuck in a 1940's time warp. I handed her $15 and told her to keep the change. "Are you sure," she said, "it's over two dollars."

"It's okay, we enjoyed the food and our compliments to the chef," I replied.

"You are so sweet," she said as she gave me a big hug, "but I cooked this all myself."

On an impulse, I asked her if she happened to know

an old Mr. Van Sickel. "Outhouse Van Sickel?" she asked. "Sure, but I don't think I ever heard him referred to as 'mister.' He can usually be found over at the Wagon Wheel Bar on the east side of town. Go to the first stoplight, turn right and go about five miles. You'll see the place at the bottom of Suicide Ridge. Oh, and by the way, my name is Jean," she said, holding out her hand.

Peggy Sue and I introduced ourselves, thanked her for a wonderful lunch and for the directions to the Wagon Wheel Bar. "We'll see you again soon," I said as we headed out of the restaurant.

"If we can find this Outhouse guy," I said to Peggy Sue once we were outside, "he may be able to tell us a few things about the house that we need to be looking out for…like more hidden doors. You know he helped build the house years ago and might know the locations."

Peggy Sue agreed. "It's a great idea to find him. I sure don't want to get lost in another dark room any time soon."

We found the Wagon Wheel Bar with no trouble. It was located at the foot of a large ridge. Jean had referred to it as Suicide Ridge, but it looked pretty benign to us. What did not look harmless was the bar!

It appeared to have been there since before World War I, and seemed like a perfect hangout for a motorcycle gang. The building was sitting kiddywampos to the street and the roof had many shingles missing. It had probably never seen a coat of paint and the bare wood was weather-worn and cracked. A broken sign advertising some kind of beer was dangling from one end, slowly twisting in the wind. I began to wonder if it would be safe to enter the place.

I left Peggy Sue safely locked in the car and headed toward the door. The door appeared to be hanging by a single hinge, but I gave it a tug and it opened.

When I got inside, I was surprised that the place was not so bad at all and it was not nearly as dirty as the basement of my new cottage at the lake. About 15 people were seated at tables, with a few more patrons at the bar. I wanted to appear friendly so I ordered a draft beer and took a couple of swigs.

When the tough-looking bartender came over with his damp towel to wipe down my side of the bar, I casually asked him, “Do you know Mr. Outhouse Van Sickel?”

“Yeah, that’s him over there in his usual place in the corner. I ain’t never seen you in here before. You a bill collector?”

“No, nothing like that,” I said as I walked toward Mr. Outhouse. I could see the small, white-haired man, dressed in the town’s required attire: bib overalls, plaid shirt and a baseball cap. As I approached him, I noticed he was quite elderly and might have weighed about a hundred pounds. His face was as weathered as the wood on the outside of the bar and his features were craggy. A cigarette hung from his wrinkled lips and a glass of beer and two shots of whiskey sat before him. I stopped a few feet from his usual hangout and he noticed me through the cigarette smoke. He looked up at me as I said respectfully, “Excuse me. Are you Mr. Van Sickel?”

“Who the hell wants to know? And what’s with this ‘Mr. Van Sickel’ bullshit? You selling something?” His response was not what I had expected to hear from such an old, slightly-built man. I almost laughed, but managed to keep my composure.

“No, sir,” I said, “but I would like to talk to you about the old house on Irish Hill if you have a minute. Your son Lance said you helped build it years ago and that you might answer a few questions for me.”

“Oh, so you know my millionaire banker son. Well, I don’t hold that against ya. Yeah, I worked on the place. I delivered wood and mortar up that hill with a team of horses and a few years later did some work for the old guy that lived there. Whatcha wanta know?" All of this he delivered with a slight smile on his face.

"Well," I began, "first there are a couple of rooms that are locked down real tight. Do I need to hire a locksmith or do you know how to open them?"

He took a long drag on his cigarette and said, "I know of one room up there I worked on several years ago. I took out a window on the second floor and bricked up the opening. Then I removed everything from the walls and covered them with some kind of padding that old man Levison gave me and told me to put up. Then, he had me take down the bathroom door and replace it with a handmade one that I carved from solid oak. He said he wanted the inside of the door covered with tin and equipped with sliding locks so it could only be unlocked from the bathroom side. I thought this was a crazy idea, but he was paying me real well, so I didn't ask any questions. I just did as I was told. If you don't know how to open those sliding bolts, you'd have to tear down the whole damn wall to get in there. And that door in the hallway is fake. It's part of the wall and wasn't made to open."

"Wait a second," I said, "you are going too fast for me. Who is this Levison person?"

"He's the old fart who built the place back in '26," Outhouse said as he knocked back one of the shots, chasing it with a sip of beer.

I told Outhouse I remembered seeing that name on the old abstract. "It referred to him as a judge; is that right?" I asked with a great deal of interest.

"Yeah, that's right. He was from Detroit. Some said back then that he was in the rackets. Hey, listen, I gotta go home and take my medicine. Maybe we can talk some more another time. I enjoy talking about the past and, as you can tell by how I look, I don't have much of a future. You can usually find me here in my office," he chuckled.

He picked up his Marlboros, threw down his last shot

and finished off the beer. As he started to leave, I said, "Thanks very much for the information, Mr. Van Sickel."

Turning toward me suddenly, he said, "Look! Just call me Outhouse and drop the 'mister' crap!"

"Okay, then, Outhouse, would you mind telling me how to get into the room off the bathroom?"

As I followed him to the door, Outhouse said, "Look closely and you will see three small slots in one side of the door. Take a screwdriver and turn them all so they are vertical to the doorjamb, then pull on the doorknob and it should open if no one has changed anything. I'll talk to you again, but next time, you owe me some drinks." He declined my offer of a ride, saying he'd rather walk the short distance to his home.

When I got back to the car Peggy Sue was taking a little nap. When I rapped lightly on the window to wake her, she said "I thought you were never coming out. I'm cold and I'm bored!"

"Just wait 'til I tell you what I found out. I know how to get in one of the locked rooms and Outhouse actually met Judge Levison, the old man who built our house," I told her excitedly while starting the car heater to warm up my sweetheart.

We needed to stop by the hardware store to get a flashlight, some bug bombs and a screwdriver. I was hopeful they might have some old skeleton keys I could try in some of my locked doors. I dropped the gearshift down into "drive" and felt that big V-8 tug at my foot. I followed the directions Jean had given us at the restaurant and in just a few minutes we were in front of the hardware store. By this time, we had covered most of the town which was small enough to prevent getting lost. The population sign had read 750 souls.

We were greeted at the door of the hardware store by a very polite, slightly heavyset woman who introduced herself as Mrs. Galovan and asked how she might help us. "I'm Zack and this is Peggy Sue," I replied, "and we need some industrial strength fumigation bombs for spiders in our basement; and we need a flashlight and a screwdriver."

Mrs. Galovan assured us that would be easy to take care of since she had just received an order of commercial grade Black Flag bug spray. "Have a spider problem, do ya?" she asked.

"Yes, a big one…they look like black widows to me. Think that Black Flag'll kill 'em?" I asked, speaking loudly enough so Peggy Sue could hear me.

Mrs. Galovan replied in a hearty voice, "Why sure, it'll kill 'em deader'n a doornail!" That reminded me that I wanted to ask her about old skeleton keys that might fit our locks. She said she would take a look in the back of the store in some old boxes she was ready to discard. As she walked away, I hastily said I had noticed there were only 750 people in town and was wondering if they had a cop.

"Sure we do," she said, "that would be Constable Schultz and he lives over on Elm Street." She disappeared into a dark room at the back of the store and soon returned with four old skeleton keys. "You can just have these since I was getting ready to pitch 'em out anyway. Now, let's see, two cans of insect spray, flashlight and a screwdriver: that will be $8.20."

As I was paying my tab, Mrs. Galovan remarked to Peggy Sue, "You must be new in town." My wife replied that we were indeed newcomers, having just bought the house out by the lookout tower.

"Oh, I know the one. I hope you'll be happy living way out there, but it's so remote. And be careful with that bug killer. It's strong and should kill anything and everything crawling around in that basement. I've been told it's very dark and damp down there."

Peggy Sue, not wanting to carry on a long conversation because it was getting late, said her goodbyes and we were soon back in the car heading toward the hill.

As soon as we arrived at the house, I thought I should go ahead and set off one of the bug bombs in the old sauna while there was still light outside. It was so dark down there in the daytime I couldn't imagine how black it would be at night. I pulled out my new flashlight and a can of the Black Flag, went to the hidden basement door, pushed the woodwork and walked through the open door. I flipped the switch to turn on the lone 60-watter and headed down the stairs. As I entered the old shower room, I turned on the new flashlight. What a difference from the single-cell! I could see clearly now, but was glad Peggy Sue was not with me. In the new brighter light I could see that we had passed through an area with even more spiders than were in the small steam room. I hurried over, opened the sauna door, and propped it open with a piece of old pipe. I pulled the tab on my H-Bomb and it started spewing at an alarming rate. I set it down quickly, ran up the stairs and closed the door just before the gas cloud reached the top of the stairs. It crossed my mind that I probably needed a license and operating instructions to use that powerful stuff.

Peggy Sue was at the top of the stairs jingling the four keys and holding the bag with the screwdriver and extra can of bug spray. "Which one shall we try first?" she asked. I suggested we go upstairs and try the screwdriver on the door in the bathroom. "At least it's light up there and there are no bugs," I said.

When I got to the locked door in the upstairs bathroom, I was ready. I had the screwdriver in my hand and was going over in my head the instructions Outhouse had given me. The door looked even more formidable than I remembered and I could tell it was built from solid oak or other hardwood since it made a deep "thunking" sound when I tapped it with the handle of the screwdriver. I looked on the side of the door and found the three recessed and nicely hidden slotted screw heads. I put the blade of the screwdriver in the first one, told Peggy Sue to cross her fingers, and I twisted! Just as smooth as silk that screw turned effortlessly until it was vertical with the wall. I did the same thing with the second one. Closer inspection revealed that the third screw was already in the proper position. I grasped the glass door handle, told Peggy Sue to step back out of the way, and pushed on the door.

The door opened just a little and then stopped as if it had bumped into something. I put my shoulder against the door and pushed as hard as I could. There was quite a lot of resistance but I managed to shove the door partly open.

Immediately, we heard a tremendous buzzing sound. The room was alive with thousands of the biggest wasps I had ever seen…and assorted other flying creatures. Peggy Sue had retreated behind the door to what would be the boys' bedroom. I hollered at her to bring the extra can of bug spray. She grabbed the can, ran over and handed it to me and then ran out of the way. By now the bathroom was filling with all sorts of flying insects. They dove into my hair, my ears and under my shirt. I felt I only had a few minutes to take action because I was starting to get dizzy from holding my breath! I didn't want to inhale one of those bastards. I knew I had to kill them somehow, so I cautiously, but quickly, pulled the pin on the gas bomb and started the flow of gas. Then I threw the fizzing canister into the room of whirling, frenzied insects.

I barged into the boys' bedroom where Peggy Sue was, and slammed the door closed. She began frantically brushing off the flies, wasps, hornets and even a few bees from my head and clothing with an old piece of newspaper. Luckily, I was not stung, just completely out of breath. For an instant, I had envisioned myself as a foot soldier attacking an enemy pillbox with a hand grenade!

Outhouse must have been right about the padding in the room. With that much buzzing going on behind the door and we hadn't heard a thing, the room must be soundproofed.

"Have you ever seen so many wasps?" I asked Peggy Sue.

"My gosh, no. Are you all right? If you had been stung by that many insects you could have been killed. It's a good thing you had that extra can of spray. What are you going to do now?"

I took the skeleton keys from her hand and said, "I'm okay. That gas smelled strong. Let's go try each of these keys in the door in the library and then come back and take a peek inside this room in about an hour. That should be enough time to kill anything flying around in there."

We proceeded down the hallway, past the wall mural and into the master bedroom, then entered the small library. Peggy Sue had not yet seen this room and was amazed. "Wow, look at all these old books. What a neat room. And look over there; it's an old-style telephone lying on the floor behind that desk. I wonder if it works."

I told her I had found a similar one downstairs and that it had a dial tone when I picked it up. Peggy Sue was eager to try this telephone, too. "Let's see if it works. If it does, I can call the kids and tell them we will be a little late," she said. The phone worked and we decided Jake had left in such a hurry he forgot to have the service shut off.

When Peggy Sue reached the kids, they had a million questions about what was going on and had we seen the school yet. Peggy Sue said she hadn't seen the school but she would answer all their questions when we got home.

While she was on the telephone, I had been trying to slide that heavy-duty bookcase far enough to the side so that I could get to the keyhole in the door. I asked Peggy Sue to help me, thinking if we both pushed the bookcase might give. Still, nothing doing. It would not budge. I looked around for something I could use as a pry bar and found two broken chairs in a corner. We retrieved them and Peggy Sue and I placed both between the doorjamb and the bookcase. Using the back legs as levers and pulling with all our strength, the shelves begin to move. Slowly, ever so slowly, it slid to the side just enough to expose the door lock. There was no way this thing could have been moved in the last year or so—or maybe in the last ten years!

I started the first key toward the old lock. My hand was shaking so badly I had to steady it with my other, but the key went right in. I turned it. Nope. No dice! It didn't fit. The other keys looked much the same except one was a bit longer and had a few extra notches on it. I slipped this one into the keyhole and Bingo! A perfect fit. I heard the tumblers click.

I turned the knob and tried the door. Talk about squeaking—it did that in spades, but at least it opened. There was a long, steep set of stairs going up, to what I supposed must be the attic. We both went up because Peggy Sue did not want to stay alone in that library since it was beginning to get dark.

No one had been up these stairs in years. The dust was at last a half-inch deep. The stairway ended in an enormous attic. Even in the dimming light, I could see that everything was painted white, including a high vaulted ceiling. There was a complete hardwood floor that ran the entire length of the attic, and there were large windows at each end. Both windows had several broken panes. I played my flashlight around the deep recesses of the large hall and the beam fell upon a large pile of what appeared to be cots or beds. I moved cautiously closer, not knowing how much weight the old floor could hold.

They were old-style single beds, and there must have been 25 of them. Just adjacent to the beds were rolled up mattresses, several with their padding scattered about and torn apart by birds or mice. Everything had been rotting up here for years.

Peggy Sue and I decided we had discovered what

appeared to be an infirmary ward or an army barracks. A whole company of men could have bedded down up here. We were about to explore further when suddenly we heard wings flapping and a squeaking, high-pitched sound. Looking up we saw *bats*, hundreds of bats in the air and hundreds more hanging upside-down from the rafters just over our heads. It was getting dark and they were becoming active. "Run, Peggy Sue, I'm right behind you," I shouted. "Those things could be rabid for all we know."

We scampered down the dusty stairwell and slammed the door to keep them in the attic. I said to Peggy Sue, "The hell with this. I've had enough for today. Let's head for home. Spiders, giant flies and now bats! What in the world have we gotten ourselves into. This place is going to need a major clean up and I just don't know if I'm up to it." We left, hoping things would look better tomorrow in the daylight.

We both fell heavily into the front seat of the Caddie, totally exhausted. The interior had a new-car smell and was comfortable, clean, and a far cry from the filth we had just experienced in our "mansion." I clicked on the heater and soon it was toasty and warm and a perfect place to relax. We talked about the discoveries the day had brought.

I asked Peggy Sue what she was thinking about and quietly she said, "I'm just wondering what to feed the kids. I didn't put out anything for dinner." I laughed and told her the kids had probably eaten all the chips and drank all the soft drinks they could find. "I'm not hungry at all, are you?" I asked.

"No," she replied while rubbing her tummy, "I'm still burping liver and onions."

Touching my own stomach, I said, "You know, I'm feeling a little nauseated just thinking about that mess we just went through. All that bat poop. Yuck! It's so filthy and dirty, I don't think we need to be going in there again. It may be really bad for our health. We need to hire someone to go in there and clean it up and redecorate for us. I know it's gonna be costly, but we got the place at a bargain.

"After going through the house a couple of times, what do you make of it?"

Putting her hand on her forehead as if trying to soothe an apparent headache, Peggy Sue said, "I just can't decide whether I love it or hate it. The appearance of the house outside is just magnificent and the surroundings are breathtaking, but inside, deep in its bowels, it's kind of rotten and decaying.

"It seems obvious to me that with all those hidden doors and rooms someone, probably Mr. Levison when he built the place, was trying to hide something from any strangers that might visit…or maybe even burglars. I think it was a place for large gatherings of people, and those people wanted to have very private meetings. That's why the house was built so large and in such a remote and secluded area. Don't you agree?"

"Yeah, I'd go along with that," I said. "Maybe it was built as some kind of private club, like the Elks or the Masons, but I don't think they use hidden, soundproof rooms in any of their ceremonies. I think we both agree on hiring a home remodeler or an interior decorator."

Peggy Sue replied, "One of my girlfriends just had her house remodeled by a fellow named Lefty Walker. I could get in touch with him and see if he would be interested in taking a look at our place and giving us an estimate. In fact, I'll get right on that in the morning."

When we got home, we found the kids fast asleep on the sofa with the TV blaring away. Mama woke them and whisked them off to bed and I jumped in the shower. I was never so happy in my life as to wash off all that stink from the gas bombs and the dirt and slime I had picked up from the basement, the attic, and the encounter with the insect swarm from hell. I noticed, however, when toweling off that I had actually been stung a few times on my chest. I guess I was too scared even to feel the bites. I hoped I wouldn't ever again have to experience the terror I had been through earlier in the day.

5

Peggy Sue arranged a lunch meeting for me the next day with Lefty Walker; and I was pleased to see how professional he looked. Dressed in clean white painter's coveralls, a starched shirt and a Sherwin-Williams Paints cap, he impressed me as a nice guy with lots of knowledge. After I had given him my description of the house and all its problems, he said "It all sounds very interesting but I would like to see the place so I can give you a better estimate."

With a smile on his face he told me it sounded like the deal that would make his retirement very comfortable! I knew then that this project was going to be expensive, even though Lefty had probably been kidding. Little did he know!

Lefty wanted to see the property as soon as possible and I was eager to get started on the improvements, so we hopped into his white pickup right after lunch for the long drive out to the Irish Hills.

As we pulled up to the foot of the driveway, his face showed the same expression mine must have when I first saw the place. "Man, this is unbelievable. I can't wait to see the inside of that house." He got out his estimate forms and a really big pencil!

After Lefty had spent several minutes telling me how impressed he was with the premises, we went into the house for the inspection and got down to business. Lefty found the main floor to be structurally sound and thought new carpets and a fresh coat of paint on the walls and a good cleaning of the woodwork was all that was required. The ceiling needed to be re-plastered where some leaks had caused considerable damage.

Lefty believed the kitchen appliances needed to be replaced with modern ones or that the existing appliances should be rebuilt if we wanted to maintain the character of the kitchen.

The assessment of the upstairs was pretty much the same: new wallpaper, fresh coats of paint and new carpet would take care of things quite well. Still, Lefty had not yet seen the soundproofed room.

We had discussed the horrible insect swarm on the way to the Irish Hills, so Lefty wasn't surprised at the vast amount of dead insects and bats that lay about in the bathroom when we entered. I managed to push open the door to the secret room so we could both slip inside.

Never in my life had I seen such a mess. A couple of bricks had fallen out of the area where Outhouse had sealed up the window opening. This had evidently resulted in every flying insect in the country and all their bat cousins to make themselves right at home in this peculiar, windowless room.

The walls of the room were completely covered, floor to ceiling, in a filthy, deep-purple heavy padding which had come loose from the walls in several places. The pressed-tin ceiling held a lone light fixture covered by heavy wire mesh. A cot, similar to the ones in the attic, and a dirty mattress were leaning against the wall next to the door, preventing us from opening the door without a mighty effort.

The smell was overwhelming. The remains of the fumigation gas, the dung all over the floor, and the dead birds and bats made it necessary to open all the windows in the other part of the house in an effort to prevent some serious puking!

Lefty muttered a comment while holding his nose…something to the effect that he could replace the missing bricks, tear down and throw out that ugly padding and wash down the walls with a water hose.

He said his crew could shovel out the mess in the room but it would take a long time to get rid of the stench. Once the stench was gone, Lefty said he could put some nice heavy oil-cloth wall covering on the walls. "Forget that," I said, "Who in the hell would want to sleep in a room with no window, just four bare walls and a door that locks only from the outside? That would be just like living in a cell. Do whatever you have to do to clean it up; and install a new doorknob that operates from both sides just in case someone forgets and closes that door and gets locked in."

Thinking to myself that the room would probably be used only for storage, I told Lefty I'd like to show him the attic.

On the way to the master bedroom and the entrance to the attic through the library, Lefty commented on the condition of the wallpaper in the hallway. He said it was very unusual and he thought it was probably made in France. He said he would attempt to clean the wallpaper but he did not want to touch the mural because he might damage it.

When Peggy Sue and I had moved the heavy bookcase away from the door to the attic so we could climb the stairs, we left it with the door exposed. Therefore, Lefty did not notice that the bookcase would slide and cover the door. We took the stairs to the attic and I told Lefty we would probably find a large infestation of bats…but he assured me they would probably be asleep because it was still the middle of the day. Surely enough, when we reached the top of the stairs, we could see them dangling everywhere from the attic ceiling.

We were not interested in using the attic for anything so I asked Lefty just to clean up the mess of old beds and mattresses, replace the broken window panes and to get rid of the bats.

"This will probably be the easiest of all the jobs in the whole project," Lefty assured me. "I'll just get some of that industrial strength spray you used in the bathroom. If it doesn't kill 'em, they'll vacate the premises quick as a wink through those broken windows. Then I'll replace the broken panes."

We left the attic and all the upstairs windows wide open to air out, and then we headed for the basement. I wasn't sure how I would respond to all Lefty's comments on the amount of work required in that particular area!

Lefty thought it was pretty cool the way the basement door was secreted into the paneling, but when he looked down that long, dark stairwell he said, "The first thing we have to do is get the light fixtures operating down there."

Using a big spotlight Lefty had brought, we hit the bottom of the stairs and he turned his attention almost immediately to a ballroom-size, windowless room that was located just to the right of the stairs, through a large archway. Using his strong spotlight, we could see that the whole area was large enough to hold large banquets or dances. From the huge oak beams that spanned the ceiling hung four chandeliers, one intact, but the other three broken in pieces and dangling from their electric wires.

The floor was carpeted, wall-to-wall, in a design right out of the 1920's, deep maroon in color with big gold flowers cascading everywhere. Not only was the carpet old, but it was well worn from the many feet that had danced across its surface. Several large holes were torn in the carpet and those were covered with mildew and moss. The smell was rank. The ballroom was a stinking mess right now, but had once been a thing of exquisite beauty.

I could visualize the 20's—hear the band playing, and the dancers twirling round and round. What a place for a party!

Lefty's voice brought me back to the present when he said he would need to put in a couple of de-humidifiers to get some of the moisture out of the air before he began any renovations to the room.

The walls were covered in the same beautiful solid oak paneling found in the upstairs living room and other parts of the house. It only needed extensive cleaning.

Our light revealed another smaller archway at the far end of the room where the boiler heating system was still operating quietly, sending heat to the small radiators in most rooms and to the garage, as well. There were also old concrete washtubs and what appeared to be water purification filters for the well water, and boxes and junk scattered here and there. There were lots of the ever-present cobwebs, but not a single creepy-crawly thing. Apparently, the heavy-duty gas bomb I set off earlier had done its job. Encouraged by this, I told Lefty I wanted to show him an old shower room and sauna on the other side of the basement.

"Let's go," he said, "I've never seen anything like this place." We passed by the large wooden wine racks and Lefty made a wisecrack: "I see they left you some booze, but I bet that stuff is strong as hell."

I chuckled and told him, "I'm not even going to take one sip of that stuff. Who knows, it might turn me into a zombie."

Lefty's appraisal of the shower room wasn't too bad. He said it really only needed cleaning. When he turned on the squeaking valves and water spurted out getting both our feet wet, we were pleased that it went quickly down the drain.

He also felt the ceramic tile on the walls and floor was in excellent condition and would need only a good cleaning. There were three fittings for toilets in the shower room and he asked if we wanted toilets installed. I decided one would be convenient. Lefty also believed the sauna room could be fixed by a good hosing down because the drains were functional. I told Lefty about the large number of spiders we had encountered in this room. A play of his flashlight against the walls and floor revealed hundreds of bodies of large spiders, obviously the victims of my gas bomb. That did my heart good because not only did I despise these creepy crawlers, they terrified my wife and I didn't want her to be uncomfortable in our new lake house.

"Well, Lefty, that just about does it," I said. "Let's go upstairs where it's warmer and get some fresh air." When Lefty said he had seen enough to make his assessment, we decided to go out to his truck and talk over this project we were faced with.

The bright late February sun had warmed Lefty's truck nicely. I watched him as he got out his legal pad and began to write. Every now and then he would murmur something while wetting the end of his large pencil with his tongue. After he had written about half a page, he turned to me and said, "If you and the missus will pick out your carpet and have it delivered we'll install it. The same goes for the paint and wallpaper. She can select her colors and just let us know what room to put it in. You can have everything delivered here and we will do all the labor. I think this would be the easiest way for us to proceed. And if you could set up a small charge account at the hardware store, we could then pick up the small things we might need like the windowpanes, light fixtures or door fittings and any wood we might need to replace."

We talked about the exterior of the house which was in really good condition and decided Lefty and his crew would only work on the interior.

I watched as Lefty continued to write his list, adding money figures for each item. When he reached the bottom of the page, he got out his calculator and started adding up all the numbers. I peeked and saw the total at the end of the column: $15,000.

"I will do the entire job for this amount, labor only with you providing all the materials," he said while pointing to the total at the bottom of the page. "You might need a few days to think about it…or are we ready to get rolling?"

I thought about it for a moment and realized I needed to do something right away. The place was uninhabitable in its present condition. I was sure the horrible condition of the interior of the house was the primary reason Jake had spent most of his nights at the hotel in town and never actually occupied the house. I really wanted to see the house returned to its original condition, back to the image that was painted on the mural wall in the upstairs hallway. Because I'm a pretty good businessman, I had a figure in the back of my head and Lefty's matched up pretty well with my own estimate of what it would take to fix the place up. So, without hesitating any longer, I said, "That sounds like a fair deal to me. When can you get started? Soon, I hope!"

"Well, Mr. Heikel, you sure don't take long to make up your mind," Lefty replied while looking at the calendar on the back of his clipboard. "You also seem to have hit my schedule just perfectly. We can finish up the job we're on now and get over here and start cleaning up the place the first of the week. But, you will need to get a couple of de-humidifiers in that basement right away to get rid of some of the dampness down there."

Lefty said he didn't require a deposit but he would appreciate getting the charge account opened at the hardware store in Clinton and hoped we would get the paint, carpet and wallpaper ordered as soon as possible.

"My wife and I will get started on that tomorrow," I told him as I signed the bottom of his work order. We shook hands on our deal and Lefty said he needed to be heading back home.

I remembered all the open windows upstairs so I hurried off to close things up so we wouldn't find any new flying or crawling creatures when we came back.

As Lefty and I made the drive home, we speculated on what use the mansion had been put to and why it was built in such an unusual manner. Lefty said he thought it might have been some sort of private sanitarium because of the padded cell and the fact that so many people could be accommodated in the vast interior spaces of the house. The conversation went on and on with neither of us ever reaching any type of conclusion. As we talked, I kept wondering if Lefty would run into any other mysteries hidden in the house. I was fairly confident, however, that we had discovered all of them. What surprises were still in store for me!

Soon we arrived back at the restaurant where my car was parked. I gave Lefty an extra key to the house, said goodbye and drove home, happy that I had finally made a start on the interior renovation of my mansion in the clouds.

Peggy Sue and I spent the entire weekend going over paint charts she had picked up at the local paint store. Our final choices were moss greens and beige throughout most of the house, with white enamel for the woodwork. We planned to order the wallpaper and carpeting from the hardware store in Clinton. We could look at carpet samples and wallpaper books there.

When Monday morning arrived, we were eager to get on the road. I dropped Peggy Sue off at the store to make her selections, told her I would meet her for lunch, and then headed off to the house.

When I arrived at the top of the hill, I saw that Lefty and his crew were already hard at work and had been for some time. A large dump truck and a couple of pickups were being used to hold the trash that was being hauled out of the house. The upstairs windows were all wide open and I could hear a shovel banging against the floor as I walked in the front door.

Lefty came running up to me and said, "I've got it! I've been thinking about it all weekend. It's a state run boys' dormitory."

I laughed at him and said, "Lefty, are you still thinking about that? One thing I am sure of is that this was never a state owned property. I have the abstract. But, you just keep thinking and maybe you'll come up with the right answer. How's the work coming?"

Lighting up a cigarette and taking a deep draw, Lefty said, "Well, we have only been here for an hour or so, but it's going pretty well. The slow parts will be the repairs, the painting and the carpet laying, but I'll tell you one thing. You're going to have a beautiful place here when I'm done. I guarantee it.

"I've got two men upstairs cleaning the bug room and two guys in the attic chasing the bats out through the windows. They tilt open, you know; and I have two guys in the basement power blasting the shower and that smaller room. We're going to start pulling up the rug in an hour or so, but we've got to figure out how to get the lights turned on down there. Let's go take a look."

Commenting that Lefty wasn't wasting any time, I followed him down into the basement where I could hear the power water system blasting the walls and floor in the shower room and the guys shouting orders to each other.

"There's got to be a power box with fuses somewhere down here," Lefty said as he searched the walls with his spotlight. When we looked in the boiler room, we found the main electrical power box which held old-style fuses with the window in the end that showed whether or not the fuse was blown. Lefty played his light on each one and we found there were three blown 40-AMP fuses.

"I figured we'd find these old style fuses here, so I picked up a few on the way out," Lefty said. He reached in his pocked and took out a new fuse. "Well, let's see what happens when I screw in the first one." Nothing! Then he removed the other two blown fuses and replaced them. Instantly a light came on in the boiler room, illuminating a large panel that contained several light switches. Lefty flipped all the switches to the on position and we heard the men yell from the shower room.

"Hey, the lights just came on in the shower."

One of the chandeliers in the ballroom came on and we could finally see what we were doing. It beat the heck out of working in the dark! Lefty took one look at the three other chandeliers that were hanging precariously by their electric wires. They would have to be disconnected and repaired to prevent a short circuit.

Even in the light of one chandelier, the ballroom looked even bigger than I had imagined. My first thought was that there was a lot of carpet on the floor. I wondered if the dump truck was big enough to hold it all.

Lefty told the crew working in the shower room to finish up in there and then bring the water blasters into the ballroom to take some of the dirt, grime and mildew off the wall paneling. He and two other men took out carpet knives and began cutting out sections that were small enough to be carried easily to the dump truck.

I walked over to the shower room and was thrilled to see that all the spider webs, dead spiders and dust were completely gone and that I was surrounded by bright, vivid colors on all the shower walls. The floor was a beautiful rose-colored ceramic tile. I peeked into the sauna area and found it to be spotlessly clean as well.

It was evident that the crew had also used the water blasters on a low power to rinse off the wine racks. The old wine bottles were a beautiful green color and the shelves were made of heavily-grained oak. It was amazing to me that after a really short time, everything was beginning to look livable.

I was startled out of my reverie when I heard Lefty shout, "Zack, come here. You've got to see this!"

I hurried out of the shower room and into the ballroom. I could see the men were peering down at the floor where they had just cut out a large section of carpet.

"What is it?" I asked breathlessly.

"It's…it's a cement door in the floor," Lefty stuttered.

"Well, can we open it?" I asked excitedly.

"I don't know. It looks heavy," Lefty said. "See those two steel rings? I think we'll have to slide something through them like a pipe or something and maybe with a man on each end we can lift it out of the floor."

There were some discarded water pipes on the floor in the shower room and Lefty sent one of the men to get one. We slipped the heavy water pipe through the steel rings and, with Lefty and me on one side and the two other men on the other end of the pipe, we lifted.

Surprisingly, the door was not all that heavy and it came right out of the floor. We set it down with a thud and Lefty directed his light down into a large pit with eight steps leading down to the bottom of an opening about four-feet by five-feet. Lefty scampered down the steps and said he could see the opening of a cement-lined tunnel that headed out toward the front of the house. He used his bright spotlight to examine the recesses of the tunnel and said it was about six-feet square and headed downward at about a 15-degree angle. A small set of steel tracks was anchored to the floor of the tunnel and appeared to travel all the way down to the foot of the hill and exit on Collier Road.

"My God, Lefty, don't go in!" I shouted at the top of my voice, startling all four of us.

"You don't have to worry about that," Lefty managed to gulp, "I can't stand tight places and the Lord only knows where this thing goes. Whatever it is, it certainly hasn't been used in years, but I'd say it's big enough for a man to pass through."

One of the men standing next to me looked down into the tunnel and said in a terrified voice, "That tunnel looks evil to me. It's pitch black in there and it's heading straight down to hell. It's the devil's hole!"

That did it for me. It just sounded too spooky and his

voice seemed to echo all around the empty hall.

I told Lefty in a quivering, but my best "bossy" voice, "Get on up out of there and let's get this cover back over this hole. Who knows who or what could come up through that tunnel. It could be full of rats for all we know."

The four of us quickly replaced the cement door and I said, "Lefty, you and I will talk about this later. We need to decide what we can do to seal up this hole. Maybe, fill it with cement. Let's get on with taking up this rug."

The two other men set out again removing the carpeting and they were soon joined by the men from the attic. In a few hours, they had all the old carpeting and pad cut out and thrown in the box of the dump truck. Then they turned the high-pressure hoses on the wall panels.

All the while the men were working, I couldn't stop thinking about the tunnel and wondering what it had been used for and where it might end. I did know one thing for certain: the mysteries in the house were multiplying and I wouldn't sleep soundly until I unraveled them.

Now I was beginning to understand what Jake must have been going through and why he had lost so much sleep. I didn't know whether or not he had penetrated any of the strange hidden spaces, but he was obviously losing sleep over something. What could it have been? Even though he probably never spent a night in the house, something he had experienced had kept him awake.

It was almost noon by this time and I remembered I was supposed to meet Peggy Sue for lunch. I told Lefty I would see him in a few hours and he reminded me I needed to pick up a couple of de-humidifiers and some more gas bombs for the attic.

I drove straight to the hardware store but didn't see Peggy Sue anywhere when I peered in the windows. I glanced across the street and saw her waving to me from the front window of the restaurant at the Clintonian Inn. I hurried across the street, eager to tell her about the day's new find at the "cottage," but she was so excited about her choices of rugs and wallpaper that I couldn't get a word in edgewise. She described her selections and told me they would be delivered in just a few days. On and on she went. Finally after a good ten minutes, she slowed down long enough to take a breath and I jumped right in and told her about the secret door in the basement floor that had been concealed under the old carpet.

"Oh, no, not again," she said. "A secret door to where? When is all this going to end?"

"We lifted the door off and found a hole in the floor with several steps leading to the bottom where there was a tunnel heading out toward the front of the house with a set of small tracks. I think it might exit at the bottom of the hill on the road. I can only speculate; but, personally, I think it's an escape route of some sort or it was used to transport debris down from the top of the hill when the house was under construction."

Forgetting all about her decorating and with a concerned look on her face, Peggy Sue said, "This I have to see for myself. After lunch you can show it to me."

I told her the cover had already been replaced but I could show her the secret door in the floor. I thought maybe I could talk the guys into lifting it once again so my wife could see it for herself, but I was a little hesitant because I didn't know what might have come to the surface in the meantime!

After a quick "blue plate special" lunch of catfish, coleslaw and hush puppies, we stopped at the hardware store, picked up the two de-humidifiers and four cans of Black Flag. Then it was off to the house to show my beautiful wife the day's latest mystery.

Lefty and his crew were outside finishing up their lunches when we pulled up the driveway. Peggy Sue and I walked over to them and I told Lefty I had mentioned the tunnel to her.

"You know, I've been thinking about that during lunch and I think maybe it's what we in the construction business call a slouch box. That would be a fast exit for water if the basement should somehow be flooded."

I thought about it for a minute and then replied, as if I knew what I was talking about, "Yeah, Lefty, you've got something there but it certainly doesn't explain the rails on the floor of the tunnel. Also, how would the water get into the slouch box with that concrete slab on top of the hole? And, what are the chances of a flood this high up on a hill?"

"Gee, I don't know. Guess I'll have to think about that one some more," Lefty responded, scratching his chin.

Lefty sent one of his men to our car to retrieve the dehumidifiers and bug bombs. Lefty hurriedly hooked up the machines in the basement to start removing the moisture from the air and his helper hurried to the attic to set off a couple of the bombs to kill any bats that hadn't vacated the premises through the open windows.

Peggy Sue and I walked slowly over to the mystery in the floor. She was amazed at how large the ballroom was and how beautiful the oak paneling was shining in the glare from the chandelier. I commented that it didn't look too bad down here with all the rotten carpet gone and the walls shiny clean and she quickly agreed.

As we got to the far side of the ballroom and approached the mysterious cement slab in the floor, she looked down, shaking her head from side to side. "What could we possibly have here? This is nothing short of bizarre. I would say that Levison fellow certainly had a weird imagination about building a house or he hired a mentally-disturbed architect."

"I agree with you on that," I replied. "Do you want to look in the hole? I'll get the guys to open it up for you."

Still shaking her head, she said, “Absolutely not! I was just starting to feel good about this place and now I’m scared. This is all just too spooky. The hell with it! I don’t think you’ll ever get me to spend even one night in this house. I want to go home!” With that, she headed up the stairs toward the front door with me following quickly behind.

“See you tomorrow, Lefty,” I said as I hurried by him on my way out the door. “I’ll probably be by myself. Don’t work too late.”

My bride was very quiet on our trip home and, in order to break the silence, I asked, “Are you all right?”

“I’m just doing some real deep thinking. I’m not at all sure we did the right thing by buying that place. Until you figure out what the house is all about, I’m not going back in there. Not me and not my kids.”

“You’re right, Honey. There are just too many questions that I’ve got to get answers to. I’m sure there is a reasonable explanation to all of them and it’s just a matter of time until we figure it out. But, don’t worry, I’ll get to the bottom of all of it. Maybe if I could find a set of the original plans, that would tell us a lot,” I said thoughtfully.

6

At breakfast the next morning, I was preparing to go back to the house by myself. Peggy Sue was adamant that she would not be going with me. She was so upset I told her I would cancel my trip and stay at home with her to talk it all out. Even though I wanted to get back to the mansion and see what Lefty and his crew might uncover next, I was hopeful they would find nothing new and that everything would eventually settle down to something approaching normal.

I knew if I was going to keep my mate happy and get on with our plan to have a beautiful "cottage" at the lake, I would have to at least answer one of the many questions we had about the mansion on the hill. Getting the building plans would be wonderful but I was sure they were not available. Then I thought about the old abstract I got when I closed the deal on the house.

I went to my file cabinet where I had placed the abstract along with the other business papers. There was not much to be learned from the three-page document because Mr. Levison was the only person besides Jake who had ever owned the property. The abstract stated that Mr. Seymour T. Levison, a single man, had purchased the land, 224 acres, from the state in 1926 for the sum of $5,517.

This wasn't much help, but I knew I needed to find out something about this Mr. Levison person.

I remembered that Outhouse Van Sickel had told me Mr. Levison had been a judge in Detroit so maybe I could contact someone in the city judicial department and ask them to check their records for a Judge Levison.

I decided I would let my fingers do the walking, so I

picked up the yellow pages for the Detroit area and found the number for the clerk's office. The lady who answered the telephone sounded like she was at least 70 years old. I identified myself and told her I was inquiring about a judge who had served on the bench in the 1930's or possibly the '40's and I wondered if she could help me with something like that.

I heard a shaky giggle on the other end of the line and the nice lady said, "Why, my dear, I've been around here almost that long."

"Well, you're definitely the person I need to speak with," I said. "could you possibly check your records for the Honorable Judge Seymour T. Levison and let me know if you have a record of any such person."

"Judge Seymour T. Levison," the voice said; and, then after a short silence, I heard that same little chuckle, "I don't have to check our records. I remember him well. He was a judge in our Fifth District Court during those dates you mentioned and maybe even a little earlier. But, I must say, his departure in 1937 was something other than honorable.

"He was involved in a long criminal trial that year, not as a judge, but as a defendant accused of money laundering. He was also implicated as a silent, behind-the-scenes, member of the Detroit Purple Gang. This all came about by his handling of a trial years earlier when he found gang members not guilty of shooting and killing three members of a rival gang over on Collingwood Avenue in 1931.

"In, I believe it was, 1936, one of the gang members that he had found not guilty confessed to the killings on his death bed and implied that Judge Levison was on the take and one of the mob! This confession by the killer led to a Grand Jury investigation of the judge and a call for his resignation.

"I don't know why I'm telling you all this, but your questions just seemed to strike a chord with me. However, I think your best bet would be to contact the *Detroit News* because they ran a story about the complete trial and I'm sure they could get you a copy. What are you doing, writing a book or something?"

Pausing a moment to let everything she had said sink into my head, I said, "No, I'm not writing a book. But I must say you certainly know your stuff and have helped me a lot. I think I'll take your advice and get in touch with the *Detroit News* and ask about the article you mentioned."

I thanked her for her time and hung up the phone truly flabbergasted to learn that the man who had built the mansion in the sky might be some kind of mobster and a criminal masquerading as a judge!

I wasted no time, did the yellow pages thing again, and came up with the number for the newspaper. I called the number and told the young man who answered the phone that I was interested in getting copies of articles about a Judge Seymour T. Levison and the events surrounding his life and activities that ran in 1937.

The voice on the other end of the line asked nonchalantly, "Are you a *Detroit News* subscriber?"

"Oh, indeed I am; and I certainly enjoy the paper immensely," I said, crossing my fingers at my complete lie. I needed to get that article.

The young man said he would check on the information I had given him and get right back to me. I was on hold for about five minutes before he came back with positive news. "Sure we have it," he said. "What's your address. I will mail you a copy and a bill for $7 for the photostatic copy. You should get it in three or four days."

I gave him my address, amazed at how easy the answers were coming about one of the mysteries surrounding our mansion. I hoped the article would reveal information about the Detroit Purple Gang and who, or what, Judge Seymour T. Levison was.

When I related my two conversations to Peggy Sue

she was very relieved to learn that Mr. Levison was a real human being and not some kind of bloodsucking apparition that hung upside down from the ceiling at night.

She also pointed out something I hadn't thought about. "The story about the judge may sit well with you, but all it does for me instead of answering a question is bring up two more. Who was this guy and what is the Purple Gang that you mentioned."

"I don't know, Honey, but we'll know more when we get the newspaper article. I think it's some kind of miracle that we got this much information this fast with so little effort," I said, shrugging my shoulders.

The following morning when I took off to see how Lefty was doing with the clean-up job, I left Peggy Sue in the kitchen baking a cherry pie. She said she was going to spend a quiet day doing a little baking and some housework.

When I arrived at the lake house, I was happy to see everyone busy at work sweeping floors and washing down woodwork and wall paneling. I was really pleased at how well the wallpaper cleaner was working in the upstairs hallway. With all the old rugs gone and the secret padded room cleaned up and aired out, not only did the place look a lot better, it also smelled like crisp mountain air.

A workman was on some scaffolding, re-plastering the gaping hole in the living room ceiling while another crew of two men was replacing the broken windowpanes in the attic. Down in the basement, I found Lefty and another man reattaching the doors that had fallen off the large wine rack.

"Good morning," I called out cheerfully to the guys.

"Good morning to you, Zack. How is everything looking to you?"

I looked around the basement as far as I could see and noticed that the damaged chandeliers had been repaired and were hanging from the ceiling, glowing brightly. The four light fixtures bathed the basement area with bright light and there was no odor in the air at all since the area had almost completely dried out.

"Boy, those de-humidifiers really did the job, huh, Lefty?"

"That's right, Zack, but you will have to keep at least one of them running all the time to prevent the new rugs we'll be installing from wrinkling," Lefty said to me as he walked over to where I was standing.

I agreed there was no point in putting down new carpet just to let it get damp and mildew. "How late did you guys work the other night,?" I asked him as I made my way over to the area with the infamous concrete slab door.

"Well," Lefty answered, "we worked quite late, until almost 10 o'clock, but then a weird thing happened. Maybe it was nothing at all, but one of the guys thought it was terrifying. We were about to leave and we were all standing in the living room in front of the fireplace planning the next day's jobs when one of the men said he thought he could hear something like a wind chime very faintly. We all quieted down and sure enough it was a real low, tingling noise coming from out of the fireplace.

"For some reason Leroy—you remember Leroy, the guy who made the comment about the Devil's Hole—took off running out the front door and he said not to count on him coming back here the next day and he would not be back to work on my crew! Then he sped away in his pickup. I haven't seen him since and I still owe him some money.

"Anyway, it did sound a little eerie, but it's probably just something dangling loose in the chimney making that sound."

Somewhat frustrated, I said, "Man, this is all I need. If Peggy Sue hears about this, I'm positively going to have to sell the place. Lefty, please keep this to yourself. I'm sure there's a simple explanation for the noise and there's no use getting my wife all worked up."

"Well, Zack, as far as getting your wife worked up, what are you going to do about that tunnel? Should I just fill it up with cement? I could put a piece of plywood in front of the tunnel so the cement wouldn't run in and just fill her up and smooth it over flush with the floor."

"Lefty, that's the best thing I've heard today, but until we find out exactly what the tunnel is for, we had better not fill it up just yet," I said rather sharply. "I think I'll take a walk outside and look around. I haven't had much chance to see the surrounding area and anyway I need to let you men get back to work. If you need me, I'll be out in the back forty."

As soon as I left the house, the barns out back caught my eye. I wondered what might be in them and headed out that direction. The first one was nothing but an oversized brick garage and it appeared to be as old as the house. There was a huge padlock on the doors and it was so rusted it appeared to have been hanging there for years. I thought a couple of good blows with a heavy hammer would probably break open the lock. I walked over to one of Lefty's tool trucks and picked up the biggest hammer I saw. Then, I went back to the barn to attack the lock. With two hard blows, it broke in half. I pulled open the two large wooden doors and stepped in. The floor was so covered with dust and junk it looked like it was just dirt. In reality it was concrete.

Hanging on all four walls were all kinds of gardening tools, straw baskets and some old clothes laying around. There was a workbench on one wall. On top of it, amidst all the dirt, were old mechanic's tools, a pair of greasy coveralls, dirty rags, dust and an old bird nest…all of it making quite a mess.

In the middle of the floor there was a large mound of old boxes with *Canadian Club Whiskey* printed on the sides, several bales of hay, steamer trunks, old tires and a few old spoke wheels. I tried to move one of the top boxes to look inside but I caused a slight avalanche when the whole lot of them fell, hitting the floor in a big cloud of dust. I closed my eyes and covered my mouth. When the dust settled, right in front of me sat what appeared to be the hood of an antique automobile or truck.

I made my way around to its front and brushed off the nameplate. It read, "Packard 8." The car seemed to be completely intact except for missing front tires and a broken headlight. I moved carefully around to the rear and saw a Michigan license plate, 040536, dated 1937, on the rear bumper. Just below the bumper I noticed dual exhaust pipes which were very unusual for a car of that year model.

It appeared the Packard had been stored in this garage for years. An old tarpaulin covered most of the vehicle. Pulling it off slowly to minimize the dust clouds, I saw that it really wasn't a car at all but an old black hearse. In the lower rear door, six perfectly-round small holes were visible just below the window. I instantly thought "bullet holes."

I glanced into the rear seat and could see where the slugs had torn up the upholstery. There was a large spot of what looked like oil, or maybe even dried blood, all over the back seat.

I picked up a stick lying on the floor and stuck it into one of the holes in the door. Surely enough, it pointed straight toward the rear seat. It wasn't hard to imagine someone or something had been shot in this car. I took hold of the tarp, pulled it back up over the old Packard, and again concealed someone's secret from long ago!

Unnerved, I sat down on one of the trunks and tried to collect myself. It was beginning to seem that every time I opened a door or stepped into a room on this place, I encountered more unexplained and disturbing things.

Maybe my mind was just attuned to finding mysteries in everything because of the things we had already discovered on this property. Maybe my mind was playing tricks on me and these things were just normal and ordinary—not likely!

I left the barn and closed the door. I decided right then and there that I would call a junkyard first thing in the morning and ask them to come and tow that old hulk away. I didn't want any part of it—or what had happened in it—to be around the place. I had enough problems already. Why couldn't there have just been hay or something normal in the barn. That's what barns are for! Nah, things were not that easy here at the house on the hill. I decided my best course of action was to expect the unexpected because that seemed to be the norm on these premises.

Another outbuilding proved to be an old stable with a small loft. As I stepped through the split door I left the top half open for air ventilation and walked inside. There was a water pump on my left. I couldn't resist and started moving the handle up and down as vigorously as I could. Low and behold, water came pouring out, proving the well must still be good. The stalls in the barn needed to be cleaned and several boards needed replacing. Old hay bales appeared to have been there for years, but all-in-all the building was what it seemed to be, just an old stable. It was hot and sticky in the stable, so I moved outside in the cool breeze and walked to the next outbuilding.

The last barn, and the largest of the three, had a big hayloft full of old hay and a couple of surprises in store for me. Under the usual few inches of dust, cobwebs, and bales of hay, there was an old sleigh and, next to it, a buggy, both of them appearing to be in pretty good shape. Hanging on the wall was a complete harness and tack for both. All I would need now was the horse! This area would be a great place for horseback riding.

Forgetting all about the old Packard, I was now getting good vibes about my home in the woods and I could imagine myself next winter flying along in the blowing snow behind a muscular horse pulling that beautiful sleigh. This summer, if we got that horse, we could all go over hill and dale in the buggy and explore the whole countryside with ease.

Leaving my fantasies behind, I started back toward the house. I passed some tall, thick evergreen bushes about five feet high that lined the small dirt track that led to the barns. Imbedded in them were two old gas pumps about ten feet apart with their hoses lying partly covered with dirt and leaves. Their glass meters were broken and the dials so rusted you could hardly read them. "Wow," I thought, "these would be very convenient if I can get them working again. It would save so many trips to town for gas for the lawn-moving and snow-removal equipment I knew I had to buy."

I wondered how many gallons the underground tanks might hold, and how many cars' gas tanks might have been filled using these old pumps…and why back in the 1920's this much gas would have been needed by the occupants of the house.

Things were beginning to come together in my mind about this old place and they all seemed to be converging on one fact: that something in the late '30's or early '40's caused this place to become nearly abandoned and time to stand still. Everything, from my point of view, seemed to indicate that most activities and operations, whatever they were, must have ceased rather suddenly. It also seemed apparent, with the neglected condition of the house and grounds, that old man Levison must have become either a hermit or a non-resident!

The air was so fresh and sweet smelling outside, it made me suddenly think about the cherry pie Peggy Sue had been baking this morning. It was late afternoon, so I called out to Lefty and told him I'd see him in the morning.

"Maybe the carpet and wallpaper and paint will be in tomorrow," I hollered, "and, by the way, Lefty, there are some old gas pumps buried in those evergreen bushes over there. Would you take a took at them and see if they are connected electrically. Maybe they just need a fuse and we can get them working again. Good night." I replaced Lefty's hammer, gave him a wave and headed to my car for the trip home to Peggy Sue and her great cherry pie.

All the way home I debated with myself as to whether or not to tell her about the old Packard hearse with the bullet holes in the door. I decided to stay quiet or to put a positive spin on things until her attitude got a little better about our house on the hill.

When I walked into the house, Peggy Sue got my dinner out of the warmer oven and I immediately started my positive retelling of the day's adventures. "You know, Honey, I've been thinking about that cherry pie all day, so I think I'll have a piece now with a cup of hot coffee. Come on over here and let me tell you all about the beautiful old sleigh and buggy I discovered today in one of the barns. We're going to have so much fun riding around in them. All we need is a nice, docile old horse," I said while diving into the pie which was delicious.

Peggy Sue seemed intrigued by the idea of the horse and buggy so I left her with that good thought of my day's findings. I wanted her to become enthusiastic again about the house. Maybe when she saw the results of her decorating skills, she would have a more positive outlook—because if she wasn't going to be happy at our house on the hill, neither would I.

7

The next day's visit to the remodeling job started out beautifully. It was a rather warm and beautiful sunny day. I was alone again because Peggy Sue still wasn't comfortable with coming back to the house, although she was quite pleased with the idea of the old sleigh, the buggy and horses. She had said she knew she couldn't live in the barns, but she still had a creepy feeling about the inside of the house. Her comments made me want to pressure Lefty to do the best job possible and return the house to its original grandeur.

I met Lefty in the kitchen where he was painting some of the woodwork. The paint gave the kitchen a fresh, clean smell as well as a fresh and clean look. The newly-sanded and shellacked floors and cabinets looked terrific. I could hear hammering going on in the living room.

Lefty explained that the crew was installing carpeting. "It came first thing this morning," he said, "along with that pile over there of wallpaper and 35 gallons of paint." He kept right on painting and I hurried to the living room to see a big crew of men installing the new carpet there and also in the sun room. It was a beautiful moss green, overlaid on thick padding. The walls of knotty pine had all been cleaned and polished. Repairs to the ceiling were complete and it was painted a soft beige color that emphasized the massive wood beams that spanned the width of the room.

The place was really starting to shape up and look wonderful. I returned to the kitchen to give Lefty my compliments. "Your men really work fast. How long do you think it will take them to finish the carpeting in the rest of the house?" I asked.

"With the nine men I have working, we ought to get finished with the carpet today or, for sure, by tomorrow."

I was so excited. "And what about the painting and wallpapering?"

Lefty estimated he and the crews should finish the house by the middle of next week.

Lefty told me he had looked at the old gas pumps and believed they could be made operational easily. "I found an old lever-type electric switch in the garage," he said, "and when I flipped it, I heard one of the pumps kick on.

"However, in order to get a real good test, you'll have to get some gas dropped into the tanks in the ground. Just be sure the guys hand-pump the tanks out first and test them for water. Those old tanks have been empty a long time and we just have to hope they aren't rusted through and pray they don't leak."

I remembered one of the telephones in the upstairs library was working. I decided to call into town to see if I could get someone to bring a small load of gasoline out to the house. When I got to the library, I found an old telephone book dated 1948. I turned the pages until I found a gas station. I dialed the number and, surprisingly, someone answered "Holmes Service Station, may I help you?"

"Of course," I tried to tell myself, "this all makes sense. It's not 1971 here in this town; it's still 1948! After all I've bought a house near a town that time forgot."

I inquired as to whether or not someone had a small tanker truck that could deliver a few hundred gallons of gasoline out to the house. "Sure we can," came the quick reply. "We do it all the time for the surrounding farms."

I gave them my address and was asked, "You mean that house on that hill out by the lake?" I answered affirmatively and was told they would have to come in their newest tanker truck since it was the only one that could pull the hill. I explained that the tanks had been out of commission for a long time and asked if they would check for water before filling the tanks. I was assured that testing for water was a standard procedure and a simple one as well. "We do it by putting a green type of substance on a long stick and lowering it into the tank. If there is water in the tank, the green stuff turns red. Then we have to hand pump the water out. We don't want your car's gas lines to freeze up."

These people were definitely from another time, I thought. They were very cordial and thoughtful and only charged a $20 delivery fee and nothing for the water testing or pumping if it was necessary.

I was feeling pretty lucky this morning, having completed this small task because I was using a telephone that hadn't been manufactured for over 30 years and had spoken to a gas station that had had the same telephone number for almost the same length of time.

Sitting on the edge of the desk in the library, my eyes fell upon the shelves of old books. I went over and started going through them. Some were lying on the sides and others were stacked one upon another. A few were lying on the floor opened. There must have been close to 80 books. Brushing them off, I placed them upright on the shelves in an effort to straighten up the library. I noticed that most were old law books, some dating back before the turn of the century. The most recent one I found was published in 1944 and addressed the World War II legal position on gas and food ration stamps. A few others addressed general accounting principles, an unusual subject. I was almost finished with my hasty arranging when high in a corner on the top shelf, beneath a stack of old papers I found a strange, large black book. I pulled it down with my fingertips, blew off the dust and noticed that the cover had the image of what appeared to be two golden triangles stamped on the front of it. No title, just the triangles.

The book was large, about 10 inches by 15 inches, and it appeared to have several hundred pages. The printed triangles looked peculiar because the ends of each touched, giving a look, almost like the letter Z sat on its side. Then I remembered the hazy outline on the wall of the small altar area in the master bedroom suite. Taking the book over to that area, I compared the two and they looked identical. Something in this book might tell me the meaning of the lazy Z that hung over the altar.

I could hardly contain my excitement, so I took the book and went outside to my car where I could be comfortable and could read the book in private.

I turned over three blank pages; then, suddenly the golden triangles appeared in the center of the next page. Written above them in gold-leaf gothic letters were the words, *The Knighthood of Zion.*

The text began with the statement that in order to be a member and wear the ring of The Knighthood, a person must be of the Jewish faith. It went on to say that soldiers, underlings or workers could be of any religion. The text contained a smattering of German and because of my own German descent, I recognized several of the words. There were also Hebrew words and phrases sprinkled throughout the pages. There was a lengthy description of the origins of the double triangle, as it was referred to in the time of Christ. It seemed that this emblem was also imprinted on the shields of a secret society of Jewish warlords known as "The Knights of Zion."

The triangles again appeared prominently on the banners and standards used to lead the Roman legions and the emblem's presence also seemed to indicate that the organization was heavily involved in the Roman war effort.

The triangles surfaced again in medieval times on the battlefield coat of arms of a little-known Hapsburg Family.

Reading further, I learned that the knighthood, which

really was a group of mercenaries who sold their services to the highest bidder, continued using the double triangles as their insignia. Eventually, over many years, the so-called "knights" evolved into a German-Jewish crime syndicate, which operated all over Europe and eventually in the United States before and during World War I.

The book's unnamed author speculated that during World War I, Adolph Hitler was a corporal in the German signal corps who came in contact with the knighthood and was treated very badly by the Jewish hoodlums who were running wartime scams in the German Army. Several of the Knights beat Hitler almost to a pulp for trying to crash into their organization. The beating they gave young Hitler drove a hatred of Jews into the future leader of Nazi Germany that he would never forget and vowed to avenge.

Hitler turned to politics to further his dream of someday ruling over all of Germany. He was arrested and sent to prison for causing riots and political unrest and during this time wrote his manifesto on how to rule the world. In his *Mein Kamp* (*My Struggle*, in English), without calling the Knights by name, Hitler insinuated that the Knights, whom he often referred to as Zionists, and all the Jewish people were responsible for most, if not all of Germany's woes. He also preached to the masses hysterically that the Jews had sold out the nation to the French and English to end World War I with the Treaty of Versailles.

When Hitler eventually took over Germany in the late 1920's by virtue of his political shenanigans, including murder and other treachery, he went after the Jews with a vengeance—especially the Knights of Zion who now controlled the rackets throughout all Germany.

According to the book, the Knighthood controlled most unions, several banks and the protection racket. They wielded tremendous political power and their illegal activities netted them millions of Duetsch Marks each year. Using his military power, Hitler essentially declared war on the knighthood and within several months had either killed or captured most ring-wearing members and sent them to concentration camps where they died in the gas chambers.

The few who survived fled Germany and went to Argentina and to New Jersey in the United States. They immediately set up as many racketeering operations as they could get into and, after only a short time, had developed an extensive crime syndicate.

The tentacles of the crime syndicates would soon stretch into other major cities in the United States: Cleveland, Toledo, Detroit and Chicago, among them. The crime wave swept across these cities with stunning results.

However, with the advent of prohibition, according to the book, their operations became even more successful. The book listed several mobs across the northern states, including the infamous Detroit Purple Gang, as part of this Jewish crime syndicate which included the Capone organization in Chicago and other lesser support mobs.

The book did not list names of gang members or syndicate bosses but spelled out the hierarchy and how the organizations were assembled and functioned. It explained the method of transferring money within the mob, using letters of transit. The book also detailed a certain silver ring with Hebrew words engraved on its face. The ring identified the wearer as an upper-echelon member of The Knights of Zion. The signet ring was used to seal secret communications with hot wax, a system that had been used for years in Europe by those who wanted to insure their correspondence was recognized as being from a member of the Knighthood.

As I examined the book closely, I decided it was nothing other than a book on how to organize and run a successful crime syndicate. And, then a thought crossed my mind: does the Michigan police need to see this book? Nah, all this happened so long ago that the statute of limitations must have run out by this time!

I kept reading until I got to the mob organizational charts on page 55. Thinking that there were several hundred more pages to go, I was surprised when I turned the next page and encountered a piece of black metal. Lifting it, I uncovered a hollow space in the center of the book which held, of all things, a German Luger pistol wrapped in a white handkerchief. The gun looked brand new. I picked it up to examine it, removed the bullet clip and counted nine rounds of ammunition through the holes in its side. It was fully loaded and the safety was off. A date of "1925" was stamped on the top of the barrel, apparently the date of manufacture.

I quickly snapped the safety on, reinserted the magazine, replaced the weapon in the book and closed it.

Getting out of my car, I went to the trunk, opened it and placed the book and its contents into a bag of old clothes for safekeeping. The gun might have been for old man Levison's personal protection, but something told me it was somehow otherwise connected.

I convinced myself I should tell no one, not even Peggy Sue, about the Luger or the book. The house was already making me keep secrets from my wife, which I had never done before. Keeping these things to myself, I felt I was somehow protecting her from over-reacting and wanting to get rid of the house. I knew this was something I could not do because, by now, the house had me mesmerized. I was beginning to love it!

Suddenly there was a loud, roaring noise behind me. I turned to see a small tanker truck just clearing the top of the hill with its engine at full rev. I pointed over toward the two gas pumps and the fire-engine-red tanker pulled in beside them. An older man jumped spryly out of the truck and bid me a good day. He said, "I'm here to check your tanks and deliver you some gas. Are you the man of the house?"

"Yes, my wife thinks so anyway," was my quip in

answer to his question. I asked him if he minded my staying to watch him work and he had no objection.

He took out a large pipe wrench and a can of something from his truck, along with a long calibrated stick. He proceeded to remove one of the threaded caps that covered small pipes protruding from the ground. He opened the can, placed a green, greasy substance on the stick, and lowered it into the hole. It went down about halfway and then he pulled it out and exclaimed, "She's dry as a bone. There's no water in this tank and should hold about 500 gallons."

He repeated the procedure with the second tank, but this time when he pulled out the stick he said the tank was half full of water and the tank had cracks in it and would not be serviceable.

I assured him that one tank was perfectly adequate for my needs and asked him to put one hundred gallons in the tank.

"Let's see if the pump works," I suggested.

He attached a large hose that ran from a large metal tube along one side of the tanker to a spigot. Turning a valve, gasoline began to flow through his meter. When the meter read 100 gallons, he stopped and asked me to turn on the pumps. I did so and the trucker dug out a one-gallon can from his vehicle and placed the end of the hose into it and pulled the trigger. Nothing but air came out at first, but soon a small trickle of gasoline, and finally a steady stream of gas emitted from its end.

Nonchalantly, while pouring the gasoline back down the filler pipe, he said, "You've got yourself a nice little gas-dispensing system here."

I pointed across the road where another pipe extended above ground with a screw cap on its top. I asked him if he thought that was also a gas pipe, but his reply was, "Nope, it's painted green, so that would be your fuel oil for your furnace. I think the Mobil dealer has had this account for many years. The old guy that lives in that shack at the bottom of the hill usually calls them, orders 1,000 gallons each month and pays the driver in cash. It's kinda the talk of the town. He always seems to have a supply of greenbacks on hand."

I told the delivery man that I was the new owner of this property and would like for him and his company to fill my gas and fuel oil tanks monthly if he wanted the account.

"You bet I'd like to have the account," was his enthusiastic reply. "I could start filling them up next month, but just be sure the old guy in the shack doesn't call the Mobil dealer. I don't want any trouble. They may be unhappy about losing the account."

"By the way," I said, "I won't be paying cash. I prefer to give you my check if that's all right."

"That's fine by me," he said while putting away his equipment and handing me a bill which I promptly paid with my check. He shook my hand and got back in his truck, thanking me for my business. "I will handle your account personally. Just call me at the number on the invoice when you need a refill."

As the tanker rolled slowly down my hill, for some strange, but pretty neat reason, I felt very independent. I had my own little gas station right here at my house!

I decided I'd better take a walk down to the bottom of the hill and inform the old fella who lived there that I would be getting my fuel oil from another source in town. I wasn't sure where Jake had ordered last month's supply, but I certainly didn't want to cross up my new delivery service. Anyway, this was a good excuse to meet my only neighbor.

When I got to Collier Road, I walked along it to the east for about a quarter of a mile and then I saw the shack…and that's exactly what it was. Just a small one-room shack with a 1947 black pickup parked next to it. Chickens were everywhere pecking at the ground, with a few perched on top of their coop which was nearly as large as the small cabin.

The place sat way back off the road and was surrounded by heavy brush and trees. The roof was so old that moss was growing three inches thick on its surface. There was smoke curling out of a small vent on one side. The exterior of the shack was covered with plain weathered raw wood. Next to the front door was a small window that had yellowed newspaper applied on the inside. As I approached the door, I noticed that the steps consisted of two old cinder blocks stacked one on top of the other. Several of the deck boards on the porch were missing.

Being careful where I stepped, I knocked lightly on the screen door several times. Shortly, a small crack of light appeared in the door and a voice from inside mumbled something I couldn't understand. I said, "Good day to you, Sir. I'm your new neighbor. I've just purchased the house on the hill." For a few minutes there was no reaction of any kind. No sound at all. Then, finally the door slowly opened.

Standing before me was a very large man, probably in his seventies, with gray hair. He was holding a black cat with yellow eyes. The man had on a pair of blue bib overalls, no shirt and mud-spattered boots—just your typical farmer's attire.

His face, however, was anything but typical. It was so horribly disfigured that it staggered me.

There was a gaping hole in the middle of his face, just below where his nose would normally be. But there was nothing! I could see all the way back into his throat. Saliva was running out past the large tooth on the side of his mouth, which he attempted to wipe away with his hand.

He said something to me again, but still I could not understand him. He motioned me to come inside. I had to think about that for a moment and I hesitated, this poor fellow looked so ghastly. I considered for a minute that I was a young guy, pretty big myself, and I could probably handle this old man. However, if he became aggressive or was crazy, I might have a real hard time. His arm was as big as my leg! I didn't offer to shake his hand because of the saliva and snot that was still on it from wiping his mouth and piece of nose.

"My name is Zack and I just wanted to inform you that I would be ordering my fuel oil from a different delivery service in town. The man who just delivered some to me said you have previously been ordering all the fuel for the house." I had said all this rather cautiously.

He shook his head in the affirmative and then turned and walked away from me while gently putting his cat on the floor. I could tell that he was not only big and ugly, but he limped slightly on his left leg and his left arm hung listlessly at his side. It was possible he had suffered some kind of stroke.

I took the opportunity to glance around the room and observed there were only the bare basics of life in it. It wasn't dirty or untidy, but all the furnishings were handmade and very rickety. I noticed in the sink a small hand pump, so obviously the house did not have running water.

There was a small lamp by the window, so he must have electricity. There was an old refrigerator humming away in the corner and a wood-burning stove was blazing away. I could hear the burning wood crackling in it and I could smell something spicy that he was cooking.

I saw bowls of milk and food for the cat on the floor by the stove. It appeared his bedroom was through a small door on what was apparently the back porch that had been closed in with untreated plywood.

He picked up a pencil and paper and turned toward me, the faint light from the lamp hitting his face in such a way that it made him look even more hideous. His appearance shook me to deep within my soul. To be honest, he scared the hell out of me.

He wrote on the paper for a minute and handed me a

note. The handwriting was very poor but I could read, "My name is Bruno and I cannot talk good. I know you said you get oil from somebody else. OK with me."

We both stood there for a few minutes, sizing each other up. It became apparent to me that he was really quite harmless, just ugly. I felt sorry for him because his appearance must have been a heavy burden to carry all through his life. As I was about to take my leave, I told him if he ever needed anything or I could help him in any way, to please let me know. I also told him he was free to go on the property any time he wished.

He again scribbled a note to me. "Thanks, but I stay here in the house most of the time now. I do not feel good anymore. I used to go out a lot to help Judge Levison; we would go on long drives. He was sometimes my friend, but sometimes he whipped me with a stick. He took care of me. He's dead now.

Concerned, I said, "Oh, that's too bad. How did he die? Old age?"

Bruno began to write again, handing me his scribbling, it read, "Not sure, I find him in upstairs bathroom. He all burned up like piece of toast. He dead. I take him to," he hesitated, swallowed and catching his breath, then continued, "place marked funeral home. They keep him three days then letter say me to come get. I buried him."

"You buried him? Where did you bury him?" I asked immediately, in response to his strange statements.

He scribbled down another weird sentence that really threw me for a loop. "In the cemetery out in the woods behind the house where the other people are."

"Oh, no," I thought to myself. "Another item on my list of unmentionables!"

"Bruno, what cemetery? What other people?" I asked as my pulse began to race.

"I will show you if you like," he wrote. "We can't

drive, we have to walk. Water took away road."

"Let's go," I said eagerly, but thinking to myself that the guy was probably a bit retarded and there would be no cemetery; just the ramblings of an old, confused man.

We took off up the hill directly in back of Bruno's shack and walked for what seemed like several miles. I was amazed at Bruno's stamina and how well he covered the ground with his bad leg. I had to hustle to keep up with him. We stopped on the top of a small knoll and I could see the house off in the distance about a mile away. I was still in awe at how magnificent the house looked even from a distance. Turning and looking to my left, I saw it, deep in some underbrush in an area that was partially cleared: a freshly covered grave. There was a wooden marker in the shape of that funny lazy Z, nailed to a post with the name *Levison* burned into it. The marker sat at a peculiar angle and was crude and haunting.

Bruno said, with much difficulty, "There is where I put Judge after I got him from the funeral parlor in town. No one was there so the undertaker gave him to me to put in the ground. I knew this was the place because I buried other people here we would get on our long car trips."

I was flabbergasted at what Bruno was telling me and I was shocked and surprised that I was beginning to be able to understand his mutterings.

"Where would you and Judge Levison get these other people?" I asked.

He spoke with so much difficulty, but I understood him to say, "A long time ago, sometimes in Detroit; and sometimes in Chicago."

"Bruno, where are they? Where did you put them in the ground?" I asked, somewhat alarmed.

Bruno said nothing, just pointed a short distance away and held up nine fingers.

"Is that how many there are?"

He shook his head, "yes."

My own head went into a spin. This was almost too much for my brain to absorb. I felt like Bruno had shot me in the chest with a double-barrel shotgun. The first barrel blast was the Judge's body being buried on my property; and now the second blast was there are nine other people also buried on my hilltop!

Suddenly, I didn't feel sorry for Bruno any longer and I had a tremendous urge to run like hell. Here I was in the middle of the woods with a huge, ugly, retarded guy I just met, who buries people in a makeshift graveyard that just happens to be located on my property.

I looked down to see my hands were shaking. "That's it, I'm out of here," I said to myself…or maybe out loud, in a voice that was shaking as much as my hands.

"Bruno, let's go back to your house because I'm getting cold and it's starting to get dark. We can talk more about this later."

I thought, "Sure we would…after I find out from the local undertaker what was going on and was it legal to bury a person in the country or was this some sort of ritual burial ground." Obviously, my imagination must be running away with me.

It seemed to take forever to get out of the woods and back to the small shack, but I was relieved when we got there. I told Bruno I'd be seeing him again soon and I hightailed it out of there. Bruno never waved or looked back. He just disappeared into his dimly-lit little cabin.

Because it was still early, I figured I had time to make it to town before the funeral parlor closed. I needed some answers now or I'd be losing sleep just as Jake had.

After seeing Bruno, I could understand why people had said he rarely came in for supplies and that he kept to himself. I couldn't imagine how a person would react if they ran into him late at night. He could scare the devil himself.

As I walked away from the cabin, I realized I was going to have a real battle on my hands with Peggy Sue and the kids. This guy looked like he was straight out of a horror movie. I didn't know how I would ever get them to accept him. I was sure they would be frightened when they saw him, just as I had been. I began to ponder whether or not I should even mention him, or the graveyard for that matter.

"Who knows?" I asked myself. "Maybe they would never see him." I decided I would just have to add the secret that lay in the woods to my list of mysteries that I kept from Peggy Sue, a list of secrets that just kept getting longer.

I didn't even say goodbye to Lefty, I just tore off to town. I remembered passing the funeral home when we went to Suicide Ridge. It was just up the street from the Wagon Wheel Bar where Outhouse hung out. I pulled into the driveway and came to a sliding halt. I almost ran inside the funeral home and announced, out of breath to the first person I saw, "I'm Zack Heikel, and I own the mansion on Irish Hill and I need some answers fast!"

"Whoa, young man. Slow down. Nothing could be so bad to get you in such a tizzy."

The middle-aged man who spoke to me sat me down in a chair. "My name is Billy," he said. "Now, what's got you so riled up?"

I took a deep breath and told him. "I just met Bruno."

Before I could say another word Billy interrupted, "Oh! That explains your anxiety completely. Poor guy, he's horrible looking, isn't he? I remember seeing pictures of harelips in medical school, but I never saw one that grotesque."

"Man, you're putting it mildly, the guy's a beast. Exactly what is a harelip anyway? And, what's this deal about you giving him Judge Levison's body to bury? You did embalm him, didn't you and what was the cause of death?"

Billy wasted no time with his reply, "Boy, you're full

of questions. Let's take this one step at a time. A harelip is a severe birth defect where the roof of the mouth, or palate, doesn't form properly. Often there is abnormal tooth development and, sometimes, the absence of lips. Usually, the condition is not as extensive as Bruno's is. Second, the official cause of death was that he burned to death in some manner. The pathologist who performed the autopsy was not all that sure exactly how his body caught fire but recorded that the deceased death could have been a very rare case of Human Spontaneous Combustion. What ever that is. And, yes, we did perform a funeral service for the judge a few months ago, and since there was no one else in attendance and no family members, we did release the body to Bruno."

"Right," I said sarcastically. "Did you know he buried the body out behind the house in the woods?"

"No, I didn't know that," Billy said with a slight smile on his face. "But, it's perfectly legal to do so. It's out in the country and out of our jurisdiction. Believe it or not, it happens more than people realize, especially in rural communities."

"Well, then I guess I have nothing to worry about other than having a dead body buried on my property," I said, feeling my body relaxing and, at the same time keeping silent about the other nine people buried out there!

"That's right, Mr. Heikel, just forget about it and in a few years Mother Nature will work her ways and nothing, not even the pine box he's in, will exist. Now why don't you stop by the Wagon Wheel Bar and have a good stiff drink and go home to bed. Everything will look better in the morning," Billy said, taking me by the arm and escorting me to the door.

It seemed I had heard that sentiment before, perhaps because I had been saying the same thing to myself every evening since buying the house—but the next morning, something else would pop up. As for stopping at the Wagon Wheel for a drink, I decided to pass on that and just go home to my sweet little wife. I could get her to baby me for a while and then hit the hay. I had really had a bad day and my hope was that Bruno didn't find a place in my dreams once I was tucked in!

As I lay in bed later, waiting for sleep to come, I decided I had gone off the deep end acting the way I had at the funeral home. And, I was ashamed of myself for the way I had bashed that poor unfortunate soul, Bruno.

My concerns about the house, even when they are explained to me as something logical or legal, always seem to conjure up something supernatural. And that poor Bruno—he's just a dumb ox with a birth defect who has always had to follow someone else's instructions.

I knew I needed to change my attitude so I could see things as they really were, strange perhaps, but natural and explainable.

After all, the house is mine; it's my money invested in it; and it has a grip on my mind. The mysteries surrounding my new house were intimidating, yes; but, at the same time, they were so fascinating I could hardly wait for another day to dawn so I could get back over to my Irish Hill.

8

The next morning, I awoke feeling very refreshed and I had suffered no nightmares at all. Peggy Sue was in the kitchen doing her thing, getting the kids ready and off to school. She looked so good, I gave her a big kiss. Holding my wife in my arms and waving to the children as they left for school gave me a real sense of comfort that all was right with the world. Peggy Sue offered me a cup of coffee and asked how I wanted my eggs.

"Just scrambled, the way my life has been for the last several weeks," I said.

Peggy Sue chuckled and went about the business of beating up the eggs and getting them in the skillet. She turned to me and said, "Why don't you take the day off and stay home with me. We can watch a good movie on TV."

As I buttered my toast, the idea appealed to me. "That's a good idea. I need a little R and R anyway. A day or two to clear my head might just do the trick and, maybe together, we can make some plans on how we are going to handle the expense and upkeep of two houses."

"Sure," she said, placing my breakfast on the table. "You know I've been wondering how the house is looking with all the new renovations. Maybe I will love the inside of it as much as the outside. The kids are putting pressure on me and they want to see the house and are really excited about a horse. I guess I could see myself living there, especially if I got a new car."

"Oh, so that's what this is all about. A nice movie, yeah. This is really about a new car isn't it?" I laughed and pulled her onto my lap.

"Well, yes, I would need a new one. You know it's a long way into town for my old station wagon, but seriously, I really do want to see the improvements on the house," she said, kissing me on the cheek. That almost stopped me from saying my next thought.

"I am really glad you're starting to think along the same line I am. I would just love to live a little closer to my Ann Arbor office. That two-hour drive is finally starting to get to me."

"Then, it's settled," she said. "As soon as Lefty is finished with the decorating, let's take a few things over we're not using here at the house—some blankets, our sleeping bags, the portable TV—and just see how things work out.

She said all that as she was clicking on the morning movie. We settled down and got comfortable. The old film classic was, of all things, a James Cagney gangster film, a real shoot-'em-up. It wasn't long, however, before I didn't care because I was soon fast asleep.

When Peggy Sue shook me awake to take a walk with her, I realized it was already past lunchtime. We decided to go for a walk and then come home for lunch. Man, this was the life.

After lunch, I did a few odd jobs around the house and about 3 o'clock I went out to meet the mailman. When he arrived and we had exchanged a few pleasantries, he handed me a stack of mail and a large yellow envelope.

The yellow envelope was from the *Detroit News* and probably contained the article about Judge Levison that I had been anxiously awaiting. I was eager to open it because I thought it would go a long way in explaining why this guy built such a large home and whether he was an upholder of the law or a common lawbreaker.

I decided, however, to wait until later to open the

envelope. I didn't need any more surprises at the moment. I was finally getting Peggy Sue in the mood for the move and I didn't want to upset her. I was afraid that if there were more unexplained episodes, it would definitely end our holding on to the cottage on the lake. I put the envelope in my desk, locked it and decided to relax for the rest of the day.

I was looking forward to taking Peggy Sue out to inspect the renovated interior of our house because she was apparently warming up to the possibility of moving out there. However, something came up at my office the next morning that required my immediate attention. I got so involved in the mini-crisis at the company that I hadn't realized it had been four days since I had visited the new property. That fact came home to me when the phone rang and it was Lefty.

"Gee, Lefty, I really haven't forgotten about you. I've just gotten so busy I haven't been able to get out to the house," I tried to explain.

"No problem," he said. "I just called to tell you I think we've completed most of the items on my worksheet and I wondered when you and your wife might be able to come out and do a final inspection."

I told him I was afraid it would take me another couple of days to straighten out my office problems, but that I would meet him the following Monday morning and would bring Peggy Sue and my checkbook with me.

All I heard on the other end of the line was a loud laugh and, "Money time! That's what I really wanted to hear. Okay, it's a date. I'll see you here Monday at 9 o'clock."

I worked diligently with several of my key employees and was able to solve my business crisis the very next day. I spent another day contacting several realtors in the Dexter area and asked one of them to meet me for lunch. We met at a local bakery that had delicious homemade pies and cakes and also served a mean tuna sandwich. After our sandwich lunch, topped off with warm apple pie with ice cream and coffee, we talked about putting my house on the market. I asked him to appraise the property and the market and give me an estimate as to what the sale might bring. I didn't want to list the house because I still had some convincing to do with Peggy Sue. Still, I wanted to get the legwork started.

The following Monday morning, bright and early, we met Lefty at the house. It had been a long time since I had seen Peggy Sue as excited as she was when she walked through the front door. She was almost like a kid again and I expected her to jump up and down and squeal, "Goody, goody!" She didn't go quite that far, but she was extremely pleased to see the living room looking like the interior of a brand new house. Every windowpane was sparking clean, a monumental task considering there were hundreds of them.

She was especially tickled with her choice of carpet and the blending of the paint colors with the ceiling and the paneling in the living room. When she got to the kitchen and saw the new linoleum, carpet, the beautifully-painted cabinets and woodwork, she said, "Now, you're talking! I'm going to have lots of fun cooking in here."

Then Lefty walked us through the rest of the house, and we found each room looking even more beautiful than we could have imagined. We were amazed at the beautiful French wallpaper in the upstairs hallway. It looked like it had just been hung even though it was almost 50 years old. The entire upstairs area, with the exception of the secret room, was now carpeted in a beautiful deep gold, designed for heavy traffic. It matched well with the new wallpaper in all the bedrooms and the mahogany paneling throughout the master suite and the library.

Peggy Sue had asked Lefty to rebuild the old altar area into a perfume bar and make-up area and it had been wallpapered in an embossed *fleur-de-lis*. The confessional booth had been turned into a closet for her fur coats.

The area that convinced us that we had a virtually new

house was the basement. Peggy Sue had picked out a beautiful reddish-purple carpet with gold roses, similar to the original carpet that had been laid in the 1920's. The carpet and its thick pad were plush and concealed from sight the secret opening in the floor that led to the tunnel. The repaired chandeliers with their antique-style bulbs were impressive and the glow from their light enhanced the beauty of the polished wood panels in the room.

The walls of the shower room were glistening and looked like they had just been built. All the showerheads were back in operation as was the new toilet. Lefty said we would need to get a plumber to replace all the old piping if we wanted to put the sauna in operating condition.

It was hard to imagine that this area, now so brightly lit, clean and fresh, was the same foul smelling, spider-infested, spooky place it had once been. One thing I was sure of: if this house had looked this way the day we first saw it, we'd be living in it right now and would have had no preconceived notions that the house was mysterious or haunted. We would have seen it as just a beautiful older home. However, I reminded myself, if the place had looked like this when we bought it, we would have paid several times over the price we gave. This affirmed for me the fact that we had made a real steal!

I turned to Lefty, gave him a pat on the back and told him what a great job he had done and how much I appreciated his attention to detail. I then took out my checkbook and asked how I should make out the check.

"Just make it out to Lefty Walker Home Decorating Company," he said. I made the check out for $15,000 and handed it to him.

All smiles, Lefty looked at the check and said, "I really got a big kick out of doing this job. The place went from a stinking dump to what we see before us now. If you need my services any time in the future, please don't hesitate to call me."

He put the check into his wallet and headed toward his pickup. As we watched his truck turning onto Collier Road at the bottom of our hill, Peggy Sue and I embraced and were thrilled to be in our beautiful palace by the lake. It was everything we had ever wanted.

Little did we know that the renovations would only thinly veil some other shocking surprises that would spring upon us at various times over the next several years.

PART II

9

A few days later, the kids were out of school for a teachers' workshop, and we thought it would be an opportune time to introduce them to the area. They were all excited when we passed through the small town of Clinton because there was an old movie theater, a pizza parlor and a small bowling alley, all of which promised them lots of fun.

Then, it was on out through the small rolling hills to the house. When we reached the steel gates at the bottom of the driveway and she could see the house on the hill, my oldest daughter Kim looked up and asked, "Are we going to live in *that*? I didn't know we were rich."

The inside of the house seemed like a giant play area to the kids. They ran up and down stairs, opened and closed the hidden door to the basement and kept asking to see inside what had once been the padded room.

We showed them the sliding bookcases in the library with the concealed door to the attic and let them go up to see how big it was. They each spent considerable time deciding which bedroom to claim. The boys decided to take the large bedroom that was the size of an entire college dormitory. The girls, Kim and Denise, chose separate bedrooms and each of them had a large clothes closet. Peggy Sue and I took the large Master Suite with its nooks and crannies. Peggy Sue spent several hours that day determining what furniture she would need and where it would all be placed. Before we realized it, time had slipped away and it was time to go home to a hot dinner and homework.

Over the next several days, Peggy Sue and the kids

worked out their plans to occupy the house. All I cared about at the time was picking out my new king-size bed that would fit in our massive new bedroom. I wondered just how soundly I would sleep in a room the size of Manhattan.

It wasn't long before the family was spending each weekend at the lake house. The four kids and I spent most of the days wandering over the property. I paid particular attention to keeping them away from the small knoll where the graves of Judge Levison and the others were located. Walking through the woods we were amazed at the wildlife we saw. Large herds of deer roamed the surrounding hills and we saw lots of squirrels, rabbits and a few foxes.

Peggy Sue spent her time playing in her new kitchen, putting together our delicious lunches which we dived into when we came back from our long hikes exhausted and starved. Afterwards, we would watch old movies on our portable black-and-white TV set. Our oldest son Forrest put in his request for a small, flat-bottom rowboat he could use to go fishing on Lake Misty.

Our main concern with our youngest son Monroe was that if he started down the steep driveway on his bicycle, he might not be able to stop and would find himself wrapped around one of the trees or smack dab in the middle of the lake.

At dusk, we would watch a breathtaking golden sun as it sank slowly below the horizon line of the lake. It looked enormous and when it neared the water's surface, it turned to a brilliant red and seemed to send up a huge plume of steam. The six of us would lie out on blankets and watch the beautiful display of sparkling stars and planets slowly pass overhead across the pitch-black sky, undisturbed by city lights. Using binoculars and a small telescope, we could clearly see the moon, the rings around Saturn and the red surface of Mars. On one occasion, we even saw what astronomers call "The Green Flash," a very unusual phenomenon to see. It is a flash of beautiful emerald green light just the instant the sun dips below the horizon and the conditions of the atmosphere are just right to bend the light rays so only the green color of the spectrum is visible.

On most of these evenings, before we were lulled to sleep by the awesome night sky, we would move into the house, each of us with his or her own flashlight to light the way. We would climb into our sleeping bags and fall fast asleep on the soft new rug in a corner of the living room. We would all awaken refreshed in the morning to a warm, gorgeous sunrise, its beams streaming through the many windowpanes facing east. Overall, we were fitting into our new surroundings quite nicely and enjoying it immensely without the slightest hint of anything unnatural or frightening taking place.

I even began to feel that Peggy Sue was comfortable enough to see the old Packard that I had decided to keep and restore someday. I was sure she would eventually want to look in the outbuilding. Maybe now was a good time. I didn't want to upset her about the old hearse with its bullet holes in the side. However, when we entered the old garage, I was pleasantly surprised that she was much more impressed with the old grape press and wine-making utensils she found, along with the straw baskets and gardening tools. She really had very little to say about the old car.

This arrangement with our family went on for several weeks until things changed abruptly one day. I received a call from the realtor who began our conversation by saying, "I know you don't have the house listed with me and haven't decided yet to put it up for sale. However, I have a family I've been showing property to in this area. When we drove by your house and I commented that it might be coming on the market in the next few months they were extremely interested in it. Have you made up your mind to put it on the market?

"Not exactly, but we may," I said hesitantly. "Hold on

a sec' if you don't mind."

I put my hand over the mouthpiece and turned to Peggy Sue. "The realtor is on the telephone and he thinks he may have a buyer for our house. Shall I let them take a look at it?"

Peggy Sue, walking over to me so she didn't have to shout, said, "I don't see how it could hurt. We may have to get off our butts and make a decision on whether or not we're going to move."

I told the realtor it would be all right to show the house. His response was almost immediate, "Would tomorrow at 11 o'clock be okay?"

"Well, we may as well get on with it. Tomorrow is fine with us so we'll see you then," I said hanging up the receiver and wondering if I had made the right decision. After all, we had lived in the house for ten years and I knew it would be tough making a move into the home at the lake that had uncertainties attached to it.

I turned to my wife who was still standing close to me, listening to what I had said to the realtor. "Are you totally convinced that you would be happy living in the Irish Hills?" I asked. "Because, if not, this is the time to speak up. These people sound like they're very interested in our house and will probably make an offer so we need to be ready for such an eventuality. As for myself, I'm ready to make the jump."

Peggy Sue put her arms around me and said, "You know I'll go anywhere with you. I can tell you're happy with the new house and, frankly, I have just loved being out there. I've become quite comfortable during the days and nights we've stayed over. The kids can't wait to move, so if the lookers give us an offer even close to what we're asking, let's do it. Let's move!"

A few minutes before our appointment time, the realtor and the potential buyers arrived. They were about our age and had three children so the house was not too big for them.

Bill, our realtor, introduced us and they began their tour of our home. They only stayed about fifteen minutes and when they were leaving, the man asked if the property really had 16 acres. I assured him that it did. Bill said he would get back to me with the listing contract or an offer if the couple decided to make one. We visited outside for about ten more minutes and then they were gone.

Bill called the next morning, saying he had an offer on the house and he wanted to come right over. "Sure," I said, "Let's look it over." Bill arrived at the door in just a few minutes. We ushered him in and sat down at the kitchen table.

"I know you thought the house might bring $175,000, but without a signed contract I could only suggest a price, so they made you this offer." He slid a piece of paper across the table.

After I cut through all the mumbo jumbo, the bottom line was $165,000 cash and 60 days for us to vacate. The offer was simple and straightforward. I looked over at Peggy Sue and said, "Remember yesterday? Well, the inevitable has happened, so what do you think?"

Peggy Sue said she liked the idea of a cash offer so we wouldn't have to be in limbo while a mortgage was applied for, but she thought we needed 90 days to vacate.

"Sounds like you're ready to sell," I commented.

"I thought we decided that yesterday," was her comeback.

Acknowledging our conversation from the day before, I told her she was exactly right. Turning to Bill, I said, "It's hard to argue with cash. Where do we sign?"

Bill scooped up the signed contract and said he would get us a counter-signed copy from the buyers. "I suggest you call a mover, because I believe these people sure have the funds to back up their offer."

The signed contract was returned the next day and we

called a local moving company to come and pack us up and deliver our belongings to our mansion in the Irish Hills.

During the next few weeks, we moved into our new home. Of course, the little wife got her wish: a new car. I traded in her old station wagon on a new Cadillac. The children were enrolled in their new school and we bought an antique jukebox they had requested for the basement. It was a perfect place to listen to records and dance.

All we had to do now was put the piano and the rest of the furniture in its proper place and get down to enjoying our new life.

The children had one small problem. They had to walk over a mile on Collier, the dirt road in front of our house, to US 12, the old main road between Detroit and Chicago, to catch the school bus. They were the last kids to be picked up by the school bus, so sometimes they had a long wait. If it was raining or snowing in the winter, they needed shelter from the elements. There was a large billboard on the corner of Collier and US 12, right where the bus stopped. I built a small three-sided structure right beside the illuminated sign, complete with a roof and bench seat, to protect them from the inclement weather and the wind which seemed to blow constantly in this area. I hoped no one would complain about the structure, but there was nobody around to ask permission—we were in the middle of nowhere!

I went back to work and everything ran smoothly for about four months. The only exception was the occasional bump in the night, the wind making strange whispering sounds around the steel-cased windows, and the water bubbling up through the heating system. Another thing we had never before experienced was the total darkness. We had to be right by our beds when we turned out the light because you couldn't see your hand in front of your face. It was that pitch black. It made getting up in the night for the bathroom really tough, so I placed small flashlights on everyone's nightstand.

One of the girls occasionally complained of what she said was a radio playing very, very low...or a faint tinkling sound. Her bedroom had a fireplace in it and I figured the noise was the same sound Leroy had heard coming from the downstairs chimney.

We often heard the howling of some foxes off in the distance, which could be a little daunting if there was a full moon in the night sky. All in all, these things were just a part of getting used to a home in deserted hill country, or so we thought.

One evening I returned home from work to find Peggy Sue very upset. She told me something very unusual had happened to her while she was outside planting a small vegetable garden.

She told me that about one o'clock in the afternoon on this beautiful clear summer day, she was on her knees turning the soil. All of a sudden, she heard a loud whistling sound, then a whoosh, as a large object the size of a beachball crash-landed not more than a few feet away from her. At first, she said, she was terrified, but soon realized she was in no danger. The object seemed to be a large ice ball and she could see articles inside its icy surface. Some were yellow and others dark blue and shaped like small stars.

For some reason, she touched the ball and, even though she was sure it was made of ice, it was hot to the touch and was melting rapidly. All the while she was telling me this, I was thinking about something falling off a high-flying aircraft, perhaps something ejected from the toilet system. The only problem with that theory was that we were not in the path of any commercial flight pattern. Neither of us could remember ever seeing any aircraft of any kind overhead.

Peggy Sue showed me where the object had fallen to the earth. It was about one hundred feet from the house.

When we got close, I could see a large indentation in the ground, still wet with some pieces of material lying in it. I picked up a stick so I didn't have to touch the items and moved them around. They were made of what appeared to be colored paper, had blurred writing on them, and were coated with an oozy substance. When I touched them, they melted and disintegrated.

Starting to tremble at the thought of her brush with danger, Peggy Sue went on to say that if she had been hit in the head with the ice ball she certainly would have been killed. She knew the object weighed several pounds and was traveling at high speed with it landed. It would have been a real mystery to anyone finding her, she said, because once the ice ball melted, she would have just been lying there dead with her head bashed in! It was obvious to me that my bride was badly shaken up.

Completely puzzled by this event, I telephoned the University of Michigan at Ann Arbor and they referred me to Professor Joyce Hoover in the department of atmospheric conditions and weather phenomena. Her credentials indicated that she was an expert on weather conditions. I related our tale about the ice ball. She agreed there were no scheduled aircraft flying over our area but she also said that things do not just fall from planes passing overhead.

Professor Hoover said she could only guess about what the object might have been. One of her guesses was that a small whirlwind had picked up some water from one of the many lakes in the vicinity and carried it to an altitude where it froze and then fell back to earth. She also said that the Irish Hills were well known by people in her profession for producing wind vortexes and waterspouts due to their rapid change in height relative to ground level. She had no guess, however, on how the paper could have become imbedded in the ice ball—or even if it was, in fact, really paper.

I ended our conversation, thanking the professor for

the information and her help. That phone call put a virtual end to the incident of the ice ball which by now had completely disappeared. However, this was just the first incident that made us aware that things might be happening in our lives that had no natural or ordinary explanation; and it changed the way we viewed the mansion on the hill and the incidents and peculiarities surrounding it.

It was only a few months later that Peggy Sue suffered through another troubling and frightening experience. She was getting over the mental effects of the ice ball that had fallen from the sky and just beginning to relax a little.

Then, in the middle of a fairly ordinary week, when the children were at school and I was at work, Peggy Sue had busied herself with the daily tasks of cleaning and laundry and had baked a tasty meat loaf for dinner.

She told me later that she had felt a little sleepy and decided to take a nap on the sofa in the living room. During the morning hours, it had rained, with thunder and lightning; but, now the sun was shining and the air had a fresh smell to it. Peggy Sue had opened the windows to allow the sweet-smelling breeze to blow through the room. Soon, she had relaxed completely and had fallen fast asleep—or so she thought.

She told me she had begun to experience a feeling of strange vibrations in her head and was hearing a low, buzzing sound. She also thought she could hear a voice whispering in the wind that directed her to go to the kitchen and look in the china cabinet. She said she felt compelled to follow the instructions and she thought she got up from the sofa and went into the kitchen to the china cabinet as she had been instructed. She stood there gazing into the glass doors and suddenly a face materialized in the reflection.

The image was that of a very old person wearing a black cape. The skin on the skeletal face was extremely wrinkled and had flaming red eyes embedded in deep hollow eye sockets. She said there appeared to be small black pinwheels spinning inside them. The teeth in the image were rotten and decayed and the sparse hair on the mostly-bald scalp looked filthy and matted with dirt. The image wore a smirk on its face that made her blood run cold. The image seemed to be mocking her and then whispered that she should go to the basement and bring up one of the old bottles of wine.

The image hung there for only a few seconds and then, just as suddenly as it had appeared, it vaporized and disappeared.

Peggy Sue thought she was having a nightmare. When she thought she was actually returning to the sofa to finish her nap, she was terrified to feel she was floating near the ceiling of the room and could see her own body sound asleep on the sofa. She could also see the curtains blowing in the breeze from the open windows.

Peggy Sue said what felt most bizarre while she was experiencing these things was that she was trying to reason with herself and she wanted to know the exact time of day so she could explain everything to me correctly.

She went back into the kitchen and noticed that it was exactly 3 o'clock. She had put a pie in the oven and it had overcooked. She took the ruined pie from the oven and set it on top of the stove. She then felt she was lying on the sofa again, but was awakening in a cold, clammy sweat.

After she reassured herself that she was truly awake, she hurried to the kitchen and saw the burned pie and the clock showing 3:00 p.m. She decided she must have endured what newspapers and books refer to as an out-of-body experience. How else could she have know the exact time? She didn't remember burning the pie...but she did remember seeing her own body asleep on the sofa and the curtains blowing in the breeze. She remembered the grotesque, whispering face in the china cabinet reflection; and she remembered what it said to her. She couldn't get these things out of her mind!

Peggy was so disturbed and afraid that she called me at the office and asked me to come home right away. She was afraid she might fall asleep again, have a recurrence of the vision, and not be able to control her body.

I rushed home as quickly as possible and found her outside, sitting on a chaise lounge, smoking a cigarette and trembling. She recounted the entire experience, detail by detail. She was positive she had gone through an out-of-body experience since she didn't remember burning the pie or knowing what time it was.

She also told me that when she got up from the sofa and headed for the kitchen, she *knew* she would find the pie on top of the stove and she *knew* the clock would read 3 o'clock. She said the image of the face had terrified her and she was scared to death of what the china cabinet might hold. I looked at the palms of her hands that were bleeding slightly from where her fingernails had dug into them. She said she remembered squeezing her hands into fists in case she had to defend herself. I was confident Peggy Sue believed all these things had really happened to her.

I told my poor, frightened wife that surely she had just had a nightmare or a really horrible daydream. I took her by the hand and led her to the kitchen to the china cabinet that appeared to be entirely normal, bright and shining. I opened all the doors, moved the cups and saucers and glasses around to show her that everything was as it should be. She had only been dreaming. There was nothing unusual about the china cabinet.

"Then, how do you explain *that*?" she asked me, pointing to the sink. An electric shock ran through me when I saw a bottle of wine, still covered with dust and without any fingerprints or marks of any kind on its surface. No one could have picked up the wine bottle without marking its dusty surface in some manner. Then, how did it get from the cellar wine rack to the kitchen sink? This was impossible to explain and I had no answer to Peggy Sue's question.

I wasn't certain that what she had experienced was just a nightmare or a daydream and I had good reason for it. From time to time, while shaving and looking in the bathroom mirror, I thought I had seen a face in the far recesses of the mirror. I had always discounted it as simply a reflection or flaw in the old glass. Under no circumstances would I tell Peggy Sue about this. She was already too disturbed to hear about my own experiences. I decided the next time I noticed the phenomenon of the face in the mirror I would look deep into the glass to see if I could make out who or what it was and what it might be trying to tell me. I couldn't believe I was thinking like this, but I was.

I also decided to drop the question of the wine bottle. We had, after all, opened the bottle and each of us had drunk a glass of the wine. It was quite thick and deep red in color with a fruity aroma. When we took our first sips, the wine was absolutely delicious, but very strong. We saved the rest for dinner!

This unexplainable experience was the second such occurrence Peggy Sue had endured in the last few months. I knew it was up to me to see to it that we had some happy moments here at the house so she might feel things were returning to normal.

We had completed all our decorating, had new furniture in place, had shown our home to both our parents, and felt it was time to share our beautiful home with others. We planned an open house for the following weekend and invited friends and family to join us for a Sunday cookout and tour of the house.

Because we have a large extended family and many friends, we had a large crowd. We rented several large barbecue pits and I had ribs, steaks and chicken cooking on the grills. Peggy Sue made her usual scrumptious desserts and side dishes. Everyone was very impressed with our home and Peggy Sue enthusiastically showed off our new furnishings and the beautiful interior of our home. Some of our guests were particularly impressed with the concealed door to the basement. Questions were tossed around about why it had been built in such a manner. We did not discuss the padded room, the tunnel or the hidden door to the attic, and I had padlocked the door to the outbuilding that contained the bullet-ridden Packard. Most of the comments, however, were centered on how beautiful, though remote, our house was, and how it blended spectacularly with its awesome surroundings.

It did my heart good to see Peggy Sue smiling and happily going about visiting with our parents and all our guests. It was obvious that she was having a good time, especially with the family surrounding her. She certainly didn't mention her bizarre experiences to anyone and I hoped she had perhaps forgotten, at least for a little while, the terrifying incident of the week before.

After dinner, everyone sat down on the front lawn with dessert and coffee and waited for the beautiful sunset we witnessed each evening. That night was particularly beautiful. The sunset was impressive and the sky was dotted with a million stars. We stayed up late and had a wonderful time. Some of our guests lived nearby and went home, but we did have several overnight houseguests.

Both sets of our parents and some of our in-laws stayed over. My brother-in-law James had brought along his mother, a recent Macedonian immigrant in her eighties. Mrs. Korrappis was from a strict Greek Orthodox background. One of the customs she had brought from the old country was the practice of blessing any new dwelling occupied by her family. James said it was a well-known custom in Macedonia and that his mother had a particularly keen sense of detecting vibrations, good and bad. While Peggy Sue was busy helping our parents and some of our guests with sleeping arrangements, I seized upon this opportunity. I took James and his mother all through the house. She would pause momentarily in each room, bow her head, and pray aloud in her native Macedonian tongue. We were almost finished with the first floor rituals when Mrs. Korrappis paused in front of the large fireplace in the living room.

She bowed her head and began to pray. Abruptly, she stopped, grabbed her son by the hand and turned to look at me. In her broken English, she said she felt the presence of a very disturbed and tormented emotion. She didn't know how to express it in English, but she felt someone had been tortured horribly in the room. She said she could detect the slight odor of burnt cloves in the air, which in her home country of Macedonia meant evil was near.

I thought perhaps she might have been detecting the smell from the burned oak timbers in the fireplace, but I must admit a chill ran up my spine when she said she felt someone might have been tortured here.

For some unexplained reason, I looked up at the old portrait still hanging above the fireplace. I gazed at Seymour Levison's twisted face and something I had not noticed previously came into focus. There were flowers painted faintly in the upper corners of the portrait. Even more puzzling, just to the right of his head, was a small picture hanging on the wall, a replica of the large portrait itself. Deep in that small picture was another replica of the same portrait, and the pictures went on and on in the depths of the portrait. Surely, I thought, my mind and eyes must be playing tricks on me. What did the old coot Levison have to do with the sense of evil in the room? Could he be the one Mrs. Korappis was sensing, or could someone else be radiating through this portal from ages ago?

Mrs. Korappis spoke to her son in her native language and I could not understand her. I could tell, however, that she was serious and agitated. James turned to me and said, "My mother wants me to tell you in English so you can understand that she thinks you should place a crucifix and Bible on the mantel to ward off any spirits or demons that may be present here. She also says she is trembling so much inside that she feels faint. She doesn't want to spend the night in this house. I know it's almost midnight, but she hasn't been feeling well lately and I think I'd best take her home."

After the initial shock of what she had said, I decided it wouldn't hurt a thing to try and please her. I did as she suggested and placed our family Bible on the mantel while vowing to buy a cross very soon.

As I said goodbye to my sister and brother-in-law and his mother, I realized that Mrs. Korappis only wanted the best for my family, but I still took her revelations to be mere superstition. I accepted that the unusual assessments came from an honest and very religious old woman and I believed the things she "detected" resulted from the essence of this old home and its atmosphere.

After they left, I decided it had been a blessing, probably, that she had not attempted any of her rituals in the upstairs bedroom where the altar had been, or in the basement over the tunnel. If there really was something to the eerie feelings the woman was having, then either of those two areas of the house might have given her a heart attack. She could have dropped dead on either spot!

As I pondered all these things, I realized that hearing Mrs. K's prognostications had reinforced something in my mind. Peggy Sue and I were not the only ones sensing something highly unusual or supernatural looming in our house. It wasn't just us. Maybe there was something to Peggy Sue's daydream after all. No matter what, the old portrait over the fireplace was giving me the willies.

Surprisingly, even though I was shaken by Mrs. Korappis's statements, I was convinced I was not going to turn tail and run away, selling this place to the first bidder like Jake had done. I was going to stay and see what the sum of all these incidents would turn out to be. I *had* to find the underlying cause of all these episodes. After all, this was 1971 not 1712. Demons, witches, ghosts and goblins just were not accepted in this day and age. So far, all our incidents were only impressions, daydreams or imaginations; and no apparitions had actually appeared before us. If only we had known what still lay in the cards for us over the coming months and years!

A few days after our weekend barbecue, I decided to take a closer look at the old painting. I climbed a ladder and tried to take down the portrait, but it was securely fastened to the wall with nails or screws driven into its frame and the fireplace wall. Because I couldn't remove the portrait, I had to stay on the ladder while examining it. I held a flashlight in one hand and a magnifying glass in the other. Under magnification I could see that the paint was cracked and uneven. The face was distorted and one side was out of proportion to the other, as though the portrait's subject had sustained an accident. The colors didn't appear right either. I concentrated my lens on the small painting within the painting. I was amazed at how deeply I could see into the picture within a picture. It was like I was looking through a time tunnel. What an eerie effect the artist had captured in this portrait of old Judge Levison.

As I moved the glass over the canvas to one of the top corners in order to examine the painted flowers, I noticed what seemed to be a screen with holes in it under the flowers. I looked in the other corner and saw the same thing—a screen with holes in it. It appeared the painting was somehow ventilating through the fireplace chimney.

I went to the kitchen and got one of Peggy Sue's cigarettes, lit it and blew some of the smoke at the holes. Low and behold, the smoke was sucked into them instantly! I was right. There was some kind of air circulation installed in the painting, as if it needed to breathe. Before I could even make a mental note to add this to my list of mysteries, my magnifying glass passed over the subject's hands and I saw it—*the ring*!

The ring appeared to be exactly like the one described in the large black book I had found in the library: silver with the word "GAD" under what looked like a Rudy gem stone set in the center. Finally! Something definite about old man Levison. His ring identified him as a member of the Knighthood of Zion, the Jewish crime syndicate.

Suddenly, I remembered the newspaper article locked in my desk. I put the ladder away and headed straight to my desk to get the envelope containing the article. The article was dated June 17, 1937 and the headline in bold letters said, **"Judge Indicted for Racketeering."** Beneath the article was a photograph of the judge. It looked very much like the man in the portrait, especially around the eyes. However the rest of the face was a little different, so the painting over the fireplace must have been completed after the photograph was taken.

The article said the judge had been indicted and convicted for money laundering, racketeering and dereliction of duty as a public servant. He had been sentenced to 12 years in the Michigan State Prison at Jackson and was to begin serving his time on May 9. However, he was still at large at the time the article was written. The article listed the judge's address on Collingwood Avenue in northwest Detroit, but there was no mention of the house here at the lake.

The article continued to say that the prosecuting attorney for Detroit believed the judge was also a member of the Detroit Purple Gang. The murders of three members of a rival gang had taken place at the exclusive apartment complex on Collingwood Avenue that was owned by Judge Levison! In addition, the article mentioned that due to a supposed lack of evidence Judge Levison had acquitted some of The Purple Gang's hit men who had murdered members of a rival gang. Three other members of the Purple Gang were convicted by a different judge for their participation in the same crime and they were serving long prison sentences.

The thought went through my mind that the prosecutor would have been able to prove the judge was himself a member of the gang if he had seen the old painting with the ring identifying him as part of the mob. The ring cried out to all who could see it that Judge Seymour T. Levison was a secret ringleader of the Detroit Purple Gang!

The newspaper article gave a basic description of The Purple Gang that fit perfectly with the one I had read in the black book. The gang was a criminal band of primarily Jewish hoodlums that got its start in the ghettos of Detroit in early 1915. Their primary activities before Prohibition in 1918 involved small-time shoplifting, breaking and entering and the protection racket. With the advent, however, of the halt on legal liquor sales, the young delinquents quickly graduated to pulling armed robberies and hijacking bootlegged liquor. The mob came of age in the 1920's and '30's when murder and kidnappings were added to their hijacking and other criminal pursuits.

Rumrunners, landing booze along Detroit's waterfront across from Canada, had to be careful and heavily armed. If they were hijacked by the brutal Purples, they were usually shot to death, their loads stolen, and no questions were asked. Some of these hijacked loads of whiskey made their way to the Capone organization in Chicago. By the 1930's, the Purples had become the dominant gang in Detroit's underworld, primarily because of a reputation of murdering anyone who got in the way. They were the hit men of the underworld and at least one of their group was involved in the infamous Chicago St. Valentine's Day Massacre in 1929 where 13 men were lined up against a wall and executed.

According to the article, the Purple Gang members were used as couriers by most of the mobs in the Midwestern United States, carrying huge sums of money between gangs in specially built, souped-up Packard or Cadillac automobiles. The reputation of the gang as a group of ruthless killers who drove fast cars and were armed with automatic weapons made any hijacking of the cash hordes unthinkable!

The Purple Gang also controlled most of the information circulated between the various horse tracks and the gang supplied this information to Detroit's illegal bookie parlors, known as "Blind Pigs." The article went on to say that although The Purples remained an effective mob at the time of writing, their power had been diminished by long prison sentences and inter-gang killings that exacted a toll on the gang's manpower. The article listed some of the alleged gangsters who were still operating in the Detroit and Chicago areas and Seymour Levison made the list—probably because he had been convicted and sentenced for some serious crimes, but was still on the lam!

"Okay," I thought to myself. "So the old judge was a crook and wanted man. But what does that have to do with my house?"

I wondered if he could have hidden out for many years in this hilltop sanctuary. Well, now he was dead and buried here on my property. My mind began to play around. "Is he or one of the other corpses haunting the place?"

All I had accomplished was to answer one question and create others. When would this all end, I wondered. I decided it would probably take me years to solve all the mysteries, but solve them I must. I was totally hooked.

I took the article back to my desk and a thought ran through my mind about the use of Packards and Cadillacs by the gangsters. I wondered if the old Packard in the garage behind the house might be registered in Seymour T. Levison's name. I had no idea how long the state kept records on license plate numbers but the telephone was certainly handy right here on my desk. I got the number for the nearest Michigan State Police Post. Dialing, I reached a desk sergeant and ran the question of tracing an old license plate number by him. I told him I had found the plate on an old 1934 Packard abandoned on some property I had just bought.

When I gave him the plate number of 040536, he said "Boy, that's an old one, but the first four numbers indicate it was issued in the Detroit area. You know, I had an old Packard when I went to college and I sure created a lot of fine memories in the front seat of that baby!

"I would suggest you call the Detroit Secretary of State's Office, ask for the auto squad and give them the plate number. Use this private number, TY 49534, and tell them Sgt. Simler okayed this request."

I thanked him profusely for steering me in the right direction and dialed the private number he had given me.

A very pleasant voice answered the phone in the auto squad office and I told her I had contacted the Michigan State Police in Ann Arbor. I told her Sgt. Simler, the desk officer, seemed to think she could help me find out who owned an old 1934 Packard with license plate number 040536. I also told her I had found the automobile abandoned on property I had recently purchased.

"Is this a request from Officer Simler?" she asked.

"Well, yes it is," I replied sheepishly to the lie.

"All right," she said. "Give me the license plate number again and I'll see what I can find out. It will take a few minutes because this is a really old number."

She said she had a new computer system and asked if I would hold while she tried to find the information. In less than 10 minutes she came back on the line and told me the plate was issued to Anthony Buglioni at an address on Collingwood Avenue in Detroit.

I must have been holding my breath because I didn't

say anything for several seconds. I had been almost positive she would tell me the plate was in Judge Levison's name. I was not familiar with the name Buglioni and he was not named in the newspaper article as being part of any gang. But, the Collingwood address was the apartment complex owned by the judge that had been mentioned in the article. There was definitely a connection there, but this new name threw a monkey wrench into my theory about the judge's ownership of the Packard.

I thanked the clerk and complimented her on her rapid retrieval of the information I needed, marveled at how wonderful these newfangled computers were, and hung up the phone before she could ask me any questions!

I knew the information she had given me was confidential and I didn't want to get in a jam because of my curiosity. It dawned on me that the information regarding the old Packard had become so important to me that I was willing to lie to get it, even to the point of impersonating a police office over the telephone.

I now had another mystery to add to my list. "Who was Mr. Buglioni and how did his Packard get into my garage?"

Several months passed without significant unexplained incidents. There was one occasion, however, that was a bit peculiar. I was home alone, outside in the front yard doing some gardening. I glanced toward the house and thought I saw a figure move across one of the upstairs windows. I turned my head away and then looked quickly back…but saw nothing. I decided it was only the sunlight reflecting off one of the mirrors and then casting a ghostly shadow across the window. I convinced myself it was only my imagination.

Something unexpected happened soon after that diverted my attention from the mysteries surrounding my new home. A large corporation listed on the New York Stock

Exchange was interested in acquiring my company. I had been marketing the corporation's products for several years, and they had decided to eliminate their wholesale dealers and go directly to retail. Their offer was very lucrative and the proposal was entirely favorable, so I agreed to sell out to them. The buy-out of my company couldn't have come at a better time because maintaining our large home had become an almost full-time job. I had always wondered what it might be like to retire at 37. Now I was about to find out what it was like to be a country squire.

During the fall of our second year of residence on the hill, I took the family on a sightseeing tour to the lookout towers about five miles from our house. The Twin Towers were on a hill and were the height of a ten-story building. Each had an observation deck at the top. The decks were reached by climbing rickety wooden steps to their tops. From this high elevation, one could see for several miles in every direction. There were small telescopes mounted on steel poles that could be used to view distant objects.

Kim, one of our daughters, excitedly pointed out that she could see our house off in the distance. It surprised me until I realized that most of the foliage had dropped from the trees because of the season of the year.

I took the telescope and trained it toward the house. When it came into sharp focus, I noticed a carriage with a beautiful white-harnessed horse standing on our front lawn. Under nearby trees was a group of eight or ten couples, some standing and some lying on the grass. They appeared to be picnicking, in clothing straight out of the 1920's.

My mind was whirling. I knew that nearby Clinton held a Fall Festival in September where merchants and residents dressed up in old-style western clothes and rode around in horse-drawn carriages. I thought that maybe some of them had stopped by the house. Then I remembered the festival had been held nearly two months ago.

Just to be sure my eyes were not playing tricks on me, I asked Kim to look through the telescope again and tell me what she saw. "Oh, Dad, what a beautiful horse. When did we get it?"

I knew immediately I had not seen a mirage. I told the kids and Peggy Sue that we needed to hurry home because I thought we must have visitors at the house. When we turned into the driveway, I was eager to see the carriage, but it was nowhere in sight—there was nothing on top of our hill. No people, no carriage, no horses, and no telltale signs of wagon or horse tracks imbedded in the soft surface of my lawn.

Obviously, this had to have been some kind of manifestation because I wasn't the only one to see the picnickers and the horse and carriage. Kim had also seen the same things. We were not both hallucinating!

I didn't allow myself to become mentally twisted over this incident because it was not the first unexplained sighting of figures and faces. I began to wonder if we, as a family, were becoming immune to these out-of-the-ordinary events. I decided I should start keeping some sort of record or journal of the events. At least, it would serve to keep these strange happenings in chronological order just in case something really major occurred.

10

February 1973

We have had heavy snowfall this year, possibly as much as 30 or 40 inches. As a family, we have been enjoying skiing up and down the hill as well as ice-skating on the makeshift rink I plowed out on our frozen lake. All and all, it has been a happy and exciting year so far. We have had several days and nights of below-freezing temperatures and, on some nights, the wind has caused it to drop to below zero.

The fuel-oil-fired boiler ran most of the night keeping the water hot and piping it up to the registers surrounding each room. I also kept a roaring fire in the downstairs fireplace and it provided extra heat as well as a quaint place to sit and stare into the fire. We enjoyed watching the flames dance high into the chimney and hearing the wood logs snap and crackle.

Just to the right of the fireplace was a small door that opened into a wood closet that could be filled through another door that opened on the outside of the house. The cubbyhole would hold about half a cord of wood and the outside door made it convenient to fill.

One night the temperature had to be well below zero and the wind was howling like hell. Unbeknownst to me, when my eldest son Forrest had filled the wood closet, he inadvertently left the outside door open. That night when the fire in the fireplace went out, the water in the pipes running parallel to the chimney, from the basement to the second-floor radiators, froze solid. It split the pipes in the basement.

I knew the next morning I had a problem when the

boys' bedroom on the second floor was ice cold. I went to the garage and brought in a large electric space heater and used it to take the chill off the room.

My next job was a formidable one because the water pipe that had broken was in the basement, directly below the fireplace and behind the heavy oak paneling on the wall. The broken area in the pipe was easy to pinpoint because water was pouring out from behind the paneling, running down the wall onto the carpet where the hole in the floor led to the tunnel.

I hurried outside, climbed down into my well pit below ground level and flipped off the water pump, stopping the flow of water to the house. Then I went to the garage and got out my tools—a crowbar, carpenter's hammer and a blowtorch and flashlight. When I got back to the basement, I found a section of paneling near the leak that I could easily pry off. Carefully, I put my crowbar in and pulled loose one of the three-foot wide panels, taking care not to damage it. I had to remove two more panels near the top of the wall to get to the frozen pipe.

I put my two boys to work, using towels to sop up the water from the carpet. I used my blowtorch, playing it up and down the frozen water pipes. I had bought a steel clamp with a rubber gasket for an occasion such as this. I screwed the clamps tightly over the gasket that covered the small crack in the water pipe and told the boys to watch for leaks while I went out and turned on the water. When I came back inside, the boys were standing there looking at the water pipes that were now completely dry. My efforts had paid off; hot water was again flowing through the upstairs radiators.

My two helpers and I were replacing the panels when my younger son Monroe noticed three large hinges protruding from one of the panels still attached to the wall. Using my flashlight, I looked behind the panel and saw what appeared to be a large door behind it. In order to be sure what it was, I would have to remove two more panels. However, my curiosity was now tweaked, so I carefully removed the first, and then the second panel. As I pulled it away from the wall, I saw a large steel door with a small window near its top, with three steel bars attached across it. A handle on the front was connected to two steel rods that ran vertically down the left side of the door, engaging hooks at the top and the bottom as a locking mechanism. The door was mounted directly onto the wall that served as the base for the fireplace. "My God," I thought, "what have we discovered now?"

I shouted upstairs for Peggy Sue and the girls, "Peggy, Girls, mysteries revealed, mysteries revealed!" They all came running down the stairs and stood in amazement in front of the odd looking door.

"What's behind it, Dad?" one of the girls asked a little anxiously.

"I don't know, but we are about to find out," I answered. As I turned the squeaking door handle that moved the sliding rods, the door cracked open revealing, to our amazement, a small concrete room about nine-feet square and seven feet high. On the floor was a small pile of ashes, covered by years of dust. In the beam of the flashlight we saw a metal plate in the ceiling. I took a broom handle and pushed up on the plate and it opened up into somewhere. I told Monroe to run upstairs and see where the plate had opened. He did that and hurried back down to tell us the plate opened under the fire irons in the middle of the fireplace.

"Why, it's just a place for the fireplace ashes to fall," Peggy Sue exclaimed.

"That's a possibility," I said, "but it's awfully large for that and we have never used it. And that's a very small amount of ashes for the huge fireplace. This must have been used for something else."

"Dad," our daughter Denise said in a shaky voice, "Dad, there is something standing over there in the corner."

I turned the beam of my flashlight in the direction she pointed. It fell on the remains of a rather large, old wooden chair resting against the wall. I moved my light around the room that was looking increasingly like a jail cell to me. My light beam fell on something that confirmed my belief. Hanging from the top of one wall and dangling about halfway down was a set of chains with some kind of metal clamp on each end. Could this be the source of the tinkling noises that periodically emitted from the upstairs fireplace?

Obviously, this room had not been built to hold ashes; it was built to hold people! What we had here was, in reality, an old abandoned dungeon and we might never have found it were it not for that broken water pipe. I was convinced more than ever that with the padded room and now the jail cell, this place—my beautiful mansion—at sometime in the past had definitely held prisoners. Who and for what reason, I could only guess.

11

July 1974

We have had an unusually hot summer and today a series of violent thunderstorms were predicted to pass through our area. Seeing a huge storm front approaching, Peggy Sue and I called the children in from outside and we all huddled together in the living room. One never knows what to expect with Michigan weather and tornadoes are fairly common. I knew we were safe because the house had never been hit and had been standing here for many, many years. We also had a deep basement and, if need be, we could scurry downstairs and be completely safe.

Torrents of rain began to fall and, propelled by high winds, soon began pounding our windows and seeping through the cracks in the steel frames. We could see lightning striking the ground in wooded areas on the next hill.

All of a sudden without any warning, a massive lightning bolt struck the huge Volkswagen-size metal vent cap on top of our chimney. The explosion of the lightning bolt sounded like an artillery shell had hit us. Kim jumped on my back and squeezed my neck so tightly I could hardly breathe. Peggy Sue and the other children were also frightened, so we all raced to the safety of the basement.

When we got to the basement, Peggy Sue said she could smell smoke. I immediately began to search. In the boiler room I saw smoke and a large hole, about the size of a basketball, blown out of the basement wall just above the wash tubs. I could see and smell the smoke, but there was no fire. Soon, it became apparent to me that it wasn't smoke at all, but a cloud of dust that had shaken loose when the whole house was rocked by the force of the lightning strike.

The rain, heavy winds and the sound of lightning and thunder continued for over an hour. These were the most violent thunderstorms I had ever experienced and my head hurt like hell from the stranglehold Kim had put on me when the lightning struck the chimney vent.

As soon as the storm passed, I hurried outside to the front of the house to check on the damage the storm and its lightning had caused our home. I was speechless as I looked at the remains of my three-story chimney and the smoke that was still rising from its interior. Apparently there had been a flash fire when the lightning ignited many years' worth of accumulated soot on the chimney walls. There was a massive hole at least three feet around, about halfway up the chimney. The huge vent that had perched atop the chimney had been blown off and had hit the ground with such force that it was half buried in the soggy lawn. The entire structure had pulled away from the house and was leaning precariously forward at about a 30-degree angle.

Peggy Sue opened one of the front windows and called out to me saying that water was running into the fireplace. I had to give her the sad news that our chimney had been blown almost completely away. Not knowing if the rains would return, I hurried to the telephone anyway and dialed Lefty Walker in Dexter. I told him what had happened and that we had water coming through a hole in our roof. Being the good guy he is, Lefty said he would grab an old tarp and he and some of his men would come out right away and get our roof watertight again.

When Lefty arrived and took a look at the gaping hole and the extensive lightning damage to the heavy brick on the teetering chimney, he said in astonish-ment, "Wow! That looks like some of the houses in Germany I saw in World War II that were hit by our 155-mm Howitzers. Let's hope the chimney doesn't totally collapse and crash through the roof. It's heavy enough to go through all three floors and into the basement."

It was a helluva job to get that canvas tarp over the hole in our very steep roof that was three stories above the ground. Eventually, Lefty and his men got the job done.

"Hey, Lefty, it looks like you've got another job," I said. "How soon can you get me patched up?"

"For you, Mr. Heikel, I'll get some men on it first thing in the morning, but we're going to have trouble matching that old brick, and I hope I can find a welder who can repair that vent cap.

"In addition, I'm going to have to give a lot of thought as to how to repair the chimney around that window. That thing is one hell of an engineering feat. I've never seen anything like it.

"Try to keep dry and I'll see you in the morning," Lefty said as he and his men dragged the twisted metal vent cap to their pickup. It was very heavy and it was all the four of us could do just to slide it onto the bed of the truck.

I watched Lefty's pickup wind its way down the driveway with the large car-sized vent bouncing ever so slightly in the bed. I looked again at the damage to the chimney.

I could see Peggy Sue through the living room window standing in front of the fireplace, staring up at the portrait. I was reminded of the night Mrs. Korrappis expressed her feelings about a tormented soul as she stood in that very spot. Now that we had discovered the small, hidden holding cell directly beneath the fireplace hearth and because the chimney had been struck by a massive bolt of lightning, I began to wonder if God, in His infinite wisdom, was trying to purge this house of a poor, tormented spiritual entity. Or, did the house and chimney just happen to be in the way of one of Mother Nature's methods that she uses to expel excess energies from our atmosphere. One thing I did know for sure was the large, rotating steel air vent on the top of our chimney certainly made a good target for the lightning bolt.

But, I also considered another possibility for the strike, even though it might be far-fetched. I knew that the hilltop home was built on a large mound of glacial dirt and that beneath the surface there had to be rocks heavily laden with iron, therefore loaded with magnetism. These iron-laden rocks might have acted as a conductor to attract the lightning. Why it had not happened before, I did not know.

There is a tourist attraction on the same hilltop as the twin observation towers and it draws visitors from all over the area. Several wooden shacks at the site have been hit by lightning, caught fire and burned to the ground. The area is referred to as Mystery Hill and it features strange anomalies: buildings that appear to the eye to be horizontal to the ground but seem to immediately tilt to a 45-degree angle when someone enters, causing the visitors to lose their balance. Brooms and shovels hung from the ceiling are dangling at a weird angle. Employees at the site give demonstrations with balls that tend to run uphill when placed on the floor. When water is pumped from underground wells on the property, it exits the faucet in the wellhead and falls into a bucket at a 45-degree angle.

Employees at the tourist attraction explain to visitors that directly beneath the outbuildings and where the visitors are standing there is supposedly a large deposit of lodestone. This lodestone is a highly-magnetic material dropped by glaciers. Some people say the laws of physics are temporarily suspended as a result of a curious confluence of magnetic fields. Researchers who have conducted experiments on the unexplained vortex say a spherical force field rings the hilltop, and no less than 15 crisscrossing magnetic fields traverse the area and create a variety of strange occurrences. Wow!

My thinking is that the mansion, being in such close proximity to Mystery Hill, may also be located above another massive accumulation of the lodestone. I remembered reading articles that addressed this, saying that sometimes areas densely influenced by magnetic fields create strange effects on physical items including human beings and their brains. If certain atmospheric conditions are right, the massive buildup of static electricity seems to interact with the magnetic rock and cause all sorts of unusual phenomena.

As I pondered all this, I knew my mind was working overtime trying to explain all the unusual things happening on my hill. I guess it was just my way of trying to make some sense out of all the things that were going on. I was not convinced at all that any of these events were connected to the supernatural or related to spirits, but I must admit my thoughts were creeping, event by event, more and more in that direction.

The next morning I was awakened at daylight by the sound of Lefty and his crew arriving. They had come in their usual pickup but one of the men was arriving in a large tow truck, the kind used to pick up broken down semi-trucks and trailers. I threw on my clothes and went out to greet the guys and inquire about the heavy equipment. Even before I got to the front of the house, they were manipulating the tow truck onto the lawn and were backing it up to about 100 feet in front of the chimney.

"Morning, Lefty. Man, you guys hit the job mighty early," I said shaking his hand.

"The weather man is predicting thunderstorms again in this area and my men are hesitant to be up that high on the house during any stormy conditions. So, I thought we'd pull down the remains of the chimney using this tractor."

While we were talking, one of Lefty's men was climbing a long extension ladder, making his way slowly up the steep roof to the backside of the chimney. He had a small lightweight rope around his waist and when he reached the top of the tilting chimney, another man tied the end of the rope to the hook on the winch cable and started turning the winch. The man on the roof pulled the rope up and eventually got the cable and wrapped it around the upper part of the damaged chimney.

With one man applying the brakes of the tractor and another operating the heavy-duty winch, they pulled the cable as tight as it would go and tried to pull down the remaining portion of the damaged chimney. The thing absolutely would not budge! With the cable still taut, the man in the tractor started the engine, backed up every so slightly, and then lunged forward in low gear. Slowly, ever so slowly, the remaining damaged portion of the chimney started to fall and then, suddenly, plunged to the ground with a huge roar. It embedded itself three feet into the soft lawn.

Lefty and his crew must've planned the night before how to attack the problem of taking down and repairing the chimney. Without any hesitation, two of the men began erecting scaffolding up the face of the damaged portion of the chimney while two other guys began to break apart the portions of the chimney that had fallen to the ground. They were trying to salvage as many of the original bricks as possible so they could be mixed in with the new replacement bricks.

I tell you this guy Lefty really knew what he was doing and I felt confident he could rebuild the main feature of this very unusual chimney with the window in its center. In the upstairs bathroom, there was a single window that was positioned directly in the middle of the chimney. When Lefty had brought this to my attention during the remodeling process, I had wondered how in the world smoke could get around the window. Because it was in the center of the chimney, it meant that the smoke from the fireplace would actually have to pass on either side of the window to exit the top.

Lefty told me he felt he could repair the brick all right but hoped he would not have trouble with the fireplace once the repairs were made. He was concerned about the chimney's drafting properly. Now that the scaffolding had been completely erected to the area where the damage began, Lefty put all five of his men to the job of cleaning and salvaging the old bricks from the pile of rubble on our front lawn. This took the better part of the day and it was almost quitting time when Lefty stood on the platform at the top of the scaffolding to evaluate the job.

I watched him as he moved from side to side of the structure, shining his powerful spotlight down into the remainder of the chimney. For some reason, he disappeared momentarily into the right-hand side of the chimney. After a few minutes his head popped up above the broken bricks. He asked me if I thought I could scale the scaffolding because he had a question to ask me.

I had been hoping he would ask me to come up because I really wanted to see the extent of the damage up close. When I reached the top of the scaffolding, I was amazed to see that I could look right into the master bathroom and I could also see a part of Denise's bedroom over the remaining section of the fireplace in her room. The devastation was staggering.

The first thing Lefty pointed out to me was that the smoke and fumes from both the downstairs and upstairs fireplaces did not pass around both sides of the window, but passed through only one side of the chimney. Looking down into the open structure, I could see clearly on one side where the smoke had passed over the years, leaving a trail of soot. On the other side, a strange hollow shaft appeared to run from this upstairs bathroom down through the first floor to the basement. Lefty thought we could examine the shaft better if we went into the house and observed it from the upstairs bathroom.

When we walked in the master bathroom, I said to Lefty, "You've got to get a tarp over this huge hole or else that plaster work you did downstairs on the ceiling will fall apart if it starts to rain again."

Lefty acknowledged my comment by nodding his head, but what we both saw before us was more interesting than any conversation about a hole in the roof. We could see clearly that this shaft was incorporated into the wall of the bathroom and, on closer inspection, we discovered a trap door that was exposed when the top of it had been broken off by the falling remnants of the chimney.

Lefty managed to work the door open. It was cleverly concealed inside the large linen closet in the bathroom. We were both puzzled by what we saw. The shaft was about three and a half feet square and contained a series of ropes and cables threaded through wooden and rubber rollers connected to a chain and sprocket drive system, coupled to a large electric motor.

Even more bizarre was that the ropes were attached to what appeared to be a chair without any legs. A large leather belt with a buckle was attached to either side of the seat of the chair.

There was a strong breeze blowing up through the fireplace and out the opening where the chimney wall used to be. The metal sprocket and cables in the shaft rattled and jangled loudly. Immediately Lefty said, "Now we know how those spooky noises were being made in the fireplace. But, what the hell is this other stuff?

I guess I was too dumbfounded even to speak and just stood there aghast for several minutes while I let my brain absorb the contents of the shaft. I tried to put everything in proper and logical perspective.

I was the only one who knew about the ventilated corners of the old paintings that hung over both the upstairs and downstairs fireplaces. I reached the conclusion that someone obviously used this secret trapdoor to enter the shaft, slide into the chair, buckle up and lower himself down the shaft into a position where he could view, as well as hear, the occupants of the rooms through the ventilated screen in the portraits.

I shared my best guess of what the shaft was used for with Lefty. To demonstrate my theory, I slid across the board placed inside the shaft that allowed a person to get to the chair. I wiggled myself into the chair lift and asked Lefty to look around for a switch that would activate the old electric motor. While Lefty was searching with his spotlight, I detected some wires running along the structure inside the shaft and believed they were leading to the chair I was sitting in. I felt around underneath the chair and found two small buttons, about doorbell size. I yelled at Lefty to tell him what I'd found.

When his head appeared in the shaft, I told him I was going to press one of the buttons and to stand by with a rope in case I wound up on the bottom of the shaft. "Here, you'll need this," he said as he handed me the spotlight.

I pressed one of the buttons and immediately heard the large electric motor begin to hum—but nothing happened. Lefty said the motor could be frozen from being inoperative for so long. Without thinking, he grabbed the pulley on the motor with his hand and gave it a jerk. Immediately, the motor began to run and I felt myself being lowered down into the shaft, very slowly and very quietly.

When I reached what I figured was the first floor, I pressed the other button on the chair and, surely enough, the chair stopped. There was no need for further debate about the use of this silent conveyor system because I was stopped directly behind the painting. Even though the holes in the painting were minuscule, I could see clearly into the living room and I could hear Peggy Sue speaking in her normal voice to the children. Pressing the button again, I found myself being lowered further into the shaft. When I felt my feet touch a solid surface, I stopped the chair. I could see nothing. I looked around the interior of the shaft with the spotlight and detected in front of me a small board with a little handle. I lifted it. There were two holes behind it that looked directly into the small holding cell under the fireplace. A similar board and handle was about two feet to the right. When I opened that, I could see into the basement ballroom just over the oak panels on the wall.

I was getting a little anxious in the tight confines of the shaft, so I pushed the "up" button and slowly and quietly was lifted back up to the second-floor bathroom. I pushed the other button and the chair stopped.

Lefty was standing there with his hat off, scratching his head and exclaiming, "Well, I'll be a son of a gun. I knew this place had a lot of strange nooks and crannies, but this takes the cake! This guy must have been some kind of pervert or just a common old peeping Tom."

"I think you may well be right, Lefty," I replied. I started to slide out of the chair into the bathroom when I remembered about the portrait over the fireplace in the adjoining bedroom. I looked over to my left and saw a long 12-inch board that ran about five feet along the wall. I slid out of the chair onto the dusty board and wiggled my way across it until I could see through the screen in an upper corner of the portrait. The view was straight into one of my daughter's bedroom. An observer, from this position, had a perfect view of the bedroom door and the bed, itself. The designer of this chair lift had a peep sight on everything in front of the old portraits and through the small holes in the basement wall.

I had seen enough, so I slid back across the board, back into the chair, and made my way out of the shaft and back through the secret panel in the linen closet to the bathroom. I turned to Lefty and, with a straight face, told him he would have to keep this secret shaft and elevator system to himself. I said I would pay him, if necessary, but I did not want this information to leak out into my community.

"You know you don't have to give me any money, Mr. Heikel. This is your business and you can depend on me to keep my mouth shut."

Hearing this, I shook his hand and patted him on the back. "Thanks, my friend. I appreciate it immensely," I said as we began our trip down the stairs so he could get back to work.

We briefly discussed why anyone would want to spy upon people in his own home. Lefty came up with the brilliant idea that I should ask "that Outhouse person" and see if he knew anything about this secret shaft.

"That's a great idea," I said. "He's done secret work for old man Levison before, but I doubt he built the shaft. It must have been constructed when the house was originally built because it's such an integral part of the design. But, it's still not a bad idea to talk to him. I think I'll go pay him a visit."

"Good luck finding him," Lefty said as he hurried away. "I've got to get that tarp on your roof because it looks like we're in for another downpour."

I took off to town in my Caddie to find Outhouse. I wanted to see the look on his face and get his reaction when I told him about the elevator system. That might tell me if he knew anything about the shaft even if he said he didn't. Whoever built the system had one hell of an imagination and was creative, as well as devious!

I decided to begin my search for Outhouse at his usual hangout, the Wagon Wheel Bar. My hunch was correct. I found Outhouse in his secluded booth at the rear of the tavern. He was dressed in pretty much the same attire and was engulfed in a heavy cloud of Marlboro smoke. When he saw me heading toward him, he mouthed "Oh, no, here comes that pain in the ass again."

I held out my hand to him as I approached and said, "Mr. Van Sickel, do you remember me? Zack Heikel, and I spoke with you about the house on the hill."

He ignored my outstretched hand and replied sarcastically, "You know you owe me a couple of drinks from the last time we talked."

"No, I haven't forgotten," I replied as I held up two fingers to the barkeep and pointed at Outhouse's near-empty shot glass.

"Well, what did you find now?" was his question to me as he took a deep drag off his cigarette.

Waving away the smoke he blew in my face, I answered, "I thought you might know someone who would be able to repair the window located in the middle of the chimney."

"Why, is it broken?"

Casually, I said, "You'll never believe this but lightning struck the chimney and damaged it so badly we had to tear it down to the roof line. The contractor I hired to do the repair work is uncertain that he can repair the window and do the brick work on the chimney. He's afraid that if it's not built identical to the way it was prior to the lightning strike, the fireplace might not function properly."

I purposely didn't mention the secret shaft and was baiting him a little to see if he would ask if there was damage to the conveyor system. I didn't want to mention the apparatus in case he knew nothing about it. He looked like the kind of guy who would spread rumors and I really didn't want to let the knowledge out into the community.

Outhouse took a sip of whiskey and said in the middle of a cough, "You know, I always wondered why that window was directly in the middle of the chimney. It was such a peculiar place for it that a picture of the window was in the newspaper several years ago in Ripley's 'Believe It of Not' column. I can see why your contractor is concerned about rebuilding it. Fact of the matter is, I don't know anybody around these parts who would even attempt that job. I'll bet those repairs are gonna cost you a small fortune."

I baited him a little more. "My contractor hasn't given me a price as yet because he doesn't understand how the smoke and fumes from the fireplace could pass by on both sides of the window or how much reconstruction he will have to do."

All Outhouse could do was shake his head from side to side. "I'm glad it's your problem and not mine. I wouldn't want any part of that headache."

In one last effort to determine if Outhouse was holding something back, I said, "Did you ever do any work on the fireplace at the house?"

His reply indicated to me that he had no knowledge of the elevator system when he said, "No, the only time I worked inside the house was in that there padded room on the second floor. Have you asked Bruno? He may know someone who has worked on the house. Hey! Are you going to have a drink with me? A couple of us guys are gonna play cards in a few minutes if you want to join us."

"Thanks, but no," I said. "I've got some errands to run so I guess I'll just shove off. Thanks for your help and good luck with the cards."

On my trip back home, I thought I might stop by and see Bruno since I had to pass right by the front of his cabin. As I pulled up to the small cottage, I didn't notice any smoke coming through the vent in the roof. I made my way to the front door, stepping around the chickens and the holes in the floor of the porch. I knocked on the door and waited a few minutes. When no one answered, I rapped again loudly. Still there was no answer. I was sure Bruno was at home because his pickup was parked beside the house.

I didn't want to irritate him if he was taking a nap, but

I hadn't seen Bruno since he showed me the graves at the back of the house several months ago. I stepped over and rapped on a window; still there was no answer. I looked through one of the windows where the newspaper had fallen off. I saw Bruno slumped over in a chair at the kitchen table. I knew I had to investigate, so I went to the front door, pushed on it with my shoulder and the door opened. It wasn't locked.

I called out to Bruno, but he didn't move. I went over to him, put my hand on his shoulder and shook him. Finally, he responded. Looking dazed, he told me he must have fainted because he had been feeling quite ill lately. He wanted me to get him a glass of water. After he took a few gulps, I asked him if he wanted me to call a doctor. He responded negatively and asked if I would help him to his bed.

He said all he needed was a couple of aspirin and he thought he would be fine in the morning. I got him another glass of water, found the aspirin on the kitchen windowsill, and took them in to him. In his usual mutters and grunts and with some gestures, he told me he appreciated my help. I asked if I could light a fire for him and if he needed food. He said no, he thought he just needed to get some sleep. He did ask if I would check on him in the morning.

"Of course I will," I said. "You try to get some rest and I'll see you tomorrow."

The poor man looked worse than usual. He both looked and smelled terrible. As I left the small home, my hope was that I would find him alive in the morning.

I didn't sleep much that night, worrying about whether or not I should have called the paramedics. I had done as Bruno requested and left him alone, but I was apprehensive about what I might find the next morning.

Early the next day, I knocked at Bruno's front door and was relieved when he answered on my second rap. He stood there holding his cat and I could smell eggs cooking on the stove. He thanked me for my concern and asked if I needed him for something. I told him about the lightning strike to the chimney and asked if he knew anyone who had done work inside the house and who might be able to help my contractor. He thought for a minute and then grunted, "Too bad about the lightning, but I don't know any repairmen," he said, shaking his head from side to side.

I asked him if he had ever done any carpentry work inside the house and he told me he was no good with a hammer or saw. The statement rang true to me because of the condition of the boards on his front porch. It was apparent to me that he was not only a poor handyman—he also didn't know about the spy system in the fake chimney shaft.

As I got ready to leave, I asked Bruno if he minded if I stopped by periodically to check on him. I mentioned that with no telephone, he was really isolated out here.

Surprisingly, Bruno reached over and took my hand. He said he would appreciate it very much because he had not felt well lately and had been losing his balance. Again, I asked if he wanted me to take him to a doctor and his answer was a resounding, "No!" He said he hated doctors and didn't need them; that aspirin was all he ever needed because they seemed to make him feel better.

"All right," I said, walking to my car, "but I'll be checking on you from time to time and I'll be sure you have a good supply of aspirin."

As I drove up my driveway, I thought I wouldn't be surprised at all if he was not long for this world because he looked so pale and ill.

My visits with both Outhouse and Bruno had dashed my hopes of finding out something about the elevator system. They knew absolutely nothing about the who, what or why of the secret shaft. I doubt that anyone living could tell me about the system. I figured no one knew it existed except the phantom that rode up and down behind the walls, spying on unsuspecting souls. Souls that were probably having a hell of a time dancing and drinking in the basement; or while some poor wreck might have been in agony chained to the wall of a cell like a wild animal. Simultaneously, others in the upstairs bedrooms could have been in ecstasy.

What kind of a thrill this sick person experienced while spying from the shaft was beyond my imagination. However, it seemed all the answers were taken to the grave by old man Levison if, indeed, he was the demon in the darkness.

About 10 o'clock, that evening Lefty called. "Are you okay over there? Got any water coming into the house? It's raining cats and dogs over here."

I told him we were nice and dry and experiencing only sprinkles at the time. He asked if I'd had any luck locating someone who knew something about the window construction, and I had to tell him I had struck out on all fronts. I recounted to Lefty all the events of the afternoon and told him he would have to figure out the riddle of reconstruction on the chimney himself.

Lefty chuckled and said he thought he was up to the challenge, but asked me what I wanted him to do about the apparatus in the secret shaft.

I instructed Lefty to leave everything intact and to wrap some rags around the chains to keep them from rattling and to tie down the cables. I said he should just rebuild the chimney to the best of his ability and secure the secret door used to enter the shaft. I thought that might help me sleep better at night, knowing the door was padlocked and no one had access to the chair. It is interesting that, even after this was done, I continued to have the sensation that someone was watching us in our bedroom and downstairs in the living room. It seemed the eyes in the paintings seemed to follow me constantly. Maybe my imagination was out of control again!

To make myself more comfortable, I even asked Peggy Sue to cover the portrait with some drapes saying I thought the painting did not go well with our new furniture. She said she would get around to it "eventually."

Sometimes if I was awakened by a noise at night, my first thought would be about that obscene contraption dangling behind the wall, just a few feet over our heads. I knew I could never reveal the secret "viewing" apparatus to anyone, particularly Peggy Sue. I would have to keep its existence solely to myself.

Over the next several days, the reconstruction job went along rapidly. I was amazed at how well the bricklayers had worked in the old bricks with new ones, creating the impression that the wall had just been cleaned, but never damaged. It was a work of art. And, Lefty had found a glass factory that reassembled the twisted remains of the window, installed new windowpanes, and applied a fresh coat of black enamel to the frames. The window looked brand new. When it was cemented in place in the center of the chimney wall, it was difficult to tell that anything had ever been damaged.

Lefty had another big surprise for us once the window was installed in the chimney. A completely reconditioned vent cap for the top of the chimney arrived with Lefty one morning. It was in the back of his pickup and it had been totally restored. Lefty used the extension boom of the tow truck to lift the several-hundred-pound vent to the top of the structure and held it there while his workman bolted and cemented it into place very securely.

The large hole that had been blown into the basement wall by the lightning bolt had also been repaired. In less that two weeks, Lefty and his crew had us back in business! When it came time for me to settle up with Lefty on the cost of the job, I was amazed that the total price was only $3,200. I said to him, "Are you sure you figured this right? I think the price is too little for the beautiful job you've done. I'd at least like to give you a tip."

He thanked me but said that wasn't neccssary. "If I ever need a reference about my work, could I give your name?"

Laughing, I said, "You bet! I'll make it sound so good they'll think I'm your brother." I handed Lefty his check and reminded him of my request to keep the contraption in the chimney shaft a secret.

His only reply was "What contraption?" As he pulled away in his truck, he joked that I should let him know if I ever found out what in the hell the shaft was all about. I told him I would, but I doubted it would ever come to pass.

12

December 1974

I recently purchased the old movie theater in downtown Clinton from a widow who was ready to sell the place to an auto dealer to store parts. I thought it would be a shame for the town to lose its only theater. Peggy Sue agreed to renovate the place. After a few weeks of general cleaning and painting inside and out, she had a company install a new screen and new seats. They overhauled the old-style projectors.

Peggy Sue hired an agent to acquire movies for us and we began showing first-run films. She hired some high school kids part-time to help out but there was one long-time employee of the theater Peggy Sue kept on. Her name was Lena Stein.

Lena was a very nice lady in her sixties, and our children got along great with her. When she came to the theater to sell tickets each night, she would bring her large, white, blue-eyed Persian cat with her. Our daughter Denise loved the cat and played with it constantly. Since the child had become so attached to the animal, Lena asked my wife one evening if she could give the cat to Denise. At the time, we had no pets at home so Peggy Sue agreed to let Denise have the cat.

The next day Lena brought the cat, its food and toys, litter box, and bed out to our house. Lena was very specific that the animal was a house cat and very rarely went outside. Lena went upstairs with Denise and her cat to help get it settled in the bedroom. Denise was crazy about her pet and for several days, everything went very smoothly. The cat had the freedom to roam about the house and was very good about using the litter box.

One night everyone had gone to bed and was fast asleep. Suddenly we were all jolted awake by the sounds of a screaming, spitting feline. The cat was running around the house in a frenzy, like someone had put a match to its tail. Denise was trying to catch her cat and hold it, hoping to calm it down; but she was unable to do it. I hollered at the boys for help and they tried to tackle the animal, but it was too fast for them. The cat ran into the boys' bedroom where my sons had partially opened a window for fresh air. The cat saw the opening, bolted out the window onto the ledge and then bounded up to the slate roof and disappeared into the night.

Poor Denise must have spent at least an hour outside calling to her kitty and trying to coax it back into the house. But, the cat did not reappear that night. Denise could hardly wait until morning to begin a daylight search for her cat. She hurriedly put on her clothes and her snowsuit and boots and ran outside to see if she could find the pet. It was nowhere in sight.

An hour later she came in the house crying, so I told her I would have a look myself. It was cold! I threw on my heavy overcoat, boots, earmuffs and gloves and picked up my binoculars as I headed out the door to try to locate the fluffy cat.

It didn't take me long to detect a white ball of fur huddled against the black slate roof on one of the attic window sills near the chimney. Denise and I hurried upstairs to the library window just below the area where the cat was scrunched up in a ball. We opened the window and called out to the kitty, but it would not budge. Denise even tried to tempt the cat with a favorite treat, but it would not leave the safety of its hiding place. This house cat was not accustomed to the freezing temperatures and was shivering and pressing its little body tightly up against the wall of the chimney for warmth. There was just nothing we could do to coax the cat back inside. It remained perched three stories up in the air on a very cold, windswept roof. When Denise was out of earshot, I told Peggy Sue I only gave the cat a couple of days to survive the exposure to the cold.

All weekend Denise tried and tried to retrieve the cat, to no avail. When the kids went back to school on Monday, there was still no indication the cat planned to return to the warmth of the indoors. On Wednesday of that week, I was filling my car's gas tank at the pump. I glanced up on the roof and saw the cat scampering across it with a bird in its mouth. I watched as the cat feverishly devoured it. The cat was doing everything it could to survive in the harsh environment. It had never dawned on us to put food out on the roof for the poor cat.

Immediately, I went upstairs to the attic and poured a large pile of cat food on the roof. When Denise came home from school, she was thrilled that I had seen her cat. For several more days, we continued to feed the cat on the roof. We also noticed that the kitty was using the troughs on the eaves of the house as a litter box. We left the attic window open so she could get inside for protection if she wanted to, but there were never any signs that she did that. After three days of leaving the window open, I had to close it because bats were again occupying the high corners of the attic ceiling.

Surprisingly, the cat lived on our roof for most of that winter, getting its nourishment from the occasional bird it could catch and the food we put out on the roof.

The cat living on our roof provided quite a conversation topic for Denise when her friends came over. They always tried to retrieve the cat. Even though the cat had spent its entire life as a house cat, there was no way that cat was coming back into our house. Something had terrified it so badly it was willing to freeze and starve rather than return to our house.

In March when the snow began to melt, our son Forrest found the cat's partially eaten body frozen solid in a snow bank. We didn't know what had happened—was it just the elements or had some predator like an owl or hawk finally caught up with the hapless creature? Who or what had terrified Denise's pet remains a mystery we will never understand. Even our local veterinarian had no clue as to what had troubled the animal. She did comment that cats are, by nature, very suspicious creatures; but she had never heard of a cat behaving that way. This was the first example of the peculiar reactions and behaviors of animals that were brought home to live with us, including a few horses I later bought to ride and pull our sleigh and buggy.

13

July 1975

We've had a beautiful spring and early summer. I decided it was time for us to buy a horse. This area was perfect for horseback riding, with its rolling hills, water everywhere and fruit trees in abundance. A friend of the family told us about a ranch that sold horses. He and I took a two-hour drive over to see what horses they might have for sale. When the foreman asked me how I planned to use the animal, I told him about the buggy and sleigh and that we were interested in riding around the countryside. I also mentioned that we had small children so we needed a horse that was completely tame and easy to handle.

He walked us over to a stall and showed us a beautiful, well-groomed, chestnut gelding. He was tall and stocky in his conformation and was three years old. "This is the horse for you," he said. "He's a hunter-jumper and very expensive. I raised him from a colt and he has never given us a minute's trouble. He's just very docile. My kids ride him all the time and he harnesses willingly."

He went on to tell me we would need to be careful on him because he liked to jump over fences. When he asked if I'd like to try him out, I was a little hesitant. I had been an excellent rider in years past, but hadn't been on a horse for several years. However, I was willing to mount him for a stroll around the paddock area. The horse handled like a dream and was so large and comfortable it was like riding on a large sofa.

We agreed on a price for the horse, a saddle and tack. We loaded the horse in my friend's trailer and headed home.

The kids named the horse Sean. He was so tame the children could climb all over him. He allowed us to harness him to the buggy with no fuss whatsoever. He was always completely under control when pulling the buggy. Not only did the kids ride him, but Peggy Sue even took a ride on his back now and then. When I rode him cross country, he was completely tranquil, even when a pheasant would suddenly fly up in front of him—a happening that would startle most any horse. Nothing seemed to bother him or spook him in any way—at least, not at first.

That changed early one morning. I was coming downstairs to have breakfast with the children before they went off to school when my son Forrest looked out the kitchen window.

"Dad, something is wrong with Sean. He's running around wildly and kicking his hind legs in the air. It looks like he's going crazy."

I also looked out the window and noticed that, in fact, the horse was acting very strangely. Although I was still in my pajamas, I quickly got some sugar cubes from the kitchen cabinet and hurried out to the corral. Leaning over the fence and displaying his favorite treat, I called to the horse. He ignored me and continued on his rampage. This kind of behavior was highly unusual because Sean would do anything to get one of his sugar cubes. I then offered him a handful of grain. He wasn't interested in that either. There seemed to be nothing I could do to calm down this violent animal.

After about an hour of frantic physical activity, the horse began to sweat profusely. I had never seen an animal act this way and I knew I needed some help from someone who knew more about horses than I did. I called the ranch foreman and excitedly described to him what the horse was doing. His first reaction was that he couldn't believe I was talking about the same horse he had sold me. "That's so strange because that horse has always had such a cool demeanor. Have you been having trouble with him before now?"

"No," I responded quickly. "He's perfect, but I'm really worried about him now because he's sweating so much. What can I do for him?"

The ranch foreman told me I should try spraying him down with a garden hose and if that didn't work I would have no choice but to wait until the horse exhausted himself. "There's nothing else you can do," he said.

I told him I would try the water hose right away and thanked him for the suggestion. By the time I returned to the corral, Sean had lain down by the gate and he was covered in lather. I approached him slowly so as not to scare him. I turned on the water hose and began to direct the spray on his back. He looked up at me with sad, big brown eyes as if to say, "Boy, that feels good." In a few minutes, he slowly stood up and let me stroke his nose. I took the sugar cube I had in my pajama pocket and offered it to him.

He took the sugar cube quickly and munched it up. Then he drank for a long time from the horse trough. Finally, he had regained control of himself.

I telephoned the ranch foreman and told him everything was under control again. We discussed some possible causes of the incident because I didn't want something like that to happen again to my horse.

He was happy to learn that things were back to normal. He asked me if we were feeding the horse too much grain. I said, "No, I don't think so. We're giving him the same amount he got at your ranch."

"Well, then maybe he's bored or he misses the other animals here at the ranch. I think however, if that were it, he would have acted up before now since you've had him for several months. You know sometimes just a strong wind can rile 'em up. They're strange creatures."

I felt like the guy was trying to help me, but he was

beginning to sound like a car salesman who was trying to get me to buy another horse. I thought about it and decided that might just be a good idea. If we had more horses, we could all ride at the same time and enjoy the countryside together…and Sean might be happier. So, voicing my feelings, I said, "I bet you'd give me a good deal on a horse today, wouldn't you?"

"I'll sell you a horse cheap today if only to keep Sean happy. For three hundred dollars and I'll deliver it to you. Now, bear in mind, it's an old horse and I was just going to put it out to pasture, but she would make a good friend for Sean. She's old and kinda swaybacked, but she's very gentle."

My mind was turning over this proposition. I had paid five thousand for Sean. Three hundred dollars—why I would have to pay that much just to get somebody to trailer the horse over to the house.

"When could you deliver her?" I finally asked.

"Would tomorrow be soon enough?" he quickly asked and I told him that would be great.

When the horse arrived the next day, the kids were ecstatic and fell in love with the old mare. She was light brown with white spots. The kids named her Cricket. Now, when you talk about docile, well Cricket was the perfect example. She would stand in one place for hours just looking at the fence. But the kids had great fun riding her and she was not nearly as hopeless as the ranch foreman had made her out to be. But still, she was very, very docile!

Sean seemed to like his new companion and sometimes they would stand together for a long time as if talking to each other. Everything was just perfect: Sean was happy and so was Cricket…for about two weeks. And, then it happened.

It was just at daybreak when I heard the pounding of hooves and the whinnying and snorting of the horses. I went to my bedroom window, looked out and saw the two horses running wildly in the pasture. I thought something had scared them, a wild animal or thunder perhaps. I stood and watched them for several minutes and became concerned when their actions turned violent.

Both the horses were standing on their hind legs, pawing the air with their front feet. Then, they were bucking up high and kicking out their back legs as if trying to protect themselves. This didn't surprise me too much since I had seen Sean acting similarly a few weeks ago, but to see Cricket so disturbed, especially at her age, was frightening.

Hurriedly, I put on my clothes and went out to the corral and saw that both horses were in a very heavy sweat and had probably been in this rage for some period of time. I tried the same thing I had done with Sean a few weeks earlier and just waited for the animals to exhaust themselves. It took over an hour, but eventually both animals were lying prostrate on the ground, sweating and breathing heavily.

I managed to spray a stream of water on Cricket who was near the corral fence, but I had to carry buckets of water to pour on Sean to revive him. The horses lay in a stupor for a few hours and then slowly got to their feet and made their way to the water trough for a long drink.

I was absolutely at my wits' end trying to figure out what in the devil was bothering these animals. I waited until I was sure the ranch foreman was up and called him again, detailing the same problem I had earlier. His response was that he didn't understand what was going on. "Something is spooking the horses, or it's something you're feeding them. It's as simple as that," he said.

"I really don't know what else to tell you. I guess it's a problem you're going to have to solve on your own. Maybe you should call the vet and see if there's something else to be done. I wish you the best of luck. Goodbye." Click! He just hung up. Guess he was just as frustrated as I was.

I knew then that I had to get some answers about what

could be disturbing the horses. At the end of each episode the horses were exhausted and I was afraid they would eventually die. I called the same vet I had consulted with about the cat. She was very nice and listened closely as I explained my concerns about my horses. She asked me where I lived and I told her out in the Irish Hills. Her memory apparently kicked in because she said, “You’re the guy with the cat living on the roof, aren’t you?”

“Why, yes I am,” I said. “I didn’t think you’d remember me since it’s been several months since I called you.”

Quickly, she responded, “Are you sure your kids are not mistreating your animals?”

“Absolutely not! They are gentle children and I would never put up with our pets being abused,” I said firmly.

In an attitude of apology, she said, “I’m sure you’re right. It was just a suggestion.” She went on to say pretty much the same thing the ranch foreman had said, that it might be the wind, wild animals or maybe something in the water or perhaps a noxious weed they were eating. She mentioned the rhubarb plant and said it was bad for animals to eat—and that some humans felt the same way about it!

Just before we hung up, she said all she could think of doing was to draw some blood to see if any toxins were present. I thanked her and said I would get back to her about doing the blood tests.

Thinking about what she had said about the rhubarb, I knew it was safe for humans because Peggy Sue had been gathering it from the orchard and making the best rhubarb custard pie imaginable and we had been eating it with no ill effects for a long time. We also ate many other fresh vegetables and fruits that grew in our orchard, including asparagus, mushrooms, apples, pears, cherries, apricots, peaches and sweet corn. We also had as many grapes as we wanted because we had a large vineyard. Peggy Sue even made several bottles of wine each year, using the old wine press we found laying next to the Packard.

However, I had never considered noxious vegetation as a source of the problem. There were many strange plants in the area that the horses probably had access to, and one of them might be causing these fits. Trying to eliminate the possibilities the vet posed, I decided to send a sample of the barn's well water to the water department in Ann Arbor for analysis. I would also stay on the lookout for strange plants.

I knew the water in the house was safe because I had it tested when we had first moved out to the Irish Hills. However, it was possible the barn's well could be contaminated because it was only 50 feet deep and the well that served the house was over 400 feet deep. I paid close attention also to any weird looking plants the horses could have been nibbling on. If I found one, I pulled it up and threw it in the trash burner.

I kept a close eye on the horses for the next few days and was careful that I wasn't feeding them too much grain. I kept them mostly on a hay ration. They had good appetites and were back to acting normal again. I would see them standing for hours completely still, one staring of into space and the other staring at the ground. They just seemed to be waiting for one of us to come out to play with them or ride.

The water test results arrived in the mail. It confirmed my suspicions that the water was fine to drink, but it did contain a high count of iron particles, just like the water in the house did. I was aware of the iron in the house water because of the extensive measures I had to take with water softeners in the basement to remove the iron. Otherwise, it stained all the toilets. Well, that relieved my mind about the horses' drinking water. Something else was at the root of the animals' strange behavior.

14

September 1975

The demeanor of the two horses I had bought was never as calm as it had been at the ranch where I bought them, or as it was the first few weeks on our hill. The animals seemed to be on edge all the time and they were becoming very skittish. I stopped giving them grain and fed them almost exclusively on hay. I continued to scour the pastures for any sign of strange vegetation.

One beautiful fall day, soon after a passing thunderstorm had cleaned the air, I was eager to take a ride on Sean. I managed to get him saddled and get the bit in his mouth, but he was very uncooperative all through the process. His ears stood straight up and his eyes were wide open as if in anticipation of something. I threw my leg over his rump and dropped into the saddle. Immediately, he began to buck and snort aggressively as he tried to throw me off.

I managed to rein him in and we started slowly down the hill toward the lake. I had to keep a tight rein on him because he was fighting the bit and wanted to take off in full flight. At the bottom of the hill, I stopped and allowed him to take an apple off a tree. He seemed to be enjoying this treat and I must have let my guard down for just an instant. Without warning, he reared up on his hind legs, dropped down again and took off at a full canter with me hanging on for dear life. He made a mad dash straight toward the lake and, with no hesitation at all, ran down the wooden dock that led to the lake and dived straight into about thirty feet of water.

When we hit the water in a huge splash, we made a geyser that must have gone twenty feet in the air; and then we sank into the murky water. When I struggled to the surface, I was completely disoriented and it was difficult to swim in my full riding gear. My boots had filled with water and my water-soaked clothing was beginning to pull me under again. Suddenly I felt a big surge just beneath me. It was Sean coming to the surface. I managed to grab onto his neck and hang on. He kicked mightily back toward the shore, but each time he lunged forward, I went under again. Then I realized he was swimming parallel to the shore and heading toward a remote section of the lake where the trees came almost to the shoreline.

I managed to grab one of the reins and pulled his head toward the shore. Finally, he got his footing on the lake bottom and waded in toward the shore that was about 75 feet ahead. The water was only up to Sean's knees and because I was draped across his body, I was completely out of the water.

I thought the ordeal was almost over when we were within 30 feet of the lake edge. Sean was standing motionless so I righted myself in the saddle and took the reins and let the horse catch his breath. Believing that everything was now under control, I pushed my spurs slightly into his underbelly. Unexpectedly, he lurched forward and fell immediately into what seemed to be a sinkhole.

Even though Sean was 16 hands high at the withers (about six feet), he had already sunk down to a point where the saddle was completely under water. He struggled with great effort to move forward, but every effort caused him to sink even deeper. Because the shore was so close, I thought if I jumped off the horse I could wade the short distance and with my weight off his back Sean might be able to make it to dry ground. When I jumped off the saddle, my feet hit what felt like the lake bottom; but, as I tried to right myself, I began to sink slowly into some kind of muck. I began to struggle; but the more I struggled, the deeper I sank into the mud. Suddenly, I realized that my horse and I were trapped in a large area of quicksand and were slowly being sucked under. I knew I had to react quickly, so I lay face down on the water. There was only about a foot of water covering the quicksand pit. I tried not to move to prevent sinking any further. I yelled as loud as I could, "Help!" but my cries just echoed over the area. There was no one around to hear me or to help me. For a moment, I thought I was a goner.

Then, out of the corner of my water-and-dirt-filled eyes, I saw a figure on shore rushing toward me. It was Bruno! He was shouting instructions to me, but I couldn't understand what he was saying. I did understand what he was doing, however, when I saw him begin to break large branches from a nearby tree. He ran to the lake edge and slid the branches across the water to me. I managed to catch the edge of one and, knowing this was my only lifeline, I held on as tight as I could as Bruno pulled me slowly toward the shore. When I hit the dry ground, I was covered from head to toe in mud and totally exhausted. But, I was alive!

I struggled to my feet and threw my arms around Bruno and embraced him tightly. This guy had just saved my life and, in spite of his hideous physical appearance, he was the most beautiful human in the world right now! He was mumbling something and pointing at the water. I turned and saw Sean slide almost completely underwater. He was fighting to keep his head above the water and I knew if we didn't act quickly the horse would be sucked completely under.

I thought about my tractor and the chain hanging on the back of it that I used to pull up small trees. I told Bruno to throw as many branches as he could toward the horse and I ran up the hill to get the tractor. I had left the keys in the ignition so I quickly started the tractor and raced down the hill toward the lake. When I got back only Sean's eyes and nostrils were above the water.

Without hesitating for even a second, I backed the tractor to the water's edge and unwound the long chain. I hooked one end to the back of the brush-cutter attachment on the rear of the tractor. The brush cutter extended out over the water about ten feet. I lay down on my belly and slid across the branches Bruno had placed in the water. Slowly I made my way toward the submerged and frightened animal. I knew I had only a few seconds to act, so when I reached the horse, I wrapped the chain around his neck and hooked it as tightly as I could. Then I shimmied my way back across the tree limbs to the shore, jumped onto the seat of the idling tractor and threw it into low gear.

As I let out the clutch, I felt the chain draw up tight and tug on the horse's body. I slowly applied the throttle even though I knew the chain was choking the horse. I had no other choice!

I looked behind me to see that most of Sean's head was now out of the water and he had turned over on his side. Bruno was feverishly moving the logs and branches and pushing them down under the horse's neck. Slowly, ever so slowly, more and more of Sean's body emerged from the death grip of the quicksand. After only a few minutes—though it seemed like an eternity—my mud-covered riding companion was lying prostrate on the lake edge. I didn't know if he was dead or if Bruno and I had been successful in saving the big animal. I shoved down on the emergency brake and ran back to find Bruno releasing the chain from Sean's neck. It had cut rather deeply into the horse's neck and blood was oozing from the cuts. My horse was not breathing. He lay there without moving a muscle. I wondered how one might do mouth-to-mouth on a horse, but I figured what the hell, I had to do something!

I put my hands tightly around his lips, inhaled as

deeply as I could and blew all my air into one of the horse's nostrils. Nothing happened, so I tried it again with the same result. I was beginning to hyperventilate and get dizzy so I lay down on my back. Amazingly, Bruno took over my position at the horse's head and he, too, began to blow into the horse's nose. Suddenly, Sean let out a huge burp, his eyes popped open and he took in a full breath of air. Almost at once, he jumped to his feet, stood there for a minute and then began shaking himself to get rid of the water and mud. Immediately, with a mighty lurch, the horse took off at full gallop up the hill toward the safety of his barn stall.

I turned toward Bruno as he was retrieving the chain. I stopped him, took him by the shoulders and looked into his sad eyes. I thanked him again and again from the bottom of my heart for saving my life and that of my horse. Bruno tried to manage a smile on his disfigured face. My outpouring of affection was obviously something Bruno was not accustomed to and I think I embarrassed him a little bit. All I could understand from his garbled speech was, "You kind to me; I help you. Just did what I could. I hope horse okay."

Then he turned and slowly limped away on his gimpy leg, probably not realizing he had just saved the lives of two of God's creatures. I knew I was very deeply indebted to this hulk of a man. I no longer thought of him as a disfigured old hermit, but as a heroic knight who had saved me from a watery grave. If Bruno had not heard my shouts or had not come to my rescue, my family might never have found my body. Along with Sean, I would have been buried under six feet of mud and water near the shore of Lake Misty. What a ghastly thought!

As I watched Bruno shuffle up the road, I looked around and everything seemed perfectly tranquil, with no hint of the tragedy that had almost occurred just a few minutes before. It was eerily silent. I could see the trees moving in the light wind, but could hear nothing. I could see birds flying across the now-still waters of the lake with the sun reflecting on its surface.

Suddenly, I felt a sense of total euphoria surging through my body and I felt light as a feather. I don't know if it was the adrenaline coursing through my bloodstream or if my brain was just firing on all cylinders. Whatever it was, I was experiencing a natural high after my close brush with death. It just seemed that all was right with the world.

And, then it hit me! I remembered the blood oozing from my horse's neck and it dawned on me that he had survived the quicksand, but might now be bleeding to death up at the barn.

I took a deep breath, mustered my energy, jumped on the tractor, and headed up the hill toward the barn. When I reached the corrals, I was tickled to see Sean on his feet, drinking from the water trough. As I approached him, I could see the injury to his neck but it didn't look quite as serious as I had first thought. But the water in the trough was a crimson red. I grabbed the reins, turned Sean's head to the side and saw a gaping, bleeding wound. I ran to the house to alert Peggy Sue and grab a first-aid kit. Peggy Sue was in the kitchen when I burst through the door, startling her.

"Quick, get the first-aid kit and bring some water. Sean has been injured."

Seeing my wet clothes and mud-caked hair, she jumped right in the middle of my sentence and yelled, "My God, what happened to *you*?

"I'll tell you later," I exclaimed. "Right now I have to tend to Sean. He's bleeding badly. Bring the largest needle and biggest thread you can find when you come out with the water." With that, I turned and ran back out to the barn with the first-aid kit and a couple of clean rags.

Sean was standing nonchalantly in the corral even though his lifeblood was running out of his body. I immediately shoved a clean rag into the area of the wound that was bleeding most profusely and pressed down as hard as I could. Peggy Sue arrived with the water and needle and thread. She had also picked up a few other items from her medicine cabinet. After a few minutes, the pressure on the wound was beginning to stop the flow of blood. That calmed me down and lowered my own blood pressure!

Peggy Sue removed the bloody, mud-caked bridle and the bit, whispering softly to Sean, “You poor animal, you poor animal.” Then she looked straight at me and practically yelled at me, “Zack Heikel, you better tell me what happened to the two of you!”

I swallowed hard and replied a little shakily, “Well, Sean took off with me and jumped into the lake. We almost drowned when we got stuck in some quicksand while we were trying to get back to the shore. If it hadn’t been for Bruno, we would both have drowned. His quick actions saved us both.”

Wide-eyed and yelling, Peggy Sue said, “Who in the hell is Bruno and what quicksand?” Before I answered, I peeked under the blood-soaked rag and saw the blood flow had slowed to a trickle.

I didn’t know where to begin my explanation. First I told Peggy Sue the kids would be safe swimming in the lake because the quicksand was in a remote end of the lake far from where the children swam. And, then I tried to explain to her that Bruno was an old hermit who lived in the little hut about a quarter of a mile up the road. I said, “You remember the place, the one with the grass growing on the roof.”

I dipped the other clean rag in the water Peggy Sue had brought and began cleaning Sean’s neck wound. All the while I continued to tell Peggy Sue about Bruno. I told her that because of his frightening appearance I had not mentioned Bruno to her before now and had decided not to tell her about my numerous visits to his little cabin. When she had heard the whole story, Peggy Sue said, “By the sound of it, I'd say he's just a poor, handicapped person that someone took advantage of and that's very sad. Regardless of what he is or how he looks I would call him a hero. Don't you agree?"

Taking the needle and thread from her hand, I responded, "Yeah, I think that sums Bruno up pretty good. Now, let's take care of this cut. You grab hold of Sean and I'm going to try to pull the edges of the wound together with this needle and thread. Now hold on tight!"

I squeezed the cut together with one hand and stuck the needle into his flesh with the other. Sean twitched, but stood still, so I continued until I had several stitches across the laceration. Then I applied some antibiotic ointment on the stitches and applied a big glob of Vaseline over the whole thing to keep flies away. Now that the injury had been attended to, I needed to hose down the horse to get the mud out of his coat.

I removed the saddle and saw that it was badly damaged. The seat was torn and twisted and had several deep scratches. One of the stirrups was missing, probably resting at the bottom of Lake Misty. Even though the saddle had cost me six hundred dollars and was now totally worthless, I figured it was a small price to pay to still have my life and my horse!

I told Peggy Sue to release Sean. When she did, the horse walked slowly into his barn stall and began to eat hay. I thought he would be all right but would continue to apply the ointment and Vaseline until he healed completely. Cricket was half asleep in her stall and seemed unaware of what was going on around her. She was munching hay and having a nice, leisurely day. As I left the barn, I could only imagine her reaction when Sean related the events of the day to her!

15

November 1975

I believe it's time to relate the tales about the table silverware. On several occasions over our years in the house on the hill, we experienced strange goings-on with the tableware. We saw knives, forks and spoons defy gravity! Many times while seated at the table, my wife, my children and I would see a piece of the silverware move—or two pieces would wiggle side-by-side. Occasionally, Peggy Sue said she would see a pot or pan that she had hanging on a rack above the stove move or clang together. Because these things happened so often, we soon just ignored these slight movements. We blamed it on the strong winds that frequently blew across the top of our hill.

The kids believed I was magnetizing the silverware using the car battery in order to impress them and their friends. Of course, I was doing nothing of the kind, but I would just grin when the subject came up. I didn't have anything I could say, really.

One incident, however, left all of us baffled. The six of us were at the table, just starting dinner. Suddenly, a spoon in front of Denise and a fork in front of Peggy Sue shot up to the ceiling as if fired from a gun and hung there. We were all flabbergasted and our youngest daughter started crying and yelling, "Dad, you are doing it again!"

I assured her I had nothing to do with what was happening, that this was no parlor trick of mine. I hurried to the garage and got my ladder. When I got back, another utensil had sailed through the air and stuck to one of the dining room's oak beams. I climbed the ladder and grabbed the spoon. I felt a slight tingling in my fingers and the spoon dropped into my hand. When I touched the other pieces of flatware, they also came unstuck from the ceiling.

About that time I heard a loud clap of thunder and I thought, “That’s it! Lightning and static electricity—they create magnetism. Maybe they had charged the atmosphere right over our house.”

Our house was almost 1200 feet above the surrounding lakes in the area, and maybe it was so high that it extended up into the electrified air. I tried to explain this to my family, telling them this must be the reason for our levitating silverware. Besides, I didn’t have any other plausible explanation!

I didn’t know if that might truly be the cause, but the most important thing was I think the children believed me. Or, maybe they just wanted to believe me in order to keep their sanity.

16

April 1976

It had been several months since my terrifying incident at Lake Misty with Sean. I had not ridden him since then because I didn't want to aggravate his neck injury. By now, however, he appeared to be completely healed and ready to ride, so I saddled him up and went for a casual walk around the acreage in back of the house. We had had lots of rain during the early spring with some heavy thunderstorms. This was the first pretty, bright sunlit day we had enjoyed in weeks.

I guess we had been on our trail ride for over an hour when we unexpectedly rode onto the small hilltop that held the makeshift cemetery.

It was the first time I had been here since Bruno first showed it to me a few years earlier. The vegetation had become quite dense in the area. As I rode around the grounds, I noticed that heavy rains and runoff down a ravine had washed away a substantial amount of the dirt around the graves. Two of the graves were exposed and I could see what appeared to be the remains of caskets, with just the corners protruding from beneath a block of concrete. It looked like when Bruno had buried these two bodies he had dumped a load of hand-mixed cement on top of the caskets. I imagined that with Bruno's impaired reasoning, he must have wanted to make sure the bodies stayed buried! I wasn't too concerned about the graves being partially exposed because this area was so remote and, after all, it was on private property. The graves wouldn't be seen by anybody and eventually leaves and brush would cover everything up again.

Quietly sitting on my horse enjoying the utter silence of the deep woods, my senses seemed to fall into a daydream. Suddenly, the silence was broken by a rustling sound in the brush a short distance away. I looked that direction and saw a large dog making its way out of a small opening, walking toward me. Sean's ears stood up, his eyes widened and he let out a loud whinny. I pulled hard on the bit in his mouth and said, "Steady, big fellow," in an effort to calm him.

The dog was a big, liver-colored coonhound and I decided he had just come through the creek at the bottom of the ravine. The dog's coat was wet and covered in mud and it was not the least bit shy, but walked to within five feet of us and just sat down. The dog had no collar but I could see it was a female who looked like she'd had a litter of puppies. I surmised she was some hunter's dog who had gotten lost. I began to talk to her and she wagged her tail and appeared to be quite friendly.

Sean and I had been out and about for a long time and I was getting hungry, so I started back to the barn. I noticed the hound dog was following closely behind us. When I got back to the house, I unsaddled Sean, brushed him down, and turned him loose in the pasture. All the while, the dog was sitting just outside the pasture fence and she seemed by be observing me closely.

I closed the gate, spoke to the dog and knelt down to pet her. She stayed just outside the reach of my hand and wouldn't allow any contact. She was a stocky dog, very muscular, and she had very strange eyes and a peculiar looking mouth. Her eyes were blood red with black pupils and when she looked up I had the impression she was seeing straight through me, and out into the distance. Her mouth was a light tan and large white fangs protruded from the sides of her lips.

I left her by the gate and went up to the house for

lunch, thinking that when I came out later in the day she would have run off to the woods looking for her master.

Entering the house, I called out to Peggy Sue, "What's cooking?" She returned by greeting with, "Just soup," and then asked me if I had enjoyed my ride. When we sat down to eat, I told her how nice it had been to ride Sean again. I then told her of our encounter with the large lost dog and that the animal had followed us home. (I didn't say a word about the old gravesite because I had never shared its existence with my wife). I asked Peggy Sue if she had, by any chance, seen me talking to the dog by the gate. She said, "I saw you and Sean but I didn't see any dog."

I told her the dog seemed to be a very nice, older coon dog with "titties as big as my old girlfriend Gwendolyn's." Peggy Sue was nice enough to chuckle at my little joke and said, "Well, that was a long time before I ever knew you!"

That evening when I went out to throw fresh hay to the horses, I didn't expect to see the dog. However, as I approached the barn, she came running out of the trees just behind it. I greeted her, "Well, hello, Gwendolyn. I didn't expect to see you here." The friendly dog was no longer shy and came up to me immediately. I bent down to pet her on the head. When I did, I was jolted by a three-inch electric spark that jumped from her tongue to the back of my hand! As she began licking my hand, her tongue was extremely hot. I continued to feel a constant tingle like you get walking over carpet and touching something metal.

Her breath smelled like ground cloves and she still had that far-off gaze in her eyes. But she was so friendly! Her tail was wagging in the air as fast as it could go. For some reason, I loved the touch of this buxom canine, so the shock I'd felt and her weird appearance didn't seem to bother me too much.

I can't explain it, but somehow I felt this was a very special dog and she really seemed to like me. I stayed just another minute or two and then went back to the house, leaving Gwendolyn at the barn.

When I came through the kitchen door, Peggy Sue was looking out the window toward the barn and I said, "Gwendolyn is back. What do you think of her?"

Peggy Sue looked at me strangely and said, "Back where? All I saw was you and the horses. I did notice you bending over by the corral gate, but that's all."

"That's real funny that you could miss seeing a dog that big, but it's getting a little dark and there's a mist coming up from the lake. I guess that explains it. But, she's probably run off by now." I was really puzzled by all this.

The next day was Saturday and I slept in until after 10 o'clock. I washed my face and combed my hair and went downstairs for a late breakfast. I said good morning to my wife and asked where the children were. "I sent them out to feed the horses," Peggy Sue told me.

I peeked out one of the rear kitchen windows and saw the four kids out by the barn throwing hay to the horses. One of the girls was filling the water trough. I was proud of my very responsible children.

My good wife was whipping up a nice breakfast of eggs and bacon, with whole-wheat toast and some of her excellent coffee. That woman can make a man feel like a king! Peggy Sue set my breakfast before me, kissed me on the cheek and suggested I go outside after breakfast. "I think you need a little sun. You've been looking a little pale to me lately."

Taking her advice, I finished eating and even though I was still in my pajamas and slippers, I walked outside and made myself comfortable on the chaise lounge. It wasn't long before I dropped off to sleep. It seemed I had just dozed off when I felt a funny tingling sensation on the side of my face. Opening my eyes, I saw Gwendolyn standing beside me, licking my cheek. How strange!

I had been daydreaming about Peggy Sue's early-morning kiss on my cheek when I felt the dog lick my face in the very same spot. Weird.

The dog then lay down in the grass right beside me, snuggled her head onto her front paws and closed her eyes. I was so comfortable and relaxed that I began to drift off again and was soon in a beautiful deep sleep. It was a sleep filled with Technicolor dreams of Peggy Sue and me cavorting naked across the beautiful rolling hills filled with every kind of flower imaginable—almost like we were in the Garden of Eden. When I awakened from my journey into dreamland, I felt totally refreshed from my short nap. As I stood to go back inside and give my wife a big hug, I noticed Gwendolyn disappearing into the underbrush just a short distance away.

When I entered the house I saw Forrest standing in the kitchen. I asked him if he had seen the dog.

"No, I haven't. When did we get a dog?"

Then, I heard Peggy Sue from the other side of the room, "I think you're beginning to see things. There is *no* dog around here."

A little angry, I replied, "I beg to differ with you. She was just lying in the grass beside me while I took a nap."

"Well," Peggy Sue said, "I think you're going nuts or you need to have your eyes examined!" Her comment caused me to forget all about the hug I was going to give her. Puzzled, I just went upstairs to get dressed.

For the next several days, every time I went outside, the dog would scamper up and walk beside me—but only if I was alone. This led me to believe she must be frightened of other people, even my own family members.

One day I started off by myself on a long walk out over the hills. I was a good distance from the house before Gwendolyn came to me. By this time, I had become quite attached to this independent and reclusive dog. I just loved to run my hand over her head and her back. I enjoyed that slight tingle and the warm feel of her smooth coat.

We had just entered a densely wooded area when she began to bark. This was new to me. I had never heard her do that before. Then, she took off running toward a small tree. When she reached the tree, she jumped high into the air and grabbed a large raccoon in her mouth. She had the face of the raccoon in her jaws and she shook it very vigorously. By the time I got to the dog, she had chewed off the entire head of the animal. She didn't try to eat—she had just killed it, apparently for the sport!

In the several weeks we'd been together, I had never seen her act in a vicious manner. I began to walk on and, in just a few minutes, she was again at my side, docile as ever. We hadn't walked more than a mile deeper into the woods when she again took off in pursuit of some prey and soon she was out of sight. I could hear her baying in the distance. When I reached the edge of a small clearing in the woods, I saw Gwendolyn chasing a small herd of deer. She was rapidly gaining on the slowest of the group and soon had it by the throat. I hurried toward Gwendolyn, hoping to prevent her killing the deer. Unfortunately, I was too late. By the time I reached her, Gwendolyn was already tearing at a young buck's intestines. When I approached the dog, her face and snout were covered with blood. She turned her head to me and her eyes seemed to make a red flash. She made a deep growl in her throat and bared her long canine fangs. She had taken on a completely different appearance. She seemed much larger, darker and lion-like in her attitude. I had thought it almost impossible for a single dog to bring down a large buck, armed with a set of antlers for protection; but Gwendolyn had done it almost effortlessly. I felt some kind of almost super-natural strength was involved.

Her growls and menacing glare gave me the distinct feeling she was about to pounce and grab me by the throat. I was terrified by the horrible metamorphosis in the dog.

Slowly, I backed away, turned and left the area, leaving the dog to her feast. As soon as I felt safe, I quickly made my way back to the house.

I couldn't, for the life of me, figure out what was wrong with the dog. She had seemed so tame when she tenderly licked my hand; and yet this same animal could tear apart another living creature with hardly any effort.

As unpredictable as her killing of the raccoon and deer were; and as unexpected as her initial appearance at the old gravesite several weeks ago had been, her disappearance was strange as well.

After that day, I never saw her again. Even stranger was the thought that I was the only one who ever could see her. A figment of my imagination? Maybe so. The devil's hound? Could be. What she was and what she was supposed to represent remains a mystery to me until this day.

My seeing things invisible to everyone else wasn't a good sign, in my opinion. I decided that Peggy Sue's suggestion I see a doctor might be a good one; but I just couldn't do it. My God, a psychiatrist would have a field day with my wallet on this one. I didn't feel sick at all. In fact, I felt terrific. Though I knew it wasn't logical and that it was impossible to explain, I still believed Gwendolyn actually existed and was, in fact, my unseen companion. I often thought of her tingling kisses upon my hand.

17

June 1976

Things around the house had been running smoothly for a while. Everything was in full bloom around the yard. The kids had done well at school and were enjoying summer vacation. I was enjoying my retirement in my own little world here on the hill. I had been feeling fit as a fiddle and until just today had not encountered any bizarre animals in the woods. For that matter, I hadn't had any visions at all!

It was just after an intense spring thunderstorm and I was out in the apple orchard spraying bugs on the trees with an insecticide so we wouldn't have worms in our apples. Using my tractor to pull a 200-gallon tank behind it, I had just finished spraying the trees and was heading up the hill to the barn to reload with spray. After that, I was going to the cherry trees to give them a dousing.

Suddenly, the weirdest sight filled my field of vision. I heard a loud whooshing sound, looked up and saw that a large vulture-like bird had landed in one of the cherry trees! The huge bird looked to be carrying something in its claws and it carefully laid it in what looked like a nest. When I moved closer to the tree where the bird was perched, I thought I must be losing my mind. The object the vulture had been carrying was a human infant!

I stopped the tractor and just stared in amazement as the bird began to feed the baby some worms. Both the bird and the baby turned to look in my direction and the baby pointed a finger straight at me, and smiled! God, I wanted to scream in terror.

I think I must have fainted because I fell off the tractor. When I regained my senses, I was looking up at a beautiful blue sky with billowy clouds drifting overhead. I believe I had been lying there for several minutes. Slowly, I turned my gaze back toward the cherry tree. All I could see in it were beautiful cherry blossoms. Initially, I thought I must have inhaled too much insecticide and that caused me to lose consciousness momentarily.

Regardless, I decided that because of the strange visions I was having, my fall and my confused mental condition, the time had come for me to have a complete physical as soon as possible.

The next morning, I made the 45-minute drive to Ann Arbor to the outpatient department at the University of Michigan School of Medicine. Dr. Edwin Piatt, a friend I had met at the ranch when I bought Sean, was going to look me over. I had felt comfortable calling the physician at his home the night before. He was a horse lover, like me, who lived on a huge spread of wooded land and knew what it was like to experience the solitude of the Michigan woods. He had been very understanding when I listed my symptoms over the phone and told me to come in the next day and he would see me right away on an emergency basis.

When Dr. Piatt came into my examination room, we spent the first several minutes talking about our horses and the Hunt Club where he was a member. When we finally got down to the business of my physical exam, he had me explain again how I was feeling and why I thought I needed the exam. I told Edwin that I was feeling fine physically, eating and sleeping well, but had been seeing strange things. As he took my blood pressure, he asked, "What do you mean, seeing things?"

I had to tell him the whole Gwendolyn story that had upset me terribly but had been almost forgotten until I saw the vulture with the human child. I told the doctor, and my friend, that I believed I had a serious problem.

Edwin quickly told me he was not a psychiatrist but he believed a thorough physical exam might uncover any existing physical cause for my hallucinations. After taking my blood pressure which was normal, he did an EKG on my heart and pronounced it completely sound. I had a chest x-ray and that, too, was normal. I wasn't overweight and I didn't have any aches or pains. Dr. Piatt said the only thing left to do was to check my liver with a blood test.

He drew two vials of blood and sent them to the lab for analysis. He said the results would take about an hour and suggested we go to lunch. We went to the cafeteria and got sandwiches and coffee. While we ate, Edwin said, "Now that I have pronounced you sound of body, you need to join our hunt club and go with us to chase some foxes."

I told him I appreciated the invitation and would give it some thought. All the time I was telling him that, I was thinking: there is no way I can picture myself on a big horse, galloping after a pack of hounds who are chasing a small, helpless little fox with the desire to tear it apart. I might be sound physically, but I didn't think my psyche could stand the reality of a foxhunt right now!

We finished our lunch and went back to his office to review the results of the blood work. I sat in a comfortable chair in his office while he looked over the lab paperwork.

It took him about five minutes to evaluate the results of the tests. He looked up at me and said, "Well, Zack, you aren't diabetic, your heart is fine; so is your pancreas. Your cholesterol is within normal limits and all your other readings are fine. However, the ferrous sulfite or iron content in your blood is extremely high and your liver functions are somewhat out of line. The iron content of the blood is a condition we doctors refer to as 'iron overload.' Do you eat a lot of liver or drink a lot of wine with dinner or take iron supplements?"

"No," I responded, "I don't. But that's my wife's favorite meal, liver and onions. The only thing I can think of is that I had my well water tested and it had a high iron content. Because of that I use a filter system that removes the iron particles from the water. Could the water be responsible for our seeing things?"

Edwin looked at me over the top of his reading glasses and then back down at the test results. "It's a possibility that the high iron content of the water may be accumulating in your blood and that could certainly disturb your mental processes and liver readings.

"I would suggest you run the iron filtering system attached to your water supply more often than you do now. I'm going to write you a prescription for some medication that will help your body secrete a lot of that iron through your urine. Then, I need to see you again in about a month. It will take that long for the medicine to do its job.

"If that doesn't work, then I will have to take some blood from your system because the body has no natural way to rid itself of excess iron. The extra iron will settle in your body's tissues and organs.

"Do not drink any booze of any kind while you take the medication. And, I would suggest you have your wife's blood profile looked at, too."

When I left Dr. Piatt's office, I stopped at the college pharmacy and had the prescription filled. I didn't hesitate to ask the pharmacist for a cup of water so I could take my first pill right away. I wanted to get that medicine in my system as soon as possible. I really didn't want to experience any more sightings and I had high hopes for the medicine. I felt good knowing I was finally doing something to help myself mentally!

As I passed through Clinton on the way home, I stopped at the hardware store and picked up several bags of water softener salt and four large cans of Sodium

Permanganate to recharge the water system and knock down the iron content to as low a level as possible. I was determined to do everything I could to find the underlying cause of the visions Peggy Sue and I had been having. I wasn't sure why the children were not experiencing these sightings. I did remember one of the girls had also seen the horse and buggy in front of the house through the lookout tower's telescope. The other kids had seen the episodes with the levitating silverware…I just didn't know. They were drinking the same water we were if, in fact, the water was the source of the problem. But, the kids left the hill for most of the day during the school term. While they were at school they drank city water. Maybe that was the reason they weren't complaining about strange visions—or maybe they were just afraid to mention them to us.

On the other hand, Peggy Sue and I were on the hill almost all the time and we both drank a lot of water. If water was the cause of our problems, we could remedy that quickly by drinking only bottled water or by running the softeners more often or boiling the water.

I had just turned off the main highway headed for my house when I passed Bruno's cabin and noticed he was working in his vegetable garden. I hadn't seen him for several weeks so thought I would stop in for a quick visit. I could also give him the giant bottle of aspirin I had been carrying around in my glove compartment for a few days. I bid him good afternoon as I gave him the aspirin.

"Thanks, these work good," he said in his usual garbled way. "How horse?" He always asked about Sean each time I visited.

"He's fine, completely recovered, and I've been riding him quite a bit lately."

I asked Bruno how he had been feeling lately. He said he had been doing all right, but had been spitting up quite a lot of blood lately, maybe from his teeth or gums. I just hoped he wasn't taking too many aspirin because I knew they could be hard on the stomach and cause bleeding. As I was thinking that, he popped several into his mouth and swallowed them like candy! Then, in an effort to be neighborly, he offered me a beer or glass of water. "No, I don't think I'll have any water, but I would enjoy a beer."

Bruno popped open a can of Miller Lite and handed it to me. At the same time, he noticed the bags of water softener salt on the back seat of my Caddie and asked if I had been to town. I told him I had stopped by the hardware store on my way back from the hospital. I explained that I was feeling fine but had been experiencing some strange hallucinations. Then, for some stupid reason, I asked him if he had seen a big liver-colored dog wandering around in the woods lately.

Stupid, stupid, stupid! What he told me certainly didn't make me feel any better or help my present mental condition.

"Oh, no. I don't see dog in woods anymore. She Judge Levison's black and tan coonhound and she die two years ago. I find her down in ravine so I bury her next to the judge. Why you ask?"

Bruno's words made the hair on the back of my neck absolutely stand straight up! But not wanting my neighbor to think I was crazy by telling him about my experiences with just such a dog, I just said I had heard a dog barking last night.

I told Bruno I needed to get to work on my water softener, drank down the last swallow of my beer and headed on up the hill. I really just needed to be by myself for a little while to try and sort out a few things in my head. I was just wondering when these complex problems were going to be resolved. No sooner would I put one behind me than it would come back to bite me in the ass—to wit, the blankety-blank ghost dog. How in the world was I seeing the ghost of a dog that had been dead for two years...and just happened to have belonged to the old judge? How could that possibly have anything at all to do with the iron content in my water or in my bloodstream? Could the dog's appearance be some kind of ghostly apparition? I'm still working on an explanation of why this long-dead dog I called Gwendolyn decided to show herself to me.

When I got home, rather than working on the water system, I decided to go up to my study and make a list of all the reasons why I should continue to live on this hill. After that, I decided, I would make another list of all the reasons I should escape and just run like Jake had done. I secretly pledged to myself that when the list of reasons to escape got longer than the list of reasons to stay—I'd be out of there! I would sell the place at some ridiculously low price to some poor unsuspecting soul, take my family, and get as far away as possible from this magnetic hellhole!

My list of reasons to stay:

How I feel 90% of the time
The silence and tranquillity of the deep woods
The smell of cut grass
The rolling hills
The beautiful sky, sunset and sunrise
The beautiful shimmering lakes
The blood-red sumac trees in the fall
The smell of the fresh mountain air
The taste of the many fruits grown right here on the hill
The beautiful panoramic view of the surrounding hills
The abundance of wildlife
The experience of watching my kids grow up

The smile on Peggy Sue's face
The long horseback rides
The smell of hay in the barn
The proud feeling I get telling people I own the Mansion on the Hill
The view out my bedroom window when the world below is shrouded in fog and the house seems to be floating on a carpet of billowing white clouds while flights of ducks are honking their way across a beautiful sky
The feeling that I am captain of the clouds in my own private world
The feeling of euphoria I often have, making me feel I'm living in paradise
The new-fallen snow in winter that turns everything pure white
The multi-colored lights of traffic in the distance on Highway 12
The fun and laughter my family and I enjoy skiing down the face of our hill
The ice skating on the lakes
The taste of hot cocoa
The feeling of satisfaction when I do solve one of my mysteries of my house on the hill

I knew if this list could stay longer than the "Reasons to Escape" list, then maybe I could stay here long enough to solve all our mysteries.

<u>My List of Reasons to Escape</u>

The way I feel 10% of the time, physically and emotionally drained; fearing I'm losing my sanity
Why the ghostly visions (first and

foremost!)?
Why was this mansion built in the manner it was?
The strange nightly noises
The creepy atmosphere of the mansion at night
The strange howls from animals in the woods at night
The bats
The strange behavior of our pets
The graves out back
The portraits
The secret shaft with its peepholes
The Packard
The secret rooms
Who was Judge Seymour T. Levison, really?
What was the strange organization he belonged to?
What is Bruno's full story?
Who in the hell is Anthony Buglioni?
The moving silverware
Peggy Sue's out-of-body experience
What fell out of the sky?

Making out my lists temporarily put my mind at ease and I was feeling better about things when I heard Peggy Sue calling me from downstairs asking if I would like to have some hot apple pie and coffee. Yummy! I couldn't get down the stairs fast enough.

When I had finished the scrumptious pie and coffee, I told my wife just how beautiful and talented she was. Then, I went down to the basement to recharge our water softener. I loaded several bags of salt into one side of the softener and turned the valve to back-flush the iron filter. The fluid that exited the vent pipe in the back of the iron filter was a deep purple in color. It ran a short distance into one of the floor drains. I continued to back-flush the filter until the exiting fluid was nice and clear. In a separate container, I mixed one can of Sodium Permanganate into a thick paste and dumped it into the recharge section of the iron filter. The smell of the back-flush was very pungent. I thought I'd better get used to it since I would be doing this every four days for a while to be sure I got as much iron as possible out of the water.

Over a month had passed when I made my way back to Dr. Piatt's office for my follow-up exam. I had also made an appointment for Peggy Sue to take her blood test at the same time. When Edwin entered the exam room, his question was pretty much the same as other doctors ask when seeing a patient: "Well, how have you been feeling?"

"I'm in the pink and couldn't feel better," I answered enthusiastically. "Edwin, meet my wife Peggy Sue." He shook hands with her and then proceeded to take my blood pressure which was normal.

Then he said, "Let's get your blood drawn and take Peggy Sue's at the same time." Almost as an afterthought he asked with a grin, "Oh, have you been seeing any strange birds or stray dogs lately? Any hallucinations?"

I was happy to report that I had not seen anything strange since my last visit. I purposely did not use the word "hallucination" because what Bruno had told me about the Judge's dog made me really question whether she was a hallucination or something else altogether.

Peggy Sue and I retreated to the hospital cafeteria for lunch while the lab processed our blood samples. About an hour later we were back in Edwin's office and he was looking over the results of our tests. He raised his head from the lab report and said, "Well, Zack, the iron content in your blood is dramatically lower than it was last month, and that's good. And, Peggy Sue, I'm afraid your iron content is quite high—not as high as Zack's was last month, but high nonetheless. I think you should start taking medication to bring it down. I'm going to give you a prescription that can be filled here at the hospital and, Zack, you can stop taking your medicine.

"I also believe, Zack, that you should send a sample of your well water to Ann Arbor now that you have been filtering it more often. Get the iron content checked again and compare it with the old report if you have it. Just be very sure you keep the iron particles in the well water as low as possible."

Dr. Piatt pronounced me in excellent health and believed I would stay that way as long as our water was treated often and properly. As we were getting ready to leave, he said, "If you experience another recurrence of those visions, then I would have to say there is a cause other than your physical health."

As I shook his hand goodbye, all I could think about was "caused by something *other* than your physical health." What *other*? I wondered. "How about something *other* being something simple like a *ghost*! God, I must be losing my wits.

18

January 1977

In early December 1976, I finally finished putting up several hundred feet of snow fence in preparation for a heavy snow season. It helped keep the blowing white stuff from drifting completely over the driveway, making it impassable. In case we got a heavy snowstorm, I had parked my Ford 8N tractor, fitted with a snowplow, in the heated garage. That made it easy for Forrest or me to just start her up and drive down the hill, flipping the snow to the right; and on the way back up the hill, flipping it to the left. Just two passes usually did the trick, but this was not the case beginning the second week in January 1977.

On the 10th, it started snowing—lightly at first—and then heavily, with the wind blowing so hard we couldn't see the lake or the road. We were in a complete whiteout as the snow fell all day and throughout the night, as well.

My youngest sister Joan had come to stay with us over the Christmas holidays and she had never seen a snowstorm like this one. She was from Cleveland where they got plenty of snow…but nothing like this. The next morning, when we looked out the windows, it was like a fairyland of white. The snow was still falling and blowing. I didn't even wonder if my snow fence had helped, because I knew it hadn't. It was nowhere to be seen, buried under at least a foot of snow.

Joan had a return flight back home scheduled for that day and we wondered if the planes would still be flying. I wasn't sure aircraft could or would fly in this stuff, but my primary concern at this point was whether or not I could make it down our driveway. I doubted it seriously; the roads were impassable. A quick phone call to the airport affirmed my suspicions. All flights had been canceled for the next several days. Joan would just have to stay on with us until the weather cleared up.

The kids and I weren't worried. We were going to have a ball skiing and riding the toboggan down the hill as long as the hot chocolate held out! I figured Peggy Sue and Joan would play cards and dominoes like they usually did when they were together. I knew they would have a great time because they were the best of friends.

But Joan was a recovering alcoholic as well as diabetic and she was concerned about having enough of her medications for the few extra days. She had only brought enough medication for her planned three-week stay with us.

At the end of our first day being snowed in, everyone was having a good time: the kids and I on the hill and Joan and Peggy Sue playing cards, cooking and baking pies. That evening we all sat down to dinner, enjoying a delicious pot roast, mashed potatoes and green beans, and marveling at the beautiful winter scene outside. We were all in a festive mood except Joan who seemed to be irritated about something. I noticed she was on her third glass of Peggy Sue's delicious Concord grape wine. That was not a good sign. I didn't want her to start drinking again and she was also diabetic. Peggy Sue's wine was pretty strong and had quite a kick to it.

After dinner, we three adults moved into the living room in front of the roaring fire while the kids cleaned up the kitchen and did the dishes. Joan poured the small remains of a bottle of wine into her glass, looked up at the portrait of Levison over the fireplace and told us how ugly she thought the painting was. She had begun to slur her words and it was obvious to us that she'd had enough wine for the night. I quietly whispered into Peggy Sue's ear not to open another bottle.

We sat for a while in front of the fireplace, watching the snow fall outside the big windows. It was really beginning to accumulate and had already drifted to the top of the outside windowsills. It was getting quite late. The children had already gone up to bed when we noticed that Joan was beginning to doze off; so we all agreed to retire for the night. After everyone had washed up and put on their pajamas, Peggy Sue and I snuggled into our nice warm bed, watched the snowflakes dance around in front of our window for a few minutes. Soon we were fast asleep.

It must have been 2 or 3 o'clock in the morning when I realized I was in bed alone. I sat up and pushed my feet into my slippers and looked around the room. Peggy Sue was nowhere in sight but I could hear the mumble of voices. I moved over to the door that led to the hallway and heard Peggy Sue talking to Joan. I opened the door, stepped into the hall and peeked around the corner into Denise's bedroom where Joan had been sleeping. Joan was cowering, trembling violently, and wringing her hands, while sitting on the floor of the bedroom closet.

Joan was muttering, saying she had fallen asleep when she was awakened by a voice coming out of the fireplace, calling her name. It had scared the daylights out of her. Peggy Sue tried to reason with her, saying it was probably a lack of her medication and the fact that she had drunk three full glasses of strong wine that had her imagining the voice. I stepped into the room and suggested that it could have been the wind whistling through the chimney that she had heard.

Joan said she was afraid to go to sleep again because of what had happened, so I suggested we just sit with her for a while with the lights on. We did, and after just a few minutes, Joan had fallen asleep again. Peggy Sue and I left the light on and went back to our own bed.

The rest of the family had been up several hours the next morning when Joan finally came down to the kitchen looking for a cup of coffee. After she took a sip of coffee, she said, "I had the weirdest dream last night of a voice calling to me and it seemed to be coming out of the fireplace." Peggy Sue reassured her, saying it must have been a nightmare or it was the effect of the alcohol in her system. Joan said that nevertheless it had scared the hell out of her and she wanted to sleep downstairs on the living room sofa from now on. We told her that would be fine and that she should sleep wherever she felt the most comfortable.

Peggy Sue whipped up a fantastic breakfast for Joan and I sat with her while she ate, enjoying my second cup of coffee. We talked about the still-falling snow and about how badly she wanted to get home. We didn't realize it was going to continue to snow steadily for three more days and accumulate to several feet deep on the hilltop.

When the snow finally did stop, I began to try and figure out a way for us to get some supplies up the hill. With seven people holed up in the house for a week, lots of groceries had been consumed and we needed some more staples. I knew it would be impossible for us to get off the hill, but if the phone lines were open I might be able to get the snowmobile dealer to agree to bring us some supplies if I paid him for his trouble. The secretary at the sales office answered the telephone in a cheery voice, "Happy snowmobile riding, may I help you?"

I asked to speak to the manager and when he came on the line I explained my situation.

I told him I would pay him $100 to go by the supermarket, pick up a list of supplies and bring them out to us. He was happy to accept the challenge and said he would come on his lunch hour. Most snowmobilers are proud of the fact they can get around in conditions others can't, and they like to have a chance to prove it. Surely enough, about 1:30 in the afternoon, we heard the roar of an engine and could see the yellow Ski-Doo plowing its way up our hill through the deep snow. Soon, there was a rap on our front door. When we opened the door, there he was, the snowmobile store manager, standing proudly beside his Ski-Doo with several boxes strapped to its back seat. He was smiling from ear to ear and proud of his accomplishment in covering the thirty-five miles to our house in less than an hour. He unstrapped the boxes and brought them into the house while I shoved $37 for the merchandise and a hundred-dollar bill for his trouble into his hand. Peggy Sue pushed a cup of hot coffee into the other. We offered him a chair and a chance to get warm but he said he needed to get back to town. He hurriedly drank his coffee and then headed out the front door, straddled his machine and was soon disappearing down the hill in a blur of snow!

I was relieved to see that he could make it out to the house and we did have some physical contact with the outside world. Our kids could have cared less that we were snowed in and only reachable by snowmobile. They were having a blast sledding and riding the toboggan up and down the hill.

On this particular day, I thought maybe the kids and I could do something a little different. The five of us, armed with our snow shovels and ice skates tied to the toboggan, slid down the hill to the lake, leaving Joan and Peggy Sue busy in the kitchen putting up our groceries. When we reached the frozen lake, we used the shovels to clear the snow and fashion a large skating rink. While the kids skated, I found some dry kindling wood and lit a fire with the matches and newspaper I had tucked into my parka. When the fire was in full blaze, I laid a few logs on the top and we soon had a roaring bonfire where we could roast the hot dogs and marshmallows I had brought along.

While the children and I were enjoying our winter picnic, Peggy Sue was going through a troubling experience with my sister. Later, she told me about it.

Shortly after the children and I left for our adventure

at the lake, Joan had begun to act peculiarly. Her sentences didn't make sense and Peggy Sue soon figured out the reason for her incoherence. Joan had sneaked down the stairs to the basement, brought up a bottle of wine, and hidden it in the wood box next to the fireplace. She had drunk about half of it!

Peggy Sue said she knew the intake of the alcohol, coupled with the fact that Joan was out of pills, was very dangerous and told Joan so. Then, Peggy Sue decided to go to the basement to finish the laundry, thinking that if Joan were left alone she might think about her situation and straighten herself out.

My wife had been in the basement for about half an hour and was stacking some of the laundry on a folding table that was situated on the wall directly under the fireplace. She heard a faint voice. She couldn't make out what was being said, so she moved closer and put her ear to the opening in the cell door behind the paneling. As Peggy Sue listened, she realized it was Joan who was speaking. "How long are you going to be in Cornwall?" my wife heard her say. Peggy Sue had no idea what her words meant and thought Joan was coming totally unglued. She heard Joan repeating and whispering the same question for several minutes and then all was quiet.

After about 15 minutes, Peggy Sue had returned to her task of removing clothes from the dryer and folding them. Suddenly, she looked up and saw Joan standing in front of her with a meat cleaver in her hand! She wore a blank expression on her face and was quietly repeating the same questions, "How long are you going to be in Cornwall?"

Peggy Sue was now terrified. Joan appeared to have lost her senses and was in some kind of trance, waving a dangerous weapon around with a wild-eyed look on her face. Peggy Sue knew she had to act quickly to disarm Joan, so when she uttered the same cryptic question again, "How long are you going to be in Cornwall?" Peggy Sue decided to answer her.

"A few days perhaps," Peggy Sue said, repeating the phrase over and over again while she slowly approached Joan. When she reached Joan and touched her softly on the shoulder, Joan seemed to suddenly awaken from her stupor. Peggy Sue quietly took the cleaver from her hand and asked Joan what she was planning to do with it. Joan's reply startled her.

"The voice from the fireplace terrified me so badly that I felt I needed something to protect myself from the voice and everyone here in this house."

Trying to reason with her close friend and sister-in-law, Peggy Sue assured her no one in the family would ever harm her in any way. She suggested they both go upstairs and lie down for a little while. Joan allowed Peggy Sue to lead her upstairs to the sofa in the living room. She agreed to lie down and Peggy Sue covered her with a blanket and placed a warm towel on her forehead.

My wife then hurried outside and called to me, saying I needed to come up to the house right away. Although we were about to have our wiener roast, I could sense the urgency in Peggy Sue's voice; so I let the kids fend for themselves and hurried up the hill. When I entered the kitchen door, I found my wife terribly shaken and my sister fast asleep (or maybe passed out!) on the sofa.

Peggy Sue recounted her frightening experience and I could tell it was time for me to get my sister out of our house one way or the other! I felt it was also for her own good to get back to Cleveland and her doctor and medications. I had no idea what was going on with her physically or mentally, but I knew she was acting completely out of character. I realized that in her mental state she could become dangerous, especially at night when we were all vulnerable while sleeping in our beds.

I wasted no time in calling American Airlines. The ticket agent told me flights had resumed and were leaving on time but passengers were having a hard time getting to the airport. I knew it would take some doing on my part, but I was determined. I thought of Tom, the snowmobile expert, and wondered if he might like another challenge. When I got him on the phone I told him it was urgent that I get my sister to the airport to catch a plane at 7:00 p.m. I asked if I might use his snowmobile to get her from the house, with her luggage, down the hill to an automobile. I asked if he thought he could hire someone to take her to the airport, and said if he could help me with all this there was two hundred dollars in the deal for him this time!

Tom said he wasn't sure the roads were passable to the airport but he would call me back shortly to let me know. Half an hour later he called back. This guy was really on the ball and wanted that money. He said his wife had agreed to drive the snowmobile out to the house to get Joan and her luggage down the hill to the main road where he would be waiting in a four-wheel-drive Jeep. He would see to it that Joan got to the airport in time to make her flight.

It wasn't like me to want to get rid of some part of my family, but I must say I was really happy to see Joan disappearing down the hill in a cloud of puffy white snow as she held on to the back of the Ski-Doo. I was relieved for her, too, because she seemed to have been in such real agony the last few days. I had given her instructions to call us as soon as soon as she arrived home. At about 6 o'clock she called from the airport to say the plane was departing on time and she should be home three hours later. Her husband Merle was going to pick her up at the airport.

Three days later I got a disturbing telephone call from Merle. He told me Joan was not herself at all when he picked her up and she had horrible nightmares that night. The very next day he had taken her to the doctor. When he examined her, the doctor said apparently she had been exposed to some terribly traumatic episode. He prescribed a sedative to calm her down. A blood test to check her sugar level had also indicated an unusually high content of iron in her blood, so he also gave her medication to deal with that problem as well as upping the dosage level of her insulin.

The physician was also concerned that she had been drinking again. Even though she told him it was just wine that she had been drinking, he said it was as bad as 100-proof whiskey.

Merle was upset with us, thinking we had purposely given her the wine. I told him that was not the case at all and that she had slipped into the wine cellar without our knowledge and hidden a bottle upstairs in our living room. When I explained how things had happened, Merle was apologetic but said we should have kept the wine under lock and key since we knew she was a recovering alcoholic. I knew he was probably right but told him it was virtually impossible to lock up the hundreds of bottles downstairs in our wine racks.

Merle was puzzled by how her blood chemistry could be so totally out of control. I admitted to him that she had drunk a lot of water on her visit and we had a problem with our water having a high iron content. I also told him I had been filtering the water twice a week and that had kept the iron levels in check. I expressed our concern for Joan and asked him to keep us posted on her health. Having said that, I quietly said my goodbyes and hung up.

About a week later I heard from Merle again. He apologized for having been so short with me the last time we spoke. He was calling to give us an update on Joan's condition. "She is feeling much better and is her old jovial self again," he said. "Her medication has helped the iron problem and her insulin levels have stabilized."

He also said Joan had not been drinking which was

great news to us. We told him we were happy things were better and looked forward to seeing them again soon.

After I hung up, I looked back over the entire situation with Joan and it confirmed my thinking that something at or in our house caused people and animals to act irrationally. My sister was usually a completely happy person, just as she was when she arrived for her three-week visit over the holidays. Yet, when she left, she was a basket case. I couldn't believe it was just because she drank a lot of water or that she got into the wine. Something else had been acting on her psyche, just like it was on ours. The difference was that we had almost come to expect the unexpected or grown immune to strange occurrences.

I vowed to think long and hard about possible causes of the personality changes occurring in our animals and our guest, so that I might explain them rationally. That's what I've always tried to do with all the incredible situations that have reared their nasty heads on our hill.

My brother-in-law's remark that we should have kept the wine locked up gave me an idea. Maybe I should find a way to secure the wine just in case she ever visited again. When the children got a little older, they might become curious about alcoholic beverages and the wine supply shouldn't be easily accessible to them either.

I grabbed my flashlight and went down to the basement to examine the old wine racks. Over the years Peggy Sue had gathered lots of Concord grapes from our vineyard; and, using the old winepress from the garage, she had put up enough wine to keep the hundred or so old bottles full all the time. There were still a few of the original old bottles high on a shelf, at the rear of the shelves. Even though Peggy Sue was a "clean freak" and kept all the bottles dusted, the cobwebs removed, and the shelves clean, there were a few of the old bottles that were impossible for her to reach.

I got my stepladder, placed it against the shelves and

climbed to the top to examine the old, untouched, still dusty and cobweb-covered bottles. I also wanted to see how the shelves were attached to the wall. I thought it might be possible to place a wooden frame with some kind of screen in front of the bottles that could be locked. When a bottle of wine was needed, the screen could be unlocked and moved to the side.

I played my flashlight back and forth across the very top of the racks adjacent to the wall and accidentally bumped one of the bottles, sending up a plume of dust. As the dust bunnies floated in the air, my light beam caught the dust being sucked rapidly between the top board of the rack and the wall, and on into the darkness. I reasoned there must be a hollow space behind the wall, or the dust was just venting somehow to the outside of the house. I continued to look at the shelves and moved my ladder to the other side of the rack, looking for a place to attach a screen door.

When I got to the top of my eight-foot ladder and leaned over the side of the top shelf, I noticed a metal handle that had been hidden from sight by all the cobwebs. It was set in a deep recess in the wall and not visible even in the basement light. My first thought was that the handle could have been some kind of lock that secured the wine bottles, so I brushed away the cobwebs, grabbed the handle and pulled on it as hard as I could.

All of a sudden, I felt the heavy wine rack start to move. The next thing I knew, I was on the floor with the ladder on top of me. My flashlight had fallen to the floor and was shining into a huge room that had suddenly appeared behind the wine racks. The racks had swung open like an enormous door!

I jumped to my feet, grabbed the light, stepped over the ladder and then knocked down the cobwebs that covered the entry. As I looked inside the room, I felt like I was in a time warp. On one side of the threshold was the year 1977, but stepping into the room I found myself suddenly in the year 1930! Dirt and dust and cobwebs covered everything and there was an awful musty smell to the stale air. In the beam of my light I could see several rows of old desks, each with its own wooden chair. Some of the desks held old hand-operated adding machines. On nearly every desk, like lonesome sentinels, were pedestal telephones like the antique one in our upstairs entry hall.

Shining my beam on the wall adjacent to the door, I saw two light switches and flipped them both up. One lamp out of about 12 dangling from the ceiling came to life. The bulb had a funny green lampshade and was suspended over one of the desks, casting a strange greenish tint to the dust. I could see an ashtray, still filled with the butts of dried out cigarettes; and a coffee cup still sat in its saucer next to it.

On other desks, I could see old beer bottles, some standing and others tipped over on their sides. An empty whiskey bottle and shot glass was on another desk. When I stepped further into the room, I turned my light to my left and saw, behind me and off by itself, a large roll-top desk. It was also covered with all sorts of debris and scraps of paper. Old-style accounting ledgers were piled one on top of the other. A rickety wooden chair with a torn cushion and an old telephone sat off to the side. As I moved over to the desk to examine its contents, I noticed a black box about the size of a fishing tackle box on the right side of the desk. The box was closed but not locked. I lifted the lid, directed my light beam inside, and saw money! Lots of money—greenbacks of unknown denominations tightly secured with bank wrappers and in neat stacks. There must have been 14 or 15 bundles of bills and I was hesitant to touch them because they were filthy and dusty.

I decided I'd better get myself upstairs and tell Peggy Sue to find some gloves and come down here with me to investigate this latest mystery find in our home. I didn't need to hurry things, I figured, since this stuff had obviously been here for years and years and it wasn't going anywhere anytime soon. Still, my curiosity was really getting the best of me and I excitedly rushed up the steps and told Peggy Sue that I had found another secret room in the basement behind the wine racks. I rattled on, telling her the room was filled with old office furniture and a black metal box full of money! She had been washing dishes when I came flying into the kitchen but when she heard the words "full of money" her ears seemed to go "pointy." She said, quite calmly, "As long as there aren't a bunch of spiders in there, I'd be happy to take charge of the money."

Then she got in high gear, grabbed some rubber gloves and, still wearing her apron, hurried down the basement stairs behind me. When we got to the bottom of the stairs and she saw how the wine rack had swung away from the wall, she couldn't believe it. She had been working around it for years and never had any indication at all that it was some kind of door. Together, we stepped through the time warp, into the room. She didn't even hesitate a second, but went straight to the cash box which I had left open on the desk. She reached in the box and started removing the packets of money, shaking the dust off each one and then dropping it into her apron, all the time saying, "It looks like a lot…it looks like a lot!" She wasn't the least bit interested in the dust-covered desks or the chairs or the rusting antique office machines. This woman could really focus on the important things…and she was focused on the money!

It reminded me a little of the day I took her out to see the Packard. She hadn't paid a bit of attention to the old vehicle but had focused on the things hanging on the walls, the gardening tools, the winepress, the baskets, and the contents of an old steamer trunk.

I was just amazed that uncovering this secret room after six years in the house wasn't a big deal to her. I guess to

Peggy Sue it was just another room in a very big house that she would have to keep tidy and worry about cleaning. I, on the other hand, was amazed that a room like this had been hidden from us while it was right under our noses. This room obviously had to be added to my ever-growing list of mysteries connected to our mansion on the hill.

Standing there looking at the interior of the room and its contents—the vintage office furniture, the adding machines, ledgers and multiple telephones—I soon started to put two and two together. I came up with the idea that this room, particularly with all the cash and phones, could have been some type of accounting department or collection agency. However, I could more easily envision it as an old time bookie joint right out of the 30's and 40's. This room reminded of those rooms referred to in movies and newspapers as "boiler room operations." What in God's name was this kind of operation doing out here in the middle of nowhere in the house I had bought? I hoped that the journals and papers left scattered about on the desks and floor might give me a clue as to the kind of operation that was going on here so many years ago.

As Peggy Sue headed back upstairs with her apron bulging with the wads of money, I cracked open the first journal on top of one stack and began to read. The heading at the top of the first page read, "Cicero area, 1944."

My concentration was broken by Peggy Sue's calling from the top of the stairs, "Honey, please come up here." I picked up the book and left the room. Before going upstairs, I pushed the wine racks back against the wall. Without much effort, they swung back into position and locked tightly against the wall with a loud "click."

When I got to the kitchen, Peggy Sue had spread the packets of money out on a newspaper, taken off the paper bands that held them secure, and stacked the bills in three piles by denominations. There were hundreds, fifties and twenties. “Do you know how much money you have just found?” she asked.

“I have no idea, but that stack of 100’s is pretty high,” was the only thing I could think of to say.

With a smug smile on her face Peggy Sue announced, “Three thousand eight hundred and seventy bucks. We’re going to keep it, right?”

“Sure we are,” I said, picking up and fanning through a stack of the twenties. “After all these years, who knows it’s here but us? I’d say these bills are worth even more than their face value to collectors. Some of the things are silver certificates and no longer in circulation.”

All Peggy Sue could manage to say was “Wow, I wonder if there is any more money hidden around the room.”

“Greedy little devil, that wife of mine,” I thought but certainly didn’t voice aloud. I, too, wondered what more we might find when we went through all the desks.

I thought of the journal in my hand and looked at it, thinking, “What are you gonna tell me, old fellow?” I walked into the living room, sat down in my favorite chair and began to read the notes and study the rows of numbers on the lined pages.

Under the heading on page one was a row of what appeared to be the names of business places and, to the right, another column with dollar amounts in it opposite each name. At the very bottom of the page and marked, “Total September” was the figure, $57,812.00. I thumbed through the journal, glancing at the pages. Except for the different months and amounts, all the pages were similar: rows of business names in one column with amounts of money in a column opposite the names; and then a total figure listed at the bottom of the page.

Each page had sub-titles for different areas like Highland Park, Shaker Heights, Chicago (east) and Chicago (central). It appeared the numbers represented sales or other income from these various businesses in towns across Illinois. I counted twenty-seven different towns, did some quick math in my head and added the figures at the bottoms of fifty pages. I figured the total income from the state of Illinois in 1944 as $3,876,751.00 and this was just *one* ledger book.

I put the book on the coffee table, went back downstairs, pulled the hidden handle to open the wine racks, went in and picked up several more ledger books. I hurried back upstairs with them so I wouldn't lose the train of thought of where these numbers were leading me. I took a minute and paused in the kitchen to give Peggy Sue a peck on the cheek. I dusted the books with a damp washcloth and told my honey she'd better make a pot of coffee because I might be at this for a long time. I was certain I was on to something. Back in my comfort zone in my chair, I opened another journal.

The heading at the top of page one in this book was "East Detroit 1944," again with rows of business names on the left, dollar amounts on the right and the total at the bottom of each page. East Detroit's total at the bottom of the first page was $31,612.00. Other towns listed in this ledger were Flint, Saginaw, Jackson, Detroit, Northville, and Lansing. My quick math again came up with a total of $2,156,117.00.

The first page of the third book read "Toledo, Ohio 1944" and subsequent pages listed other towns and amounts in Ohio. This book's total of all the pages was $1,723,423.00.

I had also brought another interesting book upstairs. It listed names of various men, with money amounts in a column labeled "Cash Amounts Received" opposite their names. Opposite each name was a figure of more than several thousand dollars. At the back of this particular ledger were some pages that listed expense items. The categories were eye-opening: bribe, auto, pay-off, and the most intriguing one of all, HIT.

A notation on one particular page of the third book

made my pulse quicken as I read a list of men's names. One almost jumped off the page at me: Anthony Buglioni, with the notation opposite his name "guard and special job, $8,000!"

There was that name again, the one the license plate on the Packard was registered to. He must have been a guard of some kind for the Judge and he must have performed some special job for him. Could the job have been a *hit*? I could only think of one kind of *hit* that might fit these circumstances—and it didn't have anything to do with baseball!

Eight thousand dollars would have been a high monthly wage for guard duties. These books were beginning to make a lot of sense to me, but I wasn't sure I was enjoying figuring it all out.

The last book brought up from the basement began with the year 1943 and listed all the same cities in Illinois as the first book I looked at. This book appeared to be a catalog of just one more year. There had to be at least 20 of the volumes stacked on the old desk, so the rest of them probably covered other years.

I took another sip of the coffee and found it stone cold. Then I realized I had been looking through these old books for over two hours.

I meditated over the books for a few more minutes and came to the conclusion that these books from 1944 recorded cash money collected from businesses in various states. As I studied the notations in the expense column and the transactions made in cash, it was quite apparent to me that this was all ill-gotten money, probably from the rackets. Throughout the books were telltale notations in parentheses detailing the sources of some of the cash. They included things like horses, numbers, loans, and booze—all pointing toward mob activities. That's all I could come up with. Nothing else made any sense. Whatever operations the money figures represented, legal or illegal, it was obviously very profitable and netted someone or some group over eight million dollars! That was a huge sum of money in 1944 and my thought was that Judge Seymour T. Levison was probably the beneficiary of the money!

I now believed the room behind the wine racks could very well be the master link to unraveling the mystery of the mansion on the hill and its owner, Seymour T. Levison. I wondered just what his role was in the entire operation. I really wanted to figure out exactly what kind of character the former owner of my house really had been.

My curiosity was beginning to run wild and I really wanted to get back down to that room. I hollered at Peggy Sue and told her I was going back to the room and might be down there for quite a while and asked her to hold dinner for me. I picked up my trusty flashlight, grabbed four 100-watt light bulbs and my stepladder and went back inside the secret room.

As soon as I got into the room, I replaced some of the light bulbs in the overhead fixtures so I could get a better view of everything. Now that the secret chamber was out of the darkness of the past three decades, I could make out things in the room very well.

The room itself was about 30-feet by 40-feet and had the appearance of an underground bunker. The walls, floor and ceiling were all made of gray-colored concrete; and, in the shadows of the far back wall, there were two black doors. I jumped down from the desk I had been standing on while changing the light bulbs and headed over to the doors. As I got close, I switched on my flashlight and turned its beam on one of the doors to get a good look. The door was made of steel, slightly smaller than a standard interior door.

The other door was not a door at all, but astonishingly was the entry to a steel vault about seven feet high and five feet wide. The vault door held a large circular combination lock in its center, next to a large steel handle. At the top of the safe in bold gold letters was the manufacturer's name: Diebold. I knew this brand was popular in heavy-duty bank vaults. Human nature caused me to reach out and attempt to turn the handle; but it was, of course, securely locked.

I turned my attention to the other door and found it unlocked. When I opened the door and looked inside, my flashlight beam revealed a dark passageway that seemed to lead off to the left…in the direction of the underground tunnel we had discovered in the ballroom floor of the basement. I couldn't resist the temptation to go down a few steps and look into the passageway as far as my beam could penetrate the darkness. But I could tell that this passageway would intersect with the other tunnel! I couldn't go any further into the passageway because my claustrophobia kicked in, so I retraced my steps back into the "counting" room. As I thought about the passageway intersecting with the tunnel, I knew it was some kind of escape route that led underground somewhere out in front of my house.

As I was closing the steel door I noticed the flashlight at my side was illuminating the dusty floor. I noticed there were faint impressions of footprints in the dust other than just mine. I could tell they weren't fresh prints, but someone had been in this room, other than Peggy Sue and myself, within the last several years. The footprints seemed to lead from the wine rack entry straight to the vault door. I guessed that Judge Levison had been in this room shortly before he died because I could think of no one else who would have known of the existence of this room.

I was extremely intrigued with the vault door so I walked over to it and spun the combination dial. It was sluggish, but it did turn. Turning it in several directions had no effect on the door that remained securely locked. I stood there trying to figure out how I could get into that vault. I pondered the possibility of calling a locksmith…or even contracting for the services of a safecracker! I quickly dismissed the latter thought.

I had to find someone I could trust to help me because I felt this was vitally important. After all, this was a safe I was trying to break into and it was housed in a secret room. Not your run-of-the-mill situation! There were already too many rumors surrounding the house and I didn't want to raise any additional suspicions.

Then a light bulb went off in my head. I thought of my old friend Chuck Christiansen, a man I knew and trusted who owned a junkyard in Dexter. He had a heavy-duty acetylene torch and I believed he could use it to cut through the outer shell of the door and expose its inner workings. I was sure we could then spring the lock open. There was a drawback in using the torch, however. It would destroy the door and might even set fire to the contents of the vault so I had to consider my options carefully. I decided to think about it a little later.

Again, I turned my attention to the old roll-top desk and the papers scattered over its surface and in the pigeonholes across its top. I pulled out a bunch of papers stuffed into one of the pigeonholes and looked them over. I found a delivery receipt signed with the initials *S.T.L.* and I knew that Seymour T. Levison had accepted receipt of a shipment of money in the amount of $11,300. Just below the initials was a wad of red sealing wax. The wax had the impression of the face of the silver ring with the Ruby stone in the center!

I was holding in my hand hard evidence that the judge was definitely in charge of accepting large sums of money from some source. The Detroit District Attorney's accusation that the judge was laundering money for the Purple Gang was most likely true. I found several more receipts for money shipments and also documents detailing transfers of money in amounts of several thousand dollars. All the documents were initialed and sealed in wax like the first one.

My mind was reeling and I realized I'd had enough excitement for one day and needed to take some time to evaluate everything I had found in the underground bunker.

I swore Peggy Sue to secrecy and we agreed we would not even tell the children what we have found behind the wine racks. Another thought crossed my mind. I wondered if Peggy Sue should attempt to pass a few of the "greenbacks" that we had found in the black box. She could use them at the grocery store and we could, at least, determine if the bills were numbered or had been marked as being from a bank robbery or something.

On the other hand, the bills might be counterfeit. I decided if anyone was going to take the risk, I should be the one passing questionable bills. If one of us was going to get caught doing something wrong, I certainly didn't want it to be Peggy Sue. Still, I had to find a way to determine if the money was good.

I left the room, turning off all the lights, and pushed the wine racks back in place, making sure they were secured. It might be a while before I returned to the room that existed in a time warp.

I wasted no time and set out on a plan to check the greenbacks. I asked Peggy Sue if she needed anything from the grocery store. She gave me a list of some things she needed and I told her I was going to use a few of the twenty-dollar bills to buy the groceries...just to be sure the money was genuine. Peggy Sue was nervous and asked if there were not some other way to determine if the cash was safe to use. I explained that I felt we needed to get some of the money into circulation to see if anyone from the government or law enforcement got suspicious. I was fairly sure the bills were all right because they had been in storage in that cash box for many, many years.

On the other hand, if the bills were somehow bad,

there was still the possibility so much time had passed that no law enforcement personnel were on the lookout for any of it.

I drove to the supermarket in town and collected all the groceries on Peggy Sue's list. I walked to the checkout counter, handed the cashier two of the old bills in payment, and held my breath. The cashier did not hesitate and put the bills in the cash drawer, gave me my change and told me to have a nice day. She didn't realize she had just made my day! All I could do now was wait to see if our town's constable came knocking at my door.

19

March 1977

About two months had passed and I hadn't seen hide nor hair of the frowning face of Constable Schultz or any men in black, flashing badges. I was beginning to feel comfortable about spending the rest of the money we found in the box. I told Peggy Sue she could use some of the money for her seeds and any other things she needed for her spring garden. She was going to get started early this year because we were having a warm spring with heavy thunderstorms and the soil was ready for planting.

But, something happened that would temporarily cause Peggy Sue to lose her enthusiasm for the garden. It was in the middle of a dark, moonless night after a storm had just passed over. We were awakened by the sounds of loud banging noises, coming from the barn. It sounded like the horses were kicking the walls of their stalls and they were whinnying, snorting, and shrieking. Peggy Sue and I ran to the window that overlooked the horse barn and looked out.

In the utter darkness, we could barely make out the outlines of the barn, but we could see a glowing green cloud drifting around the barn, suspended about three feet above the ground. At first, I thought we were seeing a large swarm of fireflies, but this was nothing like that. It looked like some kind of plasma that seemed to be pulsating. All the time, we could hear the horses going crazy, apparently scared to death by the green haze.

I threw on my shirt and pants, slipped on a pair of boots, grabbed a flashlight from my night stand and headed out to the barn. The sounds coming from the barn sounded like the horses were fighting. I was in such a hurry to get to the horses that I didn't realize I had walked right into a part of the glowing green fog. Then, the strangest thing happened.

The moment I touched the cloud, it just went "poof" and completely disappeared. I smelled a slight odor that reminded me of the fabric softener Peggy Sue uses in the laundry.

The horses were still fiercely battling. I swung open the barn door and my flashlight illuminated a scene of utter carnage. Sean, the big gelding, was terrified out of his wits and had jumped out of his stall. Cricket, the mare, had tried to do the same thing but had not been able to clear the top of her stall completely. She was hanging over the top rail where it had caught her between her belly and rear legs. For some unknown reason, Sean had attacked Cricket who was totally helpless and unable to defend herself. Sean had kicked her several times in the head and she was bleeding profusely, hanging listlessly from the top rail. Both animals were completely covered in a heavy lather.

Even with my shrieking at the top of my voice at Sean, he continued to kick at Cricket mercilessly. Finally, I grabbed a horse blanket from the tack room and threw it over Sean's head, covering his eyes. In a few minutes, he was calm enough for me to halter and I was able to lead him back to his stall.

In all the confusion, I hadn't noticed that Peggy Sue had come into the barn. She was kneeling over Cricket's horribly injured head. She screamed out at me, "Quick, get over here. She's not breathing."

When I saw the poor animal with her head in a pool of blood, I realized Peggy Sue was right. She wasn't breathing. I didn't know what to do, but thought if I could just get her body off the top rail she might be able to breathe again. I ran up to the house and got one of my tree saws. When I got back to the barn, I quickly sawed through the rails of the stall and Cricket's body fell to the ground with a loud thud.

The mare just lay there motionless in the blood although it was being quickly absorbed into the sawdust on the barn floor. I took a deep breath and tried to blow air into her lungs through her nostrils, but all I succeeded in doing was getting my hands and face covered with blood. I then raced over and filled a bucket from the well, returned and poured it over the mare's body, hoping the cold water might shock her into taking a breath.

Peggy Sue and I just stood by dumbfounded when nothing happened. After about 15 minutes it was apparent that our sweet mare was dead. Sean had succeeded in kicking his companion to death. This was impossible for us to understand because the two horses had gotten along so well and seemed to really enjoy each other's company. Sean had never shown any violent behavior toward Cricket. I thought he had just gone completely crazy when he saw the mysterious green cloud floating around outside the barn. I told Peggy Sue right then that I was going to get my horse off this hill and out of his misery. He had never seemed really happy since we brought him here.

I made plans to call Dr. Piatt and ask if the hunt club would like to have the animal. Peggy Sue and I were both terribly upset by this macabre incident. I tried to console Peggy Sue who was silently weeping over her dead pet. After a few minutes, when she had regained her composure and dried her eyes, she turned to me and asked, "What in the world was that green mist? We really did see it, didn't we?"

I could only answer, "Sure, we saw it all right, but did you notice how it disappeared when I walked through it?"

Peggy Sue was walking over to Sean's stall with the

hope of comforting him in some way with a little grain and some water. She turned to me and said, “Yes, it kind of went out just like you would turn off a light. It was totally spooky. What do you think it was?”

“I’m not really sure,” I answered quickly, “but I think after I call Dr. Piatt, I’m going to call that college professor at U of M and ask if she has any ideas about it. I’m also going to have one helluva time burying Cricket.”

We walked wearily back up to the house, arm in arm, trying to console each other. We went into the house and made a pot of coffee, waiting for the sun to come up. Just as surely as day follows night, the sun rose on the horizon bright, golden and warm.

When the kids came down for breakfast, I told them they didn’t have to feed the horses before school today, that I would take care of it myself. I didn’t want any of them to see Cricket, so we rushed them off to school and Peggy Sue and I went about the task of getting Cricket’s body out of the barn. Sean was standing in his stall next to the lifeless body of his companion as if nothing had happened the night before.

Using my tractor, I backed up to the barn door, extended the chain from its attachment, wrapped it around the carcass and slowly dragged it out of the barn. I pulled Cricket down the hill into one of the small sinkholes in the ravine and covered her body using the blade on my tractor. Peggy Sue, being the sentimental and religious person she is, had me bow my head as she said a prayer over the grave. Then she climbed up on the tractor, slid onto the seat next to me and we drove sadly up to the house, not saying a word.

After we ate a light breakfast, I put in a call to Dr. Piatt. I explained to him what had happened the night before and he expressed his sympathies and said he was sure the hunt club would be happy to take Sean off our hands. He felt they could put him to good use, training young riders enrolled at the club’s new school. I asked if he would arrange to have the horse picked up as soon as possible.

"For a gift like Sean, I'm sure we can arrange to have him picked up today," he assured me. He asked me how Peggy Sue and I had been feeling and I told him we were doing well. He expressed his gratitude for the gift of the horse to the club and said he would send a trailer to pick him up about noon.

My next call proved to be more interesting. I dialed the University of Michigan and asked for Professor Joyce Hoover. When she came on the line, I reminded her that I had called previously about the strange ice ball that had fallen from the sky. She remembered me!

Professor Hoover asked if I had learned anything additional about the ice ball. I told her that the ball had completely melted and the materials that were left on the ground after the melt just seemed to disintegrate when I touched them. She was amazed and told me she had never heard of anything like it in all her years of teaching. And then, as if she were in a hurry, she said, "What can I help you with today?"

I began my tale by telling her how we were awakened in the middle of the night to the noise of the horses and about the glowing green haze we saw hanging just above the ground out by my barn.

"You saw what?" she exclaimed.

Not wanting to sound like a crank caller, I said clearly and sincerely, "Professor, I am not kidding around. It was a glowing green cloud that seemed to be pulsating. When I accidentally walked into it, it just vanished."

She laughed and asked me if I was taking any kind of special medications; but then she told me quite seriously that the area I lived in must have low-lying marshlands since we were so close to the lakes and hills. I interrupted her briefly and said there was, in fact, just such an area only a short distance from the barn where the cloud appeared. She thought this was important and said in her opinion what my wife and I had seen was nothing more than low-drifting swamp gases.

"Swamp gases," I sputtered. "You've got to be kidding!

The professor was adamant and said, "I kid you not, I believe that's what you saw. This time of the year, methane gas from rotting vegetation, confined by ice, suddenly comes to the surface. If conditions are right, it emits a greenish glow and would certainly dissipate when you walked through it. Without knowing other details, this is about all I can tell you."

Not wanting to irritate her, I told her that I appreciated the information and hung up. I turned to my wife who had been listening to my side of the conversation and said, "Swamp gas!"

Looking quite puzzled, Peggy Sue said, "Swamp gas, what is that?"

I tried to sound like I had learned something from the professor, but quite frankly, in relating the information to Peggy Sue, I just didn't think it was plausible. Lacking any better explanation, I decided I would just have to accept what I was told as the cause of the eerie green haze. Whatever the cause, I believe the green haze was the reason one of my horses was dead and I was going to have to give away a five-thousand-dollar dear riding companion. I felt I had to do it before he, too, turned up mysteriously dead.

When the children came home from school that afternoon, I missed my chance to intercept them before they went out to the barn to do their chores. When they came running back to the house to tell me the horses had gotten loose, Peggy Sue and I sat them down and explained that we no longer had the horses. We told a tiny white fib and said we had given them to the hunt club. We just couldn't tell those kids that Cricket was dead; there just was no reason to hurt them that way. Not having their horses anymore was hard enough on them emotionally. They were heartbroken because they loved the horses and had had so much fun riding them. I tried to comfort them by explaining that their mother and I would also miss the horses. I told them to look on the brighter side—they would no longer have to tend the horses and do all the chores around the barn.

There was, however, a happy outcome to this episode in our lives. A few weeks after we had given Sean to the hunt club, the children were bugging us to go out to see the horses. I quickly called Dr. Piatt and asked him to call the club and get a story put together that would spare our kids' feelings about Cricket. He said he would have the people at the club tell the children that Cricket had been sold to a good home. Something that simple would be acceptable to the kids.

Later that day, we piled into the car and drove out to the club. Sean looked absolutely magnificent; he was well groomed and perky and seemed happy to see us. When we inquired about Cricket for the children's benefit, the club's hunt master told the children the story we had concocted. They seemed to accept this as a disappointment but one that was soon shrugged off.

The hunt master was full of praise for Sean. He said he was a willing and eager jumper and very cooperative when being saddled or bridled. He said they had not had any trouble at all with his attitude. After we watched Sean's workout on the jump course for a few hours, we left for home feeling much better about Sean's new life.

We received another happy surprise a few weeks later when Dr. Piatt informed us that Sean was being used for workouts by the Canadian Olympic equestrian team that practiced at the hunt club. This was quite an honor for a hunter/jumper horse.

Even though Sean was gone from our house, each time I was out in the barn and got a whiff of alfalfa hay, I expected to see him standing expectantly in his stall, just waiting for one of our serene rides into the deep woods. I missed him a lot, but was relieved he didn't have to suffer the mental agony he had gone through trying to escape whatever was haunting him here on our hill.

20

June 1977

The song, "June is Busting Out All Over" would be a perfect description of the beautiful flowers and blossoms on the fruit trees that surrounded the Mansion. The grass was a deep green and very healthy. Of course, being healthy means that it grew a lot; so, I was constantly on my Ford tractor mowing the lawn. One day, I had my Sidewinder brush cutter mounted on the rear of the tractor and I was attempting to cut down brush and small saplings in an overgrown area I had not previously cleared.

The area was just adjacent to a large gravel pit that had formed naturally off to one side of the hill near the front of the house. The brush cutter was doing a good job, knocking down the small saplings. Suddenly, it hit something with a loud clunk as if the blade had hit metal. Immediately the cutter became wedged and it stalled. I jumped off the tractor and carefully climbed back through the brush and over-hanging vines to reach the Sidewinder. Before I could attempt to clear away whatever had jammed the blade, I stepped into a large muddy spot on the ground.

When I lifted my foot and looked at my boot, I could see the sole was coated with a deep purple mud. Immediately, I recognized it as coming from the fluid that was ejected when I back-flushed the filters that removed iron from the house's water. I began to speculate on how the purple-colored fluid could somehow be migrating to this area so far from the septic tank that was high on the hill. I retrieved a shovel I always carried on the side of the tractor and began to dig several feet above the mud puddle in a small alcove in the side of the knoll where I was working.

I had only moved a few shovels-full of dirt when the blade hit a metal object. When I looked down, I could make out what looked like the metal housing surrounding a door. Taking the blade of my shovel, I pushed straight down against the metal and could tell by the sound that it was scraping across a large metal object.

I frantically began throwing dirt every direction and soon I had uncovered the outline of a steel door. Purple fluid was oozing out from beneath it. The door had a small broken glass window in its center and I could see through it a short distance. I saw dirt, gravel and rocks filling what seemed to be a very small room with a caved-in ceiling. The purple fluid made me realize I had just discovered the exit to the tunnel that had its entrance hidden in the room behind the wine racks. I speculated that because I was running the iron filters so often, the septic tank where the fluid accumulated had overflowed and the excess runoff had reached the top of the tunnel. It had then seeped its way down its entire length, accumulated in a huge puddle in front of the exit door, and was then absorbed into the sand and gravel in the area.

In my mind's eye, I could envision people trying to escape a bust by the Michigan State Police…or the Untouchables. I could see them all rushing through the entrance door in the accounting room and scampering down the tunnel, exiting here through this single door in the side of the hill. Then they would jump into their Packards or Cadillacs parked at the secluded gravel pit and race away up the small gravel road to freedom! My imagination was having a great day.

I stopped daydreaming any further, threw down my shovel, unhooked the Sidewinder, jumped on my tractor and drove up the hill to get Peggy Sue. I walked into the house and found her reading a book. I grabbed her by the hand and told her not to ask any questions but just to come with me. She squeezed herself onto the seat of the tractor with me and we were soon pulling up in front of the exit door in the hill.

As she jumped to the ground, she said "Okay, what have you unearthed now?"

I was quite proud of myself and said nonchalantly, "Oh, nothing much, just the exit of the tunnel." For some reason, I thought she would be pleased with my solving one of the mysteries of the house. However, it was apparent she was not at all impressed when she said, "You mean you took me away from the best part of the novel I was reading to show me this? Everyone knew the tunnel had to end somewhere, it just happens to be here. Why don't you do something important, like break into that old safe in the basement and maybe find some more money. Take me back up to the house so I can finish my book."

Boy, I was really disappointed that she didn't appreciate my detective work and now I, too, had lost the sense of excitement I first had when I realized what I had dug up. So, I snapped at her. "If that's going to be your attitude, then I guess you'll just have to walk home."

As I struggled to free my wedged brush cutter, I watched her stomping angrily up the hill toward her chair and her book. As I watched her I wondered if this was always going to be the reaction I'd get as I solved other mysteries surrounding the house. Had she and the kids become disinterested in the weird events of the past or had they just come to accept the bizarre and unexpected happenings as if they were just the norm here on the hill?

My nose was still out of joint from Peggy Sue's sarcastic remarks, and I didn't want to be around her for a while. I sat on my tractor for well over an hour listening to the birds and letting my mind contemplate a line of attack against the vault door. The longer I sat there and thought, the more I began to believe that my wife's suggestion of opening the vault was the correct thing to do. It had been several months since we had spent the last of the money we'd found, so I was quite sure no one was after us.

I figured it was about time to go on up to the house. The singing of the birds and the warm sun and beautiful spring flowers had calmed me down to the point that I was no longer mad at Peggy Sue. I started up my trusty Ford tractor and headed to the garage. As I looked back toward that exit door deep in the underbrush, I could see how it had stayed hidden for so many years. I just wondered what else might show up the next time I was out minding my own business, taking care of my property.

When I reached the house I went to the kitchen for a glass of water. I felt Peggy Sue behind me as she put her arms around my waist and gave me a big hug. "How about some iced tea?" she suggested.

As we sat there drinking the refreshing beverage, I told her she was right; it was time to do something about the safe. I told her I was planning to call Chuck and have him come out with his acetylene torch. She thought it was a good idea but said I should tell her when he was coming. "I don't want to be here. The kids and I will go to the movie in town," she said.

I called Chuck at the junkyard in Dexter and told him that I had found an old locked vault in my basement and wondered if he might be able to use his torch and cut out the locking mechanism so I could get in it. When I had explained what I wanted him to do, his response was typical of Chuck. "Man., I never thought I'd ever get a chance at safe cracking, but I've just bought a new cutting torch that's sure to do the job. It should penetrate the steel door with no problem."

I told him if he was ready to give it his best shot, he could come out at his earliest convenience. I gave him directions to the house, told him to throw the torch in the back of his pickup and come on over.

"I knew you would eventually have some more work for me," he said. "I welded that big vent cap that sits on top of your chimney for Lefty. Now, I'll finally get a chance to see that mansion Lefty and everybody else in Dexter is talking about. How about day after tomorrow around six in the evening?"

"That's great. I'll see you Friday evening at 6 o'clock," I replied, hanging up the telephone. I noticed that Peggy Sue had been listening to my side of the conversation, trying to interpret what was being said on the other end of the line. She's always been good at that!

She said Friday would be fine with her for Chuck's visit. "I can take the kids into town and we'll have an early dinner and go to the movie. I've been curious about how it's been operating since I sold it to Mrs. Fitzvasser. I'm eager to see how she's doing."

We had sold the theater to the very responsible Mrs. Fitzvasser when it began to be a big hassle, staying in town late at night until the movies were over and then making the long drive back home in the middle of the night.

Exactly as planned, Chuck arrived right on time on Friday evening. He waved as he passed Peggy Sue heading down the steep driveway. I could see two large tanks in the back of his pickup that were connected to his cutting torch. This was indeed a commercial rig, plenty capable of cutting through my steel vault door.

"Wow," I heard Chuck exclaim as he got out of his truck. "What a house!"

I helped him lift the cutting torch rig out of the truck and we rolled it into the house. Carefully, one step at a time, we lowered the unit into the basement. I had opened the wine rack door and turned on all the lights, hoping he wouldn't realize the room had been, in fact, hidden from prying eyes for many years.

When he looked around the room and saw all the old office furniture, he said, "Look at all this old junk. It must have been sitting here for years."

I told him to forget all that stuff and showed him the safe. "This is the monstrosity you have to break into," I said. He turned his eyes to the large black door that seemed to stand there like a sentinel guarding his master's wealth!

"Man, this is going to be a challenge," Chuck said. "The steel looks as heavy as the plate on a battleship. I'd better get at it 'cause this looks like a tough job."

Chuck rolled the tanks up to within ten feet of the door, removed a stool attached to his cutting rig and placed it about two feet in front of the door. After he put on his heavy leather apron and his gloves and welding helmet, he ignited the torch with a sparkler. The torch sprang to fiery life with a loud pop. He warned me not to look directly at the welding arc and then he set to work. He put the blazing torch against the steel door about four inches above the combination lock.

He applied the enormously hot flame to the spot and when the metal was a bright pink, he pressed a lever on the torch releasing high-pressure oxygen that sent sparks cascading all around him as they fell to the floor. It looked like he was sitting right in the middle of a miniature fireworks display. The air in the room became heavy with the very pungent smell of melting metal, the oxygen and acetylene, and Chuck's sweat. Every now and then, Chuck would pound away on the spot where he had been cutting. He was using a heavy steel hammer. Then he would immediately resume the cutting. This process went on for over an hour. Chuck stopped only once to smoke a cigarette and drink a bottle of the beer I had given him.

I sat most of the time just hypnotized by the light from the torch flickering on the walls of the room, and dreaming of what we might find inside the safe. Chuck was an eager beaver and soon was back to work, applying the torch to the door and sending sparks every which way! Another hour passed and it seemed to me that he had cut a complete circle around the dial in the middle of the vault door.

He shut off the torch, picked up the steel hammer and a large chisel and began using them on the lock. With one final blow, the entire combination dial fell to the floor. The hole in the door exposed three steel rods about an inch in diameter. Chuck said he would have to cut these in half and hoped they would then slide out of the doorjamb, thereby unlocking the door. He cut the rods, struck them with the hammer and they, too, fell on the floor. Then he used a huge pair of pliers that he applied to the half of the rods left in the door. By twisting them, he managed to slide them out of the doorjamb. Then, he turned the huge doorknob on the front of the vault door. Low and behold! It popped slightly open.

Immediately, I told Chuck to stop right there. He was surprised and disappointed because he was very curious about the contents of the safe. But I told him he had gone as far as I wanted him to go and stepped between him and the vault door.

He began rolling up his hoses and gathering up his equipment. I told him that I wanted the privacy of examining the contents of the safe alone and reached into my pocket and pulled out five $100 bills. I slipped them into his hand as I shook it. When he glanced down and saw the bills, a big smile spread across his face and there was real pleasure in his voice when he said, “That’s just fine with me. You’re the boss. You can consider that I was never here!”

I helped Chuck get all his equipment back up the stairs and into the back of the pickup. I told him how much I appreciated his hard work and that I would call him again whenever I needed welding work done around the place. I also told him I appreciated his trustworthiness and knew I could depend on him not to talk about the safe in the mansion on the hill.

We shook hands again and he went merrily on his way with $500 of my money in his pocket. I considered the money very well spent. I waited until the taillights of his pickup had disappeared into the darkness and then I practically ran back down the stairs to the basement. Once I got back into the hidden room, I was almost hesitant to open the vault door. I approached the black monstrosity with caution, apprehension and lots of excitement.

I played my flashlight beam on the door. Somehow it looked much larger than it really was. My imagination was running wild with all kinds of possibilities regarding the contents of the safe. As I reached for the handle of the door, I noticed my hands were trembling almost uncontrollably. I grabbed the handle and slowly pulled on it.

The door glided gently open as if operating on a cushion of air. My excitement turned to despair when I saw yet another set of steel doors. They were beautifully covered with a hand-painted picture of a yacht floating on a deep blue sea. There was another combination lock and small handle on this set of doors. Of course, I thought to myself, "Have I let Chuck and his cutting torch leave too soon? What an idiot!"

But I wasted no time. Without touching the combination dial, I grabbed the small handle on the inner doors and gave them a turn and a tug. The door opened with a click. I held my breath, opened both the inner doors and saw something that was unbelievably thrilling and spectacular. What I saw caused me to think about the treasure hunter and explorer who had discovered King Tut's tomb, saw the riches and uttered the now famous words, that he saw, "fascinating things."

The interior of the vault was well over ten feet square and was stuffed full of all kinds of documents and journals like the others I had found on the old desk. These journals were neatly stacked on a large metal shelf and laying next to them was, of all things, a revolver—and next to it, a 45-

caliber sub-machine gun with a drum magazine and red-painted handle. However, that was nothing. The most impressive sight of all was the rows and rows of dust-covered greenbacks!

The bills were lined up neatly on steel shelving and probably explained the need for the heavy artillery. Piled on the other side of the room were huge canvas bags, resembling army duffel bags, but these were a dirty off-white and most of them were stenciled with the words, "Detroit Bank and Trust." I was dumbfounded!

There was too much in the safe to look at with just a flashlight, so I looked around for a light switch, found one and turned it on, bathing the interior of the vault in a bright white light. I stepped inside the vault.

Money was everywhere, on the shelves in stack after stack and in small piles on the floor where packets had fallen out of an upturned canvas bag. I looked in one of the canvas bags. It, too, was full of money, most of it wrapped in the customary wrappers used by banks to bundle cash. Several of the packets had the figure "$2,000" marked on their bands

Had I discovered the Knighthood of Zion's mother lode of cash? I wasn't sure whom this money belonged to, but there had to be thousands, perhaps even millions, of dollars in this vault.

My head was spinning, but I knew one thing for sure: it would take a helluva long time to determine exactly what all the contents of the safe added up to—not only in monetary value but in the contents of all the documents. Those would go a long way in explaining the true meaning of the mansion itself.

It was getting late and I knew Peggy Sue and the kids would be getting home at any minute. I needed time, lots of time, to figure out just what to do about this latest and most impressive revelation my house had shown me. I had to keep this situation totally secret. Revealing the contents of this safe to the wrong person could get me and possibly my family members a bullet in our brains.

I heard Peggy Sue's Cadillac pulling into the garage, so I quickly shut off the light, closed both the inner doors and the massive outer doors to the vault, shut the wine rack and hurried upstairs to greet my wife and kids. I worried that I might have just put all of them in jeopardy by opening the safe. I knew I would not be sleeping well at night, knowing I was taking my rest over a branch of the Detroit Bank and Trust. I was very possibly a closet millionaire!

When I asked Peggy Sue how she had enjoyed the movie, her comment was, "It was fine. Did you get in the safe?"

"Oh, yeah!" I said, trying to contain my excitement. "As soon as the kids are in bed and we're sure they're asleep, I'll take you inside the vault and let you see for yourself."

Naturally, because it was Friday night, the kids stayed up late and it was after eleven before they finally went up to bed and to sleep. About midnight, Peggy Sue and I headed down to the basement and the room full of money.

As we reached the bottom of the stairs, I could just see in my mind old man Levison taking this same path to the vault. He had probably been living on this cache of dough right up until his death.

I opened the wine racks, stepped into the bookie parlor, turned on the lights and walked straight over to the safe. I opened the heavy outer doors, then the smaller inner doors, and stepped inside the vault with Peggy Sue clinging onto my shirttail. I knelt on the floor and scooped up a handful of $100 bills. Raising the "fistful of dollars" toward Peggy Sue, I asked, "Well, what do you think of this?"

"Oh, my God, what a horrible letdown it would be if all this money is counterfeit." She had also said this when we opened the small tin cash box that held a mere $3,000.

"No, it's the real McCoy," I said from my position on

the floor. By now, I was leaning my head back against one of the large canvas bags full of cash. "You know it is, I know it is…the real question is what are we going to do with all this money? For our own safety and that of the kids, we've got to keep this room and its contents to ourselves. We can't even tell the kids. We need to take our time here and not make any mistakes. It's gonna take us a long time to count all this cash."

As I was speaking to her, she took a few steps over to the metal shelves and lifted the machine gun by its handle and said, "Is this thing real?"

I yelled out loud enough to wake the kids, "Look out! That thing is probably loaded to the max."

She let go of the gun and let out a loud shriek. "Damn," I said, "I hope that one didn't wake up the kids. I don't want them sneaking in here and seeing all this stuff—and, what the hell were you staring at?"

"Honey, there's a glass jar on that shelf over there and it looks like it has human fingers in it," she said rather calmly.

"Human what?" I sputtered and I jumped to my feet and stepped over to the metal shelf. I reached to the back of the shelf and slid a big dust-covered jar toward the front. I used a $100 bill to wipe off the side of the jar and Peggy Sue and I stared through the glass. Surely enough, it held several human fingers that obviously had been severed from somebody's hands, at the knuckle. The glass lid had a knob in the center. I took hold of it and lifted the lid off the jar. The strong smell of formaldehyde assaulted my nostrils.

We looked down through the clear liquid and counted nine fingers neatly stacked like rows of pickles! As I studied the ghastly contents of the jar, I nearly died when I saw that three of the fingers wore the signet ring of the Knighthood of Zion, similar to the one, less the precious stone, Seymour T. Levison wore on his finger in the portraits.

Nine human beings had lost fingers in some kind of ghoulish ceremony or as a means of keeping track of dead people. I thought that way because I remembered seeing Bruno hold up nine fingers when he told me about the graves on the remote knoll at the back of the property. He had mumbled the number "nine" the day he showed the graves to me. There were exactly nine graves in addition to the judge's. The fingers in the jar could only mean that three of the bodies buried out there belonged to members of the knighthood! I also realized that Bruno had not come clean with me about the bodies buried in the makeshift cemetery. He knew a lot more about these deaths than he had told me. It was now up to me to find out what he was holding back.

God, I would have to think about this tomorrow. It was the wee hours of the morning by now and Peggy Sue and I were excited but emotionally, more than physically, exhausted. We closed the vault doors and the entry to the secret room and headed back upstairs to bed. I really hoped a good night's sleep would clear my head and that I would have a better picture of the whole scene waiting for me behind that vault door.

I did feel better the next morning after having slept on all the questions I had about the things I'd discovered. I was convinced that I had a good plan mapped out in my head. First, we had to count the cash to see how much money we had uncovered. Then, I was eager to look at the documents that were in the safe. And, lastly, I had to confront Bruno and get more information about the graves.

I was drinking my morning coffee when I heard Peggy Sue ask the children what things they wanted to pack for summer camp, scheduled for the following week. I was thrilled to think they would be gone for a week and knew this would be an opportune time for Peggy Sue and me to go to work on the vault.

I had decided to purchase a bill-counting machine,

thinking this would be critical for handling that much cash. I had a week to track one down before the kids went off to camp.

On Monday, I contacted Lance at the bank and asked if he knew of a secondhand bill-counting machine that I might purchase. I was surprised when he said he had a couple of them and I could get one for $50. Jokingly, he asked me if I planned to start my own bank. Nonchalantly, I told him I was going to be the treasurer of a charity raffle event and felt the machine would be handy in counting all the one-dollar bills I would be getting. I thanked Lance for saving me lots of legwork and told him I would come by the bank later in the day to pick up one of the machines. As an afterthought, I asked if he would mind showing me how the machine worked.

"No problem," he said laughing. "A bank president needs to be knowledgeable about how all his equipment works. Sometimes I even have to repair a toilet."

It dawned on me that I was getting quite good at stretching the truth about things relating to my mansion. I never used to do that.

The remainder of the week was spent cleaning out the old barn and mowing several acres of the lawn. I might have appeared tranquil to my family, but inside I was jumping with excitement. I wanted to get that bill-counting machine clicking down in that vault! I thought about our windfall constantly. I just couldn't get it out of my mind. Even though Peggy Sue and I were well set financially and living, pretty much, on easy street, the piles of money I had uncovered in that musty old room would go a long way in securing my children's financial future. Still, deep in my heart, I didn't think I would do anything illegal to jeopardize my freedom. On the other hand, I also knew I wasn't going to turn the money over to the state and I sure as hell wasn't gonna give it back to the mob. If, in fact, it was mob money—hell they were probably all dead or in prison. The money had been resting in that vault for at least the seven years we had lived here and no one had tried to claim it. Little clichés were going through my mind like: possession is nine-tenths of the law; and the famous one I remembered from being a kid, finders keepers, losers weepers! The little mind exercises were just my own way of justifying the fact that I planned to keep the money.

The day finally arrived for all four of our children to go off to the Baptist summer camp for a week. We drove them to meet our church bus, loaded all their bags, and bid them farewell as they sped away happily toward camp. Peggy Sue and I raced back to the house and headed down to the basement with the counting machine, a big bag of potato chips and a couple of cold Cokes. We knew we had our work cut out for us.

We had agreed that Peggy Sue would assemble the hundreds of documents that were scattered about the vault and get them into some semblance of order so we could go through them sometime later. In the meantime, I would start the main task of counting the money. I set up a small workstation on one of the old desks and plugged in the counting machine. I was so excited!

We decided to start at the doorway and work our way back into the recesses of the safe. Peggy Sue began picking up papers and documents off the floor and I grabbed the loose bills that had tumbled out of the canvas bag.

I took the loose bills, the open canvas bag and some more bills I had thrown into a box I found in the safe and moved to my workstation. I loaded a handful of bills into the machine, and turned that sucker on. In a flash, they were counted. I could hardly believe my eyes when I read on the meter, 114. I did quick calculations in my mind and realized I had $11,400 just from a fistful of random bills. I looked at the bag beside my workstation and realized that entire bag was almost full of $100 bills. I had counted all the canvas bags in the vault and knew there were 47 bags. I wasn't even certain how many stacks of bills were also lining the steel shelves along one side of the vault. I realized it was going to be a monumental task to count all this money and I didn't think we could possibly do it in a week, but we were willing to give it our best shot.

Again, I began feeding the $100 bills through the counting machine, recording the amount on a blank page in one of the half-filled journals I found in the vault. This went on for over an hour and I wasn't even a third of the way through the partially-filled canvas bag. Then I remembered that Lance had another of these counting machines. I bounced upstairs, telephoned Lance and asked if he still had the other machine. When he told me it was still available, I told him a cock and bull story that the first one I bought was malfunctioning. I didn't know what else to do. I couldn't tell him that I was using the counter to tally up bags full of $100 bills.

I felt a little bad when he said, "That's too bad. It was pretty old anyway. Just come on down here and pick up the other one. You can have it for nothing and just throw the other one away."

I insisted on paying for the second unit but he wouldn't accept my money. We agreed I would buy him lunch sometime. I felt like a fool when I picked up the so-called replacement machine. I mean, after all, I had $100 bills spilling all over the floor of my basement. Still, I rushed back to the house, showed Peggy Sue how to operate the counter and we put the second machine to work.

Peggy Sue and I were both feverishly loading the machines with bills, stacking the counted ones on some of the empty shelves, and recording the amounts in the journal. Finally, after three more hours, we had successfully counted the partially filled canvas bag. The face value of the bills in that bag, all $100's, was $111,700. We were exhausted and dirty, so we stopped for food and took the time to put a pencil to our arduous task. While Peggy Sue made tuna salad sandwiches, I figured on my math problem. "Let's see, time involved in counting: over 4 hours. And that was for just one bag. Take that, times 47 bags, and it comes to over 141 hours of constant work. That figures out to be almost six days at 24-hours a day."

I figured if we worked a 10-hour day, it would take us at least 14 days to count just the bags. I realized, using my calculations, there was no way for us to get this stuff counted in one week unless we hired a small army—a proposition entirely out of the question!

So I calculated the approximate amount of money in the bags. I penciled together a figure that was absolutely unbelievable. Assuming each bag contained $111,700, then 47 bags would total $5,249,900. And that was *just the money in the bags*! The sum was even larger than I guessed it would be and I checked my figures more than once. When Peggy Sue asked me what my calculations totaled, I was almost afraid to utter it aloud, so I whispered it to her as if the house were full of spies; but here we were alone in the middle of a pine forest, high on a hill. I guess just the thought of it scared the shit out of me.

We sat there silently looking at each other for a long time, daydreaming about all the things we could buy with this much money…all the 'round-the-world trips we could take, the beautiful homes we could buy for our children, all the new Cadillacs! I broke the silence, finally, and said, "I'll bet you're thinking of how you're going to spend all this money, aren't you?"

Her answer to me summed up our problem, "How in the world are we going to be able to keep this a secret? And how in the world will we be able to spend it without causing a lot of questions?" She was dead right and I answered her with a statement that seemed a little ridiculous at the time, but just might be a credible solution.

"We could always move to another state or even another country, like Australia and just say we became rich when we hit the Irish Sweepstakes lottery."

She laughed half-heartedly and said, "Hey, I guess that could work. But speaking of work, we'd better get back to it."

When we got back to the vault and I took another look at the huge job before us, I turned to Peggy Sue and said, "Hell, what's the use of counting it? There's more here than we could ever spend, so what difference does it make what the exact amount is."

Her answer surprised me a little, but she said, "Maybe you're right, but we should at least tidy up the place." For the first time that day, I had a really good laugh. I laughed until tears ran down my cheeks, but thought we might as well act on her suggestion and at least put things in order.

I thought we should first stack the canvas bags. I reached out and slid one off the top of the pile and set it on the floor. I had a tremendous urge to look in it, so I removed the hook on the end of the bag, opened it up and peered in. I was surprised to see a letter-size piece of paper lying on top of the bills. I picked it up and realized it was a shipping receipt. Neatly printed across the form were the words, "Letter of Transit." My eyes scanned to the bottom of the page and saw a total penciled in on a line at the bottom of the page. The figure was $37,120. I looked further into the bag and saw that this one was filled with $20 bills. Then it hit me, if all the bags contained a shipping receipt or a letter of transit, our counting job just got a lot easier.

Immediately, I pulled down a second bag, opened it and found another receipt. The penciled total was $42,080 and this bag was also filled with twenty-dollar bills, all of them neatly bundled and secured with Detroit Bank and Trust bands, the amount of $2,000 stamped in blue ink on each packet.

I handed the two receipts to Peggy Sue and began tearing into the other bags looking for more receipts when she said to me, "You know, in your haste, you didn't even notice the date printed at the top of this sheet of paper. It's dated August 14, 1944."

I stopped in my tracks and turned to her, "My God, this bag has been sitting here for 33 years. Is there a date on the other page?"

Peggy Sue looked stunned about the time frame as she examined the second receipt. She shook her head "no" to my question about a date on the second piece of paper. I told her to sit down at the desk and we would record the dollar amount on all the receipts in the bags.

Meticulously, she cleaned off the desk and wooden chair and sat down to record the amounts I gave her from each of the bags. It took us several hours because it involved moving the heavy bags, unhooking each one, and retrieving the form that recorded the bag's contents. Physically, I handled 56 bags and all but 11 of them had receipts inside.

The 45 bags that were totaled held different denominations of greenbacks. Some held all $20's; others all $50's and several contained only $100's. Peggy Sue calculated her long list of amounts and concluded that the 45 bags with receipts totaled $2,840,120! The amount was surprising; and the fact that some of the receipts were dated as far back as 1937 was startling.

The older receipts gave us something else to be stunned by and concerned about. These receipts contained a red glob of sealing wax with the image of the signet ring pressed into it! Of course, the seal on the letters of transit was evidence to me that this money once belonged to some of the gangs controlled by the Knighthood of Zion. It also convinced me that Judge Levison was a major player in the hierarchy of this ancient organization.

A scary thought crossed my mind. Maybe I'd better start practicing with that sub-machine gun on the shelf. I might need it. I tried to allay my own fears by reminding myself that one, Judge Levison was definitely dead; two, most of the gang members were probably dead or so old they could barely walk; three, the cash had been here untouched for at least 33 years; and, four, I owned the house that contained the money. Maybe I wouldn't need that target practice after all.

I did make one concession to my cautionary thoughts. With all this cash just lying around, it might be prudent to have a little protection. I thought immediately about the German automatic pistol hidden inside the black book, but I had taken it to a safety deposit box at the bank 45 miles away. So, I took the old revolver, still in a well-worn leather shoulder holster, from the shelf of the vault, along with several boxes of ammunition lying beside it.

Peggy Sue and I left the vault, closed everything up and went upstairs. I went to my library to examine the revolver. It took some effort to remove it from its tight holster. I was amazed to find the gun was not at all rusted, only a little stiff from disuse over so many years. Now that it was in full view, I could see by the stamping on one side that it was a Smith & Wesson, 38-caliber. It was marked with the words, "Police Special." On the other side of the gun, just in front of the trigger guard was imprinted, "Detroit Police Dept." and below those words was the number, S631387. The fully-loaded gun held six bullets which I carefully removed.

I took a little sewing machine oil, applied it to all the moving parts, squirted a little down the barrel and replaced the shells. Now the question, "Would it fire?" I took the gun down to a small ravine at the back of the house, pointed it at a large pile of dirt and squeezed the trigger. A deafening "kerpow" echoed off the nearby trees. The gun had a hell of a kick to it, but it worked. I went back to the house and put the gun in the drawer of my nightstand, the one I could lock. I hung the key under the bed on one of the rails. I now considered myself armed and definitely dangerous!

Peggy Sue and I got down to work over the next several days. We counted up the bills in nine of the bags without receipts and these totaled $692,500. The other two remaining bags without receipts had a mixture of denominations. These bills were completely mixed up and appeared to have just been scooped up and hastily thrown into the bags. We didn't bother to count these and decided that occasionally we would take some of this money and spend it. Not only would it be a hassle to count it, but using some of it would give us a chance to be sure the money was legit. We were pretty confident that it was.

We took the easy route in counting the dust-covered bills that were stacked on the vault shelves by counting only the money bundled in the bank wrappers. Using the amounts printed on the bands, Peggy Sue came up with the figure of $342,000. The money that was not counted was lying loose on the shelves and we stuffed it into the two bags of money we were going to spend.

Finding the receipts in most of the bags enabled us to easily complete our inventory of the currency in the vault and we had three days to spare before the children returned from camp. The total of all the cash, not counting the two bags of mixed bills, came to the staggering total of just over *three and one-half million dollars.* We were rich…I mean richer!

Having counted all the cash, we finished up early in the morning of the fifth day by assembling and putting in piles all the documents, legal papers, what appeared to be a set of house plans, and lots of newspapers from cities in several states. We didn't take time to study any of them, but planned to do so later. There was a large filing cabinet against one wall and that would also have to wait until later. The wife and I decided that after five days of steady work we deserved to celebrate our entry into the stratified air of millionaires. We decided to have a party—a private party, just the two of us.

I told Peggy Sue I wanted to take her to the Clintonian Inn restaurant and buy her the best liver and onions dinner they had on the menu and that we would eat until we were almost sick. She quickly nixed that idea and said she would prefer to cook us a nice pot roast with carrots, onions and potatoes and open a bottle of our vintage wine from our racks in the basement…maybe even two of them. I decided this might lead to a possible amorous encounter with my lovely wife, so I quickly agreed. Even though we had been completely alone for five days, I had not once had a sexual thought. I was so fascinated by the volume of cash that lay behind the hidden vault door that I had hardly even taken time to eat. Man, was I hungry!

I helped Peggy Sue prepare dinner by peeling the veggies while she seared the meat and then assembled everything and got it into the oven. While she went upstairs, took a hot bath and put on her nightgown in anticipation of our party, I went downstairs to get the wine. Instead of getting one or two bottles, I got three bottles of the old wine. These were the bottles that had sat unmolested on the top shelf of the wine rack for so many years. I brought them upstairs, washed them under tap water, wiped them dry and put them in the refrigerator to chill. I was excited about serving the perfectly chilled wine to my bride with our dinner. I showered in the kids' bathroom. Thirty minutes later, we were sitting together on the living room sofa, holding hands and daydreaming about our future days of luxury. The party had started.

Later, Peggy Sue and I sat at our massive dining room table, took generous portions of the roast and steaming vegetables and began our meal. It was peaceful and quiet—not like the pandemonium that sometimes happened when the four children were also at the table.

I poured us full glasses of wine and it was wonderful with the meat. Soon, I was opening the second bottle, which we downed with the remains of our wonderful dinner. We were comfortable and relaxed as we finished dinner and took our wine glasses into the living room.

Looking out the windows at the darkening sky, I started pouring from the third bottle. We could hear thunder off in the distance and the lightning played a light show on the far horizon. Soon, it began to rain lightly. The tranquilizing sound of the falling rain on the roof and windows made the wine go down way too easy! That old stuff really had a kick to it and before we realized what was happening, we were both pie-eyed, but very jovial.

Unfortunately, the two of us were so out of control that lovemaking was out of the question so, laughing all the way, we helped each other upstairs to the bedroom. We both fell limply on the bed and were probably asleep before our heads hit our pillows. What a beautiful evening…at least I thought so for a while. What happened later bordered on the macabre.

Sometime in the middle of the night, I began having trouble breathing and felt as if I was struggling under a tremendous weight. I tried to move but found I could not. Then I started choking. I heard a huge thunderclap and opened my eyes just in time to see, a very distorted and hideous face illuminated in the lightning flash. Some kind of wild person was sitting on my chest and looking down on me. He was tightly squeezing my throat with his hands, trying to strangle me and was beginning to succeed!

Without thinking, I struck out with my fist and connected with it right into my assassin's temple. The blow was hard enough to knock him off my chest and loosen his hands from around my throat. He hit the floor with a huge thud.

Lying there, a few seconds I finally caught my breath, then jumped out of bed only to trip and fall flat on my prostrate assailant. Looking down on the body, I was suddenly, shocked and very confused when I realized, "Oh my God! It was my WIFE! I had knocked her unconscious. Crawling into the bathroom, I ran some cold water on a towel and applied it to Peggy Sue's forehead. I could not ever imagine hitting my beloved, but at that instant, it was as if some strange creature had possessed her. I had no other choice because she had been doing her damnedest to kill me. Something was wrong, radically wrong. Sure, the wine had a kick to it, but what had happened in our bed was horrifying.

Peggy Sue was finally coming to, complaining that she had a terrible headache, felt sick, was dizzy and couldn't see straight. She asked me what had hit her. About then, another bright flash of lightning from the storm illuminated her head and I noticed she was bleeding from the mouth and one of her ears.

When I saw the blood, I knew I had to get us both to the hospital, but I wasn't sure I could make the forty-five-minute drive in my condition in the rain, that was now turning into a downpour.

I got Peggy Sue into her bathrobe and put mine on, too. I struggled with her down the stairs—the very ones we were laughing on just a few short hours ago. I managed to get her out to the garage and into the back seat of the car. As I attempted to open the garage door, I doubled over in pain. My stomach was killing me and, all of a sudden, I threw up. I immediately thought about the wine and wondered if it was poisoned or if we had drunk far too much of it. I was sure of only one thing…we were both deathly ill.

It took well over an hour in the driving rain to reach the emergency room at the University of Michigan hospital facility. I almost collapsed as they wheeled us into the hospital, but I did manage to explain to the doctor what had happened. I asked him to inform Dr. Piatt just before I slipped into unconsciousness myself.

Eventually, I heard faint voices and opened my eyes to see Dr. Piatt standing over me while the ER doctor was putting an IV into my arm. Dr. Piatt began talking to me. "Zack, you gave us quite a scare when your blood pressure fell so low, but we have it stabilized now. But, I'm afraid we're going to have to give you a few units of blood to replace what we had to draw from your system. Zack, it's that old iron content again, extremely high, in both you and Peggy Sue. We are transfusing her now. This time the levels were high enough to wreck your liver and do both of you in. Are you drinking that water again?"

I could only shake my head "no," because it hurt too badly to do or say anything else.

I spent the next two days drifting between sleep and consciousness, but was coherent enough on one occasion to ask Dr. Piatt to call my mom and dad and have them take care of the children. The only other thing I worried about was where Peggy Sue was and how she was doing. Each time I thought of her, I remembered hitting her in the temple with my fist. I just couldn't believe I had done that, and I played that traumatic event over and over again in my head. What in the world had caused this bizarre incident? I was adamant I would do whatever I had to do to see that it never happened again—up to and including moving off the hill!

I awoke one morning from a troubled sleep and felt hungry for the first time since coming to the hospital. I rang for the nurse to come and asked if I might have something to eat. She said she had to check but soon came back to ask if I would like to be wheeled into Peggy Sue's room to have breakfast with her.

"I sure would, but there's no need to wheel me. I'm sure I can walk," I said happily. The nurse helped me out of bed and held on to me as I tried to stabilize myself. I did make it to Peggy Sue's bedside chair and we enjoyed our breakfast together. I was happy to see her rosy face and bright smile, but was saddened when I noticed the large blue bruise over her left eye. I lifted myself out of the chair, placed a kiss on the spot and told her I was so sorry I had hit her.

Peggy Sue said she didn't understand anything that happened that night. "I heard that storm approaching and suddenly had the haunting feeling that you weren't lying in bed beside me. I saw that awful skeletal face I'd seen in the china cabinet glass door, but it was attached to your body," she said trembling.

It had seemed so real to her. She said the ghost, or whatever it was, whispered into her ear that it was going to rape her and afterwards he was going to eat her children. He said her husband would not be able to help her. Peggy Sue said her head seemed to be vibrating violently every time it thundered; that she couldn't see and thought she was going insane.

She said she believed she had to protect herself and the children somehow, and that's why she was trying to strangle the face with the red spinning eyes. "I didn't know it was *you*, Zack," she said, on the verge of tears. She went on to say that when I hit her she immediately felt relief from the vibrations and that "when the floor came up to meet me, I passed out."

Peggy Sue said she couldn't explain her actions but told me she believed the house was somehow at fault and she wished we had never moved into it. I told her I sympathized with her completely and that I also thought it was time for a change. "But, Peggy Sue, have you forgotten what's in the basement at home?" Thinking for a second, she agreed we would have to stay at the house but felt we should get professional, scientific help to determine what had caused this terrible thing to happen.

Just as we were finishing our breakfast, Dr. Piatt came to check on us. We told him we both felt well enough to go home. We also told him we had decided to spare no cost and to spend as much time as necessary trying to figure out what was causing living things (referring to the horses, the cat and ourselves) to act so violently on our hilltop. Again, Dr. Piatt told us he felt sure it was all connected to the high iron content in our bloodstreams and the weird geophysical conditions present at the location of our home.

I told Doc Piatt I wasn't sure what he was referring to, but if he had suggestions, we were eager to try them. I told him about my conversations with Professor Hoover and about her familiarity with atmospheric conditions in our area. He said he thought that might be a good place to start. He also said he was acquainted with the professor and might be able to get her to pay us a visit before we left the hospital.

"Peggy Sue and I would be eager to talk with her and would appreciate it so much if you could arrange it."

That evening, just before 6 o'clock, we were finishing dinner in Peggy Sue's room when Professor Hoover stuck her head in the door and asked how we were feeling. We almost simultaneously said we were feeling much better and made that typical statement of patients, "We're ready to go home."

The professor said she and Dr. Piatt had been discussing our unusual situation and they were not sure about a couple of things. She said they couldn't figure out why the iron content in our blood was so high or how the house and its location might be interacting with this blood condition. She said she remembered our telephone conversations about the green fog, the behavior of the cat and the horses, and the freaky falling ice ball. She said she was almost convinced that atmospheric conditions during heavy thunderstorms must be contributing to our altered mental behavior. She said she was now so intrigued by the things happening on our hill that she was willing to spend some time with us at our home to evaluate the situation. She asked if that might work for us and if it might be possible to bring a colleague along to assist in her evaluations.

We agreed willingly and told Professor Hoover we just hoped they might come up with answers to the strange events that were driving us almost to insanity.

As she left our room, she commented, “You needn’t worry. It may take us a while, but we will determine exactly what is occurring. I’m almost certain, however, that our results will be startling.”

21

About three weeks after we left the hospital, we got a telephone call from the professor asking if the next week would be convenient for her to visit. She said it would be a good time because the weather forecast for the coming week predicted some heavy weather in our area of the state. Peggy Sue and I were both feeling exceptionally well, so we told her to make her plans for the visit. The professor said she and her colleague would arrive on Sunday evening. We told her we would prepare two bedrooms for the visit and that we were looking forward to their arrival on Sunday.

Sunday evening, just as we had finished cleaning up the dinner dishes, we saw a Volkswagen bus come to a stop in front of our door. Professor Hoover stepped out of the van. Accompanied by a short, heavyset gentleman, she made her way to the door. Peggy Sue and I greeted our visitors and welcomed them to our home. Professor Hoover introduced us to Professor Otto Schweitzer. She said that he had his doctorate in electrical engineering and was currently working on a theory of using super-cooled magnets to levitate and propel trains along a track. She said he had also been working with NASA to determine the possibilities of propelling spacecraft with magnets, interacting with the magnetic field of the earth.

Professor Hoover said she considered her colleague to be a genius and one of the leading experts in the country in the field of electromagnetic engineering. Dr. Schweitzer held out his hand to us and said he had never had such a glowing introduction and was embarrassed by the praise being heaped upon him.

The doctor, in addition to being short and portly, had an enormous mane of white hair, thick busy eyebrows, and was probably in his seventies. He resembled photos of Albert Einstein and certainly fit the image of an esteemed scientist. I pumped his hand enthusiastically in welcome and told him we were honored to have someone of his reputation and stature involved in trying to solve our strange problems here on our hill. We invited our guests to join us in the living room while we discussed the strange phenomena that seemed to invade our home in the Irish Hills.

Dr. Schweitzer said Professor Hoover had told him about a few of our bizarre experiences and that they always seemed to occur during or immediately after violent thunderstorms. He said she had been so excited in telling about the incidents that he, too, was eager to participate in evaluating our situation. He said he felt his findings here might aid in his study of magnetic levitation, and he felt fortunate to be able to participate. He also said if we were going to spend several days together it might be nice to be on a first-name basis. "Please, just call me Otto," he said with a little grin.

"Oh, and please, by all means, call me Joyce," Professor Hoover piped up before anyone else could say anything. We all agreed to these informalities.

I helped our two investigators with their luggage and showed them to their respective bedrooms. Otto asked if I would assist him in bringing in some of his equipment.

I had never seen anything in the world like the various scientific measuring devices he had. One of them was so large it had to be placed in the garage. All the devices were complicated looking contraptions and I was sure that only a guy like Otto would possibly know how to operate them. I figured they would probably do some really unique and fascinating stuff!

Otto wanted to place his equipment downstairs, but I wanted to protect the sanctity of the basement and suggested the two super sleuths use the study upstairs, just down the hall from their bedrooms. I really didn't want these guys poking their noses into our business in the basement.

We had sent the children off to spend a week with their grandparents, so it was just the four of us who sat down in the living room for a cup of coffee and a piece of Peggy Sue's fabulous apple pie.

What an interesting couple they were. Joyce was young enough to be Otto's daughter and she was a pleasant looking woman. She also had amazing academic credentials, but she didn't seem to flaunt them. However, the one drawback was that both of them smoked. We tolerated it because we didn't want our guests to be uncomfortable. Joyce smoked her cigarettes in a long-stemmed holder, similar to the ones depicted in the mural on the wall in the upstairs hallway. When I commented on the holder, she said it kept the nicotine stains off her fingers. Otto smoked a pipe filled with a very pleasant, sweet-smelling tobacco.

That first evening, we visited for a short time and then headed upstairs to bed. As Peggy Sue and I made our way to our bedroom, I thought, "If magnetism and high-voltage electricity in storms have anything to do with the weird happenings on our hill, these two will be the ones to figure it out."

At breakfast the next morning, Otto told me he had been thinking about some causes for the high ferrous sulfite in our blood that had sent us both to the hospital. Otto was aware of the problems with our water but said, since we were filtering it twice a week, it should not be the cause. Surprisingly, he asked if he might examine some of the wine, we were drinking the night we became so ill.

I chuckled and told him we had finished off three bottles of the stuff that night, but I could bring up another bottle from the cellar for him to analyze. Without giving him time to reply or attempt to accompany me to the cellar, I jumped up and hurried to the basement and got one of the bottles from the top shelf. When I handed the dusty bottle to him, he asked how long it had been in the wine rack and I said, "A long time, years."

With a smile on his face he said, "If this checks out okay, it would be a shame to waste such a fine vintage, so why don't you and I just drink it?"

I popped the cork from the bottle and said, "That'll be all right with me." We took the open bottle upstairs to the study where his diagnostic equipment was set up. Otto poured a small amount of the wine into a test tube and added several drops of other liquids to the tube. Then he played the flame from his portable Bunsen burner over the bottom of the tube to heat it. In a few seconds, the mixture turned a deep red and Doctor Otto exclaimed, "Aha! Just as I speculated, concentrated ferrous sulfite. Zack you and your wife were drinking what amounted to a highly toxic cocktail and if you had consumed enough of it, it could have killed you. Where did you get this wine, and do you have any left?"

I explained to Otto that there were almost a hundred bottles on the wine racks when we moved into the house seven years ago and we had been refilling the bottles with wine made from pressed grapes from our own vineyard on the back of the property. Otto jumped out of his chair.

"Let's go get some of those grapes right off the vine." We both scampered out to the vineyard and, grabbing a handful of ripe grapes, hurried back to the study. Otto mashed up the grapes in a mixing bowl, poured the juice into a clean test tube and performed his test again. In only a few seconds, the deep crimson color of the iron sulfite appeared in the bottom of the tube.

Otto looked at me over the top of his glasses and said, "I would not be at all surprised to get this high a reading from most anything that might be growing out there in that orchard. Just to be sure, I think we should analyze a shovel of dirt from about 12 inches below the topsoil. I'll bet it contains high amounts of iron sulfite."

It took us less than an hour to determine that the old professor was right. Everything on the hilltop was growing in soil heavily laced with iron. Otto thought for a minute and said he would also like to check the water for its iron content, in order to complete his report. We drew a pail of water from the outside well, the one where the horses watered, and the doc put the sample through the test. He found that the water also had high concentrations of iron, but when compared to the wine…the wine had ten times the amount of ferrous sulfite in it.

Otto began a short lecture, telling me how this heavy concentration of iron was essentially the lodestone the glaciers had piled up to make this hill eons earlier. He said that not only did the lodestone contain tremendous amounts of iron, it was the reason why compass needles always pointed north. Lodestone is highly magnetic.

Otto explained that in essence our home had been built atop one of these anomalies. "Unfortunately, you and your family have essentially been living on what amounts to an enormous dirt magnet. By eating the grapes and other fruits and vegetables grown in this soil, you have been consuming huge doses of iron."

The old guy was really living up to his reputation. In only one day he had solved the mystery of why we were accumulating the deadly concentration of iron in our blood. We were drinking it in that sweet-tasting wine from our basement wine racks and eating it in my wife's delicious cherry pies and the vegetables from our garden. Not only were we affected, but our animals were as well. The horses were driven crazy just from drinking the water and eating grass and perhaps the apples from the orchard.

Another thought came rushing into my head. People living here in the past, namely the judge and his long-term visitors, must have had the same problems with the iron content in their blood. They were doing the same things in this house we were doing: eating, drinking the water and, especially, the wine. The only difference was their illnesses and bizarre behavior must have gone on indefinitely because they had no idea that the very soil and water they lived on was poisoning them. Maybe, that's what killed some of those people buried out in the back forty.

The following day, about three o'clock in the afternoon, the professors got a chance to study the atmosphere with their sophisticated equipment. Far off on the horizon we could see a black line of angry looking storms. We could see lightning bolts shooting out of the dark, rapidly-moving clouds that were headed our direction.

The very minute Otto heard the thunder, he asked me to help him wheel outside the large apparatus we had stored in the garage. We moved it to the middle of an open field about five hundred feet from the rear of our house. It took the storm about an hour to reach our hill, but when it hit, our personal scientists were ready for it.

Otto had on his heavy black raincoat with a black rubber seafarer's hat, high black boots and a pair of heavy black rubber gloves. Joyce was dressed similarly, but her outfit was a feminine, ladylike pink. The violent lightning bolts that seemed to be striking all around our hill did not seem to frighten them at all. Looking like the Wizard of Oz and a female helper, Otto and Joyce studied their dials as the several weather vanes attached to the contraption swirled in every direction. One of the instruments that looked like a large voltage meter occasionally lit up when the lightning would strike.

Professor Schweitzer then did something really interesting. He inflated a rather large red balloon at the side of the machine and let it sail high up into the air, keeping it tethered to the instrument by a long line. While Otto was performing his "Ben Franklin" experiment, Joyce was walking to the bottom of the hill with still another instrument to take more readings.

The weather balloon was being buffeted by the high winds while Otto was studying the instruments. After a bit, he took one of the instruments from the front of his contraption and went into the house to look at the readings. Once he had removed all his rain gear, he used a waterproof slate and grease pencil to make some notes. As he worked he asked if Peggy Sue and I were feeling all right. We assured him we were fine, but I thought his question was peculiar until he said, "Did you know that your hair is standing on end?"

Peggy Sue and I looked at each other and laughingly told him this happened to us all the time during a thunderstorm. "In fact," I said, "the kids tease about it and just call it the frizzies. We thought it was resulting from static electricity in the carpets."

The professor said we were correct, that it was a form of static electricity, but the highly charged atmosphere surrounding the house was responsible for it. He then made a strange request of us. He asked us if we would mind getting two spoons from the kitchen pantry and lay them on the floor in the center of the hallway. We did as he requested. The moment we set the spoons on the floor, they began to vibrate. Suddenly, one of them flew to the ceiling and hung there, just as we had seen happen earlier.

I spoke up, "This has happened before when we were all sitting at the dinner table. The kids accused me of performing tricks!"

Otto said, "Yes, but those tricks were being played by Mother Nature. The spoon will fall when the storm weakens."

We heard Joyce come into the mudroom through the garage and Otto went out to speak with her. We overheard her saying that the atmospheric pressure was significantly lower here at the top of the hill than it was down below by the lake. She also said the wind speed seemed to accelerate as it hit the bottom of the hill. Then, she said the wind seemed to spiral to the top of the hill in a swirling vortex, then jettison itself up into the atmosphere. She described it as a giant wave of air that created a kind of lifting mechanism to the electrically charged particles surrounding the house.

I looked at Peggy Sue and said in a low mumble, "They might as well be speaking Greek. It sure doesn't make any sense to me. Maybe when everything calms down they can tell us what this all means in language we can understand."

I guess I didn't speak as quietly as I thought I had because Professor Schweitzer turned to us and said excitedly, "I thought I would never observe this phenomenon in my lifetime. But based on what Joyce has just told me, and my own measurements, I am pretty sure what we have here is an enormous, naturally occurring, oscillating magnet! It is changing from negative polarity to positive, then back again with each nearby lightning strike. Amazing, truly amazing!"

Just then, we saw a lightning bolt and immediately heard the spoon hit the hallway floor. Otto was really excited. "See, there…it has reversed. Fantastic!

"We almost have enough data to reach some definitive answers to your perplexing problems. I need a little time to recheck our figures and get the final readings from the equipment that's still running outside. We should have the results in a few hours,"

With that, he donned his rain gear again and walked out into the rain toward his big machine that was still gathering data.

Several hours later, the storm had passed and the rain

had stopped. The two scientists worked behind closed doors in the upstairs library, going over their final analysis of what had just occurred in the atmosphere during the intense electrical storm. They remained secluded until dinnertime when Peggy Sue called them down for one of her scrumptious meals.

After we had finished dinner and were enjoying steaming cups of coffee, Joyce began an explanation.

"If you recall, when I left your hospital room I told you that our findings might surprise and shock you. Well, I must say they truly have surprised and shocked us both. We agree on some important points, but the only way we can be totally certain is to do a brain scan on one of you after you have drunk at least one bottle of wine during an electrical storm.

"I'm not sure either one of you would want to go through that experience. First, based on the amount of lodestone just beneath the surface of this hill with its huge magnetic pull, Otto is convinced this house is right on top of part of a huge dirt magnet. Secondly, we applied my findings of the extreme variances in the atmospheric pressures and the tremendous acceleration and lifting effect of the wind, and reached some conclusions. We believe that each time a lightning bolt expended its energy nearby it would actually produce a temporary change in the polarity of the magnetic field. It would change from negative to positive and then back again, thereby completing the oscillating magnet.

"But now, here's the most important part. Living creatures in this proximity would also be affected. If they had a high concentration of iron in their blood streams and coursing through their craniums, these living creatures would become completely disoriented each time lightning would strike in the vicinity, activating the magnet and disrupting their brain's electrical impulses. This is almost akin to a person taking a shock treatment for some kind of mental psychosis.

"Due to the fact that both of you had such high concentrations of iron in your bloodstream, during thunderstorms you had to be hallucinating, almost in a state of insanity! We have both agreed this would also have been the cause of the strange behavior in your animals."

Otto and Joyce had also analyzed the amount of ozone gas that was created in the atmosphere during the lightning strikes. The amount was so high and so concentrated they believed it was possible the ozone had reached a state of plasma. They also thought the ionic polarity, being changed constantly from negative to positive, might have actually caused the gas to glow green. They concurred that this was the source of the green haze that hovered around the horse barn.

They also believed our horses were affected because of the iron content in their blood, caused by drinking the well water. They said this made them susceptible to the electrical impulses during storms, throwing them into an altered psychotic state that resulted in extreme violence.

"While it's true that you folks have not been consuming water with a high iron content, your last episode was definitely caused by the thunderstorm combined with drinking the old wine," Joyce said. "We recommend you destroy the remaining bottles and discontinue consuming produce from the orchard. We also think that it might be a good idea to get off this hill if you have advance warning of an approaching electrical storm."

"We can only speculate on the former inhabitants of this house. But we would almost guarantee that, based on what we now know, if they were in residence here for more than three or four weeks and consumed the water or the wine, the first electrical storm that passed through would probably have created some temporary insanity.

"Also," she continued, "prolonged stays of several

months could have resulted in multiple organ failure and eventually death."

Turning to Otto, she asked, "Did I miss anything?"

Otto put his fingers to his temple and said, "I would remind you, Peggy Sue, that anything you may have canned or frozen should also be thrown out. That's a real shame about the pies because they are wonderful."

The scientists told us they thought their evaluation was complete and they needed to return to the university the next morning.

"Oh, by the way," Otto said, "I hope you two will be agreeable to my using your names in a scientific paper I intend to publish on this subject in the near future." Peggy Sue and I agreed that Otto could use our names.

Early the next morning, the professors left the hill taking with them their measuring devices and our appreciation, praises and blessings. We couldn't tell them adequately how grateful we were. We truly believed they had possibly saved our lives and provided us with safeguards against future episodes of terror. As absurd as it seemed, it appeared the wine we so enjoyed and the brilliant lightning shows we had witnessed, together with the very ground we lived on were essentially combining in an unintentional effort to kill us. It amounted to an enormous electrical monster!

Not only did Joyce and Otto solve our medical problems; they had effectively explained the cause and effect of several strange phenomena surrounding our home. I believed they had given me an explanation of the behavior of Judge Levison and perhaps some of his guests, and a possible reason for the existence of the padded room upstairs.

Several weeks passed after the scientists had revealed to us answers to at least one of the great mysteries surrounding the mansion on the hill. We now knew that during electrical storms, living creatures on our hill were very vulnerable. We accepted the idea that high iron content in our blood, combined with the effects of electrical storms, could have produced hallucinations. However, we certainly were not hallucinating about the many other strange things surrounding the old house. Some of those questions were still unanswered.

For instance, why was the house built with secret passages and secret rooms? Who were the weird characters who lived here when the house was first built? Why had Sean and I been almost killed when he bolted into the lake? What about that ice ball that fell from the sky? That thing could easily have killed Peggy Sue. It was a reality, not a hallucination. The green fog was real. And the money in the old steel vault was also very, very real!

The children and Peggy Sue and I had never felt healthier. As a family, we were enjoying some luxuries we had bought with some of the money from the vault. Though we were sure, by now, that the money was not counterfeit and not marked, we were still a little apprehensive about having that much cash in the safe. I was pondering about what I should do with the money; so, one day after the children had gone off to school, Peggy Sue and I retreated to the basement to finish going through the multitude of papers and the old file cabinet in the vault room. We hoped going through all that material would give us a hint on how to proceed.

The cabinet had five drawers. In the top drawer in a large folder were several clippings from the *Chicago Tribune* referring to the shootings and killings of several men in a Chicago garage on St. Valentine's Day. In one of the articles, there was information indicating that a member of the Detroit Purple Gang had actually participated in the Chicago shootings. The article said it was believed at the time that the name of one of the assailants was Anthony Buglioni. The name in the article had been underlined by someone.

Several other clippings from the *Detroit News* and the *Free Press* addressed the killings of Purple Gang members at the Collingwood manor in northwest Detroit. One of the articles looked familiar, and I realized it was the same article I had requested and received from the *News* that tipped us off to the fact that the judge was really a racketeer.

The Buglioni name appeared several times in the article and had been circled in pencil.

Another article in the Detroit newspaper indicated that in September 1936 a gang war was raging in Detroit between various members of the Purple Gang. It was a battle over control of the gang. During this time, the article indicated, most gang activities had come to a standstill. It was believed that many members of the gang "went to the mattresses" and were hiding out at an unknown location, thought to be outside the Detroit area.

In another drawer, we found the original house plans for the mansion and several hundred receipts for building materials. I went over the papers quickly, looking for any more secret rooms and found none. I couldn't see where any of the secret places we had found were even indicated on the house plans. It was apparent that only Judge Levison, and perhaps the one who built the rooms, knew of their existence.

We also found a judge's black judicial robe in the drawer. Wrapped up inside the robe were some folders containing several case histories—one of which was a file on the Collingwood massacre.

To my wife's utter delight, we also found some pieces of antique jewelry. There were three beautiful necklaces in red velvet boxes; and there were also six of the most exquisite rings with diamonds and other precious stones Peggy Sue had ever seen.

In the very bottom drawer, wrapped in an old pillowcase, was another journal, similar to the others in the vault. This one was different, however, in a curious way. The pages in the book were blank except for nine names written on the first page of the book. Next to each of the names was noted a city and a date, one date as far back as 1937.

Also stuffed into the old pillowcase were more newspaper articles from various cities. Front page headlines described several killings. In dramatic detail, one article described a firefight involving several automobiles on opposite sides of a lonely stretch of road in Ypsilanti, Michigan. Apparently, several cars were riddled with bullet holes and dead bodies littered both sides of the road. Most of the dead were later identified as members of the Purple Gang. The Detroit newspaper attributed the homicides to an ongoing gang war.

Also mentioned in the newspaper articles were drive-by shootings and gangland style executions. Another article mentioned a well-known gang member in Toledo, Ohio. The gang member and the service station attendant who was filling his car with gasoline at the time were hit by machine gun fire which created a tremendous fireball when the gasoline exploded.

Each of these articles corresponded to a man's name written on the front page of the journal and to the date written beside it. Most articles mentioned the fact that the victims had no immediate family and that the bodies had been released from the morgue to Buglioni's Funeral Home.

This information explained the old black Packard in my old outbuilding. That hearse was registered to a guy named Buglioni, but that didn't give me any information other than the fact that he was someone who picked up dead bodies! It was evident, however, that Judge Levison was keeping score on guys that he killed or had killed by someone else. One thing was definite: those same guys were buried right here on this hill.

There was a large yellow envelope mixed in with the newspaper clippings. The envelope contained medical records from Eloise General Hospital in Ypsilanti, Michigan for a victim of gunshot wounds to the face. The initial medical report stated that the gunshot wounds were probably fatal, but subsequent reports indicated the patient's condition had stabilized.

According to the medical file, extensive surgeries followed in an attempt to repair damage to the patient's face. Bullets had torn away most of the jaw and cheekbone from the right side of the face, as well as the right eye. The bullets had also irreparably damaged a small portion of the lower brain. Multiple operations included grafting bones into the face, implanting an artificial eye, dentures and extensive plastic surgery. Speech therapy and rehabilitation were noted as being necessary follow-ups to treatment.

The records indicated a nine-month hospitalization, from December 1937 until August 1938. Charges for the services were several thousand dollars. All the medical bills included in the file were stamped "Paid in Cash." The patient's name was Seymour Levison!

Peggy Sue and I agreed that if the judge was in the hospital for nine months during 1937 and 1938 that would explain why the mansion was vacant for such a long time during that period. It was possible that during this time Bruno began acting as caretaker of the house, looking after things until the judge was able to return home.

I hadn't seen Bruno around the lake or in the fields for a long time, and I felt it was high time I paid him another visit at the cottage.

About a week later I was on my way to town and had a little extra time, so I thought I would stop and visit with Bruno. I pulled into his dirt driveway, noticed his pickup in its usual place beside the house, covered with the customary flock of chickens. The chickens had done their "business" on the pickup, causing the black paint to appear painted in polka dots. I got out of my Caddie and slammed the door. The noise sent the birds scattering in all directions. I hoped they wouldn't decide to perch themselves on my car that I had just washed the day before.

I went up to the door and knocked. When there was no answer, I knocked again; and then, once more. Then I walked over to a side window and knocked as hard as I could without breaking it. Still there was no response from inside. I thought it might be possible that Bruno was out walking in the fields, or maybe down at the lake fishing, but something just didn't feel right.

I tried the front door and found it locked. I went around to the back of the house. I knew there was no door in the back, but hoped that I might be able to see through a window. My first glance into the small bedroom at the rear of the house proved my hunch to be correct.

Bruno lay on the bed with his feet on the floor. It was apparent to me that he was either dead or extremely ill. I wasted no time, rushed to the door and kicked it with my foot as hard as I could. The door sprang open and I hurried through the small kitchen into the bedroom and Bruno. The stench in the room was awful. Bruno had vomited several times and had lost control of his bladder and bowels. His face was covered with what looked like dried coffee grounds and he didn't appear to be breathing.

I finally detected a faint pulse in the jugular vein in his neck. He was alive, but just barely. I knew I had to get medical attention for him quickly. I ran out to the car and drove as fast as possible back up the hill to a telephone to call for medical attention. The lone policeman in Clinton, Constable Schultz, answered my emergency call. I quickly told him about Bruno's condition and that I needed help immediately. Schultz said he was familiar with the location and would come out himself but it would take about 30 minutes to get there. He asked if I could give Bruno some basic medical attention myself. I assured him I would do my best but begged him to hurry and bring help with him.

I told Peggy Sue what had happened and she handed

me the small first aid kit she kept in the kitchen. I tore off back down the hill to see if there might be something I could do to help Bruno until medical attention arrived. When I got back to the cabin, I opened the first aid kit and took out the smelling salts. I opened the bottle and waved it under the opening where his nose should be. He squinted up his face and I noticed he was trying to open his eyes. I told him in a loud voice that help was on the way and he was going to be all right. I was absolutely convinced that my statement was totally false because he looked as if he had already died and was just waiting to be buried.

Thirty minutes after my telephone call, I heard the siren of the constable's police car. I went outside to direct him into the house. Constable Schultz was accompanied by three Clinton Fire Department volunteers in an ambulance. Bringing up the rear of the three-car caravan was a white, four-door Buick driven by an elderly man.

The firefighters hurried into the cabin with their emergency equipment and began working on Bruno. Constable Schultz also came in and checked out the premises for any indications of mishap or accident.

The medics were strapping on oxygen mask over Bruno's face. Then I saw them open his shirt and push a long needle into his chest, injecting a white substance directly into his heart. Another of the emergency workers was taking his blood pressure and a third was injecting something into Bruno's arm. After working on him for about ten minutes, the firefighters slid Bruno onto a gurney and headed out to the ambulance. These guys really seemed to know their stuff and when I asked about Bruno's condition, I was told hurriedly, "He's still alive."

Just as they were about to slide the gurney into the back of the ambulance, I noticed the person in the Buick was standing nearby. I asked him if he was a doctor. He was wearing a three-piece suit and a hat and looked like a professional to me. He told me he was not a physician but was on his way home to his cottage on the lake several miles up the road when the emergency vehicles raced past him and turned on Collier Road.

He said he knew there was only one house out here and thought he would follow the ambulance to see what had happened. Holding out his hand, he introduced himself as Clarence Sullivan. I shook hands with Mr. Sullivan and gave him my name. I told him I now lived in the house on the hill. His response to me was intriguing.

"Oh, I once knew somebody who lived up there." Just then, he looked down at the body on the stretcher as it was being loaded into the ambulance.

"Hey, I know that guy! He's got a face I could never forget," he said. I asked how he knew Bruno and his response staggered me.

"Bruno? When I knew him, all us guys just called him Mumbles because you couldn't understand half of what he said."

As the medics closed the door to the ambulance, I asked them where they would be taking Bruno for treatment. They said they were headed for the University of Michigan Medical Center. I quickly yelled out to them to notify Dr. Piatt and tell him the patient is Zack Heikel's neighbor. As the ambulance drove away, I quickly turned back to Mr. Sullivan.

"Are you sure it's the same person? He's an old man in real bad shape, so you could be making a mistake. Where did you know Bruno and what guys are you talking about?"

He hesitated a minute before answering, like he was trying to avoid my question. "Yeah, it's the same guy. How could you forget him. I just hope Mumbles, or Bruno as you call him, doesn't suffer much longer. He will probably welcome death. He's had a real tough life."

"What in the world are you talking about? Please, Mr.

Sullivan, where and when did you know Bruno?" I asked, returning immediately to my initial question to Mr. Sulllivan.

Getting back in his Buick, he said very nonchalantly, "Man, it's a long story. I'm almost eighty years old now and will probably take it to my grave. But, who knows, maybe I'll get it off my chest and tell somebody some day, maybe even you." Without another word, he slammed the Buick's door and drove off in a cloud of dust, leaving me gagging on it because my mouth was so wide open!

My mind was racing with all kinds of possibilities as I followed the ambulance to the hospital. That guy had just appeared right out of the blue and sure seemed to know something about Bruno and the house. I knew it was mandatory that I speak with him again before, as he put it "he takes it to the grave." Apparently, he had several missing pieces of the puzzle which, if they fit, could put the entire mosaic together and finally unravel the mystery of the mansion.

How this guy knew what he knew I could only speculate about, but I figured I'd just have to wait until I met up with him again to find out. My main concern now was getting to the hospital and making sure Bruno received proper care. I was almost certain he had no medical insurance, but for some reason I felt duty bound to cover his medical expenses, regardless of the cost. After all, I had millions in cash in my own house.

I was certain now, more than ever before, that Bruno, the house, Judge Levison and the cash were all intertwined. How they were all connected, I wasn't sure, but I was willing to bet that after I talked to Mr. Sulllivan again, I would have my answers.

I turned my thoughts back to the present as I hurried into the emergency room. I arrived to find Dr. Piatt and several nurses hovering around Bruno. He had tubes coming out of the nasal hole in his face and IV's in both arms. Dr.

Piatt addressed me, "Zack, do you know this poor, unfortunate person? When the medics told me he was your neighbor I took it upon myself to admit him. Does he have any relatives or any kind of health coverage that you know about? If he doesn't, I can't keep him here. If he lives, which I don't think he will for very long, he's going to need constant care. It's a miracle this guy lived to be as old as he is with the kinds of medical problems he has.

"We found several old gunshot wounds on his body and two of the slugs are still in him. And that's in addition to the terrible deformities to his face. He's got to be at least 80 years old and has suffered plenty."

A thought passed through my head. Mr. Sullivan was right; Bruno had done a lot of suffering.

I told Dr. Piatt that I appreciated his admitting my neighbor to the hospital and that I was quite certain he had no relatives. I also said that if Bruno did not have health insurance, I was prepared to cover the costs for him.

"That's fine," Dr. Piatt said, "but there's one more thing. What is this man's name? I admitted him as a John Doe."

I stammered around a little bit myself and said, "Well, as a matter of fact, I don't know what his last name is. I have always just called him Bruno because that's what he said his name was. I guess until we can ascertain what his real name is we could just call him Bruno Levison. I think that would be appropriate because the judge employed him for years as a caretaker."

I explained to the doctor that Judge Levison had owned the house I now lived in and that Bruno still lived on the property. "For that reason, I feel a little bit responsible for him."

Dr. Piatt told me he would do his best to make Bruno comfortable but he was afraid there was little else that could be done. "He has cirrhosis of the liver and most of his other organs are damaged and shutting down. I would give him a few days at best."

I asked Dr. Piatt if Bruno had regained consciousness and was told that he was awake and stable, at least for the time being. Dr. Piatt said I should wait until the next morning to talk with him.

The next morning I arrived at the hospital and was told by a nurse that Bruno's vital signs were weakening and I should keep my visit short. I knew that any questions I asked Bruno would have to be asked now because it was apparent he wasn't going to live much longer. When I entered his room, he was awake but connected to life-sustaining equipment. I said hello and, telling another little white fib, said he was looking much better. Essentially, he still looked like he was already dead.

I asked him if he felt well enough to talk for a few minutes and answer some questions for me. He nodded his head affirmatively. I quickly asked him what year he became the caretaker at the house. When he spoke, his utterances were worse than usual and I couldn't understand one thing he was saying. I stepped out to the nurses' station and got a pad and pencil.

I repeated my question and he scribbled haltingly on the pad, "1937. Not caretaker. Judge's driver and bodyguard"

My next question was "Where did you drive the judge?" Again in his scrawl, he wrote, "Where he needed to go. Sometime pick up bags of money."

Then, I asked a most important question, "Bruno, what happened in 1937 when you were driving the judge? Was he injured?"

Bruno wrote, "Judge shot by gang. Want money." I immediately asked him what gang had shot the judge.

"Bad guys from purple gang shoot judge in face. I take to hospital, he stay months. I not work this time and hide in room on Collingwood. They look for me. I have bags."

Now that I had him thinking I quickly asked. "Were you driving the big black car that is parked in the garage on the hill when the judge was shot?"

He wrote quickly as if he knew what I was going to ask him. "Yes, but I get even. I kill them with my red devil."

I thought for a minute and remembered the red-handled sub-machine gun and I asked, "The Red Devil is a machine gun isn't it, Bruno?" He answered yes.

Finally, he was opening up to me about a lot of things he had done, so I asked him another question, "Are these the men that are buried on the hill?"

"Yes," he wrote, "except three. Two die in cement room in basement, one upstairs."

"You mean in the cell that is under the fireplace?" I asked, and again he indicated I was right. I could tell Bruno was getting very tired but I had to keep him writing. I had to know why these men were in the cell. "Bruno, why were these men locked up?"

He wrote, almost seeming to gain strength, "When judge get out of hospital, he find they bad. They bosses, wear ring, but steal money from mob. Judge say to me no shoot, bring to hill. He sentence them to years in small jail, silent room upstairs. They all die. I going to die? Hope so. Belly hurt bad."

Bruno has asked me the question with a sincere but pained look on his face. He was coming clean with me so I thought I had to tell him the truth. "Yes, Bruno, you are going to die; we are all going to die."

His reply tugged at my heart when he wrote, "You nice with me. Can you bury me? Want nice tombstone. I have nobody. You take cat?"

I told Bruno sympathetically, and with a catch in my voice, "Yes, Bruno, I'll bury you and I will see to it that you get a nice headstone. And, the cat is already at my house. Don't worry about your hospital bills. I'll cover them for you."

Quickly he grabbed the pad and wrote, "No need. I have money, lots of money in chicken coop in steel box under bench and you take this,(he took off a ring from his hand and gave it to me saying,) is very valuable, but you never put on finger." I accepted the ring and slipped it into my pants pocket. Of course, when I read the line on the note about the metal box and money, I envisioned another sight like the one that greeted me behind the vault doors in the basement of the house, but I knew that would be ridiculous.

I thought of another question for Bruno. "Were you ever in the silent room upstairs?" I hoped his answer would clear up some loose ends. But his answer startled me.

"Many times. When my head hurt, when thunder and lightning scare me. Judge bring food and water. Sometime I stay in room many, many days. Could not control anger."

Just as I was getting ready to ask Bruno my next question—had he ever cut off three men's fingers—a big burly nurse walked in and said in a huff, "You know you're grilling a dying man. Why don't you leave him alone a while; say, like come back tomorrow." I'm glad I hadn't got that last question out of my mouth as she was walking in the door.

I figured, anyway, his answer would probably have been the same. "Yes."

"Okay," I said, "you're right, but I had to get some answers from him and, quite frankly, he has made my day. He has solved a lot of riddles that have been going through my mind for years. Would tomorrow morning at about 10 o'clock be all right for me to visit again?"

Her soft-spoken reply was, "Yes, if he's still alive."

As I left the hospital, I was feeling very sad. I was probably about to lose my neighbor, a quiet man who loved his cat. Sure, he was extremely ugly physically, and he was sorta spooky; but I knew he wouldn't hurt a flea now.

He had shared the bounty of his garden with us and, often, he would leave a basket of vegetables beside the driveway at the bottom of the hill. But, most of all, I would be eternally grateful to the hunchbacked, deformed old man who had pulled me from the sure death of Lake Misty. Then, it suddenly flashed through my mind about the dialogue that had just passed between us. I realized that Bruno, in spite of his diminished mental capacity and quiet nature, was nothing but a *cold-blooded killer*.

On the drive home, I thought about the machine gun and the fact that it had been used as a murder weapon. Somehow I felt that implicated me in the killings. I thought maybe I should notify the police about its existence. But then, I considered that if I turned it over to the police, I would be opening up a big Pandora's box and would surely not be able to keep the money I had found in the vault. I also thought about the fact that the men killed here were all notorious mobsters and they probably had no living relatives; the judge who had passed sentence on them—either to have Bruno kill them or to lock them up in the small cell—he was dead; and Bruno himself was about to be put in his own grave.

I knew that keeping the money might not be the right thing to do, but there sure was a lot of it and I would put it to good use! I was feeling better about it. I had accepted the responsibility to pay Bruno's hospital bill and I would buy him the biggest, most outlandish tombstone I could find around here with some of the loot.

As I passed by the now-empty cabin where Bruno lived, I thought about the metal box in the chicken coop. I whipped my Caddie into the driveway and jumped out in the silence of my neighborhood. Except for the occasional cluck of a chicken, it was eerily quiet. Quickly, I headed for the chicken coop. Shooing several of the fowl out of my way and off the bench, I knelt down and looked under it. Behind several old boxes, I saw it—an old black steamer trunk, like the ones in my garage that obscured the old Packard. Reaching in, I slid it from beneath the bench. I could see clearly that it wasn't locked. The latch had been broken off. Lifting the cover, I saw a tray with handles on each side. The tray held several pairs of socks, some old suspenders and moth-eaten shirts. Beneath one of the shirts lay a black revolver. I picked it up and saw that it was a 38-caliber police special. Stamped above the caliber-mark was "Detroit Police Judiciary," indicating it had been issued to a member of the judicial bench for personal protection.

This had to be Judge Levison's handgun because it was in Bruno's trunk. I was willing to wager he also used it in some of the shootings in which he was involved. Bruno must have planned to use this gun to protect himself and his stash because the pistol was fully loaded.

I grasped the handles and lifted the tray out of the trunk. The bottom was littered with empty money wrappers, each one with the customary $2,000 printed on it. I scooped most of them out of the old locker and dropped them at my feet. There must have been hundreds of them, all empty. Then, in one corner of the locker, I noticed more wrappers but these were not empty. They still contained $100 bills. I removed nine packets of bills, which I figured contained $18,000. I figured this was all that was left of an original small fortune. Judging from the size of the trunk and the number of empty money wrappers, I figured there had once been as much as $200,000 in it. Now, I understood the reason for the 38 being in the top tray. I wasn't sure if the judge had given this money to Bruno or if maybe this was the loot the gang was trying to take from the judge the night he was shot.

I had a pretty good inkling that the judge had given the money to Bruno to live on and it had sustained him for several years. I noticed some legal-looking documents in the bottom of the trunk. Without reading them, I shoved them in my back pocket. Then, I noticed an old brown briefcase on the very bottom of the trunk. I picked it up, carefully opened it and saw it was stuffed with papers and several articles.

One of the articles was a small tin box, opening it revealed the diamond stick pin that Judge Levison wore in the portrait that hung over my fireplace. Other items in the briefcase were some loose coins, a few dollar bills rolled up with a rubber band holding them together and a black box which contained of all things, the silver signet ring the judge also wore in the painting. I reasoned that these things were probably personal items the judge had on when he died and were given to Bruno by the funeral home when he picked up the judge's body. I noticed a yellow envelope and opening it I removed a tattered and very brittle document. As I carefully unfolded it, I got the shock of my life. It was a birth certificate, written in what appeared to be Italian. Though it was hard to decipher, I was certain of two items recorded on it. One was the birth date of April 5, 1896; and the other was the name of the child whose birth this document recorded, *Anthony Buglioni.*

I could hardly contain myself. I was completely overwhelmed by what this document revealed. Finally, I knew who Anthony Buglioni was, but I needed to hear it from his own lips.

Replacing everything I had found back into the briefcase and before closing it, I remembered the ring Bruno had just given me, so for safe keeping I dropped it into the briefcase also. I slipped in the revolver, the money and all of the empty money wrappers. I did not want these to be found someday and create suspicion. I certainly did not want the pistol to be found especially this particular gun! Ballistics might be able to link it to some of the shootings mentioned in the old newspaper articles—and that would be it. I would have blown the whole secret. I took the briefcase out to my car, placed it in the trunk for safekeeping and headed off to the hospital to confront Bruno with the birth certificate.

There wasn't a night nurse at the station, so I walked directly into his room. It was empty. At first I thought I had the wrong room, but just then the nurse appeared and asked who I was looking for. I hesitantly said, "Why, Anthony Buglioni," then quickly caught myself and said, "Oh, I mean Bruno Levison, the man who was in this room.

The nurse softly said, "He expired and is in our morgue waiting for the family to designate a funeral home."

I was so saddened by his death even though I had known it was imminent. And, I was disappointed I hadn't had a chance to ask Bruno if he was, in fact, Anthony Buglioni. I told the nurse I was responsible for his body as well as his hospital costs.

"What mortuary will you be using? Hill Brothers Funeral Home is the closest one."

I said that would be fine and asked the nurse to tell them to use the very best casket available and that I would be contacting them in the morning. I also told the nurse I would visit the accounting department the next day and take care of all the hospital charges.

Suddenly, I felt very tired, mentally and physically. I took my leave of the nurse and told her I would be back tomorrow.

"All right, then. I will call Billy or Harold, the Hill boys, and have your friend's body picked up," she said as she disappeared up the dark hall.

I dropped into the front seat of my car and pulled away from the hospital; and, before I even realized it, I was pulling into my own driveway. I went straight to bed without dinner and slept better than I had in weeks, having solved several of the mysteries that had been playing with my mind for years.

The next morning, I told Peggy Sue what I had found in the steamer trunk in the chicken coop behind Bruno's cabin. I tried to help control her astonishment when she learned that Bruno was, in fact, the mystery man Anthony Buglioni. After I had convinced her that the birth certificate was valid, she finally believed I wasn't just kidding her. One of the documents I had stuffed into my back pocket turned out to be a bill of sale for the old shack and four acres of land, sold to none other than Tony Buglioni and signed by Judge Seymour T. Levison.

The old judge knew Bruno was born Buglioni in Italy and might have used it against him. It did appear that Anthony Buglioni was an illegal immigrant because there was nothing in the trunk indicating U.S. citizenship. Maybe the judge had been threatening him with deportation if Bruno refused to do his bidding. Maybe because Bruno was slightly retarded and in the country illegally, he fell for that ploy. I did a lot of speculating, realizing that most anything was possible where the judge and Bruno were concerned.

Finally, I picked up my checkbook and headed back to the hospital. The accounting department had all the charges neatly calculated for the hospital stay of only three days. The cost of the drugs and equipment used, and the doctors' services came to $9,267. I wondered if the hospital would accept cash or if I would have to give a check. The clerk said cash would be fine, so I removed an envelope from my jacket that contained $100 bills from the vault. I counted out 93 of them. The clerked stamped the bill, "Paid in Full in Cash."

After settling the account, I tracked down my old friend Dr. Ed Piatt and thanked him for his courageous attempt to save my neighbor's life. He was curious about one thing, however, and asked me if I knew if Bruno had been in World War I because he had so many old bullet wounds and injuries to his body.

Not letting on that I knew anything at all about Bruno's violent past, I just said, "Who knows? Your guess is as good as mine. Maybe it was hunting accidents."

Trying to change the subject, I asked Ed for directions to the Hill Funeral Parlor. He told me it was just up Highway 12, past Suicide Ridge. Then, I remembered that I had visited the funeral home several years ago when I first met Bruno and found there were bodies buried on my property. I got on the road and when I passed the Wagon Wheel Bar where Outhouse Van Sickel held court, I knew I was getting close to the funeral home. Shortly, I saw it on my right, just about half a mile away.

Walking into the funeral parlor, I passed the office just inside the front door. I noticed a familiar face at the desk. Stepping inside the office, I said, "Hello, Billy, remember me?"

His response was immediate, "Sure, you're Matt, the guy who lives on the hill and who Bruno scared the shit out of that day a few years ago. Yeah, I remember when you came rushing in here all scared and flustered."

Irritated by the rough description of our first meeting and getting off on the wrong foot, I said, "Almost correct, you got part of it right. I'm Zack, not Matt. We need to get our names straight. As a matter of fact, I almost called *you* Hillbilly when I found out you were one of the Hill boys!" I let him soak that in for a second and then I said, "And speaking of correct names, I have a flash for you. That's not a guy named Bruno you have in there in the casket."

Billy stood up and brushed doughnut crumbs off his shirt, took a sip of coffee and said rather indignantly, "The hell it ain't; there's only one guy in these parts with a face like that. It's him all right."

I really didn't want to get in an argument with this joker, especially in a funeral home, but I had narrowly missed doing that by jokingly reversing his name. I wondered how he would react when I told him Bruno's real name.

"You have the right body and the face that goes with it, but his name is not Bruno, it's Anthony Buglioni.

Billy got all uppity and showed me the papers from the hospital that indicated the person he picked up was Bruno Levison. I jumped into the middle of his conversation to try and calm him down. I told him he hadn't made a mistake.

"I gave the hospital the name Bruno Levison because I didn't know what his real name was until I went through some of his old papers. I found his birth certificate," I said as I pulled the document from my hip pocket. I handed the fragile document to Billy saying, "Take a look at this."

His response, after looking at the birth document, was "You're just in time. I was getting ready to go to the hospital for the final death certificate in the name of Bruno Levison. Now we can at least get the poor guy buried with the correct name. I need to make a copy of this birth certificate for the coroner's records."

While he was at the copy machine, he turned to me and said, "Do you know if Bruno, I mean Anthony, would want a religious service?"

"I doubt that very much," I said, "knowing what I have just recently found out. His soul is probably already in the smoking section of hell."

Raising his eyebrows, Billy then asked, "Have you selected a grave site for him?"

"Yes, I have. I want to bury him out on the same small hilltop that the judge is buried on. Does the law still permit me to do that?"

Billy was slipping on his suit coat and straightening his tie in preparation for the trip to the hospital to get the death certificate. He began to look very professional! "It's perfectly legal and I can get you a couple of men with strong backs and a horse-drawn wagon that can get the casket through the woods and up the hill," he said. "They can also dig the grave by hand. It will only cost you a couple of hundred."

I told him that was mighty kind of him and asked him to make the arrangements as soon as possible. Then I asked him how much the service and the casket would cost. He pulled open a drawer on his desk and took out a form and pushed it across the desk at me. I picked it up and saw it was an invoice for $3,715. Looking down at the total, I asked what was beginning to be one of my favorite questions, "Is cash okay?"

With a smile, Bill said, "That works best for me." I quickly pulled out the envelope containing the $100 bills and counted out 38 of them. I laid the pile of money on the desk and told Billy to keep the $85 in change.

Smiling again, he said, "It's really unusual for us to receive a tip, but I really do appreciate it." I noticed he slipped the whole wad of bills into his pocket. He asked if I wanted to "view the remains," as well as the casket I had purchased. I said I would like to do that.

As we approached the parlor to view the body, Billy put his fingers to his lips as if telling me to be quiet. "We don't want to disturb the person who is in with Bruno, paying his last respects." As I stepped through the doorway, I was almost floored by who was kneeling alongside the casket. It was Clarence Sullivan.

Billy said in a whisper, "Do you men know one another?" I told him we had met. "Well, then I'll leave you two alone and get over to pick up the death certificate," he said as he headed out the door.

Clarence and I shook hands and I asked him what he was doing at the funeral home.

"Paying my respects to the newly-departed as any good Catholic would do, and God knows this guy needed praying over." I was still a little irritated from my conversation with Billy Hill and Sullivan's comment didn't help my condition much.

So, I said sarcastically, "You know, Mr. Sullivan, you keep hitting me with these insinuations that you know a lot about Bruno. When the hell are you going to let me in on what you are referring to?"

His reply was just as elusive as ever when he said, "In

time, my friend, in time. I first need to find out what kind of man you are. I must say I am impressed by the way you are handling Bruno's death and arranging for his funeral. I also heard you paid his hospital bill in full. Not only am I sure he would appreciate what you did for him, I do also. I can tell you are a kind and compassionate guy, but can you be trusted?"

"There you go again, damn it, can't you say anything that makes sense?" I sputtered. "As far as what I'm doing for Bruno, that's between him and me. It was something I promised him and I always keep my promises." I just shook my head as I tried to figure the guy out.

"That must have cost you a pretty penny. What did you do, inherit some money or hit a jackpot?" Sullivan's comment sent a quick shudder up my spine and made me think, "does he know something about the vault or is he just fishing?"

This guy was as cagey as I had ever seen. I knew the way I responded would go a long way in defusing any further questions he might have about my spending a large sum of money on a neighbor whom I really knew little about. Finally, I spoke up after a few seconds of us eyeballing each other. "I don't see where it's any of your business how I spend my dough, but in this case, seeing that you are a self-admitted old friend of Bruno's and someone I want to continue talking with, I won't insult you and just tell you to go to hell.

"You see, I plan on getting back the four acres and the old shack where Bruno lived. It was part of my place at one time, so I think it's worth my investment in Bruno's affairs, so to speak. It might give me some leverage with whoever inherits the place."

Mr. Sullivan replied with a little chuckle in his voice, "I don't think you need to worry about any of Bruno's relatives coming out of the woodwork. There aren't any. The guy was smuggled into this country as a kid from Italy to do certain illegal things for a kind of club—a sportsmen's club, so to speak."

All the while he was speaking, I was thinking. This guy is talking in nothing but riddles and just when I get rid of the mystery of Anthony Buglioni, then this joker shows up on the scene and takes his place!

One thing I knew for certain. He said he was a Catholic so that eliminated him from being one of the old knights. They were all Jews. This guy wore no rings on his fingers. He might have been in one of the mobs, but certainly he wasn't one of the bosses and thereby not privy to any of the knights' secrets. However, I was sure he had most of the puzzle pieces I was missing. I just had to coax them out of him. To do so, I felt I needed to befriend the elusive old fart.

Finally, Sullivan's mouth stopped moving and I started talking, "Mr. Sullivan, you say you knew someone who once lived at my place. Were you ever in the house?"

He got that sheepish smirk on his face again and said, "Ever in that house? Many times, my friend, many times, although it was a long time ago."

"Then you must have known Mr. Levison pretty good?" I asked, leading him on.

His answer did not surprise me at all when he said, "Yes, I knew him. Not well, but I knew him even as far back as when he was on the bench in Detroit. Very few people ever got real close to him. He was a real strange person and trusted no one."

I could feel this guy really beginning to open up to me. I felt that if I could get him up to the house he would eventually spill the beans. So, I took a chance and said to him, "You know, Mr. Sullivan, my wife and I have done a lot of renovations to the old place and I bet you would be surprised at the changes we've made. I was just thinking, my wife is planning a Christmas party in a few weeks and we are going to have cocktails at our house and then dinner at the

Bauer Manor. I was wondering if you would like to attend. You would get a chance to look around the house; and, on top of that, you'd get a nice free meal."

Looking somewhat surprised at my invitation, he said, "Boy, it's been a long time since I've been to anything. I more or less restrict myself to just a few trips to town a month for supplies. The rest of the time I spend fishing or reading. Being without family, I find it lonesome sometimes, but it's not a bad life. Yes, I would like to take you up on your offer of the guided tour and, of course, the free dinner. I never pass up anything that's free of charge.

"I don't have a mailing address," he continued. "So, when you need to reach me about the exact date and time, you can leave a note in the odd-shaped mailbox on the point, at the south shore of Evans Lake. I'll get it. You see, I live on an island in the middle of the lake and get back and forth using an old speedboat. You can't miss the mailbox. It has my name on it, Speedy Sullivan. That's the name I go by and, if you like, you may call me Speedy. Also, my Buick is always parked nearby."

Clarence Sullivan held out his hand for me to shake and started for the exit. I didn't invite him to Bruno's burial because I didn't want him to see the judge's gravesite. I just said, "All right then, I'll just leave you a note a few days before the event. Take care of yourself, Speedy."

He waved as the door closed behind him, but I managed to hear him mutter, "If I don't, nobody else will."

I guess Billy Hill wasted no time getting in touch with the gravediggers, because he called early the next morning and said the men were ready to leave for my place. He asked if I had the spot picked out where Bruno was going into the ground. He reminded me, also, that I was to pay the guys the two hundred bucks.

I was a little surprised by the suddenness of it all but said, "Sure, come on out. I have a nice spot picked out and I have the money. Are you sure they can get back up into those hills?"

"No problem!" he said. "Following the hearse with the body will be a pickup truck and trailer with the cart and a couple of nags in it. Don't worry, they'll get Bruno in the ground. And, if you're real nice to them they might even say a few words over the grave."

"That's okay," I replied. "I planned on doing that myself, but thanks for the suggestion; and, by the way, thanks for everything. You've been very kind."

Very business-like in his manner, he replied, "You are certainly welcome; it's just part of our service. As for being kind, I think you take the cake for kindness. For a guy that had the shit scared out of him by Bruno, you sure have changed. The way you have befriended him and handled his funeral, you're the one who should be complimented."

I was a little embarrassed by that. "Well, the poor guy had nobody and he was always friendly toward me, so I thought a decent burial was the least I could do." Actually, in the back of my mind, I was starting to question my true motive in all this. Was I trying to keep people away to avoid any questions about the strange happenings on the hill? Was I thereby protecting my main concern, *the money*…or was I being, as Billy had said, "kind?"

I managed to convince myself that I really did like the old hunchback. Even though he had a sordid past, I knew him as only a good neighbor and, on one occasion, my lifesaver!

About an hour later, the hearse and pickup arrived. I met them and directed them to a side road next to Bruno's cabin. They unloaded the horses and the small cart, harnessed the horses to the cart, threw a few shovels into the back along with some rope, and tied the casket to the small conveyance. Then, it was off to the knoll at the rear of the property where the makeshift "cemetery" was located and the other people were buried.

It proved to be relatively easy going for the two-horse team. The horses had plenty of muscle power and in a short time, with my leading the way, we arrived at the burial site. This summer's heavy growth of vegetation had almost completely obscured the small hilltop and the handmade grave marker Bruno had made for the judge. However, one of the men did see it and both guys became very inquisitive. They started asking questions, which I didn't particularly like.

I tried immediately to put their minds at ease by telling them that the Hill brothers knew all about the grave; that it was perfectly legal, and it was registered with the funeral home. The reply I got told me I had said just the right things.

"Well, that's all right. If they know about it, then it must be okay to bury someone out here. I guess we're a long way from any city limits anyway."

I hurriedly directed them to the area where I wanted the hole dug and they set out with a man on either side, armed with shovels. The guys could really move a lot of dirt and in less than an hour they had the hole down to about six feet in depth. Then they placed ropes under the casket. With a man on either side of the hole, they worked their way into position over the open grave. Using the two ropes, they lowered the casket into the yawning hole.

I asked the men for a moment of silence, said a small prayer aloud and listened to my words seeming to echo off the silent cedar trees. Then, I asked the men to fill the hole, which they finished very quickly.

When they were done with their work, the workmen began to meander around the hilltop. Suddenly, I heard one of them shout, "Hey! It looks like there are more graves dug in this area."

Lord, on hearing this, I shuddered and quickly called the men over to get the two hundred dollars I owed them. I took two bills from the white envelope I had refilled with hundreds. I showered the men with compliments and commented on how easy they had made the job look. I patted them on the back, I smiled a lot.

"Will you guys be able to find your way back down to the road?" I asked, hoping against hope they would take the hint and get out of there! Surprisingly, they did. They jumped up onto the wagon seat, clicked at the horses, and were soon disappearing in the woods. Was I ever relieved!

I understood that my anxiety about the men just being on the hilltop was getting way close to paranoia. But, I knew I was getting paranoid because I had to keep the secret of what was residing in my basement. It was just that—a secret!

As I stood on the hilltop next to Bruno's resting place listening to the breeze rustle through the leaves and enjoying the sweet smell of autumn in the air, a lone songbird whistled in low tones—as if playing Taps for the old guy. I thought about how peaceful it was here and how Bruno was finally at rest. In death he had been mercifully separated from the horribly disfigured, aching old body he had occupied for over eighty years.

I thought about the twisted and frightening memories he must have constantly endured and been haunted by. Those long road trips, the loud staccato noises made by firing the Red Devil, the sounds of pumping out the slugs pounding his eardrums; the smell of gunpowder; the gruesome sight of the bodies torn up by bullets that exploded into their flesh—all that was gone now. Bruno was finally removed from the pain and misery of trying to recover from gunshot wounds or other injuries received in some of the raids. He no longer had to remember the long days and nights spent in the padded room when magnetism caused his brain to misfire and he couldn't control himself. No longer did he have to relive the anguish of doing the bidding of the sinister Judge Levison. The memory of all that mental and physical torture was now put to rest. At least Bruno's body was settled here on a peaceful knoll. Sadly, I figured his soul was somewhere else…I'm certain, in Hell.

As I looked at the pile of fresh dirt heaped upon the new grave, I visualized where I would place the elaborate headstone I had promised Bruno would be erected.

As I pondered this, I also thought about the other poor souls buried on this hilltop. True, they were probably all evil and bloodthirsty gangsters and killers, but they had been human beings. Once, they were all smiling little children whose mothers loved and doted over them. I wondered why they went wrong in life. Was it just a matter of chance? Some people believe we are all preordained to take a particular path in life. Well, whatever the cause, these were all bad guys in every sense of the word. Nevertheless, I felt a strange kind of kinship to the men buried up here, especially to Bruno and, in some small way, even to the despicable old judge. Those two had occupied the deep and hidden recesses of my mind for several years and they had occupied my thinking on many a sleepless night when I wondered about their lives and activities.

It sounds bizarre, but for some reason, I worried about the other men on this hill in unmarked graves. I wanted to acknowledge them in some offhand way, but I didn't want to arouse suspicion about who they were or why they died. I just wanted some little something to let the world know these men were at one time alive on this earth.

Then, it came to me. I decided that when I ordered the tombstone for Bruno I would also have a small stone marker made. In generic terms only, revealing no names, the stone would just acknowledge those buried on the peaceful little knoll.

The very next morning, I thumbed through the telephone book for the Ann Arbor area. I found a large ad for monuments and took off for town, leaving Peggy Sue at home after telling her I felt a need to do this alone.

The monument company was quite large and had an array of headstones from which to select. The stones could be cut in any number of ways. I explained to the stone cutters that I wanted a large piece of black granite, at least seven feet tall. I wanted the stone highly polished and I wanted the words etched in white on the face of the marker. I was told that this was not an unusual request, that they had supplied many stones in the same fashion. I talked with them about the smaller marker, saying I wanted a tablet in rose-colored Italian marble. I explained that the markers were to be placed in a small private cemetery on my own property. I thought they might be surprised to learn that the graveyard was actually at my house, back in the woods of the Irish Hills, but I was relieved to learn the only concern was whether or not an automobile or pickup could get to the site.

I explained they probably would need a farm tractor pulling a small flatbed trailer to carry the stones to the site.

The manager who was taking my order said they would probably have to come out to the site and pour a concrete base, sturdy enough to hold the heavy black granite stone. After the cement was poured, he said it would be necessary to wait to set the marker until after the first frost had hardened the ground. I said there was no hurry and that erecting the stones in the winter would be better anyway. Frequently, at warmer times of the year, the ground is often wet and almost impassable.

Now that we had selected the method of transporting and erecting the monuments, it was time for me to give them the inscriptions I had decided to use. I had been thinking a lot about the wording I wanted cut into these headstones. I wasn't concerned about the vital statistics like name, dates of birth and death, but about the statement that would summarize in a few words the life of the deceased. After thinking about it for more than an entire day, these are the words I selected for Bruno:

Here Lies
Anthony Buglioni
"Bruno"
April 5, 1896
November 19, 1977
This is not a handsome man
In fact, he was ugly and lived
A horrible and terrifying life
He did, however, on occasion
Show great compassion and once
Saved a man from death by drowning.
This man's life might have been
Completely different had he not been
Taken advantage of due to his
Diminished mental capacity...
And, who knows
He might have become someone
Loved and famous.
May his soul finally rest in the peace
That always seemed
To elude him here on Earth.
A Friend

The other tablet I ordered inscribed in this way:
All those interred here
Were once loved by someone
Their lives did not turn out happy
But very sad.
Where their souls now reside is left
To the Almighty
But those reading this are now aware
These humans once lived...
And the reason for this marker
Is Fulfilled.
A Dreamer

Once I finished giving the manager the order, he exclaimed that with so much engraving the stones might have to be much larger. I told him I understood that and asked that he figure the complete price of the stones, the engraving, the pouring of the base and the erecting of the stones. He told me it would take a few minutes. I waited until he had completed his calculations.

When he returned, he said the total price for the stones and their engraving and installation would be $17,000.

My only reaction to the price was to ask when he wanted to set the base for the gravestones. He said he could arrange for the work within the next few days if I gave him a deposit.

I pulled out my cash envelope and counted out the total money for the markers, saying, "I would like to pay the full amount now if I may, and in cash, if that is acceptable."

The guy, taking the money out of my hands and feeling the weight of the stack of $100 bills, said, "I didn't realize $17,000 was so heavy. Sure, it's okay. Cash is still king around here. I'll get my men out to your place in just a few days; you just show them where you want the markers erected."

Two days later, a man from the monument company showed up at my door. Soon after I took him out to the grave site, he had two foundations poured in fresh concrete. I guess the old saying that "money talks" still applies to most everything, even tombstones.

About three weeks later, and after the first freeze, I heard the engine of a heavy-duty truck laboring hard to get up my steep driveway. Behind the truck was a flatbed trailer loaded with two headstones and a backhoe. I threw on my jacket and went out to meet the guys. They unloaded the backhoe and used it to carry the massive black slab. I told them to follow me out to the back of the property and the grave sites.

During the three weeks since ordering the stones I had managed to clear away most of the underbrush and erect a nice post-and-rail fence made from small cedar saplings. My work gave the hilltop the appearance of being set aside from the surrounding wilderness.

Slowly, the backhoe made its way to the site. The large slab of black granite was lowered onto its concrete base at the head of Bruno's grave. Once the stone was placed, it looked awesome even if somewhat out of place on the wooded hilltop. It looked like some kind of manicured outcropping from the earth. It was secured in place by special bolts that, when cemented over, were completely invisible. After being sure that Bruno's stone was properly secured, the men made their way back to the trailer to get the second marker.

Once the workmen had erected and secured the second marker with its inscription acknowledging those also interred on my hilltop, I had a wonderful sense of fulfillment, satisfaction and completeness. I felt confident in a job well done. Not only did Bruno have his elaborate headstone as I had promised him, but the small cemetery looked exactly as I had envisioned it. It was peaceful, secluded and serene. Hopefully, this place had taken into its soil the last person involved in the Purple Gang or the Knighthood of Zion.

22

December 1977

The month of December began with my usual chores of setting up the snow fences so drifts would not plug up the driveway, and weatherproofing the water pipes so they wouldn't freeze. I took the sidewinder off my tractor and replaced it with the snowplow, getting ready for the snowy white onslaught I knew would eventually come to our hill.

Sure enough, as though written on some unseen appointment book, the snows blew in one night while we all slept snugly in our warm beds. We awoke to a beautiful white wonderland. My eldest son and I put the snow blade to good use and cleared the drive while Peggy Sue got the other children ready for school. After breakfast, the kids all went happily on their way to catch the bus, pitching snowballs at each other all the way down the hill. Peggy Sue and I watched them out of sight while we enjoyed our second cup of coffee and discussed the Christmas get-together and dinner she was planning. When she asked me how much she could spend on the event, I replied with a smirk on my face, "Honey, you don't even have to ask. Let's have a real ball. The sky's the limit. Just take whatever you need from the basement."

She looked me straight in the eye and said, "You know, you're right. I can do that and I will, but we sure are getting nonchalant about that money. Eventually, we're going to have to do something about it. I'm so afraid someone will find out about it and sneak in here some night and kill us all in our sleep!"

I guess I had become so accustomed to knowing the money was in the basement that I had forgotten it was dangerous. Certainly, people had been murdered for a helluva lot less than what lay in the old vault. Trying to put her fears to rest, I said, "Honey, don't worry, I'm working on it. It's just that there's so much of it I don't know where to hide it other than where it is. But you are definitely right, we are going to have to do something with it.

"Lets put the issue aside and have a good time this Christmas because we have a lot to be thankful for. Let's go over your list of guests for the party." We went over the names and then she asked if there was anyone I wanted to add to the list of guests. Suddenly, Speedy Sullivan came to mind. "We don't want to forget Speedy," I said.

"Speedy who?" she asked.

Then I realized that, in all the confusion of Bruno's death and the revelations that surfaced at that time, I had never told Peggy Sue about Speedy so she was completely in the dark about this new mysterious individual.

I started at the beginning, telling her about my first meeting with Speedy at the cabin the day I found Bruno unconscious. I told her about his following the medics and Constable Schultz to our hill and how he seemed to know Bruno.

Then I told her about my second meeting with Sullivan at the funeral parlor and about the things he had said about Bruno, indicating he knew him quite well; and that he mentioned he knew the old judge and had even been in the house many years ago.

I told Peggy Sue that I had thought if I befriended the old guy, I might be able to find out more about Bruno and, for that matter, God forbid, the vault. So, I invited him here for the Christmas party.

With her mouth agape, she said, "You what? We were

just talking about keeping ourselves safe and the money a secret and then you tell me you've invited some man that could be anything—even a killer—right into our house. Why in the hell don't you just take him to the basement and show him the money?"

Oh, my goodness, my wife was mad! I could see how steamed she was so I tried to explain to her that we had to find out who this Sullivan guy was and what he knew if we were ever going to be able to really enjoy the money without looking over our shoulders at every turn. I said, "Speedy is in his eighties and he's somewhat feeble. I think he's completely harmless."

Finally, her tone softened a little, but I couldn't ever remember her speaking to me so sharply. "Well, you'd better introduce me to him as soon as he arrives so I can keep my eye on him." It was obvious Peggy Sue was very concerned about my new acquaintance, Speedy Sullivan.

The next few weeks were filled with the hustle and bustle of the holidays and the planning for the celebration we were hosting. Peggy Sue soon forgot about Speedy, but I didn't. I wondered constantly if I had, indeed, done the right thing inviting him here to the house. I didn't have long to wait to find out because the party was almost upon us.

The day before the event, I went to the basement and made sure there were no telltale signs of the secret room at the foot of the stairs, and that the wine racks were tightly closed. Upstairs in the library, I made sure the door leading to the attic was securely hidden behind the bookcase, and I checked to be sure the secret door in the linen closet of the bathroom, opening into the chimney shaft, was not visible. I was satisfied that everything was in order. If Speedy knew anything about these secret rooms, it was from previous knowledge because Judge Levison's unknown carpenters had very cleverly concealed them. On second thought, maybe Speedy could have been one of the carpenters. I would find out the next evening, I was sure.

Peggy Sue had completely outdone herself with the decorations for the cocktail party and the *hors d' oeuvres* she had prepared to serve before we went to dinner at the Bauer Manor. All preparations were in order and Peggy Sue was receiving some early guests when I noticed, from my upstairs bathroom window, the white Buick was slowly making its way up the slippery driveway. I felt a slight lump start to rise in my throat and my pulse quickened when I saw Speedy step out of the car and head for the front door. He was also headed straight for my wife!

I made a mad dash down the stairs in order to intercept him before he made it to the open front door; but, I was too late, and he was already shaking hands with Peggy Sue. I noticed she was eyeing him suspiciously. Immediately, I called out, "Well, look who's here. Welcome, Speedy."

When I reached the door, I held out my hand. "Honey, this is the gentleman I was telling you about. Remember, the one who visited this house so many years ago?"

Speedy, quicker on the draw than I realized, said, "Zack, don't make me out to be so old in front of a good looking woman like your wife." Well, that did it! Peggy Sue is a pushover for compliments and I could see her relax on the spot.

We escorted Speedy into the living room. Wide-eyed as he looked around, he said, "Oh, my. You sure have changed this room. I see you even got rid of the old man's portrait."

"No," Peggy Sue responded, "actually we haven't. It's just hidden behind all that red drapery."

We had our confirmation that he had been in this house before. Now that Speedy had tipped his hand, knowing about the portrait of the Judge, I was determined to find out how well he had known the judge and if he had knowledge of any of the secret rooms. I knew I would have to tread lightly with this guy. This burned out, derelict of a man, if I made a misstep, could blow up my entire financial future and maybe even my life.

Wanting to be a good host I asked him if he would like a beer or something harder. He replied, "Beer is for boys. When I drink, it isn't often any more, I like whiskey and water, no ice." I motioned him over to the bar where I poured him a stiff one. He took a deep drink, and holding his glass up to the light, said, "Can you imagine the government at one time trying to stop the entire population of the United States from drinking this stuff? Prohibition, they called it. Hell, no one quit; everything just went underground. Lots of money was made with illegal booze. Places like this one were built with that kind of money. Man, those were the days. Of course, I was young then; and full of piss and vinegar."

As if to agree with him in regards to the government, I said, "Well, that's the way the politicians work in Washington. They make changes and see if the public bitches. If they don't, they leave the laws in place; if the people do complain or if they just keep right on doing the thing that was outlawed and Washington's not getting its cut of the pie, they simply repeal the law. Then they tax the shit out of everybody."

In a complete about face like he'd had second thoughts, Speedy said, "Every now and then, however, they surprise me and do something good."

Not wanting to spend any more time talking politics when I needed answers, I changed the subject by asking him if he knew anything about a huge pool of water under the garage floor. I was just on a fishing expedition and so I was surprised when he started in the direction of the garage with *me following him*. He walked into the garage and went right up to the doors in the floor. Looking down, he said, "I see you have padlocked the entrance; good idea with kids around."

I opened the lock and lifted the doors. He looked into the dark water and said, "Turn on the light. I want to see if the water is still as clear as it used to be." I walked over to the switch, flipped it on and turned back to face him. I saw that he had already descended the steps and was bending over, feeling the water. "Just as I remember, crystal clear and lukewarm. You can swim in this, you know."

Surprised at how sharp his memory was, I played it dumb and said, "You can? It looks a little spooky down there to me."

He came right back with, "It's really not so bad once you get in; and it feels great on a cold winter day." I was getting a sinking feeling in my knees. This guy probably knew everything about this house, including the secret rooms and the vault.

I asked him if he wanted to see more of the house and he said he would like that. I closed and locked the pool doors and we headed back into the house. As we passed the bar, he asked if it would be impolite to ask for another highball. Telling him that was no problem, I took his glass and really loaded this one with whiskey. We turned and walked into the sunroom. When we entered, Speedy said, "This was always my favorite room. I read a lot of pages from those books over there." He nodded toward the bookcases lining one of the walls. We talked there for about thirty minutes or so. Then, I noticed his drink was almost empty again and offered to freshen it for him. "Sure, why not," he said with a little slurring in his voice. "What brand is it?"

"It think it's either Crown Royal or Canadian Club," I replied.

This statement stirred some memories for old Speedy. "I brought a lot of that stuff into Detroit in the old days," he said. Sensing this was my opening to get some more information and a feel for what this old guy did back then, I asked a loaded question.

"Oh, were you in the import business?

He laughed heartily, drank down the remainder of his drink and said, "You might say that; yeah, kind of."

At any minute, I thought, he might drop a bombshell about his past. I was convinced the booze was loosening his lips. Pointing to his empty glass, I said I'd get him a refill.

"Do you think I can take it with me?" he asked. "I hear your lovely wife calling us to the cars. She says it's dinner time." I was irritated. Here I was, just getting somewhere with this character and now it was time to eat. I guess I had lost track of time.

I looked at my watch and realized we had been talking for almost two hours. I wasn't going to let Speedy out of my sight. I would just have to arrange to have Peggy Sue seat him beside me at dinner. I really needed to pump him further. Driving the eleven miles over to the Bauer Manor, following closely behind Speedy's car, I noticed he was weaving from one side of the road to the other as if slightly out of control. The liquor was starting to hit home. Fortunately, we made it to the Manor before he ran off the road.

I helped the staggering Speedy up the steps and into the inn and finally over to the chair Peggy Sue was holding for him. Somewhat exhausted, I sat down beside him.

The waitress who was to be our server for the evening came to our table and asked if anyone wanted a cocktail before dinner was served. Before anyone else could utter a sound, Speedy barked out, "Hey, Babe, com'ere." The young woman, not knowing what she was about to get herself into, walked over to Speedy and stood by his side. Speedy, putting his arm around her small waist and, slurring badly, said, "You know, Honey. I knew a good looking broad like you many years ago and boy could she drink and do the Ooo LaLa. Go get us a couple of whiskeys and grab a seat here with me and I'll tell you the story of my life."

Knowing how to handle this kind of situation, the

young woman said, "All right, it's whiskey for this gentleman. Who else needs a drink?" She then slithered away from the clutches of a dirty old man.

Just for a moment, while Speedy was propositioning the poor waitress, I tried to visualize him as a young man. He wasn't a bad looking guy even now in his eighties, so he must have been a real ladies' man in his earlier years. His hair was all salt and pepper now but still wavy, and it must have been very attractive when it was jet black. He was tall, well over six feet, and without his gut and the forty pounds he had acquired over the years, he might have been quite handsome in his heyday. One thing was certain: he wasn't at all bashful and came across as a take-charge kind of guy. He had in the short time I had known him, and probably because of his tough-guy image, become immensely interesting to me. This evening, however, would not reveal any further information from the old Don Juan. The now-attentive waitress, who appeared almost to relish Speedy's hands being all over her attractive derrière, had been steadily bringing drinks. After several more highballs, Speedy abruptly stopped talking and his head hit the tabletop with a bang. He had passed out like the proverbial light!

After dinner, when Peggy Sue started the singing of Christmas carols, it looked pretty bad to have a drunk slumped over on the table. It didn't seem to fit the scene so I told Peggy Sue I would either take him home or put him in his car to sleep it off.

Grabbing my overcoat, and with help from another guest, I manhandled the old drunk out to his car. He came to just long enough to get sick all over the hood of the Buick and to tell me, "You never should have moved me." I stepped out of his way and ask him if he wanted to sleep it off in his car or go home.

Blowing his nose on the dinkiest handkerchief I'd ever seen, he said, "No, take me home. I haven't been this sick in years." I told Speedy I'd be happy to take him home but he might have to remind me how to get there. I had only been as far as his mailbox when I dropped off the date and time of our party.

"Can you direct me to your place? Can you stay awake long enough to do that?" I asked him. Speedy attempted to straighten up his clothes and told me just to take him to the south shore of Lake Evans.

"I can take it from there," he said. "Here's the keys; drive the Buick. If I pass out, it knows the way." I guess he was trying to be funny.

I was familiar with the lake point he was referring to and, because there was a full moon, I was able to negotiate the winding, slippery, snow-covered road through the hills. It only took me about twenty-five minutes to reach the south shore. A couple of minutes after I turned off the main road and onto a dirt driveway, the Buick's headlights illuminated the shore and the unfrozen waters of the lake. Also in the glare of the headlights, I saw the old rum barrel with a hole cut in its side that served as Speedy's mailbox.

When we got out of the car, Speedy headed straight for the lake and out onto a long wooden ramp. At the end of the ramp, hanging from a hand-operated boatlift, was the most beautiful, well-preserved vintage Chris Craft speedboat I had ever seen. Then I remembered that Speedy had told me he lived on an island in the middle of Lake Evans. Speedy went to work lowering the boat into the water while flipping a switch that turned on a small green blinking beacon. Getting into the boat, he motioned that I should get aboard also, saying he was in no condition to motor out to his island home.

I explained that I wasn't very handy with boats, especially one like this. Speedy told me not to worry that the boat handled easily. He started up the motor. It was a good thing we were in a remote area of the lake because the boat motor came to life in a tremendous roar.

Speedy, being tanked, held the throttle wide open so I had no choice but to jump aboard and idle the engine down so it wouldn't blow up! I sat down behind the steering wheel and before I realized what had happened Speedy had put the transmission in gear and we were racing away from the dock out onto the silvery, moonlit waters of Lake Evans. I yelled to Speedy over the noise of the motor and the rushing freezing wind, "How the hell am I supposed to get back?"

By this time Speedy was slumped down in the boat and he had covered himself with a small canvas to protect himself from the icy wind and the water spray. "The same way we're going out. Just head back to shore and follow the green beacon or 39° northeast on that dash compass. You can read a compass, can't you?" Oh, my Lord, I was thinking!

"Right now," Speedy continued, "just hold her on a 225° southwest heading and wake me up in twenty minutes." I suppose he was trying to make it all sound easy. Well, it was easy for him. He had made this trip so many times over the years he could probably do it in his sleep. I'd have been better off just to let him try it in his sleep; because here I was trying to navigate by compass, piloting an unfamiliar boat at high speed—and dammit, he *was asleep*!

I kept my eyes glued to the 225° setting on the compass because it was the only thing I wasn't afraid of at the time. The boat was plowing through the water and kicking up a tremendous rooster tail behind it. The wind coming over the windshield made tears come to my eyes. Looking down at the speedometer, I realized why I felt so out of control. I *was* out of control. We were going over 50 miles an hour. I didn't know what I was doing, but took a chance at operating one of the controls, the throttle. I pulled it back slowly and watched the speedometer drop down to 25 miles per hour. That lowered the engine noise and dropped the wind velocity in my face considerably.

Buttoning the top button on my coat and looking out over the deep dark waters, I noticed there were no landmarks in sight and no other craft on the water anywhere. We were completely alone on what appeared to be a vast undulating inland sea. Understanding that I was right in the middle of a very uncomfortable set of circumstances, I looked around in the boat for a life vest…just in case. I didn't see one. The only thing I saw was Speedy; and the only thing I could hear above the noise of the engine and the wind was his loud snoring.

I don't think I had ever felt more hopeless in my life. I looked at my watch and saw we had only been underway for a mere ten minutes. I wasn't certain I could keep myself together. I debated with myself about waking up the old coot.

All kinds of weird visions ran through my head. I wondered what kind of fish inhabited these waters and how big they were. I thought about sea monsters. Unthinkable that a grown man would have visions of sea monsters, but I did. I also thought about what might happen if the old boat should suddenly quit running. I might be adrift out here for hours—or even days—before someone found us. Someone? Find us? Hell, for all I knew no one ever came out on this lake, especially this time of year.

My thoughts just got worse. We could be here for days. What would my poor wife do without me? What about my kids?

Thank God! Just as I was starting to think myself into a full-blown panic attack, Speedy woke up. Of course, he puked all over himself and the front seat of the boat. God, what else was going to happen?

In a little bit, Speedy dangled his hand over the side of the boat, got some water and wet his face with it. He seemed a little more coherent when he said, "We should be nearing the sand bar that surrounds the island."

"Oh, great," I thought. Maybe I should ask him to take

over the controls of the boat for the rest of the trip to the island. I didn't want to be the one to run us aground. Just then, in the moonlight, I saw the dark outline of the island and the large home where Speedy lived. It was only a few minutes later that we pulled alongside the dock. Speedy hopped unsteadily out of the boat onto the dock and tied one of our lines to a large piling jutting out into the water.

We made our way up to the house that seemed to get larger and larger as we approached. By the time we stood at the front door, the place had evolved into an enormous mansion similar to the one in which I lived. This house, however, was constructed entirely of cedar logs. We stepped inside and, even though the outside temperature was well above freezing, this house felt as cold as Nome, Alaska. I didn't know whether or not there was a heating unit, so I built a roaring fire in the massive fireplace. Soon, it took the chill out of the air.

I looked around for Speedy and saw him sprawled out on a sofa. I walked over to cover him with a heavy comforter. He opened his eyes and said he was very nauseated. "I just can't drink like I used to," he said weakly. He tried to thank me for bringing him home and said I could sleep next to the fireplace or in the guestroom if I wanted to stay until morning. I declined his offer and told him I'd better be getting home. I couldn't have stayed anyway because Speedy didn't have a telephone. I knew that, by now, Peggy Sue was worried sick. I had to get home as soon as possible since I couldn't call her.

As Speedy was slipping off to sleep again, he said, "Throw a few more logs on the fire, willya; and be careful crossing the lake. Squalls come up pretty quick this time of year. Just keep your eye on the compass with a 39° northeast heading, and in short order you will see the green beacon. And, don't forget, in the next day or two you will have to come back out and pick me up. You're taking my only means of getting off this island."

Hey, no pressure. He wasn't trying to shake me up. Surely he only wanted me to be careful. But, he didn't have to mention a squall. I'd had enough experience with this Michigan weather and the effects it can cause. But, I felt like I knew enough about the boat to get home safely. After all, I had made it all the way across what felt like the Atlantic Ocean without any problems. And, besides, if an eighty-year-old man could do it, I sure as hell could do it!

Now, if I could only remember how to start the damn boat and where the compass was, I'd be okay.

As I was leaving, I looked back into the house and all I could see was the fireplace glowing brightly. Quietly, I closed the front door and was about to lock it when I noticed there was no lock of any kind on the door. Not only was Speedy the only inhabitant of the island, it was surrounded by miles and miles of open water. Could that explain why there was no lock?

When I reached the Chris Craft, it was sitting motionless in very still water. I was amazed at how tranquil the weather had become in such a short time. I untied the speedboat and climbed on board, saw the key in the ignition switch, turned it and depressed the silver button labeled "Starter." Instantly, the engine fired. I moved a long silver lever forward, heard a clunk when she went into gear and then I was off, by myself, heading out over a vast expanse of water toward South Shore point and home.

Pulling up my coat sleeve, I saw it was just past 3 o'clock in the morning. I knew Peggy Sue was worried, but I vowed not to hurry so I could maintain complete control over the boat. I wasn't going to go any faster than 20 miles per hour. After four or five minutes, I found myself on water that was as smooth as glass and reflected the entire night sky like a giant mirror. It felt as though I was in space, floating right through the middle of two skies, one on top of the other, sandwiched between thousands of twinkling stars. I wondered if a being like myself, inhabited any of them and at this very moment in time and space was looking back at my planet wondering the same thought. It was an eerie and astonishing sight. The Milky Way and Big Dipper were very distinct on this cold, clear night and the North Star was the brightest of all—except for the huge brilliant double moons. They cast a soft pale light that seemed to illuminate the way across the water. They accompanied me like they were tied to the bow of my boat. Looking at all these heavenly wonders in all their splendor, it was easy to imagine how ancient people were so moved by these celestial bodies and why some cultures actually worshiped them as gods.

At the slow speed I was traveling there was hardly even a breeze and the only noise I heard, other than the soft purr of the engine, was the gurgling of the water as the bow of the boat pushed its way through it. I checked my compass heading and saw in the blue glow of the dash lights that I was heading 39° northeast, just as instructed. After about 30 minutes of being cradled in what seemed like the arms of heaven, I saw the green flicker of the beacon off in the distance and realized I was still on earth.

Surprisingly, I felt a little hint of disappointment that my journey was almost over. I realized I had actually been enjoying myself. I wondered if this was the way the ancient mariners felt—a sense of elation when they reached their distant destinations, using only the stars to guide them. Then I remembered my seafaring days were not yet over. I would have to do this all again in the next few days when I ventured back across the lake to retrieve Speedy from his island home.

When I arrived at the dock on the point, I had no idea how to get the boat up on the lift. After trying several times to figure out what to do, I finally just tied the craft securely to the lift using two mooring lines I found on the speedboat. I took the Buick keys from my overcoat pocket, slid behind the wheel, started her up, and headed for home and Peggy Sue.

Forty minutes later, I pulled up to the house and parked next to the Cadillac. When I got to the front door, I noticed it was partly open. I could see Peggy Sue standing behind the door, staring out the crack. Evidently, she must have waited up for me and had seen the car coming up the driveway. I ran into her open arms and held her in a tight embrace. "I see you drove the Caddie home," I said.

"Yes, and I'm still mad about it, too. You know I hate to drive alone at night, especially with snow on the roads." She continued my scolding, asked me if I knew it was almost dawn, and what the hell took me so long. Taking me by the arm, she pulled me into the kitchen and poured me a hot cup of coffee.

"None for you?" I asked, hoping she would join me.

In her very special complaining attitude, she said, "You have got to be kidding. I've already drunk two pots just waiting for you to come home!"

I was trying really hard to get on her good side. "You know, you're right. We really do drink a lot of this stuff." Her reaction told me I'd better get right to the point of why I was so late. So, after only a few sips of the delicious brew, I explained the entire ordeal of getting Speedy home. As I recounted the experience of having to traverse half of Lake Evans to get to Speedy's house and then returning by myself, she was amazed I had been able to do it. She asked me if I had been scared.

I told her I had been scared stiff going over, but that my return trip was surprisingly almost a spiritual awakening. I told her how the sky seemed to blend right in with the water and how awesome many of the planets had looked.

Her reaction…"That's it. Sounds to me like you were hallucinating or you'd had too much to drink. I think we both need some sleep. I think I can go to sleep now that you're finally home, if I haven't drunk too much coffee."

So it was upstairs to my cold bed where I would snuggle tightly against the warm body of the woman I loved. I didn't feel a need to pray that night because I had already worshiped in the vast cathedral of the sky. I fell quickly to sleep, fulfilled but extremely exhausted.

Morning came quickly and I slept only a few hours, waking just a little later than my usual time of 7 o'clock. I could hear Peggy Sue downstairs talking to the children and I could smell the aroma of the pancakes she was cooking. That did it. I couldn't resist the temptation, so I threw on my robe and scampered downstairs to get my stack of pancakes hot off the griddle

Because it was Sunday, we all gathered around the table and then dived into those flapjacks. All during breakfast, I regaled the children with my naval accomplishments of the night before. I tried to make my trip across the lake sound funny for my family, but in reality it was very serious and downright dangerous.

Then, I remembered my promise to return to the island and take the boat back to Speedy. Thinking about Speedy, I refocused on the main reason I had invited him to the party in the first place. My reason had been to pump him for information about the house and its contents, but my attempt had been aborted by his drunkenness. I knew deep down inside I would eventually have to bring him here again so I could question him about everything he knew. The sooner I did it, the better I would feel.

I knew I was going to try to get as much information as possible without him hearing or seeing anything remotely connected with us finding the money. I was certain Speedy was familiar with the layout of the house by the way he handled himself the night before. Surely, he must know about the room behind the wine racks and possibly about the vault in the wall—and probably that it contained tons of cash!

To diffuse the possibility of him finding out about the

money in the vault, I knew I had to formulate a plan. A thought crossed my mind: On his next visit while we were touring the house, I could nonchalantly let him see inside the safe and show him it was void of any money. It would be empty, because by that time *I would have already moved it*! Of course, I would have to come up with the how and where to re-hide the fortune before inviting Speedy back to my house for my low-key "interrogation."

Then, I remembered the old steamer trunks in the outside garage that had once been partially hidden by the old Packard. They were large enough to hold the contents of several of the canvas bags, but there weren't enough of them to handle all the money. I knew those old-type steamer trunks weren't manufactured anymore, so I had to come up with something to take their place. Then I thought about old army-style footlockers. Even though they were smaller, they were readily available and inexpensive.

I left the breakfast table without saying a word, went straight to the phone book and looked up the number for the Army & Navy Surplus Store in Ann Arbor. I wasn't sure the store would be open, but I got an answer. I asked if they had footlockers in stock and I was told they had plenty. "When you say plenty," I asked, "does that mean 20 or more? I'm buying these for my Boy Scout troop." There was another of those little fibs, but that's the way it had to be.

The clerk said he would check his supply if I didn't mind hanging on. In a minute he returned and said that "plenty" meant more than 20 and I would get a special price since I was buying them for the Scouts.

With my conscience hurting only a little, I asked the dimensions of each locker. Then I thanked him and hung up the phone.

Now that I had determined the containers I would use for storing the money, the next question was how I was going to move it. I needed something large and substantial on wheels and with a door that could be tightly secured. I needed something like a large box on rollers. Duh! A light bulb went off in my head. I needed a large commercial panel truck.

I was back on the phone in an instant talking to the Ford dealer in Ann Arbor and questioning a salesman about trucks he had in stock. He described one that sounded like it would do the job. I asked him for inside dimensions and the height of the truck. He read the specs to me from a brochure and told me the price was $26,517. When I asked him if he would accept cash as payment, he acted like he was talking to a kook, "Oh, sure. We even take old horses in on trade. When shall I expect you in here with the money?"

I replied, "Oh, I can possibly be in there this afternoon. Who should I ask for when I come in?"

"Oh, almost any one of us salesmen would take your cash. Bye, bye now!" With that the sarcastic so-and-so hung up the telephone.

Figuring the dimensions of the inside of the truck, I determined it would hold approximately 40 footlockers with some room to spare. Now all that was left to do was determine how much money each locker would hold. I went upstairs, put on my street clothes and jacket, grabbed my tape measure and went out to the old outside garage that still housed the Packard. Measuring the door opening, I determined that the panel truck could easily fit into the garage. Inside, I grabbed one of the steamer trunks and dragged it outside, into the house and down into the basement.

Using a yardstick and a piece of chalk inside the trunk, I marked off the dimensions of a footlocker. Now all I had to do was get inside the vault and pack as much money as possible into the chalk lines I had drawn inside the steamer trunk.

I felt reasonably safe opening the safe while the kids were at home because they were occupied upstairs with finishing pancakes and watching television. I opened the wine racks and slid the trunk into the room. Quietly, I closed the racks behind me, all the while hoping the kids wouldn't come looking for me. As long as I was quiet inside the room, I didn't think they would ever find me.

I opened the vault doors and pushed the trunk inside. Then I began placing stacks of greenbacks in it, following the chalk outline of the footlocker dimensions. I determined that I could put the contents of two canvas bags into that amount of space. Then I continued to add cash to the steamer trunk to see how much money one of them would hold. Two more canvas bags went right in. Therefore, I could put four canvas bags of money in each steamer trunk and I had six of them. Since the trunks would hold 24 of the money bags, I needed only 15 footlockers to hold the rest.

I was feeling relieved now that I had a workable plan. It would be a ton of work, but I felt Peggy Sue and I could complete the transfer of the money into trunks and then into the panel truck the next day while the kids were in school for their last few days before Christmas vacation. The only thing was, time was not on my side. I had to get the lockers and the truck today.

Without hesitation I counted out the cash I would need for the purchase of the truck and the footlockers. I stuffed the money into a large, empty old briefcase I found on one of the shelves, turned off the small light in the safe and slipped out of the secret room and upstairs. I was in the clear. No one had even missed me.

I found Peggy Sue still in her robe, half-asleep in front of the TV with the kids. Quietly I asked her if she could possibly take me into Ann Arbor and if she thought the children would be all right for the couple of hours she would be gone.

"For heaven's sake, Ann Arbor on Sunday morning? Whatever for?"

"I'll explain it to you on the way in, but I need to buy a truck," I told her in a whisper.

"Buy a truck? Well, all right, I can drive you in and the kids will be just fine, but I can't say the same thing for you. I think the episode last night knocked your trolley off the tracks a little," she said as she headed up the stairs to get dressed.

Amazingly, she was back down in a matter of minutes, not taking the time to put on makeup. Therefore, she made me promise she wouldn't have to get out of the car or see anyone. Ah, vanity, vanity!

We hustled out the door and into the Cadillac, with me carrying the old briefcase. I went over my plan with Peggy Sue on the way to Ann Arbor. She thought it was solid and expressed her pleasure at finally getting the money out of the house.

When we arrived at the Ford dealership, I told Peggy Sue not to wait for me but to head back home. Not wasting any time and just giving me a quick peck on the cheek, she looked quickly around to be sure no one had seen her in her un-made-up condition. She drove briskly away, leaving me standing in a rather large cloud of dust, holding tightly to the old briefcase.

Brushing myself off and coughing a little, I entered the dealership and walked up to the first salesman I saw. I told the young man I had called earlier about a heavy-duty cargo truck. He inquired if I had spoken to anyone in particular. I told him the salesman I talked to had said any of the salesmen could sell me one of the F-150 panel trucks in stock. "So," I said, "I assume you're him."

"Oh, absolutely, sir," the young man said smiling. "You are exactly right. My name is Bob. Would you like to drive one of the vehicles?"

As I walked out toward the lot I told him that a test drive wasn't at all necessary. "I just need to look at the cargo area."

Bob showed me two identical trucks and, after looking inside, I told him either one would do fine. "I believe I will take the blue one," I said.

Bob, wanting to be sure I would take the truck asked me again about a test drive.

"No, I'm sold. Let's just do the paper work," I said. Bob shook my hand vigorously and commented that this was the quickest of the three sales he had made so far. He had only started working at the dealership the week before and was happy as a lark to make such a large sale.

We went to his small office cubicle and, in short order, he had the forms filled out. When I glanced at the total sales price, I saw it was four hundred dollars *less* than what I had been quoted over the phone. I mentioned this to Bob and he said he had given me a special price because he didn't have to negotiate or hassle with me and he didn't have to involve his sales manager.

When I opened my briefcase and started counting out the money to buy the truck, Bob said, "Whoa! Are you going to pay in paper money?"

"Yes, that's my plan. Isn't that acceptable?" I asked.

"I don't know. I'll have to ask my supervisor." He scurried out of the office and in a matter of just a few minutes was back with a heavy-set man who introduced himself as "Lester, the sales manager."

He held out his hand to me and asked, "Are you the guy I talked to on the phone this morning?"

"Yep, that's me. You did say I could pay in hard cash, didn't you?" I asked in my very best Gary Cooper voice.

Looking a bit sheepish, Lester said, "Yeah, we still take cash as long as it's not counterfeit." Then he turned to Bob and explained to him that I was his customer because he had spoken to me on the telephone and he had spent a great deal of time pre-selling the truck. Bob's face almost fell off when he thought he had lost the sale.

Immediately, I stepped into the middle of the disagreement and said, "Lester, you said over the phone that any one of the salesmen could take my cash order and I'm going to give it to Bob. You know there are other dealers that sell cargo trucks in Ann Arbor."

Hearing my veiled threat, Lester changed his tune suddenly. "Sure, I'm willing to give the sale to Bob; anything to make the customer happy. After all, our motto is: the customer is always right." With that, he stomped out of the room.

I picked up a pen from Bob's desk, signed the forms and pushed the pile of hundreds across the desk to him, saying, "Thanks for the good sales job you did on me, Bob. There should be a few dollars over the sale price and I want you to have them. Call it a tip if you like, but I consider it as a bonus to you for having to put up with an asshole like Lester."

Picking up the keys to the truck and my paperwork, I hurried toward the row of parked trucks. As I passed Lester on my way out, I turned and said, "What a deal that kid gave me; and I didn't even have to trade in my old horse." As I drove away, I saw Lester with his finger in Bob's face, waving it and giving the kid what looked like a royal ass-chewing for taking the sale. I would bet ten to one that the kid quit and that the next time Lester answered the phone he would take his customer more seriously.

I traveled the short distance to the army surplus store. Wanting to avoid the same kind of disagreement that occurred at the Ford dealership, I asked for the person I had talked with on the phone earlier about buying a number of footlockers for my Boy Scout troop. Overhearing my request, an older man came out of a side office and said he had spoken to me earlier and would be happy to assist me.

I told the gentlemen I had calculated my needs and

wanted to purchase 14 footlockers but I needed to know the price to be sure I had brought enough money with me. The clerk said there was a price break on the footlockers at 18 and if I could use that many I could save seven dollars on each locker. I told him that 18 would be fine, thinking maybe it would be better to buy a few more in case I had underestimated the number of lockers I needed to hold the tremendous volume of money. I knew that my sons would be able to use the extra ones.

I backed up to the loading dock in my brand new panel truck and 18 footlockers were quickly loaded into the cargo area of the truck. Once again the clerk had to check with a supervisor before accepting my cash payment for the footlockers!

On the drive home with the equipment I needed to safeguard my newfound millions, a worrisome thought crossed my mind. Was I going nuts trying to keep all the money safe only to find out I couldn't spend it without a lot of trouble? Everyone seemed uptight and cautious when I was purchasing higher-priced items with cash. In reality, could my cash windfall turn out to be more of a burden than a benefit?

When I pulled up in front of the house, Peggy Sue and the kids came running out to see the new truck. The girls climbed into the cab and bounced around on the seats. My sons got in the cargo area and immediately asked what I was going to do with all the footlockers. I told them the lockers were to be used for storage and that some of them were to be used to store their things. They helped me get the footlockers out of the truck. Once they were unloaded, we took lockers upstairs to the boys' room where we placed one at the foot of each of their beds.

They began filling the lockers with all sorts of things. Toys, baseball gloves, old books and even some out-of-season clothing went into the footlockers. The boys thought it was a cool idea—sorta like the army—and when the girls saw how nice they were for storing clothing, Denise and Kim each wanted one for their rooms. My ruse had worked. The kids thought the footlockers were a neat way to store odd items and they never questioned why I had bought so many.

The kids helped me haul the remaining lockers down to the basement where they were stacked near the wine racks. Having the lockers already in place would make the work Peggy Sue and I had to do a whole lot easier.

Monday morning I hit the floor with energy and hurried to get dressed. After a light breakfast, it was out to the garage to bring in the old steamer trunks. I wanted to load them first and store them in the front of the truck right behind the driver's seat. The footlockers would go in behind the old steamers. As soon as the kids were off to school, Peggy Sue donned her work clothes and came out to help me carry the old trunks downstairs to the basement. Soon, we were inside the secret vault stacking greenbacks into the trunks.

By lunchtime we had completely filled all six of the steamer trunks and used the empty canvas bags to cover the money before we shut the trunks. We felt we were making good progress, so we took a break for a quick sandwich. Afterwards, armed with a thermos full of hot coffee, it was back to the grind of moving money.

We worked feverishly to get the transfer done before the kids came home from school. We had filled several lockers when suddenly Peggy Sue heard one of the boys calling to her. "My God, it must be after 3 o'clock," I thought.

I told Peggy Sue to race upstairs and head them off while I closed up down in the basement. Our quick actions worked and we kept the children innocent about the cash horde. After all these years of living here, they had no idea the money even existed.

The next day started out in pretty much the same manner. By early afternoon, we had all the currency stored in the trunks and lockers, covered by the canvas bags, and securely locked. The empty vault looked strange to me, somehow, and I wondered if maybe I might have been better off if it had been empty when I found it. I was concerned that in the coming months and years the money might bring us nothing but grief. As I started to leave the vault, I noticed I had left the inside vault doors standing wide open. I didn't care; the vault was totally empty now. Mission accomplished.

Now we were left with the task of dragging all the footlockers upstairs and loading them into the truck. They were heavy, but Peggy Sue and I managed to pull and drag eight of them out to the truck before we were completely out of breath. We realized we needed to come up with a better idea to move the rest of the money. I remembered seeing an old hand truck buried in the junk next to the Packard. I went outside to the garage, dug through the rubble and found it. It turned out to be a lifesaver because the steamer trunks were way too heavy for the two of us to handle. Using the old hand truck, we were able to roll the loaded boxes up the stairs and out to the truck. We used a six-foot wooden plank to make a ramp from the ground to the rear of the truck. Then it was just a matter of sliding the trunks up the plank.

If my calculations were correct, there was well over two thousand pounds of money and trunks inside the Ford. I was glad I had bought a large cargo truck because the load was heavy; but there was also some extra room in case I needed to store something else in the cargo area. After we were completely loaded, I slipped behind the wheel, started the truck and drove it into an area next to the old Packard. I got out of the truck, locked all the doors and then slid the outside doors to the garage shut. Then I padlocked the door and I was done!

I looked at Peggy Sue. She was so cute, standing there with her hair all windblown, smudges on her cheek, and wearing little green gardening gloves on her hands to protect her piano-playing fingers. I couldn't help myself, and I burst out laughing. At first, she had a puzzled look on her face and then she, too, let out a roar of laughter. Soon we were in each other's arms, laughing hysterically. We were either awfully tired or very happy to be done with the job of securing the money. Or maybe, we were just relieved that the money was somewhere else, away from Speedy's prying eyes if he came back to the house to visit. Our laborious charade to trick him might yet pay off.

23

Now that everything was safely in place, I decided it was time to go get Speedy off his island. Early the next morning, braving a stiff cold north wind, I ventured out to the Buick, hoping she would start. She did and I set off to Lake Evans. The trip took less time in the daylight and I reached the boat ramp and the Chris Craft with no trouble. The speedboat was still moored to the boatlift just as I had left it. Before I climbed aboard, I checked the green beacon and saw that it was still flashing. When I turned the key that I had left in the ignition, the engine coughed a few times and then came to life. I untied the line and headed out onto the lake as if I knew exactly what I was doing…but, deep inside my gut, the vastness of the lake was giving me butterflies.

Throttling up to 25 miles per hour and sliding down behind the windshield to get out of the wind, I put the boat on what I vaguely remembered was a southwest reading of 220° on the compass. Looking at my watch and noting the time, I figured I would have to travel about 20 minutes before sighting the island. Crossing my fingers, I settled down for the uncertain cruise to Speedy's house.

Everything was going just fine and I became almost mesmerized by the slow undulation of the waves and the beauty of the water. Finally, I glanced at my watch and stark terror ran through me. I had left the shore over thirty minutes ago and had not yet sighted the island! I bet surer than hell I had used the wrong heading. Unnerved by the thought that I might be lost in the middle of all the water, and unable to communicate with anyone, I put the boat in neutral and stopped to think. Scanning the horizon I could see nothing.

Fortunately, I had thought to pick up my binoculars as I left the house and I grabbed them out of the case. I stared anxiously into the vast emptiness and still saw nothing. "How in the hell could I miss something as big as an island," I berated myself.

For over an hour, I just sat there bobbing in the water, trying to decide what in the hell to do. Suddenly, way off in the distance, I noticed something in the sky that I hadn't seen before. I quickly lifted the binoculars and could barely make out what appeared to be a wisp of smoke on the horizon. Maybe Speedy had just lit his fireplace!

It was all I had to go on, so I started heading for the smoke. Then, I looked at the gas gauge and saw immediately that the smoke better be coming from Speedy's island because the tank was almost empty. I took off in that direction, keeping the binoculars glued to my eyes, hoping to get a glimpse of the island. It seemed like an eternity, and my muscles were knotted in a tight ball, but eventually I spotted a dark smudge in the distance. It got bigger and bigger and then it became the hazy outline of the island. What a relief I thought, because I carried no food or water. I was soon pulling up to the island's dock, coasting in on what I knew must be only gas fumes. The needle was on dead Empty.

I secured the boat and started up toward the house. I could see a large column of smoke rising skyward, but it was far too much to be coming from a chimney. Walking in the direction of the smoke, I found Speedy at the back of his house, standing near a blazing pile of brush, its black smoke rising high into the air.

Taking his eyes off the fire for a minute, Speedy watched my approach and shouted loudly, "Well, if it isn't Moby Dick. I was beginning to think you had abandoned me."

Shaking his hand, I replied, "No way! I told you I

would be back and here I am. However, I missed the island by a long way and it was lucky for me I saw the smoke from your brush fire or I'd still be sitting out there just drifting."

With a smile Speedy said, "Lucky for you; that sure is right. That pile of brush has been here for months and I just happened to think that now was a good time to set it on fire. I'd call that *perfect timing*, wouldn't you?"

"Yeah, I have to agree with you about the timing, but I'd say it was equally good timing that I made it here at all. The boat is completely out of gas and I just barely made it. I hope you have some here on the island."

Speedy shook his head in something like disbelief, "Man, you sure do cut it close. Didn't you think to check the gas gauge before you shoved off? It's the same as flying an airplane; there are no gas stations in the air and there aren't any on the lake. You've always got to check the gauges because, if you don't, you're dancing with death.

"Of course I have some gasoline. I don't take the kind of chances you obviously do. I've been around too long to do that and I've seen too many things go wrong. You dumb Shit! If you ever ran out of gas and got stranded, you could drift for days and maybe die out there. We're all alone, you know."

Then, as if he had finally finished his lecture to an imbecile, he lightened the subject. "It's okay. We'll gas up and take off. I'm getting a little low on food out here, though. You got anything to eat with you? I'm a little sick of beans and bread."

"No, Speedy, I didn't bring anything with me. I thought I'd just come on out and pick you up and take you back to the house for a nice lunch there. How's that sound?"

"Mighty good," Speedy said. "You go to the woodshed and you'll find an old oblong, six-gallon can full of gas. If you'll take it down and put it in the boat's tank, I'll tend to this fire. When it goes out, we can go get that lunch at your place. Then I can go into town for my winter supplies and refill the gas can."

I followed his instructions and took the gas down to the dock to refill the boat's tank. It took about an hour for the brush to burn down before we could finally leave. When we got to the boat, I climbed into the passenger seat and Speedy, acting like he was my dad or my boss, said, "You aren't getting off that easy. Get your ass behind that steering wheel. I'm going to make a sailor outta you yet. You don't ever know when you might have to bring me home again."

I really wasn't in any mood to argue with the old man, so I did as he told me. I got a good feeling, however, when I started the engine and looked at a quarter-full gas gauge. That was more than enough to get us home. As we pulled away from the island, I confidently rammed the throttle wide open, set a course of 39° on the compass and headed for the shore. I was starting to feel a bit more at ease here on the boat and thought maybe I could eventually become a sailor. Or, maybe my newfound confidence came from the fact Speedy was sitting beside me. He was a man who had obviously won the dance with death many times.

When we reached the shore and the boatlift, I could tell Speedy was beginning to feel comfortable with me because of the way he had been talking to me. After we had put the boat on its lift and we were seated in the Buick, he said, "I think I better drive because the way you navigate we'd end up in Chicago and I'm hungry as hell!"

And, then he had to go and say, "Look at that puke still on the hood of the car. At least you could have washed it off. And for Christ's sake why didn't you put some gas in my Buick? You know you can't wean these things…they have to have fuel. I bet you run out of gas all the time."

Would this man never quit lecturing? He just couldn't let himself get off the gas thing and he just kept bitching about everything. Here I was, a very successful businessman, happily married for years and the father of four great kids.

And he's making me feel incompetent and stupid. Maybe this was just his way of tearing me down in an attempt to dominate me. On the other hand, it might not have been a power play at all, but just his misguided attempt to be funny. Sometimes I found it really hard to understand him; he was in good shape physically, but sometimes he acted a little senile. He was obviously from the old school of thought that said older people knew best about everything.

Arriving at home, Peggy Sue greeted us cheerfully at the door. I decided to show off a little bit. Trying to act like John Wayne in the movie, *The Quiet Man*, shouting at Maureen O'Sullivan while putting his arm around his buddy Victor McLaughlin, I said, "Woman of the house, you have two hungry men to feed; now get crackin.'"

Thank goodness Peggy Sue had seen the movie with me many times. "Yes, my darling. Your demand is my command," she threw over her shoulder as the hustled off to the kitchen to prepare lunch.

Speedy and I took a seat in the living room. Trying to keep the conversation on a light note, I said, "What was the nicest thing that ever happened to you when you visited this house?"

Speedy rolled his eyes and thought for a minute. "Well, I guess I would have to say the booze and the broads, and the dances were fun; and the card games, too. Sometimes I'd win a couple of thousand; other times, I'd lose."

In order to keep the conversation rolling and on the track toward interrogation, I said, "How many times were you here as a guest?"

He put his hand to his chin and then said, "Every two or three months for maybe thirty years or so. I don't know if I would have considered myself a guest; it was more like recreation and a little rest from the stressful rackets we were in. A couple of times I wasn't a guest, but an inmate. That was tough as hell, but that's the way it was back then."

Taken aback, I said, “Speedy, I don’t understand. What do you mean an *inmate*? Did someone bring you here against your will?

His answer cracked the door a little into the hidden meaning of the mansion when he said, “I wouldn’t say that exactly. I knew what I was in for when I was told by one of the bosses to report here to Judge Levison. I had to come. You didn’t have any choice. If you didn’t show up, they would send guys to get you and then there was hell to pay.”

Just as I was starting to get somewhere, Peggy Sue called us to lunch. However, as we made our way to the kitchen Speedy almost floored me when he said, “You know, kid, I like you. You listen to my bullshit and somehow I enjoy telling it. Reminds me of old times. It’s been a long time since I told anyone what I am about to tell you. I’m sure you can be trusted to keep a secret. So, after lunch I’m going to show you something that I don’t think you even know exists.”

As we entered Peggy Sue’s kitchen domain, Speedy asked, “What’s for lunch, my dear?”

As she put plates down in front of us, she replied, “Why it’s Zack’s favorite, tuna fish on whole wheat, sweet pickles on the side and hot tea to drink. I’ve been serving it to him ever since we’ve been married.”

I laughed as we sat down to eat, “I never could get enough of a good thing. I guess that’s why I still have you around.”

I looked over at Speedy and he was smirking when he said, “You know you would have fit right in with the guys I used to hang out with. Maybe that’s why I like you.”

After we finished lunch and had dessert, I couldn’t contain my curiosity any longer. I was about to pop; not from lunch mind you, but from the suspense of what Speedy was going to show me. Finally I just piped up with, “You said you were going to tell me something. Well I’m ready. What is it?”

Speedy stood up from the table and said, “You’ll need

a flashlight."

"Got one right here," I said as I slid open one of the kitchen junk drawers and waited for him to say more. Immediately, he started for the basement, and I followed, leaving Peggy Sue to clean up the dishes.

When we reached the bottom of the stairs, he headed through the ballroom, approaching the wall where I knew the old jail cell was hidden. "Well, maybe I can't show you anything after all. I see someone has covered it up with paneling."

Acting stupid, I said, "Show me what, Speedy?"

"Well, brace yourself, kid. There's a jail cell hidden just behind this panel on the wall."

Baiting him, I looked aghast and said, "Go on, Speedy. You got to be kidding."

"No, I'm not, I've been in it," he insisted. "Hey, I know what. Let's go upstairs to the fireplace."

I thought I really had him going when we got upstairs and he removed the metal plate in the floor of the fireplace and played the light beam down into the old dungeon.

I pretended to lose it, just to go crazy…all the while knowing about the whole thing. He thought I was seeing it for the first time.

"Speedy," I said to him, "you can't keep doing this to me. Will you please just sit down, start at the beginning and tell me the entire story? Everything you know about the house—I need to know, Speedy."

I could tell he was almost as excited as I, and he seemed to enjoy reliving some of his not-so-fond memories of the past. "Do you have about a week?" he asked me. "That's about how long it's gonna take to explain what I know about this joint." I told him I had been waiting eight years for some answers, so I was willing to listen as long as he wanted to talk.

"Well, all right, then. I think I would be better able to

tell the story if we were downstairs in the basement.

"Okay," I said, "Let's go." We headed down the stairs again. Without any hesitation at all, he walked right up to the wine racks, pulled the hidden lever, and swung the door open.

"You did know this was here, didn't you?" he asked me in a tone that told me I had to be truthful.

"Yes," I answered quickly. "Peggy Sue discovered it a few years ago by accident. We just use it for storage today." I turned on the lights as we stepped into the room.

Speedy looked around and said, "Boy, it used to be a big deal just to be in this room. It was the main counting area and you had to be frisked by the guards before even stepping in here."

Looking over at the open doors of the vault, he continued, "I see you got the doors open. Man, at one time, there were millions stored in there. Did you find any cash when you moved in?"

Inside I was as giddy as a young school kid pulling his first prank when I realized my money-moving scheme had worked perfectly. Walking over to the safe with him close behind, I said, "Yes, we found some money. I have about eighteen thousand dollars left after paying for Bruno's hospital costs and his funeral and tombstone. I still have it in the trunk of my car. We weren't sure it was real but we haven't had any trouble using it. We also found a bunch of old papers, books and these," I said as I held up the machine gun and pistol.

Wide-eyed, Speedy said, "You can bet your butt the money was real, and so are those guns. Did you unload them?"

"Hell, no! I've just kept them here on the top shelf. I don't have any use for them," I quickly retorted.

"Believe you me, they have been well used," Speedy said. "Just wait til I tell you about 'em."

"Before you do that," I said, "let me run up and get

the money. I've kept it hidden in the trunk of my car for a couple of years and I want you to look at it to be sure it's the real thing."

I raced out to the car and got the cash I had taken from Bruno's shack. I hurried back down the stairs with it and handed it to Speedy. He examined the money carefully and then said, "I don't see anything wrong with it except that it's a little old."

Continuing my little charade, I said innocently, "What do you think I should do with it? Call the police and turn it in?"

That did it! Speedy went into a big-time huff. "Man, are you crazy? Don't tell anybody anything! Just go ahead and spend it."

"Well, okay, if that's what you think I should do," I said in my very best sheepish little voice.

I was convinced now that my deception had worked like a charm and I had completely bamboozled him. I couldn't help but chuckle to myself, "You fox, you." I was so sharp!

Speedy broke into my thoughts. "I would suggest, however, one more thing to you. I'd bury those guns. I recognize that Thompson from its red handle. That was Bruno's gun and I guarantee you, they were both murder weapons."

"Murder weapons? I don't understand, what's this about Bruno" I asked with a really dumb look on my face.

"Yep, Bruno, or rather Anthony Buglioni your neighbor, the nice old hunchback whom you spent so much money on for his funeral. Well, he was nothing but a killer. He was the internal enforcer for the mob. Any gang member that needed disciplined by the bosses for some mistake or someone who was caught stealing mob money was reported to Judge Levison and he would have Tony and his red devil pay them a visit. Then, it was lights out for them. *Finito*. That was it. They were either dead as a doornail or arrested and thrown in the mansion jail."

I was beginning to feel a bit overwhelmed by so much information but I was dying to hear more. I kept probing and asking more questions. "Speedy, did you know there are graves at the rear of my property and that the old judge is buried out there along with Bruno?"

Speedy nodded his head and said, "I thought that was where you would have buried Bruno, but I didn't want to say anything at the time. Did I know about the other dead guys out there? Sure, I knew there were three of them. Tony shot one of them in a bar right in front of a bunch of us guys and then dragged the body away and we figured it wound up out there. Judge Levison sentenced the other two men to several months in the cell or the padded room upstairs. They were on bread and water as part of the punishment and, for some strange reason, they both died. Malnutrition, maybe. They all worked with me in Detroit back in the late forties running numbers."

When Speedy made the comment about the possibility of the men dying of malnutrition, I knew he was dead wrong. What I had learned so painfully was that the cause of their deaths was iron blood poisoning, lightning and insanity.

But, still playing dumb, I fished a little more. "You mean that you, yourself, were in the rackets?

"Yeah, I was one of the boys in the gang."

"Do you mean the Purple Gang?"

"Well, us guys never called it that, just the newspapers. We only said we belonged to an exclusive sportsmen's club."

Hoping to dig up a little more dirt, I said, "Speedy, do you know what the Knights of Zion are?"

"Where in the hell did you hear about them?" Speedy asked me very abruptly.

"I found an old black book upstairs in the library with

two golden triangles on the front of it and I read some of it. The Knighthood of Zion was mentioned and it described a certain silver ring, and I saw one just like it on Judge Levison's finger in the old painting over the fireplace. There was an old German Luger pistol in mint condition hidden in that book. I've got both of them in a safe deposit box at the bank."

"Well, you're right, kid, he was one of them. There were only six of them left from the old country; all Jews and they all wore that God damned ring like it was some kind of magic jewelry. I guess now that Levison is dead, they're all in hell."

While he was talking, I had stepped into the vault and picked up the jar containing the severed fingers and one of the journals with the lists of names. This was the book that listed the men on the payroll or those who were paid for special jobs. Taking them over to Speedy I handed him the jar. "What do you make of these?"

Speedy was totally astonished. "Well, I'll be damned. Looks like about eight or nine fingers and I see three have on the signet ring. It's funny but us guys knew those three bosses must have got knocked off because they all just disappeared one day and we never saw them again. Everybody figured they got bumped but we never knew who did it. Looks like the old Judge had Tony hit them before they got to do the same to him. I'll be damned. Hey, let's see that book."

He opened the journal to the page with the list of names and, scanning it, said, "Yeah, here's Corky Dunlap, Spats Malone, and Duce Tebbits, names of three guys I worked with."

I jumped right into the conversation in an effort to encourage him to continue. "What kind of name is Spats? I never heard of that one before."

Speedy was happy to inform the greenhorn, "Spats wasn't his real name. Actually, spats were cloth things worn around your shoes in the thirties, real dressy like. He had them on all the time, so that was his nickname. It seems like everyone used a nickname or an alias back then, mainly to conceal their real identities. Most of the men were loners and had no families. I guess the mob was all the family they had.

"You see the little stars before some of these names? Well, those are the names of the bosses. There's Sol Vogelstein and Hymie Weinstein and see this one, Abe Lebowitz? He was my boss. By God, that's their fingers in the jar!"

I thought I would add something to the conversation by saying, "Bruno, or Tony, or whatever the hell his name was, told me that he also buried them out back along with six other guys.

"Sure, that makes sense," Speedy replied after a second. "Seems as though you have a nice little dumping ground for dead gangsters right here on your old homestead." That was followed by his little chuckle.

I laughed along with him and offered, "I'm getting all confused. Could you please start from the beginning and tell me how this whole damned jigsaw puzzle fits together?"

"Sure I will," Speedy said. "Just get me a few shots of whiskey to whet my whistle and I'll go over as much as I know."

I headed toward the wine rack doorway and said, "Let's go upstairs so we can be more comfortable." Once we were in the living room, I mentioned to Speedy. "I'm sure you know about the tunnel that leads down the hill to the front of the property, but please, please tell me about the elevator shaft!"

Looking really surprised, my informant said, "Yeah, I know about the tunnel. It was used a few times to get away from the cops. It was not all that easy to get to the bottom of the hill and once a guy and a babe got stuck in it and it took two days to get them out of there. It wasn't used much after that. Anyway, the cops just got tired of trying to find out what the hell went on out here and eventually they left the place alone. They were just a bunch of hicks, anyway, and didn't know nothin'.

"But, what's this about an elevator shaft? If you mean the one between the floors, it was nothing but an oversized laundry chute."

"No," I said, "the one that runs parallel to the fireplace."

Now Speedy was really perplexed. "Well, that's a new one on me; this I gotta see. Lead me to it."

I took Speedy upstairs into the bathroom and then into the small cubbyhole that contained the concealed door to the shaft. When I unlocked it and opened the small door, Speedy and I peered down into the shaft. Looking at the makeshift chair and lowering device, I said, "If you sit in this chair and lower it to each floor, you can see into some rooms. There are tiny peepholes in the oil paintings of Judge Levison hung over the fireplaces and small slits in the basement and attic walls."

"Well, I'll be a son of a bitch! That's how the old bastard knew everything we were thinking or planning. He could spy on us anywhere in this house, even when we were making love to our women in the bedrooms or playing cards in the living room. Now I know why he was always excusing himself early or saying he was going to bed. The old pervert must have used this contraption to see my girlfriend's ass and tits many a time. No wonder he was always so friendly toward her and often commented that she really had a great pair of funbags. And he even told her he bet when she got going in bed she could screw like a mink.

"I always wondered how he knew. I was sure of one thing. He definitely wasn't doing her because I never, ever saw him with a woman and neither did anyone else. One time I did see him in the basement shower and his Johnson was so small it looked like he coulda only had sex with bugs."

I was a little taken aback and embarrassed by the rough language and was happy that Peggy Sue was out of earshot. But, after all, the guy was a gangster. I guess you couldn't expect Shakespeare!

Now, Speedy was on a roll. "You say it goes down to the basement? He could probably see us when we were partying in the old ballroom and it would have given him a bird's eye view of the wine rack door leading to the money and the vault. Now, I know how he found out about me and another guy skimming a few bucks a week from our numbers routes. We used to laugh like hell about it over poker at a card table in the living room right where we were just sitting.

"That little piece of info got us both sentenced to 90 days in that cell I was telling you about. It was hell with the two of us in that little room. It's probably how he found out about the three bosses planning to cut him out of a new operation they were opening in Toledo; and maybe the reason he rubbed them out. He sure was a ruthless, nutty old bastard and it's too bad he didn't croak that time when he got shot in the face."

Pretending I knew nothing of the shooting, I said, "Could that be the reason his face is so twisted and ugly in the portraits?"

"Well, the old son of a bitch was ugly to start with, and that just made him look worse," Speedy said disgustedly. "Let's get that drink and I will tell you my life's story and how I first got in the mob."

We went down to the living room and Speedy plunked down into a nice, deep soft chair while I made us a couple of highballs. Handing him his drink, I sat directly across from him and made myself comfortable, too.

He began his story by saying, "It was back in 1929 and there were no jobs. I mean you couldn't even buy one, absolutely no work. I had a job at the Ford factory at the rouge plant as an assembly line worker, but I was laid off. After being unemployed for almost two years, I had to make money somehow even if it was illegal. I knew a guy named Sanford who worked at Hudson Motors who picked up numbers and I asked him if he could use me. He knew I had worked at the rouge plant and had a lot of contacts out there, so he said he would give me a tryout as a bag man and numbers drop at Ford's. All I had to do was jot down the numbers the workers would hand me, along with the money, put all of it in a brown shopping bag and then turn them over to him each night.

"My pay was five dollars a day. I would also have to pay off any hits on the book, so I started to handle quite a bit of money. I never knew what my friend did with the money, but one day a tough looking guy came up to me and asked if I was Speedy. When I said I was, he told me his name was Iggie Katonia and that Sanford wasn't around any longer and I was now the new numbers man at Hudson's.

"I was to turn the money over to him each night and my salary would be fifteen dollars a day. Really good money back then. I asked about all my customers at Ford's and he said he had already put another man in that operation, but if I played my cards right he would soon be working for me.

"I was now a full-fledged gang member; I didn't know what gang and didn't care. All I wanted was the fifteen bucks. So began my years as a soldier with the mob."

Speedy stopped for a moment and drank deep of the booze; then continued his story. "I guess I wound up doing just about everything they wanted me to do and, I must say, I was paid handsomely and eventually had men working for me. I mean I did everything: numbers, loan sharking, bootlegging, protection rackets, shady deals with mob insiders at horse tracks, you name it, I did it. I even arranged to fix a few prizefights."

I couldn't help it; I just had to ask. "Speedy, when you

said you did everything, did that include, uh," I hesitated, "killing someone?"

"Yeah, I did that, too, but they had it coming. It was either them or me. It's just the way it went. When someone starts shooting at you, self-preservation kicks in and you shoot back. You see them fall and you take off. One time I had to spend three weeks here in the attic, sleeping on an army cot, waiting for things to cool down. That's what this attic was for, you know. It was a place to hide out and also, once in a while, some of the bosses would give us classes on how to run scams; or the best procedure to follow to hijack a load of booze; so it doubled as a classroom."

Speedy was just getting started and I let him ramble on.

"I'll never forget the first time I saw Judge Levison. It was in the spring of 1931 and a bunch of us wise guys were caught red-handed with a full load of illegal booze by the cops. We were arraigned the following day before Levison. I mean to tell you, he made a mockery out of the legal system right there in front of everyone. The guy thought he was untouchable, but he wasn't and eventually got caught with his hand in the cookie jar.

"Anyway, this time he let every one of us off Scot-free. I knew then he was one of our boys. A few weeks later, I made my first visit here to headquarters for a three-day vacation. That was when I saw a man in the small cell in the basement. The poor guy must have been going nuts. He could see us having a ball while he was chained to the wall. What a bad deal for him. I don't know who he was and I never saw him again, but I know what he went through because I spent some time in that same hell hole myself. He could have been from one of the Chicago gangs. But it didn't take me long to forget about him.

"Boy, did I ever party that first time. It was booze, broads, poker and plenty of Oo La La, if you know what I mean. Then, it was back to the streets."

I was enjoying the story until he said "here at headquarters," but I was hopeful he had misspoken. So I asked, "Speedy, did you say, *headquarters*?"

Looking serious, Speedy repeated his statement, "Headquarters is the correct word for this place, Zack. The last four living Knights of Zion got together and decided to build this place. I know it's your home now, but it was built for one reason and one reason alone: to act as a base of operations, a kind of central bank, a hideout and training center for the mobs operating in the Detroit and Chicago areas beginning with its construction in 1929.

"Its remote location, the escape tunnel, all the windows giving a view of the entire surrounding area, the holding cell in the basement and the padded room upstairs—all these things were planned from the start. Of course, the bank style vault was one of the main features built into the foundation of the mansion. The only thing that was a real secret was that viewing shaft which must have been Levison's own idea. Trained as an attorney and then a judge, he was the one selected to manage the place and hand out sentences for anyone in the mob that violated the code of the underworld. I guess his position and handling of all the mob finances—acting like judge and jury—caused him to finally think he was the headman or the kingpin.

"I do remember that most of the guys in the gangs thought he was insane and that he dealt out very harsh punishment. So, none of us was unhappy when it came to us through the grapevine that he had died.

"You know, I was just thinking. None of this would have ever come out if I hadn't seen that ambulance race past me on old Highway 12 and I hadn't met you. That's the way life goes, I guess, and a guy just never knows what's just around the next corner.

"This house has been part of my life off and on for

over forty years and I have a love/hate relationship with it. I used to have a lot of fun here, but I also suffered to no end in that cell. I know I will never outlive it, but if it burned down to the ground, I'd dance over the ashes. If I had only known it came up for sale after the old Judge died, I would have bought it myself and torched it the next day. However, I was being unexpectedly detained by the feds at the time."

I could tell that Speedy was starting to get a little melancholy, so I spoke up and changed the subject. "Would you like to take a walk out back and maybe walk over to the grave sites?"

I could see his face light up at the idea and he said, "That's a great idea. I need to take a piss anyway and I can't think of a better place than on top of Levison's grave!"

We left the house and walked out to the small knoll that held the remains of the eleven gangsters. Buried there were six so-called "soldiers," three Knights of Zion, Judge Levison and, now, Bruno. As we walked, Speedy seemed to be in a hurry. When we reached the judge's grave I pointed it out to him. Right then and there, he whipped out his Johnson and took a piss like a racehorse and said with a big old smile, "Man, that felt good. I hope it runs right down into the son of a bitch's face. I guess I could say that I had the last laugh, or the last piss, as it turned out!"

Speedy couldn't believe the tombstones. "Man, I can see why they cost you seventeen grand. They're big, aren't they? Let's see what this one says over Bruno…I mean Anthony Buglioni. Yeah, I see you finally got his name right, but I think you went a little overboard on the verse. I never saw him as having even one twinge of being a nice guy, none whatsoever. What's this on the other one?"

He read the inscription and then stood motionless for a few seconds as if contemplating. Then, he said, thoughtfully, "Now, that is not too bad and makes pretty good sense. It's right in one respect. They were once just innocent kids that went bad somewhere along the way."

Looking at his wristwatch, Speedy said, "Well, this is the perfect ending to a perfect day. I really need to get into town, get my winter supplies and make the island before dark. Thank your missus for me for lunch, and thank you for the drinks. It did me a world of good, finally getting this stuff off my chest and on to someone else's—all that bullshit I've been carrying around for years. I know you don't need any grief, but you really needed to know all the facts about where you are living and the unbeliveable story behind this old mansion."

We started up toward the house. The weather was turning a little hazy and there was a funny ring around the late afternoon sun. It felt cold enough to snow. We had only walked a short distance when Speedy said casually, "Look at that old guy over there in the gully, walking his dog."

I wondered what he was talking about now, but as I turned to look in the direction of the gully, I felt a tremendous shock of terror. I couldn't see clearly, but by the wobbly gait and the bib overalls, I could make out the old man Speedy was seeing. I was certain of one thing, however, it had to be a ghost because it looked like none other than Bruno. Striding by his side was my ghost dog Gwendolyn. God! Maybe it was just a hunter out with his dog.

I was scared shitless, but said nothing. I just turned and we made a hasty trip back to the house. I continued to look in the direction where we had seen the figure, but I saw nothing.

When we got to the house, I shook hands with my gangster friend. As he drove away, he shouted to me, "So long. See you next spring."

I retreated, then, to the safety and sanctity of my home and locked the door.

When I got inside, I just felt numb all over and realized my hands were trembling. I staggered over to the fireplace, plopped down into my chair in front of the fire and gazed into the burning embers. I guess I was trying to get myself into a relaxed state of mind whereas I could put Speedy's revelations into perspective.

I was sure that Speedy had no clue that I had found the mother lode of the Knights of Zion's fortune, so I felt safe and secure about that. But, I kept asking myself if there was anything I might have overlooked that might still trip me up. Then I thought about the weapons that were still in the basement. Speedy was right. They could be very incriminating.

Even though I felt dizzy and my mind was still reeling, I jumped up and headed to the basement to retrieve the guns. Picking up the Thompson, the old revolver and all the ammo, it was my intention to bury it all in the back woods like Speedy had suggested. But, for some strange reason, I didn't want to part with them. I thought I might as well throw all the stuff into one of the footlockers in the back of the truck. After all, if the money was found, what difference would it make if the weapons were also found.

Just as I was about to leave the vault, the glass jar containing the severed fingers caught my eye. "What the hell," I thought, "I'll just keep them, too."

I wrapped the jar and a couple of the old journals in the judge's black judicial robe and then headed out to the truck where I put all the items in the footlocker just behind the front seat.

Suddenly, I felt extremely exhausted, more mentally than physically, so I stumbled into the house, went up the stairs and fell into bed fully clothed. Soon I drifted into fitfully troubled sleep.

24

January 1979

The snows finally came with a vengeance. We were almost marooned in a sea of white, but we had the trusty old tractor to plow the drive; and the state kept Highway 12 cleared enough that we could get to town for food and an occasional movie or bowling.

Although there was a lot of the white stuff, we had a blast that winter. We did a lot of snow skiing down the front of our hill and I used the tractor to clear an ice rink on Lake Misty for skating.

One dark evening, however, about 10 o'clock, things changed dramatically. We were on our way home after a family night out for dinner and a movie. As we rounded the hill at Suicide Ridge and turned onto Highway 12, I noticed a deep red glow on the horizon. I woke Peggy Sue who was dozing in the front seat and pointed out the red glare.

"What does that look like?" I inquired of her.

"It looks like a big blaze of some kind. I sure hope it's not our house." The minute she said that, I was having the same chilling thought. The closer we got, the nearer the fire seemed to be to our home. When we turned onto Collier, our worst fears were realized. We saw our home engulfed in flames. As we were turning into our drive at the end of Collier Road, I saw a white car off on the side of the road. It didn't mean much to me at the time because I was preoccupied with getting up the hill.

The way the flames were spreading, it was apparent

there wasn't anything we could do. We were completely helpless. Even if the volunteer fire department could make it up the hill, there was no water supply to fight the fire. Besides, by the time they could get here from town, the entire house would be gone.

My main concern was the outside garage and the truck that held the stuff that dreams are made of. I could see that it was in no danger since it was far from the main residence. With its contents, we could replace anything that was being lost in the fire—anything.

I had such a helpless feeling. All the six of us could do was stand there in our driveway and watch our beautiful home turn into a blazing inferno. Peggy Sue was the first to notice that the flames were no longer the brilliant red they had been initially. Now they had turned to a deep purple. An immense shaft of spiraling white smoke and steam rose skyward from the center of the house, carrying in it the still glowing embers of wood that drifted high into the night sky they then twinkled and then seemed to disappear into the black heavens.

That very moment, we heard horrible howls and bone-chilling cries emitting from the depths of the swirling fire—surely to God they weren't human.

At first, we thought maybe our ears were playing tricks on us and it was just the roar of the blaze. For just a fleeting instant, I thought maybe a burglar was caught in the fiery hell of the blaze. But, no, this was something else; something much more terrifying.

When the front door collapsed from the fire and fell away, Peggy Sue and I peered into what was once our living room. There, outlined before us in the roaring flames were images of horribly twisted faces and smoky images of figures twisting and turning while strange sounds escaped from their elongated mouths.

It was impossible to determine what or who they

were, but it was evident that these were tormented souls in unspeakable agony. We stood there in shock as this horrific scene unfolded. Then, suddenly, after just a few minutes, the shapes and faces merged into a huge ball of fire and were simultaneously swept into the pillar of swirling white smoke. They completely disappeared into the black night sky. The howling stopped instantly and everything was eerily silent except for the crackling and snapping of our beautiful oak paneling and heavy hardwood beams as everything burned.

Peggy Sue was crying. I tried to comfort her and put my arms around her and pulled her tight against me. "Don't worry," I said, "We can replace whatever is lost. Don't cry over the house. We can rebuild it better than ever."

"Oh, God, I'm not crying over the loss of the house or any of my personal things. We're all safe and that's the most important thing to me. I'm crying for those poor tormented souls that have been locked here in some kind of limbo for some reason that only God knows. I feel like they have finally been set free now that the house is gone and can no longer hold their spirits here on earth. The flames must have released them somehow from the hill's magnetism. Now, maybe at long last, they can find peace."

Just like always, Peggy Sue made a lot of sense. At that moment there was a tremendous roar as the huge chimney fell onto the roof on its way to the basement, taking with it three of the outer walls and sending up an enormous shower of sparks and debris. A few seconds after the walls fell, there were several loud bangs and popping noises. That had to be coming from the ammunition I hadn't yet removed from the house.

The final end of our beautiful mansion came with what looked and sounded like a Fourth of July fireworks display.

I can't really explain the jumble of my emotions as I watched the mansion burn. I was deeply saddened, and yet I think I had always known that we would have to leave this house someday. But, not like this, with the decision being forced upon us. And, certainly, not because something beyond our control had reduced this magnificent place to ruin.

On the other hand, surprisingly, I felt a sense of release of some kind. I think it must have been the realization that finally there was to be respite from all the years of emotional and physical torture my family and I had endured because we had chosen to live on such a complex geographical site. Now that the mansion was gone, maybe that would put an end to the weird experiences endured by anyone residing in the house. All that remained now was a pile of smoldering timbers and smoking bricks. I felt I could probably sell the property now without worrying about it. Peggy Sue and I stood there all through the night and watched our dream home burn.

At daybreak, I walked down to the bottom of the hill to the spot where I remembered seeing a white car parked on the side of the road. When I got to the spot, I looked around closely. Immediately I noticed footprints in the snow leading up the hill, so I followed them. The prints led straight toward the house. At several points along the route, it appeared the steps hesitated or stopped. Each time there was the hesitation, I noticed there was also the imprint of what could have been the bottom of a large heavy can. I continued to follow the prints until they ended in an area where the snow had been melted by the heat of the fire.

I was too tired and hungry even to speculate on who was carrying what I was convinced was a gas can. Obviously someone had hauled a can up the hill and set fire to our home; but I didn't have the emotional or physical strength to think about it right then.

I trudged back up the driveway to where Peggy Sue was standing. I told her we needed to get the kids off the hill and we all needed something to eat. Then we realized we would also need a place to stay until we could decide what we were going to do.

We piled in the car and drove into town. The kids had fallen asleep in the back of the car earlier so Peggy Sue and I were quiet as we made the drive into Clinton to get some breakfast and find a place to stay. Neither of us knew what to say anyway.

We got a suite of rooms in the old Clintonian Inn. It was conveniently located in the middle of town and the children could walk to school. Later that day, after we were settled and Peggy Sue had taken the four kids shopping for school clothes, she dropped me off at the fire department where I reported the fire.

The fire chief was astonished to learn that our home had caught fire and burned to the ground without the department's knowing about it. He asked if I had any idea how the fire had started. Not really wanting anyone snooping around the place, I just said rather sadly, "I think the boiler blew up while we were in town for dinner and a movie."

The chief expressed his regret about our house but said he was glad we were away and no one was hurt. He affirmed the notion I'd had, that even if the fire had been reported immediately, the fire department wouldn't have been able to do much to save the house. He mentioned the distant location of the house and the fact there was no adequate water supply on our hill for fire fighting.

I didn't have to fill out any reports, but the chief asked if we planned to rebuild on the site. I answered sadly that right now everything was up in the air and we weren't sure where the pieces would fall into place.

The night, Peggy Sue and I talked about what we wanted to do with our lives and what might be best for the children as well. We remembered having talked about moving somewhere in the South right after we found the stash of money. If we were going to do it, we agreed, now was the time. We didn't have to pack up for the move. We only had the clothes on our backs and Peggy Sue's El Dorado—and, oh yeah, a panel truck full of money!

We talked about rebuilding on the hill and reasoned that if we did that we would still be living on top of a lodestone mountain. That thought made us realize we didn't want to rebuild. We discussed it for quite a while and decided, for our own sanity, we were going to take our kids and that truck full of cash and head for a state down south. We wanted to get as far away from our magnetic nightmare as we could.

Sure, we knew we would miss the quaint little town and all the friends we had made—and we would miss our parents—but we thought they would enjoy visiting us in the South, especially in the dead of winter.

The kids were all for moving to another city, but they said they wanted to be closer to town so they could have more friends. Finally, the die was cast. We were going to move, but I had some loose ends I needed to tie up first. I couldn't just leave the hill in its present state. After all, it had been our home for over eight years and, at times, we were ecstatically happy there. I had to do something. Then I thought about what people do when they lose a loved one. They bury that loved one, right?

I had an idea and thought about my friend Chuck who had helped me open the secret vault. He had lots of heavy equipment and would probably be willing to help me out. When I got him on the phone and told him what had happened, he was shocked and eager to help any way he could.

I asked if he had a bulldozer at his disposal—a really big one. Chuck said he had access to a 'dozer but reminded me he wasn't in the construction business. I told him I knew that, but wondered how soon he could come out to the hill with his bulldozer and a trailer that could haul the 'dozer and an antique automobile.

"Oh, am I bringing an old car with me also?

I laughed and said, "No, Chuck, you will be taking one home with you!"

"Oh, well, I could be out there day after tomorrow in the morning. Would that work?"

I told him that would work well and asked him to pick me up in Clinton at the Clintonian Inn about 9 o'clock.

"Will do," was Chuck's no-nonsense answer.

The next day, I set out to tie up some more of those loose ends I had to deal with. I drove the Caddie into Ann Arbor to see my friend Lance at the bank. While I waited for him, I emptied the contents of my safe deposit box, including the old black book with the pistol hidden inside, into the old leather briefcase I had retrieved from the trunk of the Cadillac. When I had emptied the contents into the case, I took it back out to the car and locked it securely in the trunk one more time.

When I got back inside the bank, Lance was ready for me and he motioned me into his office and offered me a cup of coffee. I told him about the fire and, of course, he was full of questions. I tried to answer them as patiently as I could, but my mind was on getting my business concluded so I could get on with preparations for the move. When I asked him for a cashier's check that would close out my accounts at the bank, he was surprised. "Then you really are dead set on moving away," he surmised.

"Yes, after over eight years of snow and ice and fighting that damned hill, it's time we moved to a warmer climate. The fact that the house burned down just helped us make our decision," I said.

As he added up all my accounts, Lance said, "Well, I can see that your mind is made up. Let's see, now. Your total deposits amount to…oh, my, $878,473. Well, that's a tidy little sum. I'll be right back with a cashier's check."

He came back a few minutes later and handed me the check. "This ought to hold you over until you get yourself settled. But, we sure are sorry to lose you as a customer and friend. The best of luck to you and Peggy Sue and the kids. Goodbye, Zack, we'll miss you."

As I folded the check and put it in my pocket, I remembered the day I had picked up another check from Lance. It was the day eight years ago when there were a lot fewer gray hairs on my noggin that I used the earlier check to purchase "a cottage at a lake."

At 9 o'clock the next morning, Chuck picked me up at the hotel. He was driving his truck, towing the monstrous bulldozer on a trailer. We drove out to the burned ruins of my former home. He was amazed that a place that had seemed so indestructible had burned to the ground. He said the temperatures must have reached several thousand degrees to melt all the steel in the place. Even the huge vent from the top of the chimney was nothing but a melted ball of metal.

"Chuck, I want you to push the dirt from the sides of the hill down into that hole that was once my home and then I want everything covered with as much dirt as you can heap onto what's left. I don't want anything showing above the ground. Then, maybe in ten years or so, no one will ever know this place even existed. Can you do that?"

Chuck's answer assured me he knew what he was doing with that 'dozer. "Sure, if that's what you want, you got it. I'll cover up everything."

"Now," I said, "about your fee for this job. Walk over here with me a minute. I want to show you something." I took Chuck over to the outside garage and when I opened the garage doors and he saw the old Packard, he let out a yell. He was a collector of antique automobiles and he loved the old hearse! I told him I was prepared to give him the old Packard hearse and one thousand dollars to do the job. "Do you think that will cover it?"

Chuck was flabbergasted. "You bet it will," he said with enthusiasm. "I'll stay here until I get the job done even if it takes me until next week. But I better get to work. Time's a' wasting."

"Oh! One other thing," I said. "After you have taken the Packard, turn on the switch to the gas pump over there and pump all the gas you can into your truck. And fill your bulldozer if you can. Then, I want you to knock down the garage. Can you do that?"

Chuck responded as positively as ever. "Sure, that's a simple job for this baby," he said as he seated himself on the massive machine that had just started up with a roar.

As Chuck drove toward his burial project, I slipped into the back of the panel truck, opened a footlocker just behind the front seat and took out eleven $100 bills. Then I closed the locker and walked over to where Chuck was already dumping debris into the yawning hole. Over the noise of the engine, I said, "Chuck, here's a thousand and an extra hundred for doing the garage." I handed him the money and turned to leave. "I'm leaving now, but I'll be back later in the week to check the finished job. Good luck."

Yelling his answer over the noise of the bulldozer, Chuck said, "I'll probably be gone by then, but if you need me to come back out, you know where to find me. So long."

I went over to the garage, got in and started my new truck and pulled away, waving to Chuck with tears in my eyes. What my friend was burying and bringing to its final end was something that had been a big part of my life. At times it had filled me with tremendous joy; and at other times, it had brought unbelievable fear. My family had endured an ordeal of multiple strange and bizarre experiences, haunting our lives both mentally and physically. It was finally over. We had survived the house on Irish Hill, but not without some consequences.

I still had the load of money to deal with and the nagging question of who had torched my home and why. I had a short list of arsonists, very short. Speedy Sullivan was at the top of the list because he had said he would like to see the house burn. I had thought from the beginning that it was his white car I saw pulled off on the side of the road. There was also the odd-shaped imprint in the snow of the bottom of a can—and I remembered the gas can in Speedy's woodshed, the one I used to gas up the boat.

I didn't want to involve the police or my insurance company for obvious reasons, but I had no intention of letting the loss of my home go unanswered. I was going to confront Speedy. Maybe he wasn't the guilty party, but he sure had some explaining to do.

I went back to the hotel to have lunch with Peggy Sue. During the meal, I told her of my suspicions about Speedy's possible connection to the fire. All she said was, "Just let it go, Honey. It doesn't make any difference now. The house is gone and everything in it. Nothing can change that. We have all the money we will ever need and we can replace everything we've lost, so what's the point of going up against the old guy? He's unpredictable and he's probably got a gun laying around. He might even try to shoot you. Remember, he *was* a gangster."

Peggy Sue was making sense once again. Speedy was as much a killer as Bruno had been. He probably wouldn't even think twice about putting a couple of slugs in me if I crossed him. But the thought of him burning down my house while my family might have been inside was really eating at my guts.

I was going after the old bastard!

Suddenly, I thought about the loaded German Luger in the trunk of the Caddie. If it came to gunplay, and it might, I was resolved to shoot back if I had to. The more I thought about the fire the more incensed I got; and then it dawned on me…what had I become? I was actually thinking about shooting someone.

I guess my association over the years with Bruno and later with Speedy, and the fact they had killed people, had lessened somehow the seriousness of the deed I was contemplating in my mind. Was I becoming the same kind of monster they were? When you got right down to it, I guess I could be considered a thief. I was, after all, keeping money that wasn't mine.

My, my, how my values had changed since I found *it*! Then I changed course in my mind and contemplated the *amount* of money in the truck. It was a king's ransom to me and it was mine and if I had to kill to keep it, I was prepared to do so.

Peggy Sue's voice broke into my reverie. "You're awfully quiet. What are you thinking?"

Man, if she only knew…but all I said was, "Nothing. Nothing at all. I think I'm going to take a little ride and just be by myself for a few hours, so you'll be without a car for a while."

"Okay," she said, "But be careful, Zack, and remember I love you."

I didn't hesitate even for a second and headed straight out Highway 12 toward Evans Lake. It was still early in the day so I had plenty of time to confront Speedy out on the island.

When I arrived at the south shore, I parked the Caddie and moved to the trunk. I opened the black book, removed the automatic pistol, slipped it into my overcoat pocket and headed down to the boatlift.

I really expected to find Speedy's Buick parked nearby, but it was nowhere in sight. The Chris Craft was not on its lift either. What in the hell was going on? I had no way to get to the island to confront the old gangster. Speedy could be on the island and his car elsewhere…or he could be gone in the car and the boat could be in the shop for repairs or something. My mind was going haywire. I was dead set on bringing this issue to a dramatic close, but I couldn't find the one person who was the target of my anger.

I stood there in the cold wind like a fool and tried to reason with myself about what to do next. I thought about calling the police and telling them of my suspicions that Speedy had started the fire. I decided that was a good idea; but then the thought of getting the cops involved reminded me there was a gun in my pocket. I immediately ran to the trunk of my car and put the gun back in its hiding place inside the book.

I needed to get to a telephone to call the Michigan State Police, but I didn't know where the nearest telephone might be. Then I remembered there was a police outpost in Jackson, only about 30 miles away, and it might be best to talk to someone in person. So, I hopped back in the Cadillac and sped west on Highway 12 toward the outpost.

When I entered the police station, I walked up to the desk sergeant and said I wanted to report a possible case of arson. He seemed very casual about the whole thing, but took my name and escorted me into a small office.

In a few minutes, we were joined by a plainclothes detective who was going to take my statement.

"Well," I began my complaint. "I'm here to inform you about a Mr. Clarence Sullivan who…" Before I could utter another word, the detective interrupted abruptly.

"Clarence Sullivan? The guy who lives on the island in Lake Evans? You're not related to him are you?" he asked.

I was dumbfounded. "No! Why would you ask me that?" The detective headed for the door; then paused, looked back at me, and said, "You'll have to talk to my captain. I'll go get him."

All I could think was, "Oh, shit! Now I've done it. I've blown the whole thing. What a stupid place for me to be.

Now the cops will find out about everything."

Before my paranoia had time to completely take over, the captain entered the office. "I'm Captain Butler," he said, getting right to the point. "How did you know Mr. Sullivan? I believe you said you weren't a relative, but were you a friend of his?"

I told him the story of how I had met Speedy at Bruno's cabin the day of the emergency and how I had later invited him to my home; and, yes, at one time I had considered him a friend. "Captain Butler," I asked, "would you mind telling me why you are asking me about Speedy?"

"Yeah, you must have been a friend because he never let anyone call him by that nickname. I'll tell you why all the questions. He was supposed to report to us here each week. When he didn't show up for his last appointment, we took our motor launch and went looking for him over on the island. Mr. Heikel, we found Clarence hanging from a rafter at his cabin. He apparently committed suicide because he left a note. He admitted to setting a house fire and killing a man and his family in the blaze. The note went on to say it was driving him crazy because the people didn't deserve to die, but the house did. So, he said he was putting himself out of his misery.

"However, we couldn't find any reports of a house fire. Did you say you were here to report a fire?"

I stopped for a minute, trying to absorb everything the captain had told me; and trying to conjure up an acceptable answer. Quietly, through my teeth, I told another one of those little white fibs. "No, I was here to file a report that Mr. Sullivan said he was going to set fire to someone's house, so I thought you could stop him."

"Well, I would say we're too late to stop him from anything," the captain said, shaking his head from side to side. "When you first mentioned his name, we thought you were here to claim the body. But, it's too late for that, too.

We had it cremated."

I could finally take a deep breath now that the captain's attention was concentrated on Speedy and not me. I said, "You know, Captain, I'm not a student of the law, but what gives the police the right to dispose of a person's body? And, why was Speedy reporting to you people in the first place?"

The captain didn't answer for a while. Then he said, "Well, I guess it doesn't make any difference now that Mr. Sullivan is dead, so I can tell you. Sir, Mr. Sullivan was in the government's witness protection program and had been for many years. He turned state's evidence against the mob bosses in Detroit and Chicago in the 1950's and there has been a hit contract on his head ever since. We here at this office were supposed to protect him. We had him come in each week for an update on his comings and goings. We figured he would be safe being isolated and marooned on that island most of the time.

"As for the body, we don't have any information on any relatives in our file, so we did what we have to do in those situations."

I sat there for a long time, letting everything I'd been told soak into my confused mind. After several minutes, I said the only logical thing I could think of, "What happens to his Buick and that speedboat and his house?"

The captain opened the folder he had been carrying and looked through it. "According to this, it looks like everything belonged to the state. He owned nothing."

I mumbled low under my breath, "He left this earth without a trace, just as if he had never existed."

"What did you say?" the captain asked, looking at me curiously with a slight smile on his face.

"Oh, nothing. Just thinking out loud," I said, returning his smile. I thanked the captain and shook his hand, hoping he wouldn't think my sweaty palm was a sign I was hiding something. Of course, I *was* hiding something. Lots of "something." Big time!

As I drove away from the police station and my encounter with near disaster, I tried to get myself under control. If I had missspoken even a single word, it might all have been over. But, in a few minutes, a very relaxed sensation coursed through my whole body. I realized that anyone who could in any way cause me trouble about my newfound millions was dead and gone! I was completely in the clear. Even the mysterious old mansion with its many secrets was now history and buried beneath a pile of dirt just like the corpses on the hill. The money was *mine*! All mine. All *mine*! And no one could challenge my ownership. Now, what the hell was I going to do with it?

Epilogue

After the death of Speedy Sullivan and our old mansion, Peggy Sue and I felt there was no longer any need to linger in the Irish Hills.

She didn't want to have to follow the panel truck all over the South while we searched for our personal *Shangri-La*, so we decided to sell her Caddie before we started out on our newest adventure.

I followed her in our makeshift Brinks truck into Ann Arbor where we quickly sold the car to the local Cadillac dealer at a wholesale price.

Of course, I had removed the mysterious black book containing the German pistol and Bruno's briefcase from the Caddie's trunk and slipped them into one of the footlockers.

Before we set out on what might be a long journey south, we decided to take a last look at our old hilltop, which we had abandoned to the elements and to the State of Michigan—the state eventually gets everything anyway. We headed out Highway 12 and soon were pulling up the all-too-familiar driveway.

Now that the house was gone, the view from the top of that big hill was even more magnificent than ever. As we got out of the car and looked out toward the lake, I remembered the first time I stood on this exact spot over eight years ago. Sure, I had seen this view many, many times, but I was still taken aback by the awesome, almost breathtaking beauty of the setting—the sparkling waters of Lake Misty far below; the vivid green colors of the towering trees; and the splendor of the rolling grassy hills.

The omnipresent sky with billowing white clouds drifting slowly to unknown destinations made my heart ache so much that, for just a millisecond, I considered changing my mind and rebuilding on this incredible spot.

I looked over at Peggy Sue and the kids. They were all crying; then I realized that tears were running down my face as well. Big alligator tears fell like raindrops had from those violent thunderstorms we endured as they swept across the hilltop. But with those tears came haunting memories of the nightmares, hallucinations, visions and sicknesses we had experienced. I looked off into the distance toward the small knoll where the bodies were buried and I felt a twinge of sympathy, both for myself and for those unfortunate souls lying under the soil. I knew I would never look their way again. I would never see those green hills; I would never again experience the utter silence of those deep woods.

I supposed it was a normal reaction. There is always something sad and melancholy when you're leaving part of your life behind and you have to say your silent goodbyes. It's just so final—like death.

We couldn't take any more of this heart-wrenching sadness and sobbing, so Peggy Sue said a short prayer to help convince us that peace had finally come to this hilltop.

Then we all climbed into our riches-laden truck and hit the road southward, never once looking back.

After driving several hours, and just as we crossed the Tennessee state line on the expressway, I heard the shrill sound of a police siren. Looking in my rearview mirror, I saw a highway patrol car with its lights flashing and its trooper pointing to the side of the road.

I could actually feel my heart leap into my throat as I pulled over to the side of the road. The kids were sprawled out on top of the footlockers in the back and I told them to remain quiet. The trooper approached my side window that I was hurriedly rolling down. He smiled—that helped. Then he said, "Do you know that your temporary license plate has expired?"

"Oh, yes I did, Officer. But, we're moving and are not exactly sure where we are going to settle; but I have informed the dealer where I bought the truck that we would notify him when we know where we're going to be so he could send the permanent plates." God, that sounded lame and I knew it, but I couldn't think of anything better!

He looked me straight in the eye and said, "You aren't running from the law are you?"

In my sternest voice, I answered, "Absolutely not! I'm a law-abiding citizen and a family man. This is my wife and kids here with me."

He chuckled and said, "I knew you were okay when I called in your plate number. I was just having a little fun with you. This job can get pretty boring, traveling these long stretches of roads all day."

He was talking nice, but he was also looking over my shoulder and into the rear of the truck. "Boy, you have a heck of a load back there. Say, are those old army footlockers?"

By now, along with my heart, my intestines had crawled up into my throat and it was getting so crowded in there I wasn't sure I could speak. However, I was able to remain courteous and calm and I managed to reply, "Why, yes they are officer."

When he started talking again, I wanted to gag! I held on, however, and heard him say, "Do you mind if I have a look in one? I haven't seen the inside of a footlocker since my Army days."

A jillion things went through my mind in a nanosecond: "After all I've been through up to this point, including thinking of shooting Speedy to protect my stash, it looks like the jig is up and my worse fears are being realized." I thought about the loaded Luger under my front seat, but realized I was still sane and wasn't about to shoot a cop to protect the dough. I was just going to have to take the fall.

I swallowed hard to keep my insides from coming out of my mouth, slowly exited the truck cab and walked with the officer to the rear of the vehicle. Almost as if in a trance, I opened the two rear doors. The officer slid one of the lockers out and pulled it toward him. Then he put a hand on each clasp, snapped them open and raised the lid. I couldn't look down; I just stared straight ahead into the trooper's face, waiting to see the expression that would sweep across his face when he saw the piles of money. I could already feel the cold steel handcuffs tightening around my wrists.

"Looks like your kids are athletes. Yeah, the inside of one of these things always did hold a ton of stuff." Before I could faint, I saw the smile on the cop's face. Only then did I look down myself. And, what the hell did I see but my kid's old baseball gloves, a uniform, a bat and an old basketball! My son Forrest had just saved my ass and my fortune. He had placed his footlocker on top of the pile of lockers Peggy Sue and I had stacked up the day we transferred the money from the vault. Unknowingly, I had placed Forrest's locker aboard the truck in just the right spot for the highway patrolmen to put his hand on it.

I sat there in the truck and let the air conditioner blow in my face, trying to soothe my frazzled nerves, as I watched the patrol car disappear down the highway. I wondered what other surprises were waiting for me in the future as I wrestled with the surviving ghosts from our past in the Irish Hills, the ghosts that were stacked in the footlocker just behind my back. Not only was there the cash but also there was the locker, which held the mysterious black book, and the jar containing the severed fingers, on which there still sat the three signet rings. Little did I know at the time, that in the coming years, the book and these rings would have such a profound life changing affect on my entire life.

Finally, I put the truck in gear and drove away into the sunset and toward a new life. As I drove, I questioned whether finding the Knights of Zion's cash would prove to be lucky or *un*lucky. One thought continued to play around in my mind. I kept thinking that someday some unsuspecting couple might consider purchasing a lovely hilltop location on which to build the home of their dreams. I hoped they wouldn't let their visions of living in a castle in the clouds, or the lure of the mesmerizing beauty…or even the soft breezes that whispered in their ears and echoed through their minds, "This could all be yours, yours, yours," affect their rational thought and reasoning.

I knew there could be very sinister and overwhelming forces lurking just beneath their feet; or in the very air they were breathing that could pose a threat to their sanity and possibly even their lives. Instead, they should beware. Be very aware of the hill—and be frightened, *be* very frightened!

About the Author

Born in downtown Detroit in the shadow of the Tiger's Baseball Stadium and to an immigrant mother and on the wrong side of the tracks, Forrest spent his young life as well as most of his teenage years involved with his dad in the illegal rackets, mainly booking horses and loan sharking and the numbers. He managed to graduate from Northwestern High School at the early age of 16. A few years later, he was drafted into the US Army and spent over two years in Germany as a military policeman and helicopter pilot trainee.

A few months after his discharge from the military, he met a green-eyed beauty and, not wanting to waste any time, got her to marry him after a three-month whirlwind courtship. As luck would have it, upon answering a newspaper ad to sell copy machines for the 3-M company he got the job and it changed his life for the better. Haskell stayed in the copy machine business for over thirty years and, being the salesman he was, became very successful as an owner of several companies related to the office machine and leasing business.

Wanting to try something new, he sold all his offices to a large company listed on the New York Stock Exchange, moved to Texas and went into the fast lube industry. A few years later when Jiffy Lube bought out all its dealers, Haskell sold out again. This time he and his son spent most of their time racing offshore powerboats on the national circuit. When people would ask him what he did in previous years and he would tell them his life story they would always say, "Man! Why don't you write a book?" So, he did. It's entitled "12th and McGraw," a true story that chronicles life with his gun-toting strange dad.

Haskell lives near Dallas, Texas with his wife, has four children and eight grandchildren, plays a lot of tennis and enjoys writing.

Also by Forrest Haskell, Jr.

12th & McGraw

Top Publications, Ltd. Trade Paperback

281 pages   July 2004   ISBN 1-9299762-9-1

12th & McGraw is the true story of the author's coming of age as the son of a Detroit racketeer in the 1940s, his struggles to survive in his father's bizarre world of crime and fortune hunting, and his search for his identity as the result of his father's multiple personality disorder. The story recalls encounters with many weird and mysterious characters, murder, corruption, narrow escapes from the law, and the shocking discovery of his father's second family and the brothers and sisters he never knew existed!

"12th & McGraw—an unusual story! ... gets off to a great start and succeeds in immediately hooking the reader. 4 stars" ... ***Norman Goldman.***

"...a peek into the life of an exciting man who didn't play by the rules....A lovely tribute..." ***Molly Martin, Midwest Book Reviews***

Future Novels from Forrest Haskell

THE KNIGHTHOOD OF ZION

Return to Eden Series, Book II

The tale begins with the main character, Zack Heikel driving aimlessly in a truck laden with four million bucks, which he has found and taken from an old mansion he once owned in Michigan. He believes he is evading a notorious gang of Jewish hoodlums, who call themselves, "the Knights of Zion" and who are the possible owners of the found money. Along with the money, he found a jar that contained nine severed human fingers, three of which wore a silver ring. While examining one of the rings, he is shocked by a strong electric current emitting from the ring when it is touched. Wondering how this could happen, he consults an old dusty book he also found in the mansion and it explains how the rings, which can gather static electricity from Earth's atmosphere and under certain conditions, can project an image of an event from the distant past. Zack, following directions from the ancient text, connects several rings together in a circle that forms a static electric force field in which images float. Following these images and with the help of a strange old rabbi, he discovers The Holy Grail in King Arthur's tomb in England and returns with it to the United States. When the CIA investigates the disappearance of a Hebrew professor who was de-coding the ancient manuscript, they find Zack has the grail, which they confiscate and take along with Zack to CIA headquarters in Virginia.

The CIA has secretly had in their possession,....The Ark of the Covenant ..and for years have been working on it's capabilities but lacked all the necessary parts for it to fully function. However, now with the rings as its power source, the Grail as the projector and the Ark as the transmitter can be completely assembled. The CIA using personnel within a covert project called, "Enigma" puts everything together and from the top of Mount Sinai, they send a high voltage signal generated by the Ark into deep space which contacts,........... GOD....... who comes to Earth in the form of a hologram in a green laser light beam. The story ends as God speaks to the group of scientists and explains why he left the space beacon and outlines to those of Project Enigma his instructions concerning the planet Sirius, the fate of Mankind here on earth and the return of Christ.

SECOND GENESIS

Return to Eden Series, Book III

Zack Heikel, a new age apostle ordained by God, along with other scientists is aboard the massive star ship, "Shalom" streaking through the Cosmos at near the speed of light. Their mission; find a suitable planet to replicate God's ultimate experiment, MANKIND, using as a blueprint, the chapter Genesis in the Holy Bible. On instructions directly from the Almighty given them on Mount Sinai they are to re-create man through cloning and engineer him without sin and the devil's influence. They find such a planet orbiting around the star Sirius.

After terraforming the Earth-sized planet, which they christen Xanadue, they succeed in successfully cloning a race of humans, who are exact copies of some of the voyagers, with one major exception; the cloning process deprives them of reproductive or sex organs and they must reproduce using artificial wombs. These humans are far superior to Earth humans in that they are more intelligent, have perfectly engineered bodies and are a peace loving new race. However, even in this perfect "Garden of Eden" world, frictions and animosities arise when Mankind's old nemesis, the male hormone, testosterone overwhelms the space travelers and drives them to near insanity, prompting God to intervene directly to resolve the crises and save his new creations, The Clones.